The critics adore Miranda Jarrett

SUNRISE

"Enchanting. . . . loved this, Miranda!"

—*Philadelphia Inquirer*

"Poignant, endearing, tender, and charming."

—Patricia Gaffney

"*Sunrise* has all the elements that make Ms. Jarrett such a popular writer. . . . Jarrett provides her myriad of fans with an enjoyable historical romance."

—*Affaire de Coeur*

"Jarrett . . . draws her protagonists vividly and with charm."

—*Publishers Weekly*

"Lovely. Jarrett's writing is elegant, her voice sure, her characters vital. *Sunrise* is intensely emotional but never overwrought. In all ways an exceptional novel and a joy to read."

—*Contra Costa Times* (CA)

MOONLIGHT

Winner of the Golden Leaf Award for Best Historical Romance of 1999

"Five stars! Miranda Jarrett is one of the genre's best. . . . *Moonlight* will only enhance her high esteem with readers. . . . Fast-paced and delightful!"

—Amazon.com

"What a touching, heartfelt story! . . . Every detail will keep you wanting more. Beautifully written."

—*Rendezvous*

Books by Miranda Jarrett

The Captain's Bride
Cranberry Point
Wishing
Moonlight
Sunrise
Starlight
Star Bright

Published by Pocket Books

MIRANDA JARRETT

STAR BRIGHT

SONNET BOOKS

New York London Toronto Sydney Singapore

An *Original* Publication of POCKET BOOKS

A Sonnet Book published by
POCKET BOOKS, a division of Simon & Schuster, Inc.
1230 Avenue of the Americas, New York, NY 10020

Copyright © 2000 by Miranda Jarrett

ISBN: 0-7434-0356-8

First Sonnet Books printing November 2000

10 9 8 7 6 5 4 3 2 1

SONNET BOOKS and colophon are trademarks of Simon & Schuster, Inc.

Front cover illustration by Steven Assel

Printed in the U.S.A.

for Loretta,
that most illustrious Twin-Girl:
for the joy of your friendship
and fellow Gemini-dom,
and for leading me into
the land of ladies, lords, and scoundrels
(as well as tiaras and the T!)

The Fairbourne Family

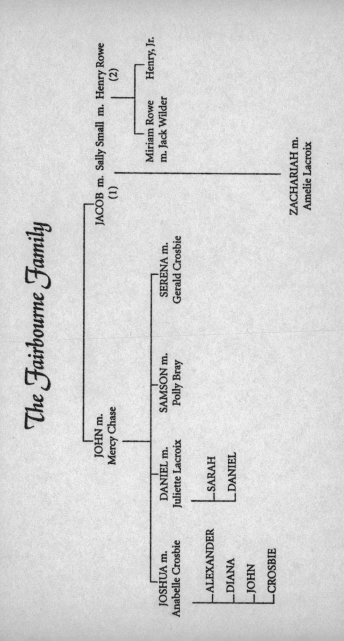

1

Ashburnham Hall,
Hampshire
1747

From the outside, the letter seemed innocuous enough: a sheet of thick, cream-colored paper, neatly folded, sealed with a blob of dark green wax, and addressed in a well-bred lady's hand. It stood on its edge, propped between the chocolate pot and the porcelain cup on the silver breakfast tray, demure and unprepossessing and waiting to shatter the blissful perfection of Diana Fairbourne's life.

"Thank you, Mary," said Diana as she hurriedly finished braiding her dark hair into a single thick plait and flipped it back over her shoulder. She plucked a slice of toast from the tray, eating it as she knelt to hunt beneath the bed for her old walking shoes.

"I'll find them for you, miss," volunteered Mary, more than a little shocked to see Diana crawling about on the carpet, and dressed as plainly as any farmer's daughter, too. For a lady and a famous beauty who'd taken fashionable London by storm, Diana showed far too much initiative in making do for herself. No wonder that since arriving at Ashburnham Hall, she'd become the subject of much head shaking and talk in the servants' quarters. "You sit now, and have your breakfast proper."

"But you see I've found them already," said Diana, sitting back on the floor to buckle her shoes on her feet in a way that was quite shamelessly common. "You may go, Mary. I won't need you, truly. I'll be on my way myself in a moment."

"But your breakfast, miss," said Mary, stern with disapproval, her hands clasped at her waist. "You must eat, miss."

"I'll be fine, Mary," said Diana, looking toward the late-summer morning beyond her bedchamber's windows. The dawn wasn't long past, the first pale sunlight drifting in through the curtains, and the hour far too early for anyone other than the servants to be awake in the great house.

Diana grinned as she flung a light shawl over her shoulders. All her life she'd risen early, and not even the fact that in four short weeks she'd marry Ashburnham Hall's master and become the Marchioness of Roxby would make her sleep beyond daybreak. "Madame Lark," the marquess had dubbed her, and promised that once they'd wed he'd give Diana reason enough to keep to their bed and forget her peculiar colonial propensity for early morning rambles.

But Diana had only laughed and kissed him on the cheek. She still could scarcely believe he'd fallen in love with her as quickly as she had with him, or that he'd asked for her hand after only two weeks' acquaintance, while showing her his collection of Roman intaglios and before she'd even learned his Christian name. He'd called her his destiny, the most romantic declaration she'd ever heard. How could she not love a man who spoke like that?

She was smiling to herself as she reached for another piece of toast to take with her, and saw the letter. The handwriting wasn't familiar, but that meant nothing; since she'd become betrothed to Roxby, she'd received many invitations and notes of congratulations from people she'd never met. Curious, she slipped her finger beneath the seal to crack it open and unfolded the single sheet. The message was short, only a handful of words, but more than enough to do what its sender had wished.

Miss Fairbourne,
If you value your Heart & Happiness, you will break off yr. Match with Lord Roxby at once. He keeps a Mistress in London, & loves you Not. Ask him if you Dare, I do not lie.

A Friend who wishes you Well

Twice Diana read the letter to be sure she wasn't imagining it, then read the words through one more time, burning them into her mind, and her heart as well. Of course it couldn't be true. Of course it must be lies. And of course the letter was unsigned. Who would take credit for such vile, trouble-making calumny?

"Are you unwell, miss?" asked Mary with concern. "Not unhappy news, is it?"

"Not at all," said Diana, her fingers trembling as she refolded the letter. She could toss it into the fire, or tear it into tiny pieces, or take it to show Lady Waldegrave, her mother's oldest friend and Diana's companion until she was wed. Or she could do the one thing that the letter's author never expected her to do. "Mary, is his lordship awake?"

"Awake?" repeated Mary with the sudden blankness that practiced servants could muster in an instant. "Nay, miss, his lordship is never awake at this hour."

"Then I shall wake him." With the letter in her hand, Diana swept from the room, determined not to let suspicion fester. "His lordship's bedchamber is in the north wing, isn't it?"

"Aye, miss, but you shouldn't—you mustn't—go there!" protested Mary breathlessly, trotting to keep pace with her. " 'Tis not proper, miss, 'tis not right!"

"In a month no one will think anything of it," declared Diana, "or remember that I went there at all."

"But miss—miss!—his lordship's not there!"

Abruptly Diana stopped. "Not there? Wherever else would he be if not in his own bed?"

An unpleasant possibility, brought on by that dreadful anonymous letter, immediately came to Diana's mind, and just as swiftly she shoved it aside. Roxby loved *her*, and he'd never once given her reason to doubt him.

"His lordship's not at home at present, miss," said the maid uncomfortably. "After you and the other ladies retired last night, miss, he and Lord Stanver decided to go to Knowlewood to play faro. On a whim it was, miss, the way the gentlemen do."

Knowlewood was Lord Stanver's estate and known to be such a gamester's paradise that a faro dealer was as permanent a part of the household staff as a butler or cook. But what Diana considered now was Knowlewood's proximity to London, only a half-hour's ride at most from the gates of the house to—

But she would *not* think that, not of her Roxby. She was sure there were other ladies and women in his past—he was nearly thirty years old, after all—but she was equally certain that he'd be far too honorable to ask for her hand if his heart wasn't free.

Wasn't he?

Her only answer was the rustle of paper as she clutched the letter more tightly in her fingers.

"We expect his lordship's return any minute, miss," said Mary, almost apologetically. "We'll tell him you wish to speak with him directly."

"Please tell him I have gone walking," said Diana sharply, stuffing the letter into her pocket, "and that I shall speak with him as soon as *I* return."

But Diana wasn't even through the door before she regretted both her words and her temper. The letter wasn't Mary's fault, any more than Roxby was guilty simply because some anonymous coward said so. No: the problem instead lay with Diana's own habitual impatience. She tended to charge headlong through life, guided by impulse and so little ladylike caution that, before Roxby, her mother had despaired of her ever staying still long enough to attract a husband.

But Diana had never been good at waiting. She'd always wanted things settled *now,* just as she wanted to hear Roxby himself deny the letter's accusations. That was what she wanted and what she couldn't have and what made her stride so swiftly that she was practically running by the time she reached the rose garden, frustration and ugly doubts driving her footsteps over the neatly raked paths.

But when she reached the end of the paths, she'd still

found no peace, and instead of following the white gravel back to the house, she cut across the open fields where, in the distance, grazed black-faced sheep and red cattle. The taller grasses brushed against her legs, the hem of her petticoats growing heavy with dew and the rising sun warm on her shoulders. Still she rushed on without stopping, farther than she'd gone on any other morning, at last coming to the stand of old oaks that marked the end of these tended fields and the beginning of the woodlands.

She blinked to let her eyes adjust to the shadows, the air cooler here beneath the trees, the ground under her feet soft with moss and old leaves. Through the branches, she could make out the glitter of reflecting water, and she remembered Roxby telling her about a long-abandoned mill and pond on his land that he fancied as his "ruin." Holding her arms out for balance, she skipped and slid down the hill to the pond's bank. A stone that she'd accidentally kicked loose rolled ahead of her, bouncing off a tree root to land in the water with a resounding *plop.*

"What the devil are you doing?" roared a man's voice. "Or did you mean to drive every fish away just to plague me?"

"And who, pray, are you to speak to me in such a manner?" Diana shouted in return. She shoved aside the last branches and overgrown vines, determined to see who this impossibly rude man could be.

She didn't have far to look. He sat at the oars of a small boat just off the shore, drifting gently on the still water beyond the rushes. The line from his fishing pole trailed from the boat's side, and at his feet was one basket for keeping the fish with another holding an earthenware jug and his half-eaten breakfast. From the rough belligerence in his voice, she'd expected some gruff countryman, the kind that regarded poaching as an honorable art, and from the man's clothes—grimy leather breeches, a checkered shirt with the collar open, a faded dark linen coat, and a misshapen old black hat— that was exactly what he was.

But although the clothes had been predictable enough, the man inside them wasn't. His features were too strong to be called handsome, his nose a bit crooked from a long-ago break, his jaw pronounced and inclined to stubbornness. Living out-of-doors had browned and weathered his skin, with little lines fanning out from green eyes that seemed to reflect the water's liveliness. The hair that poked out haphazardly from beneath his hat was light brown, gilded by the sun. His shoulders were broad with laborer's muscles, earned by hard work.

He wasn't handsome at all, not really, especially since Diana's eyes had become trained to the well-bred Londoner's ideal of handsomeness. But there was a supremely male confidence to him that she couldn't ignore, a determined sort of physical masculinity, almost an arrogance, that reminded her of the men back home—precisely the kind of man that she'd left Massachusetts to avoid.

"Are you finished gawking, then?" he demanded, his green eyes glaring at her as if she were a witch who'd poisoned his well. "Or are you just considering which stone to heave next at me and my fish?"

Diana flushed. "Why must you insist on believing I've purposely spoiled your angling?"

"Because you've given me no reason to believe otherwise," he said, openly appraising her just as she had him. "The way you came crashing through the woods with your guns all a-fire, flailing your arms about and tossing stones—what else am I to believe?"

"I did not throw the stone. I merely dislodged it with my foot, and it tumbled into the water before me." She sighed impatiently, pushing her hat back farther from her forehead. She didn't know why she was continuing such a pointless conversation, except that she hated to be bettered by anyone, and right now this man clearly held the advantage in the conversation. "Don't you know whose land you're on?"

"I'm not on anyone's *land*," retorted the man, "but I am upon the Marquess of Roxby's water. Not that his high and mighty lordship needs the likes of you defending his property."

She gasped indignantly, then remembered how she was dressed. If she told him she was the future Marchioness of Roxby, he'd laugh out loud.

"You are still trespassing," she said instead. "I could report you to his lordship's gamekeeper. I *should*."

But the man merely stared up at her, his green eyes glinting. "So who the devil fouled your temper this morning, eh? Or do you begin every day picking quarrels with strangers?"

"I should hardly call this a quarrel," she began, then broke off once again. He was right, pox him. Her temper was most definitely fouled on account of that wretched letter in her pocket. "Though I could certainly accuse you of being quarrelsome."

"Aye, you could," he agreed, "and you'd be right. I

won't deny it. I am not by nature a peaceable man, and I've started more quarrels than I'll ever remember."

He smiled, a lopsided smile burdened with bitterness, and pulled his fishing line from the water. "But I'm clearing off now anyway. No more fish to be had this day, thanks to you, and besides, I don't want you hauling me before old Roxby's gamekeeper. Why, I'm all a-shiver even thinking of it."

Pointedly he looked away from her, concentrating instead on settling the oars in their locks while Diana fumed. She wasn't accustomed to men talking to her like this—at least any man that wasn't one of her brothers—and she didn't like it, not at all.

But before she could answer, she noticed something odd: the man couldn't row to save his life. Oh, he did well enough with the oar in his left hand, but he'd absolutely no control with the one in his right, the blade first flopping clumsily over the surface of the water, then chopping deep enough to make the boat lurch unsteadily and the man swear with annoyance.

She watched and smiled sweetly. "You must dip both oars into the water, sir, and keep your elbows close to your body," she noted. "Else your vessel will never go anywhere."

He glared at her from beneath the brim of his hat, challenging, his expression black as a thundercloud. "I suppose a chit like you could do better."

A nearly-married marchioness was not a chit, but Diana let her temper simmer inside and instead widened her smile. "I could indeed."

"The hell you could," he growled. He pulled the oar free of the lock and clumsily thrust it deep into the soft, shallow bottom of the pond, pushing the boat forward that way. With two shoves, he'd reached the bank, bumping up against the moss where Diana stood.

"Aboard with you, then," he ordered, holding his hand out to her. "Come along. Take the oars and prove to me you can do what you claim."

"I'll do nothing of the sort," she said as she scuttled backward, away from him. "I don't have to obey your orders."

"I'm not asking for obedience," he said impatiently. "I'm asking for proof."

She withdrew further, shaking her head. This was madness; no, this *man* was mad, challenging her like this. If she'd any sense at all, she'd turn around and run and not stop until she'd reached the safety of the house.

"All bluster and empty air, are you?" His green eyes narrowed, scornfully skeptical. "If you don't show me how you can handle this boat, then I'll have to believe you lied about doing better. I'll have to think you don't want to show me because you can't."

That did it. She might be able to do nothing about that cowardly lady who'd written the letter, but she could put this challenging rascal in his place.

"Across the pond to that bank and back," she declared tartly, bunching up her skirts with one hand as she came down the bank to the boat. "More than enough to prove I can row circles around you."

"You've proved nothing yet," he said as he shifted benches, holding the boat steady for her. "Keep low now. I've no wish to be tipped overboard."

"Oh, yes, and be sure to warn me about tiptoeing across the lily leaves, too," she answered as she nimbly climbed over the side. She'd been born in a seafaring town on Cape Cod, clambering in and out of boats and ships since she'd been a tiny girl, and she certainly didn't need any advice about keeping low. She centered herself on the bench with her feet against the stretcher, primly tucked her petticoats around her ankles, and with practiced ease set the first oar into its lock.

"I'll need that one, too, if you please," she said, taking the second oar from him. "Otherwise we'll keep making a circle, much the way that you already were."

He grumbled wordlessly, a disdainful growl deep in his throat, and with his left hand pushed the boat free of the bank. The boat was long but narrow, with scarcely space for one man his size, let alone for them both, and as he sat facing her, she was all too aware of how their knees nearly touched.

Chin in, spine straight, she tried to concentrate on posture instead of him. Confidently she drew back the oars, dipped the blades into the water, and pulled. The little boat glided forward, and she pulled again, the rhythm of her rowing easy and sure.

But each time she leaned forward with the oars she also leaned close, closer, to the large man sitting across from her. She couldn't help looking at him, because he blocked everything else in her view. Against her will she began noticing more about him, small, intimate things: how his jaw still gleamed from his razor's morning rasp, how the neck of his shirt was open enough to reveal a fascinating patch of curling dark hair on his chest, how that same freshly washed shirt smelled of soap and iron scorch and his own male scent, a scent she'd no right whatsoever to be smelling.

"You've stopped," he said, faintly accusing. "Are you tired already?"

"Not at all," she answered quickly, though she let the boat's momentum carry them forward while the oars trailed idle in her hands and her face stayed safely apart from his chest. "I learned to handle a boat in the ocean, against the waves. To row on this pond is like rowing in a bucket of wash water."

"Then why quit? You promised you'd row to the bank and back, wash water or not."

" 'Tis not that," she said, hedging. Belatedly she pictured what another would see, the two of them so close together in a boat on this isolated pond, and tried to imagine how she'd explain this particular impulsiveness to Roxby. " 'Tis not that at all."

"No?" he asked, his eyes glowing in the shadow of his hat's brim, challenging her yet again. "Then perhaps you're simply afraid of me."

Diana's chin rose defiantly. "I'm not afraid of you, sir. Not with an oar in my hand."

"You'd use it, too, wouldn't you?" he asked, his lopsided smile now amused but also strangely approving at the same time. "Strike me across the nose like a recalcitrant donkey?"

"If you deserved it." Her brothers had taught her how to defend herself, a necessary skill for a woman in a seaport full of randy sailors. "If you were too forward."

"Ah, well, we cannot have that, can we?" To her surprise, he shifted on the bench, giving her more space. "Row on, then, coxswain, or we'll never make our landfall. Handsomely now, handsomely!"

Once again she dipped the blades into the water, considering not so much what he'd said, but how he'd said it. "You don't speak like a landsman. Have you ever been to sea?"

"Aye," he said, his expression abruptly turning guarded. "But not now."

Close to the bank, she neatly brought the boat around. But now he wasn't noticing, instead lost in his own thoughts as he stared out over the water.

"There's no shame in going to sea, at least not to me," she said to fill the silence. She'd rather liked being called a coxswain, and she was sorry he'd turned moody and stopped. "My own family's thick with sailors. That's why I can row. Likely I should've told you that in the beginning."

He sighed gloomily. "Likely you should have, aye. Lucky for me I'd staked no money against you."

"Then you concede?" she asked. "You'll say that I can row better than you?"

"Aye, you do," he growled, shaking his head with undisguised disgust, "as you know perfectly well. Bettered by some chit of a girl. Jesus."

"I'm not an ordinary chit, you know," she said, almost apologetically. Because she'd won, she could afford to be magnanimous. "Another time, and you might well have done better."

"Not in this life," he said, the bitterness returning to his voice. "The damned French have seen to that, haven't they?"

"The French?" she repeated, mystified. Her brothers and father blamed much of their misfortunes upon the French as well, for it seemed that England and France had been at war as long as she could remember. But suddenly she understood what the man was saying, the truth that she'd so blithely, blindly overlooked.

"Your right arm," she said softly. "You were wounded by the French, weren't you? That's why you can't row properly now, isn't it?"

"How kind of you to remark it." Unconsciously he cradled his awkward right arm with his left against his chest, as if to shield it from her concern.

"I am sorry," she said, and she was. She'd seen her share of battle-scarred sailors with missing limbs or shocking disfigurements earned in the king's service, and she hated to think of this man, young as he still was, already crippled for the rest of his life. No wonder he was poaching, too; there'd be precious few opportunities left for a man with only one good arm and hand here in the middle of Hampshire. "I should never have—"

"No pity," he ordered sharply. "I don't want it."

"But I only meant—"

"I know what you meant, and I'd rather you'd strike me with that blasted oar."

"Then perhaps I should, just to be obliging, and to knock some sense into your witless brain, too." The boat bumped against the bank where they'd begun, and she briskly shipped the oars. If he mistook her kindness for pity, then that was his problem, not hers. "Pray hold the boat steady for me, if you please, so I may go ashore."

"Oh, aye, please may I, pretty as pie," he said, goading her as he jabbed one of the oars into the soft bottom as a makeshift anchor. "Going back to the first man who dared cross you this morning, are you? Eager to bedevil another poor bastard?"

"I am not!" she answered indignantly, wishing she

hadn't at that exact moment remembered the letter in her pocket. "I never said I was!"

"You didn't have to," he said, grinning with the triumph she'd thought earlier was hers. "I told you I was quarrelsome by nature, and so are you. You can't help it, lass, anymore than I can. And of course it's a man that's provoked you. With a woman like you, it always is, isn't it?"

"You know nothing of me, sir, or of my situation," she said warmly as she scrambled from the boat and up the bank, "nor shall you ever have the opportunity to learn!"

"Go on, coxswain," he called after her. "Give the bastard the righteous hell he deserves. Remember how you're no ordinary chit!"

Fuming, she didn't give him the satisfaction of looking back, yet his mocking laughter echoed after her as she hurried through the trees back toward the house. She'd hoped her walk would calm her, but because of meeting this impossibly rude man she felt more unsettled than when she'd first received the anonymous letter. By the time she'd come through the last of the gardens and seen Roxby himself by the steps, she couldn't help running toward him, knowing that at last her doubts would be put to rest.

"Roxby!" she shouted as she raced toward him, her petticoats flying around her legs. "Oh, Roxby, I'm so glad you're home!"

Tossing the reins of his horse to a waiting groom, he turned toward her slowly. In that first moment she saw Roxby as the world did, an English nobleman posed on the wide marble steps of his favorite house in the country, generations of his family's wealth and position granting him unquestionable power and presence. That same presence made him seem taller than he actually was and gave the measured elegance to his bearing that had attracted Diana instantly. He had dark, deep-set eyes beneath black brows with a perpetually quizzical arch, and from his mother's family in the north he'd inherited the long aristocratic nose, one that seemed to echo the Roman profiles on the coins he collected.

Returning from Knowlewood, he was still dressed in the same clothes he'd worn to dinner—a dark red superfine wool jacket and waistcoat, only lightly embroidered with silver thread for the country, with matching breeches clasped at the knee with etched silver buckles. Even after being awake all night, nothing seemed in disarray, nothing soiled or mussed, though for riding to and from Knowlewood he'd changed into high black boots with dark red heels and silver spurs. He wore three rings on his left hand, and two on his right, four set with rubies in gold, and the last the heavy gold signet with the family's crest that had belonged to his great-grandfather.

But as she came closer, Diana saw beyond the marquess' rubies and silver lace to the man she'd come to love: a true gentleman with impeccably elegant manners, always in control of himself and his emotions, the very antithesis of the obstreperous, uncultured men she'd known in Massachusetts. Yet despite his reserve, to her joy Diana also saw pleasure light his eyes when he spied her, followed instantly by concern.

"What is wrong, Diana?" he asked, holding his hand out to her. "What has happened?"

"Nothing," she said breathlessly, barely stopping from

throwing herself into his arms the way she longed to do. Roxby had warned her before that marchionesses were expected to behave with more decorum than that, more restraint, especially before servants like the curious groom. "That is, something *has* happened, but not what you think."

"Either it has, or it hasn't," said Roxby with exquisite patience. "At this abominable hour, only you know for certain, my dear Madame Lark."

"But I don't." She pulled the now-crumpled letter from her pocket, smoothing it with her fingers before she handed it to him. "This was brought to me this morning, posted from London."

She held her breath while he read, waiting for an outburst that never came.

"Vile and scurrilous," he said with a resigned sigh. "I regret that you have had to receive such a letter."

"That—that is all, Roxby?" she asked, stunned and wounded by his lack of reaction. "You are not—not surprised?"

"My dear innocent Diana," he said gently. "I fear I have seen a great deal more of the world than you, and nothing in it surprises me any longer. Except, that is, the depth of devotion I feel for you."

"Truly?" Anxiously Diana searched Roxby's face, longing for a more passionate assurance than was in his nature to give. How desperately she wanted to believe him! "But why would this woman have written such lies if—"

"Jealousy," he answered firmly. "Malice. The illicit sport of throwing mud at her betters. There could be a score of reasons, Diana, though whomever this wretched, unhappy female may be, she clearly envies us our joy. She won't, alas, be the last. But we must ignore her, my dear. She has the power to poison our happiness only if you grant it to her."

She should have known that Roxby would offer such a perfectly logical explanation, one that was beyond questioning. That was one of the things she loved about him, wasn't it?

Yet she couldn't quite keep the wistfulness from her voice. "I know you're more experienced in such matters, Roxby, and if I'm going to be your wife, I must learn to accept such—such jealous attentions from strangers."

"I fear so." He smiled tenderly, enough to make her want to weep. "You must learn to trust me, my little bride, in this and in all things. The life I've offered you won't always be an easy one, but I pray you'll never regret your decision to share it with me."

He held the letter up before her, the sunlight catching in the jeweled rings on his fingers as he slowly, deliberately tore the letter into ragged strips, then into still smaller pieces that he let fall to the steps. Swiftly the breeze caught the tattered fragments, swirling them like oversized snowflakes around Diana's feet.

"There," said Roxby, tipping her face toward his. "All you need do is trust me, Diana, and the rest shall follow."

She wanted to trust him as much as she already loved him. He was her Roxby, and soon to be her husband as well. But even as he kissed her, she realized he'd never once denied the letter's accusations, and although the letter lay torn and scattered at her feet, the hateful words remained as unchallenged as Diana's own doubts.

And she'd never given him hell about any of it. . . .

2

With a groan, James Dunham dropped heavily onto the bench beside the back door, rubbing his outstretched thigh where the muscles were reminding him exactly how far they still were from being healed. His arm ached, too; in fact, his whole right side seemed reduced to such a jumbled assortment of pains and aches and outright uselessness that he doubted he'd ever be much good to anyone again. Certainly the lords of the Admiralty didn't think so—they'd made that clear enough—and there was precious little that James could do or say to prove they were wrong, not beached here in the middle of Hampshire.

None of that had changed, nor was it likely to. And yet on this warm and sunny morning, because of what had happened on the pond, his mood was lighter than it had been since he'd lost the *Castor*.

"The fish weren't biting, then?" asked his older sister Celia as she peered into the empty basket on the grass beside his fishing pole. "Not a nibble in all that time?"

"Oh, they were," answered James, awkwardly shrugging out of his coat, "until a young woman came crashing through the brush to frighten them all into hiding."

"A young woman?" asked Celia with considerable interest, hooking her fingers into the waist strings of her apron to listen. Celia was a born listener, though for James his sister's constant, curious empathy could be as much a curse as a blessing. "She must not have frightened *you*, considering how long you've been gone. It's nearly ten, you know."

"Ten, is it?" repeated James vaguely, now wishing with all his heart he hadn't mentioned the young woman at the pond. Celia took her responsibilities as his older sister seriously enough that, in unkind moments, he'd call it meddling.

"Ten, it is," answered Celia. "You could have stayed until noon if you wished, James. I certainly wouldn't have worried if you'd chosen to linger. A pretty young woman is precisely what you need to amuse you and help hasten your convalescence."

"Hah," he grumbled, concentrating on rolling his shirt sleeve higher over his forearm. The warmth of the sun felt good on his skin, and with Celia he didn't have to bother hiding the livid latticework of scars that crisscrossed his arm. "You forget that I'm precisely not the sort of man that a pretty young woman would choose for her own amusement."

Undeterred, Celia smiled. "She *was* pretty, then?"

James sighed with resignation. How had he forgotten his sister's inquisitions? "Aye, she was pretty. Very, very pretty. But that is all I can tell you of her, Celia. I didn't ask her name, nor did I tell her mine. I know not of her mother or her father, nor where she resides. Hell, she could well already have a husband and a brood of snotty-faced children."

"You would have known if she were married," said Celia sternly, for being the wife of an Anglican minister had also given her a certain righteousness in such matters. "Married women in this parish don't dawdle with handsome young officers."

James sighed once more. Celia's impression of him as a dashing young rake of an officer who made the ladies swoon was at least ten years out of date and in the past, back when he'd been a newly-minted lieutenant. Now he was old and wary, damaged goods, an invalid on half pay pressing thirty years, and young women like the one he'd met this morning didn't look twice at him, at least not the way he would have liked.

And he *would* have liked it if she had. She had been exceptionally lovely, standing there in the tall grass on the bank with her full, rosy mouth and her eyes as blue as the sky overhead. But what had attracted him most was her vibrancy and her self-confidence, how she'd confronted him and never once backed down, the way most girls would have done. She'd nearly glowed with it, so bright and intensely alive that he'd wanted to keep her with him, a beacon to chase away the shadows of all the death and dying that clung to him.

Which, of course, he thought with a grimace, was exactly the sort of rubbish left to bad poets. Likely the girl already had a score of lovers, strong, strapping young men with arms like hams from working in the fields. Likely, too, she'd already forgotten him; for what, really, would have been the point in remembering?

"It doesn't really matter one way or another, Celia," he said morosely. "My fate being what it is, I'll likely never see the girl again, so cease your scheming before you begin it."

But his sister ignored him. "I'm sure I know her," she said eagerly. "I know nearly everyone, rich or poor, in this part of the county. It's part of being Oliver's wife, you see. Now tell me, Jamie, was she fair-haired or dark?"

"Celia, please, I'm not ready—"

"Fair-haired or dark?"

"She had black hair and blue eyes and a green sort of petticoat," said James with exasperation, "and I swear that's all I can tell you."

"Black hair?" repeated Celia, frowning with perplexed concentration. "The only girl I know with black hair is Betsey Evans, but she is not considered a beauty, not the way a man would see, in any event. Perhaps she was one of the serving girls from the Hall. There always seem to be new faces coming down from London, and if—"

"And she rowed."

At least that brought Celia up short. "She what?"

"I said she rowed," said James. "She jeered at my sorry efforts with an oar, and I dared her to do better, and she did. Right handsomely, too."

"She *jeered* at you?" gasped Celia, shocked from her matchmaking. "Oh, Jamie, that is dreadful! What kind of impudent little baggage would dare treat you like that? After all you've sacrificed for this country, one would think she'd have the decency to show you more respect!"

"Sheathe your claws, Celia," ordered James, amused, and the blue-eyed young woman rose another notch or two in his estimation simply because she'd vexed his sister. "The girl had no more notion of who I was than I did her."

"But you're a hero, James!" declared Celia. "Everyone knows who you are!"

He smiled wryly. "To her I was merely a bumbling incompetent in a boat."

"Oh, yes, *incompetent*." Celia's eyes narrowed with the suspicion that perhaps her brother was not playing fair with her. "You, sir, are not incompetent unless you choose to be. I've heard the surgeons myself. They've done what they can for you, and the rest will or won't be your doing alone. But not if you call yourself *incompetent*. Next you'll be whining on again about being a hopeless old cripple, fit for nothing beyond a cot and a pension in Greenwich! *Incompetent!*"

She snatched up the empty basket and the fishing pole, tidying the lawn with the same brisk efficiency she applied to her parlor, and tried to do with James' life. Muttering crossly to herself, she marched into the vicarage with her apron billowing around her, abandoning her brother to the fate he'd chosen for himself, at least for the next quarter hour.

James watched her go, and though he didn't call her back, he did wonder what demon had made him tease Celia like that. They weren't children anymore—God knows she was a full-grown and determined woman by now, one whose love and attention had kept him from that gloomy pensioner's cot—but this morning he simply hadn't been able to answer her questions with the truthfulness she deserved.

Tossing his hat on the bench to let the breeze ruffle his hair, he chuckled wryly, remembering how Celia had puffed her cheeks with outrage, like the personified versions of the north wind drawn in the corners of maps. If she calmed down enough to consider it, she might interpret his teasing as another sign of recovery, one that proved he was returning to his obstreperous, wicked old self.

Oh, teasing his sister wasn't exactly the same as challenging a French ship of the line, and he wasn't going to fool himself into believing otherwise. But it was a beginning, just as being able to make his way from this vicarage to the pond and back on his own, without a crutch or cane, was a fine beginning, too. He *was* growing stronger each day, just as the surgeons had promised. For once they hadn't lied.

But his smile faded as he remembered the look on the face of the rowing girl when she'd realized the reason for his clumsiness. He hated pity, especially from women. What had happened to him was luck, abominably bad luck, a hazard of the life he'd chosen for himself. Pity was a way to soften and romanticize that bad luck until it became an excuse, and he wanted none of that.

Pity was also the reason he'd squirreled himself away here with his sister and her husband instead of facing down the stares and curiosity of his friends and superiors in London and Portsmouth. The only one in the lot he'd trusted enough to let visit him had been Admiral John Fenner, his first captain and his most loyal supporter in the entire service, almost a second father. Admiral Fenner had seen to it that James had had the best surgeons and the best attention, and had arranged to have him brought back here to Celia rather than left to rot in some wretched hospital. With Fenner's encouragement, James was determined to return to his former life. But when he did, he'd return on his terms, his way, and without a flicker of pity on anyone's face.

And especially not in the brilliant blue eyes of the girl who'd rowed him across the pond.

Carefully he raised his right hand, studying it in the sunlight. Strange how it still looked like a normal appendage, a useful part of himself. The damage was farther up his forearm, a shattered bone here, a mangled tendon there. He'd never been able to make himself listen to the surgeon's coolly impassive explanation of what the jagged wooden splinters like flying knives had done to his pitiful flesh.

Now he tried yet again to flex his fingers and make a tight fist, concentrating so hard that his whole body trembled with the effort. Perhaps his fingers did twitch closer together in obedience. More likely he imagined it, and with a bitter oath he smashed his hand against the back of the bench, howling with pain and frustration.

"Behavior like that will solve all your ills, won't it?" asked Celia, coming to stand before him, hands once again on her hips. "Baying like a wild dog at the moon! You'd do better to read *this*, dear brother, new arrived for you."

She held a folded letter out to him, and for one ridiculously hopeful moment he let himself believe it was from the Admiralty. But the Admiralty didn't send letters by common carriers, nor did they use such luxuriously cream stock with evergreen wax sealed with the arms of the Ashburnham family.

"Why would his ripe and randy lordship write to me?" he asked without taking the letter.

"Hush, Jamie, don't say such things," scolded Celia.

"That family has been good to you, very good, the same as they have been to Oliver. You never would have made captain without the old marquess putting in a word for you, and if you ever wish to have another ship in the future you'll need the assistance of his current lordship as well as dear Admiral Fenner."

"Not that my own merits matter for much, do they?" he asked irritably. "Oh, aye, his lordship will be delighted to help. Having a tame hero from your borough's rather like winning the derby with a pony from your stud. What a pity I'm not nearly as accomplished, nor as obliging."

"You'll bring us all to grief with talk like that," said Celia crossly as she finally shoved the letter into his unwilling fingers. "Now open this directly, and see what his lordship wishes of you."

Yet when he made no move to crack the seal, she snatched the letter back, opening and reading it herself, her lips pressed tightly together.

"It's an invitation," she said. "His lordship has asked you to come to the Hall for a genteel light repast and dancing in honor of his bride. I'll arrange for one of the boys to drive you in Oliver's gig, to make the very best impression. And of course you'll want to wear your new dress coat, to be sure you're properly genteel."

" 'Genteel,' hell," grumbled James. "Not if he's invited me. And since when did he find some greedy unfortunate willing to wed him?"

"I see nothing unfortunate about her at all," said Celia loyally. "By marrying his lordship, she'll be a peeress and welcomed at court."

"But she'll also have to wake with *him* atop her each morning as part of the bargain," said James cynically.

Though the marquess wasn't any less discreet about his personal affairs than most of his counterparts, there were still rumors aplenty about how he chose to amuse himself, and James had known the family long enough that he didn't doubt what he'd heard. "If she's truly fortunate, he won't let marriage change him at all, and he'll keep to whoring and gambling and leave her alone."

"That's only vile rumor and scandal, and none of it proven truth." Celia sighed mightily, a greater admission than James thought he'd ever hear, though her resolve didn't falter. "But none of that matters, not where you're concerned. You *shall* go, James, if I must carry you there on my back."

"You may have to, Celia," said James as he stiffly rose to his feet, "for I won't go under my own sails."

Slowly he started up the walk to the vicarage, leaving his sister to stew behind him. As far as James was concerned, that was the end of the conversation. Though the former marquess, an amiable old gentleman, had used some smattering of influence to help nudge him into his first command, James would be damned before he'd seek or accept such help from his son. He had his reasons, too, most excellent reasons. He just wasn't about to explain them to his sister, that was all.

"No one will call you a cripple," called Celia after him. "I'm certain the company will be too well-bred for that. And you can use your left hand, you know. No one shall be the wiser if you do."

Blast Celia for saying precisely the wrong thing! Once he'd prided himself on writing a neat, gentleman's hand, on being equally adept with a smallsword and a pistol, and splicing a line as swiftly as the oldest salt. Now he could barely dress and feed himself, and with his ham-fisted, backward attempts at using his left hand, he considered it lucky if he didn't spill down the front of himself like a dribbling baby. He didn't care how genteel the company at Ashburnham might be. None of them could avoid thinking of him as a cripple if he put on a dismal performance like that.

"And you might think of someone other than yourself, James," continued Celia, raising her voice just enough so he couldn't ignore her. "Oliver owes his living to his lordship as well, just as father did, and there's no telling what could happen to Oliver and me if his lordship becomes irked with your ungracious behavior."

That slowed him. Once granted, a living and the house and glebe that went with it were seldom taken away from a clergyman except for the most serious scandal. James doubted that the marquess would be so mean-spirited as to do that to Oliver Chase, as mild and kindly a Christian as ever lived.

But his lordship's word and wishes were as good as the king's in this county, and if he decided James had somehow displeased him, then it was conceivable that he'd vent his unhappiness on Celia's husband. James wasn't afraid for his own sake—one over-powdered marquess didn't seem like much after a broadside of French guns—but Celia and Oliver didn't deserve to suffer on his account.

He supposed he could avoid any business involving a knife and fork. And if he stayed among the gentlemen in the card room, then keeping clear of the dancing wouldn't be difficult, either, even if some lady would wish him for a partner.

"And that girl you met earlier, James," called Celia,

plaintive hope still in her voice. "She could be there, too, you know."

He snorted at the notion and his sister's optimism. If the blue-eyed girl were at the Hall, she'd be ferrying covered dishes from the kitchen, not being entertained as a guest. Not that it would matter to him. In a neat cap and apron, she'd still be the saucy lass who'd accepted his dare to row him across the pond, and he chuckled, remembering. How long had it been since he'd met a girl as pretty, as genuine, as that one?

"I can send your acceptance this afternoon," coaxed Celia. "It's only one evening, James. Consider the good that might come of it!"

He sighed, and shook his head at his own woeful sentimentality.

"I'll consider it, aye," he said softly, as much to himself as to Celia. "I'll consider it."

By late afternoon, the rhythm of Ashburnham Hall had shifted again. After the sizable midday meal, Lady Waldegrave had retreated to her chamber to loosen her stays and nap, while Roxby went over accounts and other business in the back parlor. The cook and her staff were simultaneously cleaning up from dinner and beginning preparations for supper, while through the open windows to her bedchamber, Diana could hear the giggles and gossip of the young laundry maids in the kitchen yard, hauling in the tablecloths they'd hung earlier to dry.

Diana sighed, wishing she too were out laughing and gossiping in the warm summer sun. But soon she'd be their mistress, and as such she must regard their merriment not with envy, but with an eye toward brisk efficiency. At Ashburnham, his lordship's shirts and the house linens were always washed on Monday and hung to dry in the open air, with tablecloths hung over the lines exactly in thirds. Tuesday was for washing the ladies' fine and small things and for folding the tablecloths, while Wednesday was reserved for ironing. The schedule never varied while the family was in residence, not even by a day, or woeful and dire consequences were sure to follow. All was explained in the late dowager marchioness' housekeeping book, a thick tome composed over forty years' time and filled with absolute dictates on every subject from mending gentlemen's handkerchiefs with invisible darns, to scouring the brass on the two chinoiserie tall chests in the hall without damaging the lacquer, to employing economical methods of boiling beef for the servants.

Roxby had presented this awful book to Diana soon after they'd arrived at Ashburnham, and his solemnity had made her feel as if she'd been handed down another set of sacred commandments to learn and obey. Dutifully Diana had tried to read the endless pages of exquisitely written dictates, the ink fading now to purple, and this afternoon she'd come back to her room with the best intentions of making more headway in her education as a marchioness.

But Diana was by nature too restless for reading and remembering so many details, and the precise purple words soon blurred before her eyes. With a frustrated sigh she'd finally closed the leather-bound book and used it for a pillow instead, resting her cheek on her folded hands as she let her thoughts wander back to the world she'd left behind.

Homesickness rose as a lump in her throat, a lump she tried her best to swallow. No one had forced her to come to London; it had been her decision entirely. She couldn't let herself forget that, even for a moment.

But there'd been no grim housekeeping rules to memorize in the boisterous Fairbourne family. Her mother had concentrated more on filling their large square house with laughter and love than in keeping it free of dust and beach sand—which, given her brothers and their assorted friends and pets, would have been impossible anyway. Fairbournes never did have much use for rules. Her father was a shipowner and merchant who'd made his first fortune through privateering and his second by smuggling, while her mother had been born a great lady in Ireland, the granddaughter of a duke, who'd raised an enormous scandal years before by running off to the colonies to marry for love.

Her mother had found happiness and joy in Appledore, but Diana had felt constricted by the little town's size, limited by seeing the same people every day of her life. Just like her brothers, she'd craved adventure, new faces and new places. But while her brothers had, one by one, gone off to sea like their father, Diana had chosen the only respectable path for an ambitious and beautiful young woman: she'd sailed with her oldest brother Alexander to London to find true love and the husband of her dreams.

And, oh, Gemini, had she succeeded!

With the guidance of one of her mother's oldest friends from London, Charlotte, Lady Waldegrave, Diana had embarked on a whirlwind siege of fashionable, titled London, who had been entranced by Diana's beauty, wit, and unaffected charm. In the first week, she'd caught Lord Roxby's eye as she'd glided among a sea of elegant ladies at a crowded dance. In a fortnight, he'd overshadowed every other suitor and captured her heart. Before the month was done, he'd asked for her hand, and breathlessly, ecstatically, she'd accepted.

She never imagined she'd fall in love so quickly, or with such wondrous results, and just the thought of Roxby now made her shiver with anticipation. She loved him dearly, and she delighted in the heady prospect of becoming Marchioness of Roxby, with all the privileges and riches that would come with the title. But she'd been slow to listen to Lady Waldegrave's cautions, her little warnings that no such great good fortune in life came without some ill mixed in.

Then had come this journey to Ashburnham Hall and the grim reality of her future responsibilities, as well as the realization that Roxby had other interests of his own that wouldn't include her. And finally this morning, the hateful letter that, according to Roxby, was likely to become a regular sort of occurrence in her public life as his wife.

Forlornly she poked her fingernail into the binding of the housekeeping book. Though she'd never admit it to anyone, especially not to Roxby, she felt overwhelmed and more than a little lonely. Nothing else here in England was as simple as falling in love had been. Everything seemed full of subtle, shifting layers of responsibility and significance. The only uncomplicated, easy pleasure she'd found had been a guilty one, accepting the dare of that scruffy braggart in the boat on the millpond and seeing the look on his face when she'd done exactly as she'd promised.

She sighed wistfully at the memory. The man had been rude and disrespectful, overly familiar, a poacher and a thief. But he was also so much like her brothers and their friends—the wild, rough-hewn sailor boys that she'd grown up with in Appledore—that he'd made her feel relaxed and happy in a way that she doubted she ever would here in Ashburnham, nor should she as a marchioness. Yet for that short time this morning, she'd felt rambunctiously pleased with herself, and knowing she might never feel that way again, let alone see the poacher with the injured hand, only made her savor the memory more. There'd be no advice for *that* kind of foolishness to be found in the housekeeping book, and with a resigned sigh she opened the pages to study again.

Yet when the tap came on her door, she welcomed the interruption and smiled to see the housemaid Mary enter and bustle toward the window.

"I've come to let down the blinds, miss," she explained as she reached for the cords. "On account of the sun shining in so strong at this time of day."

"But I like the sunshine!" protested Diana. "I don't see why you must draw the blinds in the middle of the afternoon!"

"Begging pardon, miss, but that was how her former ladyship always wished it to be, may the good Lord rest her soul." The blinds clacked down, shutting out the sun and the view of the garden with them. "Her ladyship said the afternoon sun must always be kept from this room, miss, else it would spoil the chairs and that mahogany press. She was most specific about that, miss."

Pointedly she glanced down at the book on the table before Diana. "But then you've already read the orders yourself, miss," she said with approval. "Her ladyship was most wise about matters of the house, miss, most wise indeed."

"Indeed," murmured Diana. When *she* became marchioness, she'd choose a sunbeam's cheer over the mahogany press, and give orders that said so, too. She'd no intention of living in the shadows for the sake of the furnishings. "Does his lordship leave orders like that for the staff, too?"

"Nay, miss, not about the house," said Mary, scandalized, as she stood with her hands linked together over her apron. "Those be the lady's decisions. But his lordship does give orders about the cattle and the stables and the grounds and gardens, miss, and about such things as the roof and drives."

"What are his orders regarding poachers?"

"Poachers, miss?" repeated Mary uncertainly. "Here at Ashburnham, miss?"

"Yes, of course," said Diana. She didn't know why such a question had sprung from her lips, but once it had, she was eager for an answer. "I have—I've heard poaching is a problem in the country, and I wondered how his lordship punished offenders."

"His lordship would have them warned first, miss," said Mary, "on account of being so generous, but then he'd have them taken up for the magistrate if they did it still. And if the groundskeeper saw a man at it, stealing his lordship's game, why, then he'd be in his rights to shoot him."

"*Shoot* him, Mary?" repeated Diana, aghast. She wondered if the man in the boat realized the risk he was running. What a sorry end that would be for a man who'd been wounded defending his country! "Surely he wouldn't do anything so . . . so *dire*."

"Yes, miss, he would," said Mary with relish, "and none would think ill of it. Poaching's the same as stealing, miss, and a thief's a thief, even if it be only an extra rabbit or fish for his cottage pot. Shall that be all, miss?"

"Quite all, Mary," said Roxby as he entered the room behind her. "You may go."

"Oh, how very glad I am to see you!" exclaimed Diana, rising from her chair to meet him. He was dressed simply today, his dark hair unpowdered and his coat plain. "I've been quite lonely here by myself."

Roxby smiled as he lifted her hand and bowed slightly over it, turning it over at the last moment to kiss the inside of her wrist, the pleated cuff of his shirt brushing against the back of her hand. She gave a little gasp of pleasure, the way she always did when he kissed her there, over the quickening of her pulse. He knew so many surprising ways to please her that she could scarcely wait until they were wed, to learn what he'd do when he didn't have to restrict himself to kissing her lips or limbs.

"So lonely that you're contemplating poaching the stray stag or hare?" he asked lightly. "I must say, dearest, I didn't know you included setting snares among your varied skills. Is that, too, part of a lady's life in the wilds of Massachusetts?"

"Oh, Roxby, please don't," she said wistfully, her initial pleasure fading. She wished he wouldn't make such jests about the poacher, or her home either, especially since they were already so oddly linked together in her mind. But like every other gentleman who thought London the eye of the universe, Roxby believed that she'd grown up among savages, making her charm an even greater marvel. No matter how much she tried to tell him about her old life, he'd persisted in pretending that her parents wore deerskin leggings and feathers in their hair and lived in a bark-covered hut. "You know I'm still an Englishwoman, only one that was born in New England instead of the old."

For a long moment, his expression didn't change, and his dark eyes so intensely focused on her that she felt her face warm. He was still bending over her hand, but his fingers had tightened around hers with a possessiveness that wasn't entirely comfortable. She'd already learned he didn't like being crossed. Gentlemen of his rank seldom did, and she wondered uneasily if she would always be expected to put his feelings before her own. She loved him, yes, but she didn't want things to be so one-sided between them. It certainly wasn't like that between her parents, and they'd been happily wed forever.

"There are parts of me that I cannot change, Roxby, even for your sake," she said slowly, choosing her words with care. "My family, and the place where I was born—they've made me who I am, and if you find fault with them, then I fear you must find fault with me as well."

At once he released the pressure on her fingers, his eyes filling with such sadness that she wondered if she'd spoken too plainly.

"Pray forgive me, Diana," he said gravely, and when he kissed her hand now it was with contrition instead of desire. "How could I ever dare think ill of your family when I have asked you to take my name and become the perfect center of my life, my own family?"

She understood what his family meant to him, and how much such an apology must cost him, too. "Of course you're forgiven, Roxby," she said softly, "especially since I wished only to explain, not take offense."

He nodded, no more left to be said, and glanced past her to his mother's book, open on the table. "I am heartened to see you take an interest in learning my family's ways. A handful of words from the minister will make you my wife, but becoming my marchioness is vastly more involved."

"I am trying," she said with a sigh, "but there is so much to learn I often feel I'll never master it."

"You will be superb, Diana," he said, silencing her by pressing his fingertip against her lips. Gently he rubbed his finger back and forth over her mouth, tracing the bow of her upper lip and pressing against the plump, sensitive cushion of the one below, tempting her again with yet one more teasing caress. "I'll never let you be anything less."

She thought then he'd surely kiss her, but instead he guided her to stand before the gold-framed looking glass. They made a handsome couple together, nearly the same height, both dark-haired, both fair, him with his dark, serious eyes and her with the sunnier blue, and she smiled proudly at the rightness of their paired reflection.

"Now, my dear," said Roxby softly into her ear, "before you change your mind, here's something that will, I trust, help convince you otherwise."

As she watched, he reached around to drape a necklace around her throat, a necklace of oval rubies that matched the one in his ring, each stone surrounded by a burst of diamonds, all glittering brilliance spilling around her throat and shoulders. For once she was speechless, beyond words or even a gasp, her smile replaced with awe at the generosity of such a gift.

"I want the world to see how much I cherish you, Diana," he murmured as he fastened the catch with a click. "I want them all to know that while I can cover you with precious stones, none of them could be more precious than you are to me."

Carefully Diana touched the largest ruby, centered to rest low over her breasts. The stone was cool beneath her fingers, the rubies and diamonds and gold settings weighing heavily on her skin. This was what she'd come so far to find, wasn't it? What woman could ask for a grander adventure than this?

But who would have dreamed that a king's ransom would also be such a burden?

"Magnificent, my dear," whispered Roxby as he kissed the side of her throat, above the rubies. "Ah, Diana, what a marchioness you shall make!"

And farewell forever to Diana Fairbourne as she'd been, the captain's daughter from Appledore. . . .

With a sigh of surrender, she closed her eyes, and gave herself over to the future that was as brilliant as the stones around her neck.

3

Fool that he was, he'd come back.

The girl had given him no reason to believe she'd return to the pond, yet here James sat again in his brother-in-law's little skiff, the oars shipped and the fishing line over the side in exactly the same patch of water where he'd been yesterday, as if they'd arranged it. This morning there was no bright sunshine to filter through the trees, but gray skies overhead and a gray mist below, gathering in wispy patches across the pond's surface, gray to match his mood.

Fool, *fool*, to think it would be any different! If he hadn't dreamed of her last night, dreamed hot, wicked dreams of her that had made him wake rammy and hard, then perhaps he wouldn't be such a damned fool this morning. Oh, she'd made him feel alive, all right, and sent his wits clear out the window. He grimaced as he remembered the particular care he'd taken with his dress, how he'd fussed at Celia while she'd shaved him, how even now time seemed to crawl as he impatiently scanned the bank for a glimpse of the blue-eyed lass.

Who, of course, having far more sense than he, did not appear.

He swore, with disappointment and disgust and in three languages, too. Oh, aye, he was a fool, all right, a sorry, pathetic excuse for a—

Plop.

At once he turned toward the sound, magnified the way sounds were on a still day like this one. The girl had kicked a stone in the water before; perhaps she'd done it again.

But this sound was different, continuing as it did with a muffled, irregular splashing, nearer to the shore where the rushes grew. Some squirrel that had tumbled from a tree branch, he thought, or one of those fish he seemed so damnably unable to catch, and idly he guided the boat closer to investigate.

With the blade of the oar he pushed aside the reeds. No squirrel or fish, but a very tired, very desperate gray kitten, its small muzzle barely above the surface of the water as it struggled to keep afloat.

"Come aboard now, little fellow," said James as he scooped the exhausted kitten from the water onto his thigh. "We've always room for another castaway in this vessel."

The kitten was shivering violently, from fear and cold, its body pitifully small beneath its sodden fur. Quickly James pulled the neckerchief from around his throat and wrapped it around the kitten, rubbing it gently to try to warm the little cat.

"Oh, sir, you are too good!" cried the woman, and when he looked up, the blue-eyed girl in the green petticoat was standing there exactly as he'd hoped she'd be. "You saved its life, didn't you?"

"It's a kitten," he said, wincing inwardly at the obvious stupidity of such a statement. "A little gray castaway."

"Ah, the sad little darling!" she exclaimed anxiously, her hands clasped before her. "Some villain must have tried to drown him, maybe the whole litter. Quick, quick, do you see any others?"

James shook his head. "Alas, he's the only survivor." Self-consciously he half pushed, half rowed the boat to the shore where she was waiting, thankful that she seemed too concerned with the kitten's fate to comment on his unsteady progress. And she'd come back here to see him, *him*, useless hand or not; that was what mattered.

"But with a dish of warm milk and a cushion by the fire," he continued, "I wager he'll be none the worse for his adventure."

"How I hate such thoughtless cruelty!" she declared vehemently. "Most men wouldn't bother to save a kitten's life, you know. But then you aren't like most men, are you? I saw that directly."

"I've spent too many uncomfortable hours bobbing in the sea myself to abandon a castaway," he said gruffly, ignoring the question of his own remarkability as he climbed from the boat to the bank to show her the kitten. "Mark this little rogue's paws. Seven toes on each foot! That's what saved him, having paddles like that."

But instead of continuing to coo over the little cat the way he'd expected, she drew back, one hand pressed to her chest with shock as she stared at the paws. "Oh, sweet Gemini, it cannot be! It *cannot!*"

"You recognize the beast, then?" he asked, keeping his disappointment to himself as he cradled the kitten in the crook of his arm. Because he'd rescued him, he'd already taken an outlandish liking to the kitten. "I was going to take him in myself, if he needed a homeport. I'd thought to call him Moses, on account of finding him among the bulrushes."

"You can't call him that," she protested. "You must call him Star Bright, on account of the white patch on his forehead. You *must!*"

He hadn't expected such insistence from her, at least not over naming a stray kitten. And to be honest, he hadn't noticed the star-shaped patch of white on the kitten's forehead until she'd pointed it out. He'd been too occupied noticing other things, such as the way her breasts swelled out above her stays. She was taller than he'd realized yesterday in the boat, and standing beside her he began speculating on how long her legs must be beneath those green petticoats. Being tall himself, he liked a good-sized woman—small, fragile women made him uneasy—and he loved long, well-curved female legs tangling with his own.

But the kitten was what she wanted to discuss now; aye, the kitten, and its name.

"Star Bright?" he repeated, dubious. "That's a precious great mouthful to call home from the kitchen door, isn't it?"

" 'Starlight, star bright, first star I see tonight,' " she recited. " 'I wish I may, I wish I might—' "

" 'Have the wish I wish tonight,' " he finished for her. "Aye, aye, I know the rhyme, but that's scarce reason to call my cat after it."

"But it *is*," she said, agitated in a way that made no sense to him. She sighed and shook her head, then looked up at him, imploring. "Might I hold the kitten? Please? For a moment?"

He'd have given her the world if she'd asked, just for the sake of having her linger with him now. Instead he merely had to dislodge the kitten's claws from his coat sleeve and pass him to her, their fingers brushing together. The kitten mewed with protest, but when she hugged him close he settled contentedly against her bosom, the lucky little bastard.

"My brother had a kitten much like this, called Starlight," she began, her words rushing over one another. "The seven toes, the white star, all of it the same except for being black, and all of it meant for luck, and for love. That's what the old woman who gave him to us said, that he'd help us find our true loves. So if you name this kitten Star Bright, then he'll find your true love for you, too."

"True love for me?" asked James, bemused. Like most sailors, superstition was so much a part of his life that he seldom questioned it, but for this half-drowned little cat to have the power of matchmaking for him—well, not even he could trust in the magic of seven for that.

"For you, yes, because he'll belong to you." She glanced up at him uncertainly. "That is, if you don't have a true love already."

"Do you believe I'd be here now if I did?" He grinned crookedly, but he meant it, too. He was old-fashioned that way, not fast and loose like the gentry. He wasn't sure he believed in "true love," but he did firmly hold to one woman at a time in his life, and if he ever did earn enough to marry and support a wife, then she would be the last woman in his life this side of the grave. "Besides,

I wouldn't need a kitten's help, anymore than a handsome lass like you would."

She blushed prettily. "Not from Star Bright, no. Not today."

"Not for either of us, then, lass," he said easily, shifting closer so that he'd be ready to slip his arm around her when the time was right. "We've managed to take care of ourselves just fine, haven't we?"

Her blush deepened. "Yes," she said. "Because of that other kitten, the one called Starlight, I've already found my true love."

"You have, have you?" Damnation, why was he horribly certain she didn't mean him?

She nodded, raising her chin a fraction higher. "Starlight first found my brother a most splendid wife, a Scotswoman, and then he found a perfect gentleman for me. We're to be married early next month, as soon as the arrangements are complete and the banns are read."

"You are." If he'd felt like a fool before, now he felt a thousand times worse, an ogling ass trying to seduce a woman promised to another. Somehow he managed to bow, the proper formal gesture so ingrained that it came to his rescue now. "Then let me congratulate you, miss, and wish you joy and plenty in your marriage."

"Thank you." Yet she didn't look happy, the way a bride should, and he couldn't help seeing how her nose had turned red, as if she were half inclined to weep. "I came here to warn you, you know. I don't want you to be shot, because you don't deserve that."

"Shot? Who the devil would want to shoot me now?"

"For *poaching!*" she cried, and impatiently dashed the heel of her hand against her eye, trying to stop those inappropriate tears from spilling over. "His lordship's keepers have orders to shoot anyone poaching on his land, which is *exactly* what you're doing!"

His brows rose with surprise. Fishing and rowing on the millpond were express privileges of the vicarage household; Oliver had been assured of that by his lordship. "I wouldn't call plucking kittens from the pond 'poaching.' Not even the marquess himself would make a mistake like that."

"Then go ahead and *fish*, you great stubborn noddy!" she cried, thrusting the kitten back into his hand. "Go ahead and be shot dead, and see if I care whatever happens to you!"

Before he could answer, she turned and ran, disappearing from his morning as abruptly as she'd entered it. For a long time he stared after her, and so did the kitten in his arm. But he didn't follow—lame as he was, he wouldn't be able to catch her even if he tried—and besides, there wasn't much left to say between them.

"Fat lot of good you've done me, old man," he said glumly as he stroked the kitten's ears. "I thought you were supposed to help me with women, eh?"

The gray kitten purred and blinked and promised nothing. And so much, thought James, for his luck changing, except from bad to worse.

"Hurry, Giulietta, hurry, *hurry*, please!" urged Diana as she sat before the mirror while Giulietta, her new lady's maid, dressed her hair. The woman was from Rome, and though she spoke little English, or at least pretended not to, she could work magic with hair and gowns. Roxby had hired her away from the Countess of

Granby, one more gift to lavish on his bride, and prepared a list of translated orders to help Diana converse with her.

But even so Diana felt uneasy around the small, silent woman with sad eyes, and she'd already decided that, once they were wed and settled, she'd let Giulietta return to the countess and find a cheerful maid more to her own liking. "Please, ah, that is, *prèsto, prèsto, per cortesìa!*"

"*Si, mía signoria,*" murmured Giulietta, unperturbed. Deftly she slicked sugar water along a curl of Diana's hair to help hold its shape, then pinned it in place with a small silk flower. "*Uno momènto, mía signoria.*"

Diana sighed impatiently, trying to sit as still as she could so Giulietta could finish transforming her hair into a glossy crown of curls and tiny braids, dotted with silk forget-me-nots and topped with a circle of lace pretending to be a cap. Roxby had asked her to go walking with him in the rose garden at ten o'clock, to discuss plans for the entertainment in her honor the following week. By swiveling her eyes, she could just see the tall clock, and just see, too, that she'd only five minutes left.

"Hurry, *hurry!*" she muttered, drumming her fingers on the edge of the dressing table. In Massachusetts she'd always dressed her own hair, except for the most special occasions when her mother's maid would help her, and she still wasn't accustomed to going through this ritual each day, twice if they were in London and she needed to have her dark hair dusted white with powder as well.

Oh, why, why had she taken so long at the millpond! All she'd meant to do was warn the man in the boat about his fishing, the briefest, most polite of warnings for his own good. It was only because he'd reminded her of home that she'd gone, and because he seemed to be so down on his luck, the very opposite of her own rising fortunes. Her concern had absolutely nothing to do with the fact that he was rather handsome in a rough-and-tumble way, or that when she'd bantered with him she hadn't had to weigh and consider every word for subtleties, the way she did with Roxby and his friends.

But instead she'd watched the man rescue a kitten from drowning and praised him for his kindness. She'd waited until he'd brought the kitten to shore so she could hold it, and she'd babbled on about magic cats with seven toes and true love and who knows what else. She'd spoken with him so much longer than that polite warning that they'd almost lapsed into private conversation. No, they *had* lapsed, and she groaned at the memory of how appallingly forward she'd been.

"Unwell, *mía signoria?*" asked Giulietta, pausing with a frown of concern. "I stop?"

"Oh, no, please don't do that!" She couldn't remember how to say the words in Italian, and motioned around her head instead. "His lordship is expecting me, and I must go to—"

"Good morning, Diana," said Lady Waldegrave as she swept into the room. "I trust you are well?"

"Oh, yes, my lady," said Diana, sliding from the bench just as Giulietta thrust the final pin into her hair. The older woman was her adviser and her sponsor and her mother's oldest friend, but she was also the dowager

Countess of Waldegrave and deserving of the curtsy that Diana hastily dipped before her. "And you, my lady? You are well, too?"

"I have been better." With an elaborate sigh, the older woman sat in a brocaded armchair facing Diana, carefully turning to be sure the daylight from the windows fell at a flattering angle across her face. In her youth, Lady Waldegrave had been a famous beauty and a favorite at court, and though age had diminished her power, she could still accomplish a great deal with her smile alone. Even at this hour, she had not left her chamber before painting her face and having her wig curled and powdered. Her gown was lavender satin with cuffs and a scarf of ecru Valenciennes lace, while diamonds and sapphires glittered on her fingers and throat. As always she seemed the elegant, composed lady that Diana feared she'd never be.

Now Lady Waldegrave flicked open her gilt-bladed fan and glanced over the top at Diana's maid. "Giulietta, go tell his lordship that Miss Fairbourne has been detained but will join him shortly."

"My lady, she won't be able to explain!" whispered Diana urgently as the maid curtsyed and left them. "She doesn't understand what we say!"

"She understands far more than you credit her, Diana," said Lady Waldegrave. "Or perhaps you do, else you wouldn't be whispering now to save wounding her feelings."

Diana frowned, wishing her own feelings might matter a bit more.

"Don't be sullen, Diana," chided the countess. "It is unbecomingly childish. Now pray stop fluttering about me like a starling and sit, sit, so we may have a civilized discourse."

Dutifully Diana sat, taking care to swing her skirts gracefully to one side over her legs the way the countess had taught her. At least she could do that much right.

"You could learn from that little Italian woman, you know," continued the countess. "She understands her place and yours. She understands that she has no feelings for you to wound, for she is a servant and a foreigner, whereas you will be an English peeress."

"I only wished to be kind!"

"Lord Roxby is not marrying you to be *kind*, Diana," said Lady Waldegrave severely. "A marriage such as the one on which you have chosen to embark holds certain obligations and expectations. Lord Roxby expects you to oversee his establishments and manage his servants, to make his home an agreeable and elegant haven for him and for his guests. You cannot do that being unduly *kind* to servants."

Diana sighed, once again seeing the looming, leather-bound specter of the Ashburnham housekeeping book. "Yes, my lady. I shall try to do better, my lady."

"Indeed." Mollified, Lady Waldegrave tipped her head back to consider Diana's hair. "I must say, Diana, that Giulietta has dressed your head uncommonly well. How clever of his lordship to obtain her for you! Yet if all he cared for in a wife was household maintenance, he could marry his housekeeper, couldn't he?"

She smiled, and winked slyly at Diana over the arc of her fan. "But that is not so, is it? No, no! You are his prize, his rarest gem, his loveliest flower, and you have made him the envy of every other gentleman in the realm. Which is expressly why I have come to speak to you this morning."

"No, my lady," said Diana uncertainly, not quite sure whether the countess was going to praise her or scold her again. "That is, in regard to his lordship's devotion for me, yes, my lady, you are right."

Lady Waldegrave sniffed. "Of course I am right. Which is why you must heed what I now say. I've heard that you have continued going out alone in the earliest hours, quite insisting upon it, despite his lordship's disapproval."

"Oh, Roxby doesn't disapprove," said Diana with relief. "He calls me his dear Madame Lark, and I hear no disapproval in that."

"Then you must learn to listen more closely," said the countess, closing her fan with a crack as she leaned forward in her chair. "In a few days this house will be filled with his lordship's friends and acquaintances, and they will be watching you, measuring your every word and step to see if you are worthy of him."

"But that is not—"

"Hush, and listen! This time will decide your entire life's success, my dear. You must subjugate your willfulness—and you *are* willful, Diana—to his lordship's wishes in everything. Your behavior must be impeccable, or you shall never recover from the talk."

"Oh, yes, and all because I have the audacity to wish to walk by myself!" Diana rose swiftly to her feet, too upset to sit still any longer. She'd had similar conversations with Lady Waldegrave before, but the countess had never spoken so emphatically, all *must's* and *must not's*. "A simple walk is sufficiently scandalous to ruin my life, while Roxby can be rumored to keep some low sort of woman as his mistress without any damage to his at all!"

Lady Waldegrave looked at her sharply. "Where, pray, did you hear that?"

"From a letter." Diana swept one of the stiff sugar-water curls back from her cheek as she paced back and forth before the countess. "Some cowardly woman sent me a letter that she did not sign, telling me that I shouldn't marry Roxby because he keeps a mistress in London."

"Oh, my dear, I am sorry." Lady Waldegrave sighed. "You shouldn't have had to hear that, not so close to your wedding."

"But it's not true, of course," said Diana firmly. "I asked Roxby himself, and he assured me it was a lie. He loves me too much for it to be otherwise."

The countess gasped, clutching the fan to her breast. "You dared *ask* his lordship such a question about his most private affairs?"

"Who better to ask?" Diana smiled confidently. "Besides, it's hardly his private affair if it isn't true."

Her ladyship shook her head, her earbobs swaying gently as she clucked her tongue with dismay. "You never, never question a gentleman's honor, Diana, even if the gentleman is your husband. *Especially* if he's your husband! Oh, child, he could have broken your betrothal over this and your heart with it! I'd have thought your own mother would have explained that much!"

Abruptly Diana stopped pacing. Her mother had wanted true love for her, the same kind of love she'd found with her father. True love had been the promise of the little seven-toed cat as well, a promise delivered when she'd met Roxby, and the memory of her seven-toed cupid with the white star on its forehead made her smile. That had been another thing her mother had told her. You don't find love, it finds you, and often in the most peculiar ways, too.

But because Lady Waldegrave had never put much stock in the kitten theory, Diana kept that part to herself and offered a shorter version instead.

"What my mother told me, my lady," she said, "was to like the man I loved and to love the man I married. And with Roxby, I do. I *do*."

"Be sure," warned the countess. "Not only about loving him, but all the rest of it as well. Because soon, very soon, it will be too late to change your mind. You cannot shame a man as proud and powerful as the Marquess of Ashburnham, my dear, not without the most serious consequences to both yourself and your family."

"I will not change my mind, my lady," answered Diana as she draped a lace scarf over her shoulders, "because I love Roxby, and I know he loves me. And that, my lady, is all that truly matters."

Truly, truly, she thought happily as she hurried down the long front staircase to meet Roxby for their walk. Yet as she did, an odd realization jolted through her thoughts.

The seven-toed kitten she'd been seeing in her mind's eye wasn't black, the way her brother's Starlight had been, but gray, like the kitten the teasing poacher had rescued from the millpond. And instead of Roxby's wonderfully modulated voice, almost a large cat's purr in itself, the voice she'd been hearing was the rough growl of the green-eyed man as he'd wished her joy and plenty in her marriage.

And in the distance, over the fields, came the first rumble of thunder.

"Rain," observed Roxby, standing before the tall window with his hands clasped loosely behind his back. "So much for dallying with my bride amongst the boxwoods."

Sprawled in a chair behind him, Lord Stanver snorted derisively. "Why do I not doubt you'll find somewhere else instead?"

"Why?" repeated Roxby with a half smile of amusement as he turned back to face his friend. "Why? Because, Stanver, you know me vastly too well for comfort."

Though Roxby took care to keep his voice wry, both men knew the uneasy truth in his words. Certainly no one did know him better than Stanver, not in this life or the next. In some remote way, the two of them were cousins, but blood wasn't what had bound them so tightly together for nearly fourteen years. That was when they'd first met in Naples, two bored, wealthy young gentlemen traveling with their tutors.

Instantly each had recognized the seeds of corruption mirrored in the other, and from then on they'd become partners in every sort of indulgence and debauchery that their titles and wealth could mask, a remarkably decadent, yet potent, basis for a lasting friendship. Neither now would ever betray the other; they shared far, far too many secrets.

Idly—which was how he conducted his life in general—Stanver studied Roxby through the drifting tobacco haze that rose from his long-stemmed pipe. "I might know you too well, Roxby, but scarcely well enough. For I still cannot begin to fathom why you need a damned *bride* to dally with at all."

Roxby smiled wearily. He was certain he'd explained this at least a score of times to his friend, but then Stanver could be remarkably dense if he chose to. "I need a bride because I need an heir, else all I own will go to some puling nephew in the north that I have never met."

"But by then you shall be dead and rotting in hell for all eternity," said Stanver pleasantly, "and past caring."

Roxby's smile lost any amusement it had held. "But you see, I care *now*. I own that I am selfish; I do not like to share. I wish my title and my lands and everything else to go to my own blood. And not even you, Stanver, have determined a way to breed without involving a female, preferably a wife, to make the outcome legitimate."

Stanver slid further down in the chair, linking his fingers comfortably over the front of his waistcoat, which, Roxby noted critically, seemed to be fitting much more snugly than it used to. "But why the devil this girl from the colonies? Why not one of the other fillies with a pedigree that the mamas parade before your nose every winter?"

"Are you blind, then, as well as stupid?" inquired Roxby patiently. "Miss Diana Fairbourne is the most ravishing young creature to appear in London in years. Every man wanted her, but I'm the only one who'll have her."

He smiled again, letting himself bask in the pleasurable certainty of that. He liked owning things that no one else could, especially not Stanver. As if to reinforce the point he plucked a priceless bit of Chinese ivory from the sideboard, turning the intricately carved ball-within-a-ball in his long fingers.

"Though her pedigree's fine enough—she's great-granddaughter to some duke or t'other, despite living off among the savages—what pleases me is that she's strong and healthy, none of your pallid hothouse misses. I'll wager you now she'll drop my first son nine months to the day from our wedding."

"Breeding stock," said Stanver sourly. "Gad. One more prize mare or bitch for you here in the country."

"Oh, I don't intend to squander my dear Diana like that," said Roxby as he tipped the ivory ball from one hand to the other. "I mean to discover considerable amusement in her as well. A beautiful, passionate young lady, by law my rightful property to do with whatever I wish once we're wed, and her father and brothers safely on the other side of the world—Stanver, you of all others, should be able to see the possibilities."

But Stanver wasn't going to see anything yet, his features set with a stubbornness that Roxby uncharitably found rather porcine. Once Stanver had had a male cherubim's beauty, but time and dissipation had turned his rosy cheeks florid and slack, and draped his china-blue eyes with bilious pouches.

"She didn't like hearing about you and Justine," said Stanver petulantly. "I'll wager she made things hot for you about that."

Carefully Roxby returned the ivory ball to its lacquered stand. "So the letter came through your hands, did it? I'd suspected as much."

"You won't be able to keep Justine now," said Stanver with relish. "You can't have them both. Your fair *wife* won't let you."

"I'm entering marriage, Stanver, not a monastery," answered Roxby, unperturbed. He was quite fond of Justine, both for her exotic beauty and her acrobat's flexibility, and he saw her as a complement to Diana, not a rival. "But since I've no intention of ever introducing my wife to my mistress, I see no problem in maintaining them both."

Stanver scowled, gnawing on the stem of his pipe. " 'Tis not fair, Roxby," he complained. " 'Tis not fair at all."

"Life seldom is, is it?" Roxby smiled expansively, and held his hand out to greet Diana, blushing and beaming as the footman opened the door for her. Perhaps life was not fair for poor Stanver, but it certainly was for him. "Ah, you see, Stanver, here is my dearest bride now, my Diana, the one true love of my life."

4

"Two letters in as many days," said Celia brightly, wiping a plate dry as she waited for James to share whatever news, good or ill, that his latest letter had brought. "That's two more messengers than we usually receive in a week!"

But James didn't care about the messengers or his sister's curiosity. All that mattered now was the letter in his hand, sealed with the familiar crest of the Admiralty Board itself. His future, his whole life really, depended on whatever was written inside. Turning away from his sister and toward the light from the kitchen window, he cracked the seal, took a deep breath, and forced himself to read the letter. He read it quickly once, remembered to exhale, then read it again.

And this time he smiled, grinning so broadly and with such unabashed relief that he had to take another deep breath before he could turn toward his sister.

"They've taken me back," he said. "The last surgeon who saw me—a rheumy-eyed old sot named Tucker—took pity on me and said I was fit again for service and for another command."

"Oh, James, that is splendid!" cried Celia, flinging her

arms and the wet washing-cloth around his shoulders to hug him. "But how could they decide otherwise for the heroic captain of the *Castor?*"

"Since the heroic captain lost that same *Castor* in the process, they could very well have left me here to rot the rest of my life," he cautioned. "It's only luck that Tucker was too drunk to realize I still cannot hold a pistol or swing a sword. This letter really promises nothing, Celia, only that I'm back on the Captain's List."

"Where you belong, Captain Dunham," said Celia staunchly as she stood back. "It's bravery and intelligence the navy values in officers, not whether you can single-handedly slay a regiment of Frenchmen."

"The navy expects all of that, Celia, and a good deal more. Doubtless this is only because Fenner's put in an extra word for me again."

"Oh, James, can't you ever be happy?" To James' surprise there were tears in his sister's eyes, tears that she dabbed at daintily with the washing-cloth. "Hasn't your luck changed? You were ready to blame that poor little cat for all your ills, yet here he's brought you the best news in the world."

James sighed, knowing he wasn't going to be able to explain how he felt to Celia, or how his happiness didn't really have much to do with the Admiralty's opinion of him one way or another. Still, if he were being honest, his lot *had* improved since he'd risen this morning, and it could be as much the kitten's doing as anything else. The little gray cat was sitting on the window sill, entirely recovered from his near drowning and now sunning himself beside a potted geranium.

"So you've brought me this fine fortune, eh, Brighty,

old man?" he asked, rubbing the cat's ears. "You've earned a place on my crew, rated captain's cat and able-bodied, too."

Purring, the cat gazed up at him adoringly enough that James grinned again. He'd have to stop doing that; the captains of frigates were supposed to be daring, heartless bastards, not grinning imbeciles.

Yet as he ruffled the kitten's ears, he couldn't help but think once again of the girl at the pond. He'd told himself before that she was likely promised to another man—she was too fair not to be—but he'd still dared hope otherwise, and now felt her announcement more keenly than he'd any right to. If the kitten truly were doling out luck, then of course he'd rather have had this Admiralty letter above everything. But was it selfish to wish he'd the girl alongside him as well, to help him celebrate?

"Now you've every reason to go to Ashburnham tomorrow," continued Celia, raising her voice as she bustled up the back stairs. "You must plead your case with his lordship, James. You know how the game is played. You must garner as much influence among those people as you can to earn another ship."

"Celia, I've told you before that I mean to stand on my own merit, not—"

Not anything, apparently, for he forgot it all as soon as he looked up and saw his sister and the captain's dress coat in her hands. His old coat had been respectable but little else, of the kind of cloth and workmanship that self-made captains could afford, and scarcely different from what a middling shopkeeper wore on shore. But this new coat told another story, midnight blue wool with white silk lining and thick gold braid that shone with the same authority as the rows of polished brass buttons, the coat of an affluent, successful captain.

"A gift of gratitude from the merchants that owned the ship you saved," explained Celia proudly, brushing away an invisible speck of lint from the coat's sleeve. "Bespoke and tailored to your measurements, James, and delivered when you were still so ill. I hadn't the heart to show it to you before, but now—now you're worthy of it once again, Captain Dunham."

Awkwardly he shrugged his way into the coat, at once feeling the difference in the cut, how it fit so perfectly over his shoulders and around his waist. A coat like this would make people overlook his useless hand and lurching walk, just as it was making him stand straighter, more confidently.

And once again he caught himself thinking of the girl by the pond. Would she have been as quick to mention her wedding if he'd been dressed like this then? Would she have judged him as something more worthy than a law-breaking poacher?

"Aye, aye, Captain!" said Celia, pretending to salute. "Clear for Ashburnham, sir, and prepare for battle!"

Clear for battle, aye, resolved James, squaring his shoulders. Enough daydreaming about lasses and kittens. Time to look to the future that was once again before him.

And forget the woman that never would be his.

"You are doing splendidly, Miss Fairbourne," said Lady Marchmont as she languidly feathered her fan before her face, attempting to find some breath of air in the crush of the party. "One would think you'd always been a part of all this wretched rigmarole of ours."

"Thank you, my lady," answered Diana, genuinely pleased by the compliment. Young Lady Marchmont had long been a friend of Roxby's, and because he valued her opinion Diana did too, flattered that the other woman had asked her to join her in this window alcove, a bit of peace away from the crowd of Roxby's guests.

Lady Marchmont wasn't as classically beautiful as many of the other ladies, but she had style and flair, and she wasn't afraid to set a new fashion instead of slavishly following an old one. Because she'd had smallpox as a girl, she painted her face heavily to cover the scars, dotting the worst ones on her cheeks with tiny black velvet patches cut in fancy shapes—hearts, diamonds, spades—that accentuated the liveliness of her round, dark eyes. She was witty and quick and forgot nothing, and because she freely, daringly, spoke her mind, she'd been labeled fast by the older dowagers like Lady Waldegrave. But all the gentlemen sought her company because she made them laugh and feel wicked, and so, now, did Diana.

"You're very kind, my lady," she continued. "But I'm not certain that Roxby would wish to hear his party dismissed as 'wretched rigmarole.' "

"Oh, but it is," said Lady Marchmont, making her eyes so round they seemed to pop from her face. "Look at all these foolish folks! They've come to pay homage to you, which of course is not foolish in the least, but they've also come to drink and eat and piss away as much as they possibly can at Roxby's expense, laying waste like locusts on the plain. Country squires and county gentry, all putting on such airs to try to outdo their betters!"

"Roxby wished to invite everyone, for tradition's sake," explained Diana, though she, too, had been horrified by the greediness of some of their guests, who pushed and shoved to reach the tables with the food and wine. There must be two hundred people crowded into the long gallery and adjoining dining hall, and the din of their voices rose above the musicians just as the heat from all the bodies made even this spacious room seem close. "He said if he played host to them now, then they wouldn't feel slighted if they weren't invited to the wedding."

"And a wise notion it is, too. Who would want this crush at a wedding?" Lady Marchmont patted the spray of diamonds pinned into her powdered hair. "Cheek to jowl, we are, and what mighty jowls some of these ladies do sport, too! And as for their gowns—I ask you, Miss Fairbourne, have you ever seen their like for artless, provincial pretension?"

Warily Diana glanced at Lady Marchmont, hoping she wasn't including in her wholesale indictment Diana's own pale blue silk damask gown, plain by comparison to the glittering *robe à la française* that the other lady was wearing. Thanks to her indulgent father, Diana had left Appledore with a wardrobe as lavish as any in the colony. But what had seemed on the edge of fashion in New England was long past the mode in London, and while Roxby had been most gallant about not criticizing her clothes, she knew that once they were wed, simple gowns like this one would be replaced with others far more grand.

"Perhaps they are following the style for this county, Lady Marchmont," she suggested, taking the side of the provincial ladies. "Or rather they wish to keep within their means."

"Oh, fah, not *economy*," scoffed Lady Marchmont with withering contempt. "One cannot expect *economy* to have anything to do with one's fashionable appearance."

"But there are times when it does," insisted Diana, remembering the unhappy frugality when one of her father's voyages failed to produce the expected profit. "And with the French wars, sometimes one has no choice but to do without."

"Not married to Roxby, you won't," said the other woman archly, trailing the edge of her fan lightly along Diana's throat, a caress that made Diana draw back. "Look at you tonight! You combine the simplicity of your gown—such a perfect virginal blue for a bride— with Roxby's rubies around your throat like some pasha's favorite houri. You have given these fat squires' wives and daughters something rare to see, something worthy. No wonder Roxby loves you so."

"A pasha's houri?" repeated Diana incredulously, touching her fingers to the necklace around her neck. "Now you're portraying me like a character from a masque or play, as if I'm no more than some—some *spectacle*."

"Exactly so, darling girl," said Lady Marchmont with a trill of amusement. "For isn't that the very essence of being Roxby's marchioness?"

But Diana didn't join her laughter. She wouldn't deny that she enjoyed Roxby's generosity, or that she found pleasure in the attention that came from being his betrothed. Yet surely even a woman as worldly as Lady Marchmont still believed that love was more important than possessions in a marriage?

But Lady Marchmont's interest had already flitted away, and impatiently she was squinting over her fan at the other guests. "How vastly vexing! Roxby vowed to me that Captain Dunham was here somewhere, but I've yet to see even the tiniest scrap of gold lace of him yet. I am so perishing to meet the man, you know!"

"Captain Dunham?" Diana thought she'd received all the guests as they'd come up the front stairs, but this name didn't sound familiar. "I don't recall him, my lady."

"*Recall* him!" Lady Marchmont shrugged with elaborate disbelief. "Captain Dunham is only the most divine hero of our time, Miss Fairbourne, the *Castor*'s master! Not only did he destroy a French ship twice his own vessel's size, but at the same time he quite saved a merchant ship full of English ladies and children from being sold into certain slavery to the Moors!"

"Gemini," murmured Diana. If even half of that was true, which she rather doubted, the man would indeed be a hero. "And you say he is here?"

Lady Marchmont nodded eagerly. "The ladies he rescued swear he was most wonderfully gallant and brave—they're all half mad in love with him—for they said he was most wonderfully handsome, too, in a manly, military way."

"A paragon among men, then," said Diana, now thoroughly sure that the stories were exaggerated. The navy officers she'd seen in New England had been a shabby, unimpressive lot, blustery and overbound by their orders and their honor, and the ponderous targets of many of her brothers' worst jests and pranks. "Mars combined with Adonis, and doubtless considerate to his old mother and spinster aunt as well."

"Don't speak so, Miss Fairbourne, or people will believe you favor the French," warned Lady Marchmont slyly, "or even worse, that you have become as wicked as I. You see, while Captain Dunham was being so wonderfully heroic, he was also wounded, near mortally they say, and no one—certainly no lady—has seen him since."

That was more sobering, and at once Diana thought of the poor man at the millpond. Though he'd been wounded and scarred in battle, too, he had no grand ladies fussing over him and was reduced to poaching to feed himself.

"It's a difficulty, yes," continued Lady Marchmont, who likely confronted no serious difficulties in her life at all. "One does prefer heroes who are quite whole, but I do pray that dear Captain Dunham may be sufficient for the role I wish for him, after I—oh, oh, this must be him with Roxby now!"

She swooped a path through the crowd, drawing Diana with her so quickly that Diana had only the most jumbled impressions of the women around her openly gawking at her necklace and men just as openly ogling her décolletage and a footman balancing a silver tray piled high with a pyramid of pink ices and biscuits over the heads of everyone else.

Then suddenly before her was Roxby, a crystal glass

of claret in his hand and his head tipped to one side as he listened to another's conversation, and beside him a broad shouldered gentleman in a dark blue coat trimmed with gold braid, standing straighter, taller it seemed, than anyone else in the room. His light brown hair was unpowdered, glinting gold beneath the candlelight, and sleeked back into a tightly braided sailor's queue and tied with a dark silk bow.

"Roxby, Roxby, you are being abominably selfish!" called Lady Marchmont with cheerful belligerence. "Miss Fairbourne and I are fair *perishing* to meet Captain Dunham, and here you've kept him entirely to yourself!"

Roxby turned toward them with obvious pleasure, looking past Lady Marchmont directly to Diana. But as Diana returned his smile, the tall man in blue behind him turned as well, and every sensible thought—and a good many nonsensical ones, too—fled from her mind. She felt Roxby's fingers envelop hers, felt his lips graze hers to prove he'd missed her in the quarter hour they'd been separated, heard him make a proper introduction to the tall man now bending over her hand.

Dear, dear Lord, what had he told Roxby? Not that she'd done anything wrong, because she hadn't—she was certain of that—but the circumstances could certainly be twisted about to make it seem that way, especially going back to the pond the second time.

Oh, what had he told Roxby? And what, oh, what, had Roxby said in return?

"I am honored, Miss Fairbourne," said the man, the gruffness she'd remembered in his voice now polished with politeness. She'd find no fault with him there, and

when he straightened from his bow his expression was
so properly impassive that it could have passed for bore-
dom: one more lady to charm and flatter, ho-hum, la-
de-dah.

And then, before Roxby and Lady Marchmont and
scores of others, he gave her fingers a most definitely un-
bored and unmistakable squeeze.

A squeeze that brought Diana's indignation into full
seething flower. Why hadn't he told her who he was at
the pond? Why had he let her make such a fool of herself, pretending he was nothing but a scarred, beggarly
poacher instead of a veritable *saint*?

"You are most kind, Captain Dunham," she replied
with a perfunctory smile for the benefit of Roxby and
the others. "But we are the ones honored by the presence
of such a famously brave hero."

She noticed how he'd used his left hand to take hers,
and how he kept his right, the one that been too scarred
to hold an oar, carefully hooked on the hilt of his dress
sword, where it wouldn't embarrass him. At least that
much about him had been true. How she wished now
that the rest of it had been, too!

He nodded solemnly, not returning her smile. "My
fame is old news, Miss Fairbourne, while yours is rising
like a star in the night sky."

"You make a pretty compliment, Captain." Her smile
felt stiff and fixed with anxiety. He *was* handsome, curse
him, and Roxby would never understand that she'd
gone back to the pond with only the noblest of intentions.

"You make a pretty inspiration, Miss Fairbourne," he
countered, and she was sure she caught a glimmer of

amusement lurking in his green eyes just for her. Blast him, he was *enjoying* tormenting her like this.

"Your beauty, Miss Fairbourne, your grace," he continued. "No one speaks of anything else, and yet nothing prepared me for the real Miss Diana Fairbourne."

Bilgewater, thought Diana sourly as she pulled her hand free. He'd already seen more than enough of the real Diana Fairbourne, while he had deceitfully hidden his own identity from her. He didn't truly expect her to believe this sort of drivel, did he? She didn't, not in the least; but Lady Marchmont was certainly willing enough to do so.

"Oh, Miss Fairbourne, did I not tell you Captain Dunham was the most perfect hero?" she purred, edging around Diana to sidle closer to the tall man. "Have you ever heard of such gallantry?"

"Not gallantry," said Roxby with proud—and reassuring—satisfaction, curling his arm around Diana's waist, "but simple truth. You've seen much of the world during your voyages, Captain Dunham. Have you ever seen any other more lovely than my bride come clear from New England?"

"New England?" The captain's brows rose with surprise. "Then I am even more impressed by Miss Fairbourne, my lord, for her to have flowered in such a place."

"You have journeyed there, sir?" asked Roxby curiously. "Diana has told me of her home, of course, but I've never visited myself."

The captain nodded as he answered but kept his gaze upon Diana. "I once had the misfortune to spend a year in Boston, a small, mean town that is the capital of those colonies, filled with canting preachers, rogues, and painted savages."

"Savages, sir?" Roxby quirked a single, skeptical brow as he sipped the claret. "Surely you exaggerate?"

"Not by half, my lord," declared the captain, that teasing, taunting glimmer in his eyes again. "Savages, smugglers and law-breaking rogues of every size and description is what you'll find in Boston, my lord."

"Oh—oh!" sputtered Diana, stunned that he'd dare say such lies. "You are most wrong!"

"I regret that I am offending you, Miss Fairbourne," continued the captain with infuriating evenness, "but based on my own experience in the colony, I stand by my observation. You are most definitely the exception, ma'am. I've never seen such a haven for thieves and rascals who care nothing for their king and only for their own pockets."

Furiously she shook her head, the ruby earrings that matched the necklace swinging against her cheeks. What he'd said had *hurt,* not just because he was defaming her home, but because after meeting him at the pond she'd thought they'd be more alike, more in sympathy, two sea-loving outsiders in a landlocked world. It made no sense, really; what was any captain in the English navy to her? She was losing her temper and she knew it, yet just as equally she knew she couldn't let his comments pass unanswered.

"But these miscreants and misfits you describe, sir," she said, her voice rising with emotion, "surely you do not mean the good people of Massachusetts—surely you do not mean my own family!—but the prison leavings and impressed half-wits that fill your own infernal, interfering navy!"

For a long—too long—minute, neither the captain nor Roxby spoke.

"Dear, dear," murmured Lady Marchmont with undisguised relish. "Dear, *dear*."

The captain cleared his throat. "Perhaps I have spoken too frankly for Miss Fairbourne's, ah, sensibilities."

"It's hardly my sensibilities that are offended," began Diana warmly, only now beginning to realize how badly she'd misstepped. "For you to say such—"

"Diana, come," said Roxby curtly, his host's smile replaced by something considerably more forbidding as he set his now empty glass down with a thump on the tray of a startled footman.

"But I do not understand why I—"

"Not here, Diana," he said, his fingers locking tightly around her upper arm. "You will excuse us, Lady Marchmont, Captain Dunham."

Diana didn't know if they excused them or not, because Roxby was already steering her forcibly through the curious guests and from the room.

"Roxby, please," she protested, trying to wriggle her arm free as unobtrusively as she could. "People are staring."

"Let them," he said, his fingers remaining almost painfully tight around her arm. The half smile on his face was clearly not intended for her but for those they were passing. "They will stare regardless of what you wish anyway."

"But consider what they will say if we—if we disappear like this!"

"I never squander my time considering what people

might say," he said as he pulled her with him up the corner staircase that led to the older part of the house. "Nor, I should venture to say after that last outburst, do you."

She struggled to keep from tripping as he drew her up the stairs, using her free hand to bunch her billowing skirts away from the high, curving heels of her shoes.

"Roxby, please," she began breathlessly. "You heard what he was saying! How could I possibly—"

"My hearing is perfectly sufficient, Diana," said Roxby, his voice frosty. "But at present I do not choose to address what Captain Dunham said, or what you deemed an appropriate reply. For now I ask only that you come with me, with the trust I expect from my future wife."

But Diana didn't trust him now. He was half leading, half dragging her down a long, narrow hall paneled in the dark wood of the last century, the happy sounds of the party they'd left growing more distant with each step. Swiftly he plucked a silver candlestick with a lighted candle from the sideboard to shine their way through the shadowy darkness that matched his own mood.

Clearly he was furious with her, not in the fist-thumping, voice-raising way that her family showed anger, but with an icy, controlled reserve and an intensity that made her wary. He'd been drinking heavily, too, the heady scent of the claret clinging to him, and the wine had given an edge to his anger that made Diana doubly uneasy.

"Please, Roxby, cannot we return to the party?" she pleaded, trying again to pull him back. "Surely we—"

"Ah, at last," said Roxby, ignoring her suggestion as he abruptly stopped, holding the candlestick high before him. "Here, Diana, here are the people whose favor you should be currying, not those twittering imbeciles in the gallery."

She looked, and gasped. The faces illuminated by the candle's light weren't real but rows of painted, life-sized portraits of ladies and gentlemen in the latest fashions at court in centuries long past.

"My family, Diana, generations of them," explained Roxby with unabashed reverence, "and yours now, too. Mark and honor them well, my dear, and what they represent."

Yet Diana found it difficult to reconcile these dour, aloof faces with her notions of family. Family were living, breathing people who squabbled and jostled and loved and cared for one another; they weren't venerated pasteboard images covered with jewels and costly lace. How could she think otherwise, when she'd grown up in a place where the past only extended as far back as one person's memory, in a town less than a century old?

"Of course I shall honor your family," she said slowly, "but I cannot forget my own either, and when Captain Dunham said such lies about them—"

"I do not recall him speaking of any one of your family by name, my dear," answered Roxby. "I should hardly wish to be accountable for defending the honor of an entire colony."

"Perhaps I did take it too personally, yes," she admitted, "but when he—"

"Captain Dunham is my guest, Diana, and an honored one at that," said Roxby with that same frighteningly icy formality. "You will never treat another of my guests in such a blatantly ill-bred way again. *Ever.*"

"But Roxby, he—"

"Your vows to me will include obedience, my dear. I don't believe this is so vastly much to ask, is it?"

Miserably Diana swallowed her objections, torn between loyalty to her old family and her new, between what Captain Dunham had actually said tonight and the unsettling feelings about him she carried from the two meetings at the pond. Though she understood obedience was part of being a dutiful wife, it would never come easily to her. When her mother had fretted over her impending spinsterhood, Diana's independence had always been at the center of her worries, and here it was again, causing all manner of difficulties between her and Roxby.

But *confound* Captain Dunham for putting her in such a predicament!

"No, Roxby," she said finally. "That's not so much to ask."

He nodded curtly, expecting no other answer. "This is my grandfather, Diana, the one I honor most. Clarence, first Marquess of Roxby. You can see the cunning in his face, can you not?"

Beneath a towering curled wig, Clarence was wall-eyed and hook-nosed and fat-bellied; he did not look the least bit cunning to Diana. "You are a great deal more handsome, Roxby," she said cautiously. "A great deal."

"Hah, and why shouldn't I be?" He shifted the candlestick to the next painting, of a woman who was everything poor Clarence was not. This lady was beautiful and languid and voluptuous, her eyes heavy-lidded and knowing, the red velvet drapery pretending to be a gown having slid down to reveal one perfectly round ivory breast tipped with a rosy nipple. "This is Lady Cynthia, Clarence's wife and my grandmother. Surely you can see how I've learned from him the wisdom of choosing a beautiful wife."

Diana smiled uneasily, not sure she liked the comparison between herself and Roxby's shameless grandmother. By the flickering candlelight, Cynthia's heavy-lidded eyes seemed to watch her with mocking indulgence. "You do favor her rather more," she ventured. "In appearance, I mean."

Roxby smiled, his gaze still fondly on the portrait. "I should favor her more, if I favor any of them. Though there's hardly shame in Stuart blood if it's old enough, and they do say Old Rowley was vastly fond of Cynthia."

"Old Rowley?" asked Diana. "What a rude sort of name for your grandfather to be called!"

"My little innocent," said Roxby lightly. "How I do forget myself around you! Old Rowley was the name of a certain licentious goat in the palace garden at the time of old King Charles, a name likewise granted to his majesty himself on account of sharing the same, ah, proclivities regarding females. Especially when the females were as *receptive* as the lovely Cynthia."

Diana caught her breath. She might be innocent in that she was still a virgin, but she was more than clever enough to understand what he was so obliquely admitting. "But for her to become the king's mistress, to never know for certain who had fathered her child—oh, Roxby, how dreadful for your poor grandfather!"

"Dreadful?" Roxby chuckled, his grip on her arm loosening and becoming more of a caress. "My dear, didn't I tell you my grandfather was a cunning man? How else would he have turned a mere barony into so much more? His majesty was most generous in rewarding understanding and obedience. Oh, yes, my grandfather was a cunning man, loyal to his king and ruthless for the good of his family."

"But that—that is not right, Roxby!" she stammered, shocked. "If you ever asked such a thing of me—if you ever expected it—"

"But I wouldn't, my love," he answered patiently, setting the candlestick down on a table so he could slip his arm around her waist. "Our King George is far too enthralled with his plain dumpling of a wife to be tempted to stray, even by a gem like you. And you are a gem, Diana, every bit as fine as the ones around your pretty throat."

Before she could protest again, he kissed her, his mouth stale with the claret he'd drunk and his arm tight against her waist in a way that wasn't so much passionate as possessive. He hadn't given her the answer she'd wanted about the king, or the reassurance that she'd expected, and for the first time she realized she didn't want him kissing her now, either.

"Don't, Roxby, please," she murmured unhappily, turning her head away from his mouth and raising her hand between them for good measure. "We should go back to the party anyway."

"Don't question me, Diana," he said sharply, pulling her more tightly against him. "I'll decide when it's time for us to return, not you."

With his hand on her jaw he roughly turned her face back toward his, kissing her harder this time and forcing her lips apart with his tongue. For a second she froze, too shocked and disappointed by this unexpected lack of respect for her wishes. Roxby had always behaved with such perfect courtliness toward her; it was one of the things she'd loved best about him. He'd never once acted like *this*.

And she wasn't his wife, not yet. She was still Diana Fairbourne, and her brothers had long ago taught her how to respond to men who'd been drinking and weren't behaving like gentlemen, even men who happened to be marquesses.

She pulled back from his kiss, twisting to break free of his arm as she swung her fist up to catch Roxby hard on his cheekbone. Anger and fear gave her blow extra force, and the heavy bracelet she wore on her wrist helped, too. He staggered back and swore with surprise, no more expecting such treatment from her than she had from him.

"That wasn't right, my lord, and you know it as well as I," she said tartly. "Now I cannot say what *you* will do next, my lord, but *I* am returning to the party and our guests."

Swiftly she turned and left, her heart pounding at her own audacity and her heels clacking on the floorboards as she hurried down the hall away from him. Though she expected him to follow, simply because he was not a man who liked anyone to better him, to her surprise he didn't.

In a way, she was relieved. Tomorrow, when the wine had left his head and her temper had cooled they'd speak again about his family and hers, and no more, she prayed with a little gulp of uncertainty, of obedient Ashburnham wives as royal mistresses.

But the farther she went in the turning, shadowy hallways of the old house, the more lost she became. The light of Roxby's candlestick had long since faded behind her, and the only light she had to guide her was what came from the moon and stars, filtered through the tiny diamond-shaped panes of the windows along one wall.

Finally she stopped, trying to listen for the music or voices of the guests to guide her back to the party, and fought back tears of frustration. This was not the way the night was supposed to have ended, not at all.

"Ah, lass," said the man's voice behind her. "My lady. So here you are."

She turned quickly, expecting Roxby, even though he'd never dream of calling her "lass."

And he hadn't now, either. Instead the tall man standing with the diamond-patterned moonlight slanting across one broad shoulder smiled self-consciously.

"I didn't mean to scare you," said Captain Dunham as he held his left hand out to her. "But I thought the kitten might not be the only one in need of rescuing."

She wished he hadn't reminded her of the kitten, or that the lopsided smile he flashed now was the one she remembered from the pond, not the sanctimonious smirk from the party.

But because she did remember that smirk and all the trouble it had caused her, she didn't take his offered help. Instead she swatted aside his hand and placed hers squarely on his chest and shoved him every bit as hard as she'd hit Roxby.

"Kitten, ha," she said. "This is all your fault."

5

"*W*hat the devil was that for?" demanded James
crossly. As strong as Diana was for a woman, she still
wasn't much of a match for him, but the shove did irri-
tate him because it made so little sense. "And what's my
fault, anyway?"

"All that stuff and nonsense about Massachusetts,"
she said warmly. "You said those hateful things—*lies!*—
to provoke me intentionally before Roxby."

"I did no such thing!" he said indignantly. "What I said
about that wretched hellhole of a colony was true, based
on my own experiences stationed there. And what I said
afterward, about you being doubly rare because you'd
managed to come from such a place to here—I meant that
as a compliment, not a *provocation*. Hell, if I'd wanted to
provoke you, I wouldn't have been half so nice about it."

She pulled her chin down low, watching him suspiciously through her lashes, more skeptical than seductive. "Like you did about the oars."

"Aye, like that," he grumbled. "And worse."

Worse? How much worse could this become? When
he'd turned around at the party to see her there, covered

with jewels and draped with silk and more beautiful than any woman had a right to be, he thought surely the world had turned upside down and inside out. Of all the undeserving bridegrooms he'd glumly imagined for her, surely the Marquess of Roxby would have been dead last.

Ever since they'd been boys, his lordship had mercilessly sought to control everything in reach, through money, force, or sheer will. A woman as unpredictable and independent as this one would drive him mad. Or was she simply a challenge Roxby hadn't been able to resist, the wildest of wild creatures that he was determined to master?

The possibility was enough to make James' anger boil up again, as if his old fury with the marquess had never cooled at all, as if the long years in between amounted to nothing. This bright, volatile girl, as exuberant as the colony she'd come from, made to bend and surrender her spirit to Roxby—but no, James wasn't going to let himself think of it. No one was making her marry Roxby. It was her choice and not his responsibility.

Diana Fairbourne. Miss Fairbourne for now, then Diana, Lady Roxby. Her ladyship. Roxby's marchioness. He'd have to begin thinking of her like that and forget that nonsense by the millpond.

All of which made his having sought her out here even more preposterous.

"But you didn't tell me about being a captain in his majesty's navy," she insisted, fortunately unaware of how his thoughts were running. "That was rather a kind of lie—a lie of omission. You let me think that you were merely some common seaman, down on his luck, instead of being this high-and-mighty *hero!*"

James frowned. Most women liked heroes. How typical of his luck with this one that she didn't.

"And what of you, Miss Fairbourne? Here you let me think you were promised to some farmer or smith or wheelwright or such, not that you'd be mistress of all Ashburnham."

She drew herself very straight, regal as a queen, let alone a marchioness. "What made you think I needed rescuing now?"

"This house rambles and roams." If she wasn't going to answer his questions with truth, then he'd be damned before he would tell her he'd feared she might come to some mischief at Roxby's hands. "I thought you might lose your way in the dark."

There came that skeptical slant to her eyes again. "You hoped to scoop me up like poor Star Bright or those frantic ladies escaping the French? To be a hero once again?" She sighed dramatically, and tossed up her hands with mock dismay. "Then save away, Captain, for I haven't the faintest idea where I am in this wretched, winding warren of a house. I'm so desperate that I won't even ask how you know your way."

She stepped forward into a patch of moonlight so he'd no choice but to feel the warmth of her smile. The pale skin of her throat and bosom seemed to glow, more luminous than either the silk of her gown or the jewels around her throat. Briefly he considered offering her the crook of his good arm, then thought better of it. By nature he enjoyed taking risks, but this one would be too foolhardy even for him.

"I was here often at the Hall as a boy," he said as he led her back the way she'd come. "My father was the vicar for Ashburnham Parish, and the old dowager marchioness felt the need for much consolation before she died."

"Then you and Roxby must have seen each other, too."

"We did," he said evenly, betraying nothing. "Until our lives took differing paths. Down these stairs, here."

"And left at this bombé chest, then down that far staircase," she said, running her fingers across the carved marble top. "I recall the rest of the way myself now."

"Not so difficult, once you get your bearings."

"But because I haven't, I do thank you." Yet she didn't go ahead; instead she leaned back with both hands on the edge of the chest. "I suppose now you'll expect me to kiss you."

That surprised him. "Meaning you expect me to ask such a favor?"

"I don't expect anything of you, Captain Dunham, good, bad, or indifferent," she said as if this were nothing more than an acceptable matter of fact. "All I'm saying is that most men will look for any reason or excuse to kiss me if they can. Some will try with no reason whatsoever. Not that I ever let them, of course, but it's happened to me ever since I was a little girl. I thought you'd be like the others, that is all."

And he was. The way she was standing with her hands braced behind her made her mostly bare breasts stand even higher above her tight-laced stays, and the artless way she tilted her face up to meet his gaze also turned her mouth toward him in an altogether too inviting fashion.

But it wasn't just a question of coquettishness or lust. It was far more complicated than that. Since he'd first seen her standing on the bank, he'd felt an odd sort of connection to her that he couldn't explain. And everything since—the boat, the kitten, and even learning she was Roxby's future wife—seemed to intensify the feeling, not lessen it. Daft thoughts, and dangerous ones too, with Roxby involved.

But oh, aye, he'd like to kiss her. What man with half a breath left in his body wouldn't? Not that he'd admit any of this to her.

"That," he said finally, "must make his lordship a jealous man."

She shrugged and smiled almost sheepishly, once again the carefree girl at the millpond. "Any other man would likely be jealous, yes. But Roxby being Roxby, I believe he rather enjoys the fuss."

James knew there'd be no "rather" about it. Roxby thrived on possessing the one thing—whether a Titian madonna, an Irish racehorse, or a breathtaking wife—that everyone else coveted. But how could she be so damned cheerful about it?

"And you, Miss Fairbourne?" he asked, more sharply than he'd intended. "Do you enjoy being his lordship's latest prize?"

Her smile faded, and her chin rose defensively. "You didn't answer me about whether you wanted to kiss me or not."

"I'm not a poacher, Miss Fairbourne," he said firmly, "and I don't take what belongs to other men. Didn't you learn that much at the pond? But I am wondering why you're so damned interested in what *I* want. Are you already so tired of Roxby that you're casting about for more entertainment?"

She gasped indignantly. "Of course I'm not tired of Roxby! I love him!"

"Oh, aye," he answered bitterly, "and that's the easy answer to everything, is it?"

She pushed away from the chest, folding her arms before her. "For me, yes."

"Then Miss Fairbourne, I wish you all the joy in the world." He bowed curtly, taking his leave. "Go down those stairs, and you'll be back at the party."

"You're abandoning me?" she asked with wounded surprise. "You're not coming back, too?"

"You left with his lordship. It would not look well for you to return with me."

She nodded, accepting that, but still she lingered. Damnation, why did she have to be so lovely, and why did she have to belong to that bastard Roxby?

"I haven't asked after Star Bright," she said. "Is he recovering from his ordeal?"

"Brighty's well enough." And feeling a hell of a lot better than James was himself, that was certain.

She smiled wistfully. "I'd like to see him again, you know."

"Then send a servant to come collect him," he said, again sharply, again unwilling to let his common sense be overpowered by one wistful smile. "We found the kitten on Ashburnham land. He's as much Lord Roxby's rightful property as—"

"As I am?" She shrugged again, her smile tinged with

sadness as she turned with a rustle of silk to leave. "You keep the kitten, Captain Dunham. I think you'll need whatever luck he brings more than I do."

As he watched her go, he told himself that she was entitled to her own opinion, just as she was entitled to Roxby and every other blasted choice she'd made.

But damnation, why did her opinion have to be *right?*

"I vow, Miss Fairbourne," said Lady Marchmont archly as soon as Diana appeared in the doorway for breakfast. "You must either have been very, very good to Roxby last night, or very, very bad."

Determinedly Diana smiled, though the flush that burned her cheeks betrayed her guilt anyway. With so many guests now at Ashburnham, she was expected to come take breakfast with the others here in the west parlor rather than on a tray in her own chamber. But after last night's party, the only person in the room was Lady Marchmont, daintily sipping her tea and feeding crusts of toast to the wriggling white dog at her feet.

The parlor was the most cheerful room in the entire house, with walls painted a whipped-egg yellow and airy French furniture, the chairs and tables gilded and sinuously carved. The paintings were by Canaletto, sweeping vistas of Venice with cloudless blue skies that almost matched the English skies outside the tall windows, thrown open now to catch the breezes from the gardens.

A most pleasant room, and on any other day Lady Marchmont would have made most amusing company, but on this particular morning Diana gladly would have hidden herself away. When she had returned to the party in the gallery last night, she'd discovered that Roxby had not, instead sending a vaguely worded excuse for his sudden absence that had raised more buzzing questions than it had answered—questions that now, with Lady Marchmont, Diana must continue to face alone.

Face, but not answer. How could she, when she had so many unanswered questions herself? She'd spent most of the night considering what Roxby had said. Even allowing for the claret he'd drunk, she still found his unexpected assumptions about him and her, his family and her own, to be troubling at best. Husband or not, he'd tried to force his kisses upon her when she refused, until she'd had no choice but to hit him to make him stop.

But what of her own shameless behavior with Captain Dunham? First she'd openly insulted him, exactly as Roxby had said. But then, for reasons she couldn't begin to explain, she'd lingered with him alone in the dark hallway, teasing him like her oldest, dearest friend instead of—instead of what? A man who hadn't been honest with her, a man she hadn't been honest with, either? A man whose career as the captain of an English navy frigate could put him in instant antagonism with her own family's affinity for smuggling? A man who was brash and outspoken and, though he was passably handsome—she'd admit that much, just as she'd admit that he seemed kind on account of rescuing the kitten—was exactly the opposite of the kind of man she'd come to England to find, and had found, in Roxby?

And she didn't even have Roxby's excuse of the claret.

"Come now, Miss Fairbourne, please tell me all," begged Lady Marchmont. "Was his lordship good or bad? How I'm perishing to know!"

But before Diana had to answer, she caught her breath with delight. On her chair at the table lay an enormous bouquet of white flowers, not sweet peas or carnations from the gardens, but creamy, fragrant gardenias from the Ashburnham greenhouse, the rarest flowers coaxed and pruned to absolute perfection.

"I would say Roxby was good, most good," she said fondly as she lifted the flowers to her face, breathing deeply of their scent. "And how sweet of him to think of me like this!"

"Sweet!" Lady Marchmont gurgled with amusement. "No one has ever called Roxby 'sweet.' It would fair ruin him to hear it, my dear Miss Fairbourne. But besotted, befuddled, bewitched: I'd call him those and more, after seeing the changes you've wrought in him. Love, 'tis love, even for a hard old nut like Roxby. Why else would he let you box his ears and then reward you with gardenias?"

"I did nothing of the sort!" exclaimed Diana defensively as she thrust the flowers at a footman to put in water, her pleasure in them gone. She and Roxby had been completely alone last night; how could Lady Marchmont already know what had happened between them?

"Ah, but Miss Fairbourne, you cannot lie to me!" Lady Marchmont pulled the little dog up into her lap, holding its face trapped between her hands as she addressed it in a high, singsong voice. "Isn't that so, Chou-Chou? She cannot lie to us because we already know the truth, having heard it expressly from Lord Stanver. Oh, how ignoble poor Roxby must look, with his face as bruised as a burst plum!"

" 'A burst plum'?" repeated Roxby as he entered the room, dressed for riding or traveling. "What a fanciful turn Chou-Chou has this morning, and how flattering, too! But how lovely you look, Diana, as fair as the morning."

He came around the table, and as he bent to kiss Diana she saw the bruise on his temple where her fist and her bracelet had hit him, swollen and angry and every bit as purple as Lady Marchmont had said.

"Oh, Roxby, I am sorry," she murmured, full of remorse as she touched the gentlest fingers to the bruise. "I didn't mean to cause such—"

"The flowers were here at your place?" he asked, pulling back from her touch and from her. "I had the best gathered for you."

"Yes, and they are beautiful. But Roxby, please, we must—"

"Good. I'm glad you liked them." He smiled as he took the cup of tea that the footman had prepared for him especially. "Just as I am glad everything is settled once again between us."

"But it's not!" cried Diana. She wanted to be the one who fixed him his tea, just as she wished he'd taken the time to pick the gardenias for her instead of merely giving the orders to have it done. She knew it would never happen that way, of course, for marquesses and marchionesses never did such things for themselves, but poignantly she wished it just the same. "Nothing is settled, not after what—"

"My dear, please recall Chou-Chou's eager ears," he said as he glanced pointedly at Lady Marchmont and her dog, both avidly and unashamedly listening. "We had certain disagreements last night, yes. But since you accepted the flowers, I can see that you've had time to reflect on your misapprehensions and errors, and that you'll now accept what I decide is best for you. There's nothing more to discuss, is there?"

"*Nothing?*" she repeated, astonished and wounded by how wrongly he'd misinterpreted her words. "How can you possibly believe there is nothing left to say?"

He sipped his tea, smiling at her over the edge of the porcelain dish. "Oh, yes, that passionate outburst from you last night. Because I love you, my dear, that is forgiven as well, and I'll gladly wear the battle scars to prove it."

"*Battle scars!*" With furious frustration she shoved back her chair and rose to her feet. "So help me, Roxby, I shall give you some real battle scars if you keep refusing to—"

"Did I mention, Diana, that I must go up to London this morning?" he interrupted yet again. "Some urgent matters require my presence for several days, I'm afraid."

"London?" Diana's eyes widened with the eager possibility. A trip to town with just the two of them in the carriage alone could solve all this unhappiness. "Oh, please, let me come with you! I could be ready in half an hour—a quarter of an hour!"

But Roxby shook his head. "I fear not, love," he said lightly. "You would find London quite empty at this time of year, with nothing whatsoever to amuse you."

With a dreadful clarity, Diana suddenly remembered the mistress mentioned in the anonymous letter, the mistress that he swore he didn't keep in London.

Slowly she sank back into her chair, doubt swirling through her heart and the fight slipping from her body. She thought what she'd asked had been reasonable enough, especially if he loved her the way she loved him.

But clearly he hadn't seen it that way. To him last night she'd been shrewish, demanding, willful. Had she driven him away now, back to his mistress?

"Not even the actors are in London in this season," he continued, ignoring her distress if he even noticed it. "I'm sure that Harriet will contrive more entertainment for you here than I ever could for you in London."

"Oh, and I have," purred Lady Marchmont, so pleased at being included that Diana, bewildered, wondered if this had long been planned between them. "That is, Roxby, if you consent. You know how my party of friends is helping confound the French in our little way."

"The 'Ladies' Ship'?" asked Roxby wryly. "Who hasn't heard of it? A ship built as a gift for his majesty's navy, outfitted entirely with pin money and what you all steal from your husbands' pockets."

"Better that it come to us than be lost at the tables at White's," sniffed Lady Marchmont. "The ship is nearly finished in the yard in Portsmouth, but I believe we could take one more subscriber, especially one as useful as Miss Fairbourne would be."

"What use could I be with such a project?" asked Diana slowly, imagining how her father and brothers would laugh at the scheme of a navy ship sponsored by a covey of titled ladies. "I am vastly familiar with boats and ships, true, but I hardly think you'd wish a woman clambering about the ways in Portsmouth."

"Hardly," said Roxby, and there was an edge to his voice that made Diana glance at him uneasily. "That part of your life, my dear, is past and best forgotten."

"But to have the new Marchioness of Roxby on our list would help our cause with those stuffy admirals," said Lady Marchmont, cradling the white dog in her arms like a baby. "Once we give them the ship, we want them to choose a captain worthy of our efforts, a gentleman who has proven himself a hero and a savior to ladies."

"Captain Dunham," said Diana, wondering why all of this felt so wretchedly inevitable, like the plot of a badly written play. "That's why you wanted to meet him last night, isn't it? You wanted to see if he was the right man for your ship."

"Not my ship, but his majesty's," said Lady Marchmont firmly. "And if Roxby says you might join us, then you shall come with me to call upon Captain Dunham at his sister's home. I fear he is going to need some persuading."

"Then Diana is precisely the lady you'll want to help with the persuading," said Roxby as he set the now empty teacup and dish on the table. "Isn't that so, Diana?"

Diana looked at him sharply, her heart racing. If Lady Marchmont knew that she'd quarreled with Roxby last night, then it was entirely likely that by now he'd somehow learned of her meeting Captain Dunham in the dark hall.

"I don't see why I should have any special influence with Captain Dunham," she said, striving to keep her voice level. "We were introduced only last night."

"And a thoroughly dismal event it was, too," answered Roxby dryly. "Which is why I am quite sure you'll try doubly hard to be pleasant to Captain Dunham when you meet him again, to oblige me."

His meaning was obvious, and his expression—the imperious half smile coupled with the heavy-lidded eyes—made it clear that he expected to be obeyed. Yet instead of agreeing immediately, Diana looked down at the table to hide her own confusion, her palms making damp rings of anxiety on the polished mahogany.

She'd never intended to deceive Roxby, nor were her conversations with Captain Dunham about kittens and kisses the stuff of great scandals, not by London standards. Where, really, was the sin in any of that?

Yet when she'd accused the captain of a lie of omission—something her mother had always deplored in her children, which was doubtless why it had come so readily to Diana's tongue—she should have been accusing herself instead.

On that very first morning, she should have come back from the millpond and told Roxby all about meeting the man in the boat. She should have told him how she'd pitied the rough-mannered stranger with the crippled hand, how she'd tried to warn him against stealing Ashburnham's fish, even how she'd rowed the boat on a dare. If she'd been especially honest, she even would have confessed how she'd let the man be more forward toward her than was proper because he'd somehow reminded her of the men from Appledore.

But instead she'd said nothing, and each day she hadn't had only confused matters more. Now she felt another invisible wall between her and Roxby, as unbroachable and troubling as the one raised by the anonymous letter. But how could she resolve matters if Roxby wouldn't talk to her?

"I'm willing to enter a thousand pounds in your name, Diana," Roxby was saying, that warning sound growing in his voice. "I want my wife well represented in such a noble project. It will make your acceptance at court so much easier. But I should also appreciate your word that you will call upon Captain Dunham and be your most agreeable self."

"Oh, Roxby, please take me to London with you instead!" she pleaded. "I don't need to go to the theater or the shops. All I wish is to be with you, so we can be together and—and *talk!*"

"And pray, how much talking would we do with Lady Waldegrave sitting like a dragon between us to guard your virtue?" His expression softened. "Until we're wed, Diana, I cannot take you with me alone on such a journey, as much as it would please me. You stay here, and amuse yourself with the company of Chou-Chou and Lady Marchmont—you must be sure to call her Harriet now, as befits friends—and when I return I promise to bring you a surprise."

"But Roxby—"

"There's the carriage. I must be gone." He bent to kiss her hurriedly, his attention already shifting toward London. "Next month, my love, on our wedding trip, we shall have all the time in the world to be together."

Next month, always next month, and a leisurely, idyllic wedding trip across Europe; other times Diana had listened excitedly when he'd explained every luxurious detail of their itinerary. But now her heart was troubled as she watched Roxby leave, and silently she prayed that next month would not be too late.

Holding her head steady while her maid dressed her wig for evening, Lady Waldegrave sat at her dressing table and clapped her hands with approval, her bracelets clinking gently on her wrists.

"To be party to the grand ladies building the new ship for the poor sailors—I am most pleased to learn of it!" she said with a smile. "You cannot ask for a higher honor, Diana, than to be included in such an admirable proposition."

"I do not see the honor in it, my lady," said Diana as she restlessly paced back and forth before the dressing table, flicking her skirts to one side with each turn. "It seemed less like an honor than a way to collect an outrageous sum of money."

"Yes, yes, but for an excellent cause, Diana," said the older woman, turning her head a fraction so the maid could comb one long white curl over her shoulder. "It's the single respectable endeavor that that wicked Lady Marchmont can claim. Such arrangements are how ladies of quality can employ their rank for good."

"More likely all they employ is their husbands' fortunes."

The countess frowned. "Diana, you must stop thinking and speaking of money this way," she said severely. "It is common, and surpassing vulgar, as if your father is in trade."

"My father *is* in trade," she said stubbornly. "And in some distant way, so Roxby must be, else he'd never be able to support his expenses."

"Ladies don't consider such things," warned Lady Waldegrave, "and if you wish to be one, you won't, either. Rather you should consider Roxby's support in this as a sign that he has forgiven you. Clouting him on the head like a Bishopsgate fishwife! Dear Lord, I nearly fainted away this morning when I saw what you'd done to his poor handsome face!"

With a disconsolate groan, Diana dropped into an armchair, sprawling in a thoroughly unladylike fashion. "Everyone keeps fussing over what I did to Roxby. No one cares what he did to me first."

"Nothing that could have merited what you did to him, I'm sure," said the older woman, peering into her mirror as she swept a rabbit's foot with chalky face powder across her forehead, obliterating the difference between her skin and her hair. "Besides, considering everything else he has done *for* you—including that splendid ruby necklace and earrings—it hardly matters."

"But it should," protested Diana. "He was drunk and he was angry, and he wanted to kiss me and I didn't want to kiss him back, not like that. He was . . . *hateful* about it, and if I hadn't hit him I don't know how much more he would have demanded of me."

But the countess merely sniffed with disdain. "And why else is he marrying you, child? He admires you and desires *you*. It is not your fortune or your title or your father's influence, because you have none of those to offer. He can hardly be faulted for that, especially since he has asked you to be his wife instead of simply taking you as his mistress. Oh, no, there is no fault to be found in Roxby's behavior."

"But that is lust, not love!" cried Diana indignantly as she thought once again of the lasting marriages of her parents, her aunts, and her uncles. "Do you know last night he showed me portraits of his grandmother and grandfather, and told me how his grandmother had been King Charles' mistress and how his grandfather had been *proud* of not knowing whether his children had been sired by him or the king!"

"Don't be so pathetically naive, Diana," snapped the countess, pursing her lips as she positioned a heart-shaped patch of black velvet to the left of her mouth. "No one enjoys a judgmental prig. Charles was married to an ugly Spanish princess that he'd not the slightest affection for. That is commonly known. But he was also a most accomplished lover, and if he favored certain married ladies with his attentions, then you can be sure they were as pleased by his skill as their husbands were with their own more tangible rewards."

"I would not lie with the king, no matter what he promised my husband," said Diana rebelliously, swinging her feet to kick her heels into the side of the chair. "Otherwise I might as well go down to a rum shop near the docks and offer to lift my petticoat and spread my legs for any sailor with a few shillings in his pocket. There's no difference that I can see."

"Then perhaps I should go deposit you there now," said the countess crossly, "and spare myself more of the considerable trouble that this match has already caused me. Rum shop sailors, indeed!"

Curtly she waved away her maid, and turned on the bench to face Diana. "You are not a fool, Diana Fairbourne. To marry for love is a glorious ambition, and I believe with Roxby you have succeeded. But you must learn not to scorn other women who are less fortunate."

"But I would never—"

"Hush, and heed me," said Lady Waldegrave sternly. "The higher one climbs in society—and you are climbing wondrously high, Diana—the more marriages one sees that are based on joining two fortunes, two estates, and nothing more. If, after dutifully bearing the children required to sustain the family, those husbands and wives choose discreetly to follow their hearts or desires, why, that is their private choice and no affair of yours. And that discretion, Diana, must include your own husband."

"Not Roxby," answered Diana, her chin raised with determination as she tried to forget the letter and the sudden trip to London. She'd had versions of this conversation with Lady Waldegrave several times before, but none of the others had had this same awful finality to them. "I would not permit it."

"You would have no choice, child," said Lady Waldegrave gently, reaching out to rest her hand over Diana's. "He is a gentleman and a peer, and he can do whatever he pleases, without most of the boundaries that restrict other men. If you wish to keep his love, Diana, you must learn what *does* please him, and then do it. It is as simple, and as complicated, as that."

Belatedly Diana remembered that Lady Waldegrave herself had been wed to a wealthy earl of her family's choosing, a man she'd barely known, let alone loved. She'd never even had the consolation of bearing children, but she had had a lover, a man endlessly devoted to her though he too was married to another. When the countess had confessed this secret—a secret that Diana was certain her mother had not known when she'd sent her daughter to be guided by her oldest friend—Diana had been shocked, but because she'd grown fond of the older woman, she'd understood and been sympathetic.

But sympathy wasn't the same as acceptance, and it most certainly wasn't what Diana wanted for herself. She *had* climbed high in this new world, and once she married Roxby she'd climb higher still. Yet none of it—not the grand houses or the title, not the jewels or the gowns—would matter without love.

"But what about his pleasing me?" she asked wistfully. "If he truly loves me, shouldn't he want to please me, too?"

Lady Waldegrave shook her head with sad resignation, the powder settling in the lines of her face making her seem as grim and world-weary as death itself.

"If you love Roxby," she said softly, "then you must find your pleasure in pleasing him. And that, Diana, is all the love, all the pleasure, that most women in our world can hope to find."

6

*B*arefoot and thoroughly disgusted, James stood on the lawn between the laundry poles and the vicarage's vegetable garden and prepared once again to do battle. He was practically panting with exhaustion, his shirt plastered to his back with sweat, as sorry an excuse for a fighting man as he hoped he'd never see.

"How—how many times d'you think I've been sent to the devil this morning, eh, Brighty?" he demanded hoarsely from the only witness to his folly. "A score at least, I'd say myself, and that'd be a kindness."

But the little gray cat only blinked and yawned, perfectly content to remain at peace with the world and the clean linens folded in the wicker basket he'd chosen as his sun-warmed nest.

James was not so fortunate. That surgeon might have passed him for duty, but he'd never survive unless he could do better than *this*. Each day he must practice; each day he must make the effort to grow stronger, no matter how it hurt.

With a frustrated growl, he gripped the sword one more time, his left hand pressed over his useless right.

The sword was not the jewel-studded one with the engraved hilt given by the grateful shipowners, but the battered old regulation cutlass he'd carried in dozens of battles and engagements. Twenty-nine inches of straight steel for the blade and a grip and hilt of cast iron, plain and serviceable and, weak as he was this afternoon, as heavy as a bar of lead in his hand.

Before him his mute adversary taunted him still, a straw-stuffed Frenchman fashioned from his brother-in-law's cast-off clothing, with a toothless rake for a spine. One more time James swung the sword, not bothering any longer with the careful niceties of wounding his enemy, but simply slashing with one sweeping stroke that sent the straw head and the vicar's hat tumbling down the hillside.

"Sweet Gemini!" exclaimed Diana Fairbourne cheerfully. "How very deadly you are this afternoon, Captain Dunham!"

He jerked around, the sword still clasped in both hands, and found to his horror that three women were watching him: the slow-witted farmer's daughter that his sister—his wretched, wretched sister, who'd gone off to make calls in the parish instead of guarding him from disasters like this—was attempting to train for service, the small, pop-eyed lady from the other night's party— what in blazes was her name, anyway?—with a white dog in her arms, and then, eclipsing everything else in his sight, Diana Fairbourne.

Ah, Diana. She was dressed completely in pale yellow, a sunny flower against the green grass, the gauzy fabric of her skirts drifting about her like petals and the bright green bows topping her wide-brimmed hat like new leaves. She was so beautiful that he almost had to squint from staring at her, and he wondered if she was smiling because she was as glad to see him as he was her. More likely, she'd never seen anything quite so ridiculous as the sight of a beached, barefoot frigate captain bellowing and whacking away at a scarecrow.

Which, of course, sobered him instantly.

"*Captain* Dunham!" the other lady was saying as she came sweeping across the grass toward him, the plumes on her hat nodding gently and the little dog's fluffy head bobbing with each step. "I am *so* honored to see you again, sir!"

He watched her come, trepidation mounting by the second. Damnation, what was the infernal woman's name? That night at the party he'd been so over-whelmed by seeing Diana again that he hadn't heard the introduction. Now he was going to have to pay for his inattention.

But worse was to come. Much worse.

"And how *vastly* exciting to catch a glimpse of the heroic master of the *Castor* at his military maneuvers!" she gushed, her eyes so round with adoration that the whites showed completely around the iris. "Why, the shivers are traveling up and down my very spine, sir!"

She tucked the miserable dog under one arm, letting its pink ribbon leash trail behind, and held her other hand out toward James, her wrist perfectly arched and her little finger cocked. Common good manners dic-tated that, once offered, he must take those plump fin-gers in his own, to kiss or squeeze surreptitiously the way he'd done to Diana's, or at least bow.

And yet he couldn't do it. His pride wouldn't even let

him try. Common good manners also said that he had to sheath the cutlass, that dropping it onto the grass would be ignominious and dishonorable. But if he tried to do so before this lady, she'd see his clumsiness at once and soon decipher the reason. Shifting the sword to one hand while he used the other to take hers wouldn't work, either, unless he wanted her to risk losing her toes when the cutlass clattered to her feet.

The lady waited, her painted brows raised with expectation, while James fought the nearly uncontrollable desire to toss the cutlass down the hill after the headless scarecrow and march back into the house alone.

And then Diana Fairbourne, bless her forever, came to his rescue as surely as he himself had rescued Brighty from the pond.

"Oh, Harriet, pray don't force yourself upon the captain," she scolded as she neatly took the other woman's waiting hand for herself, tucking it into the crook of her elbow with the ease that women friends so often had. Then she smiled, tilting her head back a fraction so she could peek out from beneath the wide brim of her hat. "You must forgive Lady Marchmont, Captain Dunham. She was so taken with your company last evening that she presumes upon your acquaintance."

She'd saved him from the dilemma of the cutlass and the hand, and she'd told him the lady's name, too, as tidy and neat as could be.

How could a woman of such admirable good sense possibly belong to a man like Roxby?

"I do not know if I should call it presumption, dear

Diana," answered Lady Marchmont archly, "unless I can presume upon Captain Dunham to accept the command of the ladies' fair vessel."

" 'The Ladies' Ship'?" asked James, his relief short-lived as he began to understand the purpose of this call. "The *Amazon*?"

Ill as he'd been, he'd heard and read of the Ladies' Ship, as ripe a bit of folly as idle females had ever concocted. A pack of titled women commissioning a frigate—it would be laughable if they hadn't succeeded in seeing the vessel built, leaving the Admiralty to scratch its collective head and wonder what to do with such a generous, peculiar gift. Under any other circumstances, the ship would have been a command desired by every captain on the list, for unlike the standard frigates commissioned by the navy, there'd been no corners cut, no corrupt economies made for an unseemly profit, no cheaper unseasoned timbers hidden in her keel or third-rate canvas in her sails.

Everything about the frigate was as trim and smart as could be. Except, of course, that the ladies who'd paid for the ship expected their influence to continue after the *Amazon*—for what else could she be christened?—was afloat. The navy's laws of seniority and rank were sacrosanct and inflexible, and so were the wills of the wives of peers. And so the poor orphaned *Amazon* sat idle at a private dock in Portsmouth, publicly a laughingstock while secretly coveted by every sailor and officer who saw her.

"The *Amazon*, and no other, sir," said Lady Marchmont proudly. "All she needs now is a captain, a master who can lead her to the glory that is her right, a brave and gallant commander who will—"

"I can't accept," interrupted James with more haste

than grace. Danger could do that to a man. "That is, I am honored, of course, but I cannot be the officer you seek."

"Why not?" asked Diana, perplexed. "Is there something that displeases you about the ship? Is she wanting in some way?"

"Because it isn't—it isn't right," he began gruffly, unable to explain without offending them. He walked away long enough to return the sword to its scabbard, looped over the back of a chair, and to buy himself another half minute to compose his words. "Ladies shouldn't meddle in affairs they aren't able to understand."

"Such as ships and boatyards and the massive pride of an average captain in his majesty's navy?" asked Diana sweetly. "Such as the way this vessel might benefit the career of any man not bound by wrongful conceptions of what is proper occupation for ladies?"

She was still smiling, but James had seen that smile before, when she'd practically seized the oars from him to row his boat, and he wasn't about to accept it as mere pleasant agreement.

"What ladies do or don't do isn't the question, Miss Fairbourne," he said, choosing his words with extreme caution. These were chancy waters here; he wasn't about to get dragged into their scheme, but he couldn't afford the ill will of these same ladies' husbands, either. "I follow whatever orders I'm given, and I don't ask questions or suggest improvements. For the good of the men and the country, the Admiralty has strict regulations about how the service is run, and they can't allow civilians to put their oar in the middle of them."

"Oh, a pox on your regulations," scoffed Diana, "and a pox, too, on where you put your precious *oar*. First it's meddlesome ladies, then Jacobites and Papists and French spies of every description, and all of a piece to you, too. If you're too narrow-minded to see what a perfect opportunity this would be for you, why then, I say you don't deserve it."

He scowled, his temper beginning to overtake his judgment. She might be a lady, but he was a captain, and captains weren't accustomed to anyone telling them where to put their oars.

"What I don't deserve," he said testily, swiping his shirt sleeve across his brow, "is some overweening virago blundering into my life to tell me how I should and shouldn't be handling my personal affairs."

"Oh, lah, Diana," murmured Lady Marchmont with interest, looking from Diana to James and back again. "If this is how Roxby believes you'll persuade Captain Dunham to command our sweet *Amazon,* then I can scarcely conceive of how you'd discourage him."

"I should enjoy it," said Diana with relish, settling her hands at her waist. She didn't really look like a virago, but she was challenging him again, all pink-cheeked and yellow-ruffled defiance. "I should begin by asking him to describe exactly how ladies are unfit for offering magnanimous gifts to his precious Admiralty."

But Lady Marchmont was looking away now, vaguely scanning the row of weeping beeches that shielded the vicarage from the square-towered church beyond. "What a pretty spot this is, Captain Dunham, peaceful and removed from worldly cares, as is fitting."

"Aye, my lady," agreed James tersely, unwilling to be distracted from answering Diana's foolishness. "This is a peaceful place. Churchyards generally are. But Miss Fairbourne, if the Admiralty can no longer be permitted to decide on its own how best to employ its officers and men, then the entire navy's discipline and effectiveness will collapse."

Now Diana folded her arms over her chest, escalating her ridiculous challenge and crushing her full breasts a bit higher over her stomacher in the process, an unfair advantage if ever there was one.

"Perhaps if your navy weren't so disciplined, there'd be no problem at all," she said, clipping each word for emphasis. "Perhaps if your Admiralty would allow themselves to be reasonable and listen to the civilians they are supposed to be protecting instead of bullying them with too many silly rules, then there'd be no question of you becoming the *Amazon*'s captain. Why, perhaps I should—Lord Stanver, whatever are you doing here?"

Whatever, indeed, thought James sourly; there were more people wandering in and out of his sister's yard this afternoon than through Winchester on market day. What the hell was Stanver doing here, anyway, overwhelming his sister's little makeshift housemaid with so much gentry come calling?

"Good day, ladies, Captain," announced Stanver. Grandly he swept his hat from his head and bowed as he made a leg with well-practiced ease, but the gallantry of the gesture was undermined by the way he huffed and puffed to rise again, the too-large buttons on his waistcoat straining and his florid face grown redder still. "Lovely afternoon, eh?"

"And how lovely it is to see you, Stanver!" gushed Lady Marchmont, fluttering and fawning with obvious pleasure. "Who would have *dreamed* you'd join us here in this humble place?"

"I fear the vicar's not at home, my lord," said James wearily. He'd wager his life that Stanver hadn't come seeking spiritual advice, but for his brother-in-law's sake he'd go through the formalities. "Though I expect him within the next hour or so if you wish him to return your call."

"Not at all, not at all." Stanver bowed again, but this time it was clear the tribute was for Lady Marchmont alone. "It is this lady I must see on, ah, a private matter. Gad, but you're looking smart this morning, Harriet! A word alone, eh? Here in the churchyard, if you please?"

He licked his lips salaciously, and Lady Marchmont tittered.

"In the churchyard, my lord? Ah, ah, you are so wicked!" Abruptly she thrust the white dog into Diana's hands. "You will watch Chou-Chou for me, won't you, Diana? I cannot keep his lordship waiting."

Before Diana could object, Lady Marchmont arched her hands over her breasts and nearly ran to Lord Stanver, making little birdlike sounds of enchantment as she gave him her hand. Together they hurried purposefully away, the plumes on Lady Marchmont's hat bobbing over the top of the hedgerow.

"Have you ever seen the likes of that?" said James with open disgust. "To be so damned jaded that you need the shadow of a church tower to give you a cockstand! I wish my sister were here, to sweep them out with her broom like she does all the rest of the filth."

Diana gasped. "Lord Stanver and Lady Marchmont? But they do not love each other! They cannot, for Lady Marchmont is married to Lord Marchmont!"

"They're your acquaintance, not mine," said James. So lack of love outraged her more than tawdry titillation; that, at least, was in her favor. "Hell, he's probably got her bent over a headstone by now."

But Diana was too busy struggling with Chou-Chou, who as soon as his mistress had fled, had metamorphosed from a passive ball of white fluff to a wriggling, snarling miniature wolf. As Diana tried to find the end to the long ribbon that served as his leash, he finally pushed free, bounding from her arms to the ground and racing across the grass toward the willow basket of laundry.

Of laundry, and of cat. At the sound of his yips, Brighty popped up, his back arching and his tail bristling and his yowl worthy of a full-grown banshee instead of a small gray kitten. For an instant Chou-Chou stopped, his paws skidding to a halt on the grass before such a brave show. Then he recalled he was at heart a masterful dog, not a mere lady's plaything, and charged forward again. Brighty conceded the battle and the basket and leaped over the side to race to the greater sanctuary of the purple-leafed beeches.

"Oh, Brighty, run! *Run!*" wailed Diana. She bunched her skirts in her hands and began to run too, her hat falling backward from her head, glancing back to call over her shoulder to James. "I'll find Brighty if you'll catch Chou-Chou!"

Without thinking James plunged after her, willing to obey her orders for such an undeniably noble cause. But the first step reminded him how long he'd been standing about after working so hard—exactly long enough for the scarred muscles in his thigh to stiffen and complain.

No matter how much he wanted to follow Diana's flying yellow skirts, the best he could do was lurch clumsily after her, grimacing and swearing at his sorry deficiency.

But when he finally did duck beneath the beech tree's sweeping branches, blinking to accustom his eyes to the shadows, the dog was still yapping and yipping and leaping up the trunk of the tree, the kitten was still hissing and spitting back at him from a branch overhead, and Diana—Diana was halfway up the tree herself. She'd draped her petticoats into the crook of one arm to free her legs for climbing, granting him a spectacular view of her red-heeled buckled shoes, her pale green stockings embroidered with roses and held by yellow silk garters, and the devil tempt him all the more, the creamy skin of her knees and one pale thigh.

He was ready to rescue the kitten again, aye. But who in blazes was going to rescue *him*?

"You get Chou-Chou's ribbon and tie him up," she ordered breathlessly, swinging up to the next branch. Jesus, he thought, she must be a good ten feet from the ground by now. "Then I can fetch Brighty down. Yes, yes, little Brighty, I'm almost there!"

"Have a care for yourself, now," cautioned James from below. The last thing he wanted was to have to explain to Roxby how his future bride had broken her neck falling from a tree. "You're not exactly rigged out for climbing."

She scowled at him over the branch and hoisted herself a little farther. "Need I prove to you that I can climb a tree as well as I can row a boat?"

"You already have," he said over the din of the squabbling animals. "I cannot begin to guess at all the talents you have, Miss Fairbourne."

"That is most wise of you." One side of her hair had come unpinned, a long, dark lock flopping over her shoulder, and impatiently she shoved it behind her ear. "Now will you please, *please* catch that wretched dog?"

He wanted to hover beneath her, the noble part of him wanting to stay to help her if she began to slip, the more base part relishing the view of so much splendid female leg so unabashedly displayed. But the sooner he captured the dog, the sooner she'd come down and be safe, and with a sigh of regret he grabbed Chou-Chou's ribbon and pulled him back from the trunk.

"Come along, you little bastard," he said as he tugged the protesting dog from under the beech. "You behave now, else I'll take you to your mistress, and you'll see how well you fare if we interrupt Lord Jackass Stanver at his pleasure."

He tied the ribbon around the laundry pole, leaving the dog to make a few final yips of frustration, then returned to the beech. Diana had managed to retrieve Brighty, curled safe in one arm, and was now inching her way feet first back down the wide, sloping branch of the tree. Her gown was going to be a snagged and grubby sight when she returned to Ashburnham; he hoped that her maid saw it before Roxby, or she'd have her share of questions to answer.

"One hand for the ship, Miss Fairbourne," he called, "and one hand for yourself."

"Oh, yes, and red sky at morning, sailor take warning, and all the rest of it," she said, concentrating on the branch instead of looking down at him. "Do not forget I come from a family of sailors, and I've heard every old tar's saying and aphorism since I was in the cradle."

"What about 'dead men tell no tales'?" he suggested. "That's the one that will apply to certain young ladies as well as old tars if you aren't more careful."

"Not to mention arrogant frigate captains," she said, reaching the trunk and swinging down to the next branch. "I should fall directly on top of you, just so you can make a new warning about the ill-timed perils of ladies tumbling from on high."

"And kittens." He leaned back a little further. "As I recall, you had some sort of foolish saying about lucky kittens, too. Isn't that so, Brighty?"

To James' surprise—for his acquaintance with the little gray cat was not thus far a long one—Brighty twisted his head around at the sound of his name, his seven-toed paws clinging tightly to Diana's bodice. He mewed once, no longer with braggadocio or fear, but merely to offer an oddly conversational acknowledgment.

"It wasn't foolishness, any more than that red sky of yours is," she said. "It was true. Because of his toes and his white star, he's the gray twin to the kitten who brought my brother true love, which most people believe equals good luck. I know I do."

Hell, her true love for Roxby was about the last thing James wanted to discuss, seeing as it practically made him retch.

"So why do you hate the navy so much?" he asked, seizing the first thought that came to mind. "Has one of your brothers been taken from his ship and pressed?"

She looked at him curiously as she slipped down to

the last, lowest branch, her face now only a bit higher above him.

"No, thank God, no one in my family's been stopped or taken up," she said. "But then our ships are always too fast for your podgy coasters to catch, and—oh, Brighty, stop, else I'll drop you!"

Now that Diana was so near to the ground, Brighty decided that he'd rather travel the rest of the way himself. He wriggled against her arm and kicked hard like a wild rabbit into her chest, breaking free and leaping forward in an effortless arc of gray fur.

Because Brighty was a cat, albeit a small cat, by nature he did this well and landed squarely on his paws. But because Diana was a human, and a lady swathed in yards of fabric, she lacked that peculiar feline ability to land on her feet, and instead toppled from the branch and thumped directly into James' chest. Of course he caught her, steadying her with his arms around her waist. He had no choice, unless he wished to let her drop completely to the dirt.

"Gemini!" she exclaimed breathlessly, flushing strawberry pink, her hands upon his shoulders, her hair tousled, her skirts fluttering around his legs, and her body pressed up close to his. "However did *that* happen?"

"The cat," he croaked, the total sum of the words he could manage. "The cat did it."

"Oh, yes, of course, the kitten," she murmured, leaning closer, and before he could do the sane, honorable thing and set her feet on the ground and step away, she'd curled her arms around his neck and was kissing him, not like a lady, certainly not like Roxby's bride, but like her own delicious self, and he could not get enough.

He pulled her closer and she came to him, curving her body easily to fit against his. Her mouth was warm and wet and eager and *alive,* and he felt as if he were the one who'd fallen, fallen headlong into a place he never wished to leave. She tipped her head to one side, letting him deepen the kiss, and as he did she bumped back against the trunk of the tree. As slight as that bump was, it was enough to end the magic, or the madness, or whatever the hell it was that was making them both behave like this, and with a little gasp Diana pulled back.

"Gemini," she whispered, her eyes enormous as she touched her fingers to her lips. "I thought you said you didn't poach."

He let out his breath in a long-drawn sigh. Resignation, regret, or relief? He sure as blazes didn't know, not the way his head was still spinning. "And I thought you didn't let men kiss you."

"I don't, as a rule," she said, her voice odd and wavering all over the place, telling him that she'd no more notion of what had just happened than he did himself. "But you—you surprised me."

Swiftly she ducked beneath his arm and away from him, gathering up the kitten from where he'd been watching them.

"You've quite muddled things, Brighty," she said into the kitten's fur. "You must look elsewhere to find a sweetheart for Captain Dunham, you little goose, and leave me alone."

James frowned, unwilling to blame this so conveniently on the cat's dubious matchmaking skills. "Why doesn't Roxby keep you under lock and key, anyway?" he asked, confusion making him moody. "Or at least keep you out of the damned trees."

From beyond the trailing curtain of leaves, he could hear Lady Marchmont's voice chirping up and down and Chou-Chou's excited yips in reply. He and Diana had to leave the shelter of this tree now, before the others noticed they'd been sharing such shadowy privacy together. He held his hand out to Diana, more to show they should leave than with any real hope that she'd take it. She shouldn't, anyway. They couldn't risk it.

She nodded, but as she began to push aside the trailing branches, she turned back toward him. "It's not the fault of the 'damned tree,' you know," she said. "It's yours. You talked to me."

"I didn't talk you into anything!" he said indignantly.

"I didn't say you did. I said you talked *to* me, and you listened to me, and—and—oh, perdition, you'll never understand anyway!"

She was right about that, sure, right as rain. He didn't understand any of this, any more than he understood why he let her flounce away across the lawn having had the final word once again.

And the sooner he got back to sea, where there were no black-haired girls to kiss or matchmaking kittens to rescue, the better.

7

*W*ith a small whoop of pleasure, Diana seized the letter that the footman brought on a tray with her breakfast. Even before she'd seen the familiar seal pressed into the wax on the back, she recognized Roxby's handwriting, full of swirls that were as elegant as he was himself. In the course of their brief courtship, she'd learned he wrote divine love letters, worthy of any poet, and worthy of constant rereading to the point that she could recite entire passages. While pretty phrases and passionate declarations weren't exactly equal to having him back from London, they were far, far better than nothing, which was exactly what she'd had from Roxby in the three days since he'd left. Swiftly she rose from the table, taking the new letter with her to a window for better light and a modicum of privacy.

But as soon as she unfolded the single sheet, her heart sank without having read a word. There'd be no verses this time, no flowery paeans to her eyes or lips.

Roxby's letter was only a few hasty lines. He was very sorry, but his business had proved more complex than he'd anticipated. He would be detained in London at least another four days, perhaps as long as a week. He knew his dear bride would be unhappy, but it could not be helped. He suggested again that she think ahead to their wedding trip, as well as continue applying herself to learning more about Ashburnham's housekeeping and management. And he did love her. She was never to doubt that.

But she already knew he loved her, and each time he ordered her not to doubt that love, she wondered perversely if there was some reason she *should*.

As for applying herself to Ashburnham's management, she had spent the last two days trapped between Lady Waldegrave and the housekeeper, dutifully reviewing each of the bedchambers to decide which ones needed complete refurbishing and which could make do simply with new bedclothes and hangings and fresh silver on the looking glasses, more than enough solemn penance for that single startling kiss with Captain Dunham.

"Is Roxby returning soon, Diana?" asked Lady Marchmont, cutting her sausages into dainty bites to present to the waiting Chou-Chou. "Ashburnham is so hideously dull without him."

Diana sighed and returned to her chair. "Not yet. His business in London detains him there another few days."

"Oh, lah, a gentleman's *business*." Lady Marchmont looked heavenward. "May God preserve us from their business! But how barbarously unfair of him to abandon you here in the country like this."

Diana nodded and sniffed, feeling thoroughly neglected and sorry for herself.

"Well then," continued Lady Marchmont. "I know how to put you to rights. You shall come with me to

Portsmouth this very morning in my carriage. I've promised to review the *Amazon*'s progress—you'll know vastly more about that than I ever will—and meet with some fusty old admirals to try to make them more agreeable. They're quite weary of me by now. How much they'll like to see your fair face instead!"

"You wish me to go to Portsmouth to be agreeable?" repeated Diana uneasily. It wasn't the thought of visiting the town that worried her, but her breezily described duties involving the admirals. She didn't seem to have a gift for being agreeable, at least not the way Lady Marchmont wished her to be. True, if these admirals were fusty and old, she doubted they'd provide the same temptation as Captain Dunham, who was neither fusty nor old but heroic and virile.

Yes, that was the word she'd been searching for all the time she'd been obediently studying worn bedsheets and pillowbiers: virile. James Dunham wasn't handsome, but even with his wounded hand and the limp he had when he tried to run, he *was* virile—most alarmingly virile. She'd realized that even before he'd broken her fall and caught her by the tree, and when he'd kissed her—no, she wasn't going to let herself think of that again.

But the part of their encounter that seemed to have confused James the most was the same part that had very nearly seduced her—he'd talked. Not *at* her. *With* her. They'd teased and jested and bantered and quarreled with an ease and freedom she'd seldom felt lately with Roxby, and—but no, she wasn't going to let herself think of that, either.

No. The safest course for her was to keep clear of Captain James Dunham entirely. Which was, of course, one more fact in favor of her going with Lady March-mont.

"Well yes, I fear we must go down to Portsmouth if you're to be usefully agreeable," Lady Marchmont was saying as she set her plate on the floor for Chou-Chou, "for I doubt either the admirals or the *Amazon* will come here to us. But you know Roxby would approve of such a journey. You will merely be ascertaining that his contribution has been put to good and profitable use."

That was true. Roxby had been most eager for her to participate in this venture with the other ladies, at least as eager as Roxby allowed himself to be about anything.

"I promise we shall stay only two nights," continued Lady Marchmont, "and take our lodging at Ports-mouth's most dour and proper inn."

But the thought of the inn raised another misgiving in Diana's mind. "Have you invited—that is, will you be bringing anyone else, my lady?"

"Oh, pray, stop that! Call me Harriet the way I've asked, instead of making me feel like the oldest crone at court," she scolded. "I shall take my maid, of course, and yours if you wish, though mine will be perfectly happy to do for you as well."

Suddenly she comprehended Diana's hesitancy and chortled merrily. "It's Stanver that's worrying you, isn't it? I know you've said nothing since that lovely after-noon at the vicarage, but it's clear enough you don't care for him."

"It's not that I do not care for Lord Stanver, Harriet," said Diana stiffly. True enough, she didn't *not* care for him, but that was only because she hated him so thor-oughly. For a man who claimed to be Roxby's dearest friend, he showed her far too much attention, looking for excuses to touch her and say lewd things in the guise of jests, and she made sure never to be alone with him. "It's that I—I am not at ease in his company."

"But that's so much of his charm, isn't it?" teased Lady Marchmont. "Our wicked fallen angel, tumbled clear to the faro tables at Knowlewood! But no matter. You have my word Stanver will not be joining us. Lud, he'd set back our cause a year!"

She laughed again and fondly patted Diana's knee. "Lord Stanver and I are ancient acquaintances, my dear young innocent. We do . . . *amuse* ourselves on occasions, true, but there is nothing more to it than that, and nothing worse, either. If you come with me to Portsmouth, I shall promise to be an absolute *vision* of virtue. I can do it, you know. Roxby knows it, too, else he wouldn't have given you over into my keeping whilst he was away. Perhaps not so respectably as your Lady Waldegrave, but well enough to impress the people who need to be impressed."

But giving the proper impression of respectability didn't trouble Diana nearly as much as did the thought of poor Lord Marchmont and their two young sons, conveniently tucked away on his lands somewhere far, far to the north. According to Lady Marchmont, the boys were in the capable hands of their tutors, and all the much older lord cared for was his dogs and his horses. Since she'd produced the two necessary sons, she'd earned her husband's blessing to "amuse" herself wherever and with whomever she pleased, ideas that went against everything Diana believed about love and marriage.

But was she being any less loyal to Roxby if she went with Harriet to Portsmouth instead of staying at Ashburnham, counting linens and looking glasses? And what of kissing James Dunham—wasn't she already trying to dismiss and discount that in her mind, simply one more of Harriet's "amusements"?

Or, as Lady Waldegrave had said, was she simply falling into the preachy righteousness of the pathetically naive, being a judgmental prig from the colonies, a prudish embarrassment to Roxby and his friends?

"In your company I shall be a perfect vestal, my dear," promised Lady Marchmont as she used her napkin to wipe the sausage grease from Chou-Chou's white muzzle and paws. "And together we shall show such *devotion* to Britannia that those odious old admirals will have no choice but to accept our *Amazon* into their ranks."

Diana didn't want to be a prig or a prude or an embarrassment. She wanted to be Roxby's marchioness, the woman he loved above all others. She'd come this far, and she wasn't going to let a few old-fashioned Massachusetts scruples make her stumble now.

Bravely she raised her tea dish in both hands and grinned at Lady Marchmont. "To Portsmouth, then," she declared, "and to the success of Amazons everywhere!"

Diana rested her book open on her knee and leaned back against the soft leather squabs of Lady Marchmont's coach, reveling in the undeniable luxury of such travel. Outside of royal governors, no one in New England kept such an extravagant vehicle, not only because of the expense—even smaller carriages and shays had to be brought in pieces by ship clear across the ocean and reassembled at considerable risk and cost—but also, quite simply, because in the northern colonies there were few roads sufficiently wide or smooth to accommodate anything as large and heavy as a gentleman's traveling coach with the horses to draw it.

Even here in the rolling hills of Hampshire, the sight of Lady Marchmont's coach, with the dark green paint gleaming like a glossy beetle beneath the dust of the road, her husband's arms painted in gold on the door, the high spoked wheels spinning, the footmen standing behind in their matching green coats, and the team of well-groomed horses, was spectacular enough to make the laborers pause in their fields and lean on their rakes to watch while children came running to shriek and wave.

But as exciting as the attention could be, it was the more private pleasures of the coach that Diana especially relished. She loved the soft cushions that eased the bumps of the rutted roads, the ever-changing view outside the windows, the soft woolen throws in case of a chill, and the hamper of food and drink for elegantly makeshift meals. Best of all was the sense of being in a snug little nest that carried her safely through an imperfect world.

An imperfect world that most likely included a perfectly furious Lady Waldegrave at Ashburnham, and once again Diana felt a twinge of guilt at how she'd escaped the older woman's watchful eye by waiting until the countess had gone out on her morning drive about the county. Diana had left an obsequious note of explanation tucked into the looking glass of Lady Walde-grave's dressing table, but she knew no matter what she'd written the countess still would be displeased with her choice of companion and entertainment.

But she refused to think of that now, and instead happily sighed her contentment, stretching her arms over her head as she grinned across at Lady Marchmont with Chou-Chou asleep on her lap and her maid dozing in the corner.

"Didn't I assure you this was the most proper thing for you to do?" said Lady Marchmont as she stroked the little dog's silky ears. While Diana had chosen a jacket and petticoat of demurely quilted blue lutestring for traveling, Lady Marchmont was again as brilliant and impractical as a tropical bird in a gown of scarlet- and peacock-striped silk and a pert little hat as flat as a dinner plate, crowned with white feathers that looked suspiciously like Chou-Chou's ears. "I vow we shall have *such* a time of it in Portsmouth!"

She chortled wickedly, leaning back to glance out the window. But as she did, the chortle swiftly turned into a frantic gasp, her eyes rounding with excitement.

"Stop the coach!" she shrieked at the driver, dumping poor Chou-Chou on the floor and twisting to thrust her head out the window, nearly knocking her hat off in the process. "Barnaby, Barnaby, stop this coach at once! At *once!*"

The maid woke with an understandable scream of confusion. Chou-Chou was barking and growling and leaping back and forth between the seats as the coachmen shouted at the horses and struggled to bring them to a halt. An oversized coach might be a luxurious way to travel, but it was the very devil to stop quickly, rocking and churning up dust and lurching so violently that Diana had to clutch at the door frame and the straps on the side to keep from being pitched from her seat.

"What is wrong, Harriet?" she demanded, shouting over the din. Lady Marchmont's head and shoulders and hat filled the entire window so there was no way to see for herself. "What has happened? Has there been an accident? Why are we stopping?"

"Because we *must*, Diana!" explained Lady Marchmont imperiously, no real explanation at all. She was fiddling with the latch on the door before they'd finally stopped, waving her hands impatiently as she disentangled herself and her hat from the window and dropped back onto her seat, exhausted by so much exertion. "Oh, why is that man being so wretchedly *slow?* I vow I have seen hoary old tortoises make more haste!"

"Here he is now," said Diana as the footman swung open the door, murmuring apologies, and unfolded the little step beneath, adding a squat stool on the ground to make up the final difference.

"Not *him*," said Lady Marchmont, frowning as she tried to hush Chou-Chou. "I meant Captain Dunham, of course."

"Captain *Dunham?*" Dismayed, Diana leaned out the open door and past the footman. Sure enough, James Dunham was trudging along the road toward the coach, his black cocked hat pointing down as he watched his footing among the wheel ruts, his long dark blue cloak blowing behind him. Though she couldn't see his face, not with his head down, she'd no doubt at all that it was him from his height, the breadth of his shoulders, and his uneven, unsteady walk.

"What is he *doing* here on this road, Harriet?" she whispered, even though he was still too far away to overhear. "I do not wish to be critical, of course, but I didn't judge him to be a man much given to walks."

"I don't expect he *is* walking, that is, walking for walking's sake," said Lady Marchmont, finally calming Chou-Chou into silence. "I rather expect he was waiting at the crossroad there for the stage to the south, when we happened by. I rather hope so, anyway, else we'd no reason to stop ourselves."

"You don't mean to have him join us?" asked Diana, appalled. "In the coach? All the way to Portsmouth?"

"If he wishes it, yes." She squeezed into the doorway alongside Diana, waving her handkerchief, while the maid hung on to Chou-Chou. "Good day, Captain Dunham, good day! Might I ask your destination, sir?"

He looked up then, the same sort of dismay that Diana felt flickering briefly across his features when he realized that she stood with Lady Marchmont.

"Good day, my lady," he said, touching the front of his hat. "And to you, too, Miss Fairbourne. I'm bound for Portsmouth, my lady."

He was smiling up at them, the expected pleasantry, but because Diana had come to know his face she could see the lines of strain and weariness that were etched around his eyes and mouth. How difficult walking this far on such an uneven road must be for him, and how much harder still to concentrate on disguising his lameness before Lady Marchmont!

"They have given you a ship, Captain?" asked Diana, her heart pounding more wildly than it had any right to do.

"No ship, no," he said, his sadness palpable. Yet she understood that as well, from all the Fairbourne men who could not be happy without a deck and water beneath their feet and a sail overhead. "But I hope that by visiting in Portsmouth, I might increase my chances."

"Then that is exactly what we mean to do as well," declared Lady Marchmont. "Come, please, do join us, Captain."

Reflexively he glanced for an instant at Diana. "I cannot impose, my lady."

"Nonsense," insisted Lady Marchmont. "I shall insist, and you will vex me mightily if you refuse."

He sighed restlessly. "I'll ride atop then, for I fear I would not be agreeable company."

"Oh, piffle." Lady Marchmont swept her hand through the air to show how little she thought of such objections. "You are quite civilized and a hero as well, and my coach is of sufficient size to host an entire fleet. You had a box or trunk with you, didn't you, Captain? Taylor, pray go back and collect the captain's trunk, and be swift about it."

But there was nothing swift about how they all sorted themselves inside the coach, with Lady Marchmont ordering her maid and Diana and James about in every conceivable combination until, finally, they agreed upon her and Chou-Chou and her maid on one seat facing forward, with James and Diana on the other, Lady Marchmont's skirts between them as a fluttering, insubstantial barrier of striped silk.

Neither Diana nor James dared look at the other. Each stared resolutely straight ahead, determined to pretend as if the other didn't exist.

And both were absolutely miserable.

All Diana's earlier pleasure in the soft leather seats had disappeared. Now she sat as rigid and stiff as if the down-filled squabs had been replaced with unyielding wooden boards, her back ramrod-straight, her hands clasped tightly in her lap, and her legs, knees self-consciously together, pressed to one side to avoid any accidental contact with the large man beside her, who, she was quite resentfully certain, was occupying far more than his rightful share of the seat.

"Well now, here we all *are*," announced Lady Marchmont, cheerfully unaware of the tension that, to Diana, seemed to be washing about the inside of the coach in queasy waves. "Hush, *hush*, Chou-Chou! You are perfectly acquainted with Captain Dunham. He is a hero, you know, so there's no need to sniff and growl so. I said *hush!*"

But though Lady Marchmont tipped her head to smile coyly at James, Chou-Chou was unconvinced, snuffling and straining so hard against his mistress' fingers in his collar that he was standing on his hind legs.

"It's Brighty he smells," said James tersely. "The blasted little devil kept trying to stow away in my dunnage this morning."

Lady Marchmont blinked. "Brighty? And who, pray, is that?"

"It's Star Bright," said Diana quickly. "He's Captain Dunham's kitten. Someone tried to drown him in the millpond, and Captain Dunham fished him out and saved his life, and now he's his pet."

"Ohhhhhhhh," said Lady Marchmont as she arched one painted brow, having heard a great deal more than Diana had intended. "I *see*."

Beside Diana, James let out a long sigh of male irritation. "Thank you, Miss Fairbourne."

"You are welcome, Captain Dunham." Still she did not turn to look at him, and from the corner of her eye she was sure he didn't look at her either. However had she been driven to lose all her senses and *kiss* this man? "Star Bright is well, then?"

"Brighty is tolerable, aye."

She heard the rebuke in his version of the kitten's name. Steadfastly she lifted her chin, determined that he'd hear the same from her.

"I am glad to hear that Star *Bright* is not causing you any more mischief," she asked. "But I doubt he's had much success in his other, ah, endeavor, has he?"

He made a grumbling, wordless sound in his throat, and she knew she'd struck home. "He is being a cat, which is all the endeavor I require of him."

Diana smiled sweetly, though she still didn't meet his eye. "Perhaps you should require more," she suggested. "For the sake of your own happiness."

"What I require, Miss Fairbourne, is that my cat simply act as a cat and not the inspiration for outlandish superstitions." Pointedly he reached inside his cloak and drew a small serious book from his pocket.

"Surely you don't mean to *read*, Captain!" exclaimed Lady Marchmont with undisguised dismay. "Surely instead you could entertain us with tales of your adventures at sea, of the maidens you've so gallantly rescued or the villainous Frenchmen you have dispensed to their maker!"

"If you wish to hear tales of adventure and gallantry, my lady, I advise you to go the theater," he said, "for there are precious few to be found in the daily drudgery of a sailor's life."

But Lady Marchmont was undeterred, and she was also a viscount's wife. "Then read to us from your book, sir," she commanded. "Pray amuse us, Captain."

"You wish to hear me read tactical considerations of navigation?" he asked dryly, holding the spread pages open for her to view. "If you wish it, my lady, I will oblige, but I doubt there'll be much amusement in such a text for you."

"You torment me, sir!" exclaimed Lady Marchmont indignantly.

"Aye, I suppose I do, my lady," answered James, settling back with his book. "I warned you that I'd be poor company, and if you wish to leave me here by the side of the road, I can still find myself a place in the Portsmouth stage."

"You shall do nothing of the sort, Captain," said Lady Marchmont crossly. "No matter how ill-mannered you persist in being, I won't have it said that I discarded the hero of the *Castor* by the side of the Portsmouth road. Miss Fairbourne and I shall simply entertain ourselves, that is all."

But with him in the coach, a grim, silent presence in dark blue wool and gold lace, scowling at his precious navigational tactics as if it contained the darkest revelations of the universe, entertainment between the two women faltered, and conversation withered away to the occasional obligatory comment on the scenery or weather. A stop at an inn to relieve the horses didn't help, nor did the lavish cold meal that was produced from a carefully packed hamper. By the time they'd reached Portsmouth late that day, and Captain Dunham had been set down before his destination, an inn with a blue-painted anchor for its sign, Lady Marchmont could scarcely muster the weakest pretense of a fond farewell, while Diana took care to keep hers only faintly more effusive.

But as the coach rumbled down the street, she couldn't help but look back at him through the window. The porter from the inn, a former old sailor himself, was already carrying James' chest inside, and another officer had stopped to greet him, doubtless offering him congratulations in a more palatable fashion than had Lady Marchmont.

Clearly James was slipping back into the world where he belonged, a world that had little to do with her. But as she leaned slightly from the window for that final glimpse of him, she discovered to her surprise that he'd turned to look back at her as well. In that instant, across the distance of a bustling street, all the discomfiture of their journey vanished, replaced by a wordless question in his eyes, a frank and open longing that she couldn't begin to answer. Chagrined at being caught and confused by what she'd seen, she quickly ducked back inside the window, praying that the other woman wouldn't notice the guilty flush on her cheeks.

"At least *that* responsibility is completed," sniffed Lady Marchmont, indignation bringing her back to life.

"That man may be perfection at sea, but on land he leaves much—*much!*—to be desired as a companion, and as for anything more, why, I cannot begin to imagine it. Whenever will I learn not to be beguiled by a handsome face and gold lace? Now, shall we drive past the *Amazon* at her dock, so you might see her?"

Although the Marchmont coach had drawn attention as it traveled through the countryside, the sight of it rumbling along the cobblestone road that overlooked the Portsmouth dockyards and harbor caused no less of a commotion, stopping work, traffic, and conversations. The fact that the coach's two occupants were handsome young ladies only increased interest, for in a bustling, crowded port town in wartime, few unattended women ventured near the waterfront, especially not ladies, and nearly every man the coach passed turned to watch.

But for Diana, all that was fascinating lay outside the coach, and she was the one eagerly gazing through the window toward the water and more ships and boats than she'd ever seen in one place in her life. She hadn't realized how much she'd missed the sea of her childhood until it lay spread before her again, and she breathed deeply of the familiar salty air. Was James Dunham doing the same somewhere along this coast, she wondered, relishing the wild, free scent of the ocean that was so different from the sleepy warmth of inland Hampshire?

"Fah, what this damp air does to one's hair!" exclaimed Lady Marchmont as she patted at her head. "I shall be completely frizzled this evening. But look there, Diana, there at the end of the dock. That pretty boat is our *Amazon*."

She knocked for the driver to stop, and Diana quickly spotted the ship in which she now had a share. It wasn't hard to spot the *Amazon;* among all the other hardworking merchant vessels and warships, her newness and the money that had been lavished upon her made her glitter like an expensive toy. Her sides were painted brick red, trimmed with glossy black, the canvas in her new sails still creamy white, and even at this distance Diana could see how her polished brasswork glittered like mirrors.

But Diana, whose family had specialized in fast ships for smuggling and privateering, could also recognize that the *Amazon* had been built for speed, with dash and style in her lines. Unlike the navy's own conservative shipwrights who favored tradition over innovation, the *Amazon*'s lady sponsors had let their shipwright copy the sleeker, swifter French frigates that could outsail most of their older English counterparts. Her father and brothers would drool over such a ship, and Captain Dunham—why, Captain Dunham couldn't consider himself a true sailor if he didn't, too, the minute he saw her. How could he not? Whoever finally became the *Amazon*'s master would receive a rare gift indeed.

"A sweet bauble, isn't she?" said Lady Marchmont fondly. "That is what sailors call ships, my dear, *she* and *her,* as if all that timber and canvas were a real lover to warm them at night. I cannot say what particular parts of our dear *Amazon* now belong to you, thanks to Roxby's generosity, but I'm sure you can claim whatever you wish and no one will dare gainsay you. Ah well, on to the inn."

She rapped for the driver to begin again, and Diana gasped with disappointment.

"But can't we go on board?" she cried. "I should love to see below the decks, to feel how she sits in the water!"

Lady Marchmont stared at her. "That would hardly be proper, Diana. To go on board, among the common sailors and shipbuilders and God only knows what other low sorts of men! That would be too scandalous even for me. We have an overseer who tends to that."

"But I thought you wished my opinion," said Diana, looking forlornly back at the *Amazon* as they drove away. "I thought that was why you asked me to join you, because of my family and how I know more about ships than most ladies."

"Your opinion about a *frigate?*" Lady Marchmont tipped back her head and roared with unladylike laughter. "My dear, what we need most from you is your pretty face when we try to coax those old admirals into agreement. Your bright blue eyes, your rosy cheeks are what will persuade them, not your opinions about *boats.*"

"What you really cared for was Roxby's money," said Diana unhappily, flopping back against the seat with her arms crossed rebelliously over her chest. "*That's* what really mattered more than my opinion."

"Well, yes, of course it does," said Lady Marchmont, unperturbed. "Having the new Marchioness of Roxby on our lists will be a great thing indeed, especially since you'll be able to have access to your husband's purse, too. He's already proven that, the besotted darling."

"Roxby has been most generous," admitted Diana, only slightly mollified. She knew she was being foolish about this, but for some reason she couldn't keep the sting from her pride. Against all reason, she remembered how she'd accepted James Dunham's dare about rowing his boat and how she'd bettered him, too. But was that to be the last time in her life that she'd do something for her own satisfaction, the last time that being Roxby's wife and marchioness wouldn't always come first?

"Of course Roxby is generous. That is his nature." Lady Marchmont snorted, dismissing any argument as preposterous. "But I meant what I said about the other, too, Diana. The last thing—the very last thing—any man wishes to hear is a woman presuming to have an opinion of her own. If you wish to make a success in this world of ours, you must never forget that."

She sighed, staring off at nothing in particular as she absently ruffled Chou-Chou's ears. "You know, at first I rather believed you and Captain Dunham might be conducting some sort of little intrigue. I thought I detected a shared *sensibility* between you. The sticking point, of course, was Roxby, for how could you even dawdle with another man when Roxby has so much to offer a woman? But then I was wrong, wasn't I? Quite, quite wrong and confused as usual."

She laughed, and halfheartedly Diana joined in. *Confused as usual.* That was what Lady Marchmont had said, but how could she be any more confused than Diana was herself?

8

"You have seen the Ladies' Ship, then, James?" asked Captain Richard Lanker, puffing gently on his long-stemmed white pipe. "What a beauty! If I'd my way, I'd give the ladies every place in Whitehall, they've done that much better than the admirals themselves."

"How could they not?" answered James wryly. He and Richard had been friends for nearly twenty years now, ever since they'd both landed in the same midshipman's berth as homesick, seasick boys, and there were few secrets between them, especially sitting together in a cheerfully noisy tavern with tankards of rum before them. "There are precious few things that such ladies do better than spend money, particularly their husbands' money."

"Ah, but the ship, Jamie, the ship!" Richard leaned closer, letting his eyes half close in worshipful admiration. "She's already been fitted out from stem to stern, down to the guns and powder, none of that tedious drudge for her master or crew. She makes every other frigate in port look like an old butter tub, and I'd wager my life she'll fly across the water like she has wings. You speak of living by our merit, Jamie. Think of what you or I could do with a ship like that!"

James only smiled, but he'd thought of it, aye. What young captain didn't? Glorious careers always seemed linked to glorious ships, one dependent upon the other.

"Think of it, Jamie, ponder it well!" continued Richard, warming to the lovely, impossible vision of such rare fortune, his face glowing nearly as brightly as his coppery hair. "There'd be no more dancing about with the French then, no more turning tail to run instead of attacking! We'd stop 'em dead in their wakes, we would, Jamie, and haul them home for prizes. You'd welcome a fair crack at that, wouldn't you?"

"You're a dreamer, Dick," said James softly. Of course he'd like to capture enemy vessels and bring them home as prizes. That was the only sure path a captain had to find any measure of security, the only way he'd ever have fortune enough to have a wife or family of his own, and a decent roof to put over their heads. But the poor old *Castor* had been far too slow to chase anything short of a barge, let alone capture it, and it wasn't an accident that his most famous action had been purely defensive.

He wasn't being overly modest, just truthful. Because he'd saved English women and children from French capture, landsmen all over England had hailed him as a conquering hero. Lady Marchmont and her optimistic friends had considerable company.

But his superiors had surely realized that there'd been more reaction than daring involved, more luck in the way the winds had favored him instead of the French captain. Certainly the Admiralty Board had recognized the facts from his report, especially the part about the *Castor*'s sinking.

"You're casting too high, Richard," he said, shaking his head with glum pessimism. "Even if the Admiralty swallows its pride and accepts that ship into service— which you know as well as I they won't—a vessel that fine will be sure to go to the next captain with influence on the list. What luck shall we have, eh, you the son of a wool merchant from the heathen north and I the lowly spawn of a country parson?"

"Ballocks," said Richard with relish, pausing to take a long pull from his tankard for emphasis. He'd been in the tavern long before James had joined him, as the glowingly rubicund tip of his nose proved, and his voice was rising to a captain's bellow. Not that anyone would particularly notice or care; the Blue Anchor was accustomed to such exuberance from its patrons.

"Ballocks, James!" he continued. "Now that you've risen fresh from the grave, you're a bona fide hero in a war that has bloody few of them. Fenner will see to it, I'm sure. Look at me, week after week on that damned blockade duty, while you've had the glory of battle."

"Oh, aye," said James dryly. "The scars are real enough, too."

"Hell, what's a little scar or two for England?" boomed Richard with the assurance of a man whose body remained remarkably unscathed. "It only adds to your value! No wonder I've heard that you've more than a few tongues whispering on your behalf."

James grimaced. "The news sheets and ballad singers might have made me out to be a seven days' wonder, but in Whitehall they know better."

"I'm not talking about ballad singers, Captain Dunham, and you damned well know it." Richard leaned over the table with a conspirator's wink, though he kept his voice at exactly the same level. "I'm talking about the grand ladies their own selves."

"Oh, aye, the ladies." James groaned. "Permit me to tell you of those ladies, Richard. I was swept up by one of them in her coach today, carried off like a prize myself, and though I pleaded in my own defense, that same grand lady insisted on running her little stocking'd toes all along my leg and thigh the whole time, bold as a five-shilling strumpet."

"The devil she did!" Richard roared with delight, shoving at James' arm. "Did you pull her up on your lap, then, and give her what she wanted, hard and strong? Oh, aye, taking a grand lady in her coach, tossing her petticoats around her ears and making her beg for more—no wonder they say the ladies are all crying out your name to the admirals, if that's how you reward 'em!"

"Do you think that's how I want to get a ship, servicing randy ladies in place of their spavined old husbands?" scoffed James. "I may have been battered about a bit, but I've still got some pride left."

Richard snorted. "I'm not hearing pride talking here, Jamie, but those overnice scruples of yours that come from being raised alongside a churchyard. You're the one that says we must rise on our merits. So I ask you, then, why didn't you show the lady how high and stiff your merits can rise, eh?"

"And earn a case of French pox for my trouble." James shook his head, thinking of how flagrantly aggressive Lady Marchmont had been in the coach. "If she wanted to be so free with me, likely she's already been free with half the other men in Portsmouth, and those aren't odds I'll take. Besides, there was another lady in the coach, too."

" 'Tis not right to disappoint a lady," insisted Richard with a salacious wink. "A disappointed lady is a royal terrible waste. And two ladies, the sad little darlings—hell, James, that's finding heaven without having to die first!"

"The second lady *is* a lady, Richard," said James as he tossed three coins on the table beside his empty tankard and rose to go. Only the fact that Richard was such an old friend kept him from hauling him into the street for a thrashing after speaking so freely about Diana Fairbourne. "She wasn't party to the other's mischief and never would be."

He left then, jamming his hat back on his head before he'd say more than his mystified friend deserved. Any other time, and with any other lady besides Diana in the coach with Lady Marchmont, he would have been there roaring and crowing along with Richard. A situation like the one he'd survived this afternoon could have provided the ribald beginnings for endless entertainment during the long tedious days and nights at sea. Yet here he was instead, defending the virtue of a woman willingly betrothed to a man he despised, a woman whose face and voice and scent and very *taste* kept haunting him with an insistence that could drive him mad if he wasn't careful.

Or maybe, God save him, he already was, and he grimaced as he remembered the bit of foolishness he'd tucked into his pocket earlier in the afternoon.

He nodded in curt farewell to the tavern's keep, and

exchanged the cheerful, raucous warmth and thick clouds of tobacco smoke for the gray early evening outside. The days were shorter now, summer beginning to fade, and the fog that had rolled in across The Solent held the first damp chill of autumn in its wispy grasp.

Yet in an odd way James welcomed it, for the fog and damp smelled of the sea, a comforting, familiar scent that he'd missed desperately while he'd been cooped up in his sister's care. He breathed deeply, walking slowly, feeling the tension in his body ease and the stiffness in his leg, worse after the long, uncomfortable ride in the coach, begin to relax with the exercise.

He'd always liked Portsmouth for its lack of pretense, a low, snug town begun so long ago on this flat island to the south that no one could remember how many centuries some of these houses had stood. Unlike London, Portsmouth existed solely to serve the sea, with every street leading toward the bays and inlets and the bristling forest of masts and spars of the ships and boats sheltered in them. Even without a ship or crew of his own, James felt as if he belonged here, just as he no longer seemed to in Ashburnham. He hunched his shoulders against the chill and crossed the street away from the lantern lights and laughter of the taverns and rum shops, instead heading down toward the water and the docks.

He knew where he was going, and he smiled to himself as he thought of how wretchedly predictable he'd become. The *Amazon* wasn't difficult to find, either. Even in the shifting fog, her beauty and grace made her stand out among her more stolid sisters like Diana Fairbourne would at a country ball. Richard Lanker was right about this, even if he hadn't been about accepting Lady Marchmont's attentions. The Admiralty should be made to gobble their pride as swiftly as possible so they could put this ship into service. He'd heard, too, how she was ready to sail as soon as she'd been granted a crew, that the ladies had even seen to filling the water casks, saving that extra month or so that fitting out a new commission usually took. To keep such a frigate sitting idle when she could be fighting the French was a sinful waste, and as for the captain fortunate enough to receive such a command—ah, he'd be the luckiest sailor in England.

"Captain Dunham?" came the woman's voice through the fog. "Is that you, sir?"

He didn't turn. Diana couldn't truly be there, not here in the Portsmouth dockyard. The voice must be one more trick of his imagination, one more sign that his thoughts were far too preoccupied with a woman he couldn't have. He'd simply conjured her up from the sea air by comparing her to the *Amazon*, that was all.

"It *is* you, Captain," she said, louder this time and with a distinctive mixture of amazement and accusation. "I should know the set of your jaw anywhere, even in the fog, so no fair pretending you don't know me in return."

No mere specter would accost him so boldly—none would dare—and at last he turned slowly around.

She was standing in the slanting beam of a lantern, her face pale inside the loose hood of her long dark cloak. The lantern was being held high by a man beside her, and with an unpleasant jolt his first thought was of Roxby, here at her side in a husband's place.

But Roxby would never go walking along the Portsmouth waterfront at dusk, not even with his future wife, and he'd certainly never be the one to carry the lantern. Belatedly James noticed that the man wore the livery of Lady Marchmont's servants, and his racing heart slowed a fraction.

"You're alone, Miss Fairbourne?" he asked and could have kicked himself for speaking so foolishly. What was it about her that made his wits flee and his tongue knot like a simpleton's? "That is, ah, Lady Marchmont is not with you?"

"Gemini, no," she said with her customary, endearing frankness. "First she'd say the fog frizzled her hair, and then she'd tell me it wasn't quite proper to go out walking from our inn."

For once he'd have to agree with Lady Marchmont. Even shrouded in the voluminous cloak, dock workers and sailors were turning to gawk at her, and he'd already overheard a few random catcalls of disrespectful approval about her person.

"It's *not* proper, Miss Fairbourne," he said, "nor is it safe. Not that *that* seems to stop you."

"No," she admitted and sighed deeply. "It doesn't. I think instead it rather encourages me. I left Appledore for London partly because my father watched me too closely. Then I left my brother's ship and keeping for Lady Waldegrave, until she became rather too watchful, too, and so I escaped here to Portsmouth with Lady Marchmont. And now the minute she decided she needed to rest, here I am, slipped free from my respectable traces yet again."

"A restless soul, then," he said, wondering to himself

how she'd ever survive with a controlling husband like Roxby. "Where will you wander next, eh?"

She lowered her chin, her guard once again in place. So she'd been called restless before, and not as a compliment, either. Had it been by Roxby himself?

"Only as far as the *Amazon*," she answered carefully. "If I have invested a thousand pounds of Roxby's in this frigate, then I mean to see and judge her for myself."

"That's where I was bound as well." He could see precisely where all this was leading, and not just to the *Amazon*, either. Likely she'd enough experience with him by now to realize it, too, which would explain part of her wariness.

But he'd had exactly the right amount of rum to drink with Richard to make every endeavor seem possible, even one as foolhardy as this. "Not to go aboard, not at this hour, but I do intend to take a long look at the ship that's the talk of this town."

"You do?" she asked suspiciously. "I thought you weren't interested in a frigate commissioned by ladies."

"Perhaps, Miss Fairbourne, I cannot keep from doing what I shouldn't, either." He stepped forward and took the lantern from the footman. "Go back to your mistress, man. I'll see to Miss Fairbourne from here."

The footman bowed, relinquishing his post and his lantern to head to the nearest rumshop without any protest, but Diana was not as accepting.

"You have no right to do that, none at all!" she cried indignantly, her hands on her hips making her cloak jut out on either side. "How can you spend hours in a coach with me and barely deign to speak a word, then expect me to come with you now, meek as a new lamb? Have you lost your wits, or do you merely believe I've lost mine?"

"Maybe we've both turned mad as hatters," he said with a shrug. "If you hurry, you can catch the footman and go back to your inn with him, or you can come with me down to the *Amazon*'s dock. It's your decision to make, mad or not."

Furiously she shoved the hood back from her head, muttering darkly to herself. She looked back over her shoulder in the direction that the footman had gone, then down toward the ship at the end of the wharf before finally glaring back at James.

"Your choice, mind," he said again.

"Choice, my foot." She reached out and snatched the lantern from his hand, skipping away with it down the wharf before he could grab it back. "I'll give you your precious *choice*, Captain Dunham!"

Off she ran, and with exasperation he swore, loud and long. Why the hell did she keep doing this to him, anyway? No wonder everyone else in her life kept trying to rein her in. Given half a moment's freedom, she'd bolt like a wild horse.

It had wounded his pride when she'd left him so abruptly at the millpond and beneath his sister's beech tree. But for her to vanish here along the waterfront, into the fog on a gray Portsmouth evening, was dangerous lunacy. There was no way he could let her go, not this time, and with another oath he hurried after her as fast as his now-aching leg would let him.

"Miss Fairbourne!" he called sharply as he lurched down the dock toward the frigate. "For God's sake, Miss Fairbourne, come back here at once!"

His ragged footsteps on the wooden planks of the dock echoed dully through the fog, his voice going unanswered over the water. The fact that this particular dock seemed empty for the night, the little outbuildings along it dark and locked, did little to reassure him. There was always a certain safety in bustling crowds, and fear for her safety quickened his pace as much as possible through the fog and shadows.

"Diana!" he called, concern making him unconsciously use her given name. "Diana! Where in blazes are you, lass?"

"Here," she called back at last, and with eager relief he turned past around an enormous pyramid of stacked barrels. She was standing alone in the middle of the dock, the lantern at her feet and her hands clasped before her as she stared openmouthed at the ship looming in the water before her.

"Isn't she a beauty, James?" she said with open admiration as he joined her, likewise using his given name without realizing it. "I do not believe I've seen a vessel with better lines, not warship or merchant. How I'd like to see her in blue water with a captain and crew to run her through her paces!"

He smiled, thinking how much she sounded like Richard Lanker and how little like a future marchioness. He'd never met a lady who could talk ships and sails and winds, but then, he'd never met one who could row a boat, either, and he let himself imagine her standing beside him on the *Amazon*'s quarterdeck as he put the frigate "through her paces," just for her.

Now she waved her hand impatiently through the air, as if to sweep aside every admiral's objection. "What a waste it is for her to be here instead of running free with the wind at sea where she belongs, tied up and useless because of some prideful male foolishness!"

James listened, his smile fading. He'd never thought he'd turn his back on a ship as handsome as the *Amazon*, but even a splendid new frigate paled in comparison to the woman before him. With her dark hair coming unpinned from running and little stray tendrils curling around her face, her lips parted, and her eyes wide in admiration, Diana was undeniably the most beautiful and most desirable woman he'd ever seen.

But it was what she was saying—what she'd *said*—that was twisting and turning through him now with the same kind of urgency he felt before a battle. And damnation, he was going to trust it, the same as he trusted his instincts instead of reason when the big guns were firing broadsides.

What a waste . . . tied up and useless because of some prideful male foolishness!

"You cannot marry Roxby, Diana."

She looked at him sharply. "What did you say?"

"I said you cannot marry Roxby. He'll ruin you, lass, destroy you so fast you'll never know when it happened."

"Why are you saying such things to me?" Her eyes enormous, she took a step back from him and out of the circle of the lantern's light, clutching her cloak tightly around her. "You've no right, and you're wrong besides. Roxby loves me too much to treat me the way you say."

"You know it yourself," he insisted, "else you wouldn't have said what you did about being tied up and useless and his pride and all. *You* said it, Diana, not I."

"You should call me Miss Fairbourne," she said, but her voice was so tiny that her order had no authority. "And—and I was speaking of the *Amazon*, Captain Dunham, not myself."

"Were you then, lass?" he demanded roughly. "Sometimes truth comes out willy-nilly when we're trying to pretend otherwise. Do you want to be a blasted marchioness so much that you'll give him your soul in return?"

"I want love," she whispered. "All I want is love, and Roxby loves me just as I love him."

"Love, is it," he said bitterly. "From Roxby. Jesus."

He had to show her now. He'd come this far and as daft as it was, he had no choice. He dug his hand into the pocket of his coat and pulled out a small lumpy bundle, awkwardly tugging aside the cloth wrapping with his left hand.

"You're the one who started this foolishness," he said as he thrust a small stoneware figure into her hand. "You can be the one to explain it. Mark this, and tell me again how much Roxby loves you."

Her fingers trembling, she crouched down to hold the figure to the lantern's light. "It's—it's your Brighty, isn't it?"

"Damn right," he said, and it was. The tiny cat sat on its haunches, its tail curled over its back and one paw raised to beg in the manner of countless other stoneware figures of kittens on the chimneypieces of countless parlors. But instead of being covered with the universal black and orange calico spots, this kitten was as gray as the fog around them, as gray as Brighty himself, with a white star on its forehead and an upraised paw crowded with seven toes.

"Now you tell me, *Miss* Fairbourne," he demanded,

"how in blazes that came to be among my shirts when I unlatched my chest at the inn this afternoon. Was it during that infernal coach ride, eh? Did you and that wicked friend of yours concoct this as some sort of rare jest on pitiful old Captain Dunham?"

"I swear I didn't!" she cried in confusion, her dark head bowed as she turned the figure in her fingers. "I've never seen it before this moment. Perhaps your sister—"

"Why the devil would a sensible woman like Celia do such a thing? To her the cat's simply a cat, nothing more."

Unconvinced, she shook her head, and lightly traced the small cat's crudely painted face with her fingertip. "Yet you said Brighty had been climbing among your clothes before you left, in the same place that this appeared, and that he cried when you left."

He grumbled wordlessly. "He didn't cast some magic spell to turn himself into crockery, if that's what you're saying."

"I don't know what I'm saying," she said, and when she turned her face back up to him, he could see the fear in her eyes. "All I know is that Brighty wanted to stay with you, to watch over you, and this is how he's done it."

"Oh, aye, and I'm the almighty king of Siam," said James with disgust. "Don't talk nonsense, Diana."

"I'm not," she said, slowly rising to her feet. "But I've always believed Brighty's a special cat, and now you do, too."

"I never said—"

"You didn't have to, James," she said, resting her hand

on his arm. "Not in so many words. But you wouldn't have said what you did about Roxby and me if you didn't believe in Brighty, too, and love, and—and—oh, all the rest of it!"

He sighed with exasperation, fighting the tug of his emotions with his common sense, the feather-light pressure of her fingers on his arm only muddling things further.

"I'm concerned for you, mind?" he said gruffly. "You're a good lass, and I don't want to see you hurt."

"I know that, and I thank you for it." She tried to smile, a wobbly effort, and looked back down at the kitten. "But I'm not like those women who needed rescuing from the French, you know."

"It would be a damned sight easier for me if you were." Gently he leaned forward and kissed the top of her head, right on the parting of her hair, as risky a kiss as he'd dare.

But she ventured more, slipping her arms around his waist to rest her cheek against his chest, and with a sigh more like a groan he parted her cloak and slid his hands inside. She leaned closer, welcoming him into the cocoon of warmth and womanly scent that her body had created, a haven against the chill and damp and the coming night around them. It was only a short step then to turn her face upward, to find her mouth with his own, and to kiss her, and kiss her again, her lips salty from the fog and the sea, and her body melting soft and yielding against his own.

"You've got 'er good now, Cap'n!" shouted a sailor from the *Amazon*'s harbor watch, and another man whooped with cackling amusement. "Toss up her skirts an' take her!"

Startled, she broke away, and James turned to snarl at the sailors on the ship. He was as angry with himself for treating her like some waterfront strumpet as he was at them. Another five minutes and he might well have done exactly what the men had suggested, and what kind of concern would he have been showing her then?

"I'm sorry, Miss Fairbourne," he said as contritely as he could manage, "and I hope you'll, ah, forgive me if you can. Here, I'll take you back to your inn now."

"Don't be sorry, Captain, for it's not your fault." She closed her eyes and shuddered, clutching the stoneware cat tightly in both hands like a talisman. " 'Tis I who should be apologizing to Roxby for being so—so *forward* with you. Oh, how shameless you must judge me to be!"

"Not shameless, no," he said, though he couldn't exactly say what kept making them behave like this together. Both of them knew they shouldn't, and yet both of them seemed unable to stop. "Impulsive, maybe. You're definitely of a, ah, a warm temperament."

"Oh, yes, and that sounds ever so much better for a lady," she said bitterly. She sighed, and opened her eyes to look at the figure in her hands, the gray glaze gleaming in the lantern light. "It must be Brighty's fault. It was the last time. He must be what is leading us into this—this trouble."

"If you believe that, then you *are* mad," he said with an uneasy sigh of his own, "madder than any hatter in Christendom. And God help us both, so am I."

9

Though the three violinists had already begun to play, the dancers would not start until Roxby had taken the gilded armchair reserved for him in the front row. Signora Benaccetto was most respectful and conscientious about such matters. He appreciated it, and in return he wouldn't keep her or her other patrons waiting. With a bow to one acquaintance and a slight smile to another, he finally sauntered to his seat and composed himself to enjoy the entertainment that had made the London house of Signora Benaccetto so celebrated in certain circles.

A silken rope, striped like candy, was stretched from one wall to a curtained window on the other, just high enough over the heads of the gentlemen below to give each one a splendid view. The signora herself tapped a small silver bell, and the curtains parted. Two young women, scarcely more than girls, really, pranced down the swaying rope, balancing themselves with heads high and arms outstretched.

But it was not the rope dancers' grace or agility that made the men below them sigh and groan with noisy approval. Their costumes, or lack of such, was what had made them such favorites. Each dancer wore bright pink stockings tied with white satin garters and rosettes at the knees, lace frills at their wrists and exuberant pink bows tied around their throats, and absolutely nothing else.

Coyly they peaked over the fans in their hands, twisting and turning and arching their backs in time to the music. In the candlelight their well-powdered breasts quivered and their well-curved hips shook, reflected over and over in the large looking glasses that Signora Benaccetto had thoughtfully hung along the walls. Every so often one of the girls would kick her plump, well-turned leg higher, offering a more revealing glimpse to the lascivious men below.

Amused more than titillated, Roxby watched with a connoisseur's jaded eye. This pair of rope dancers seemed to lack the artistry of some of their predecessors at the house, but then it was a trade that rewarded novelty rather than skill, and a willingness for seductive display over real grace and beauty. Not that such reservations seemed to be affecting any other man in the room except himself, and most assuredly not the man in the chair beside his.

"You are enjoying the performance, Admiral?" he asked, leaning across the space between them. The question was unnecessary. The man sat with his hands clenching the arms of his chair as he stared rapt at the young woman above him, his mouth open and the bulge in the white breeches of his uniform all proof enough of his interest. "You find the dancers accomplished?"

"By God, how could I not, my lord?" exclaimed the admiral without moving his gaze even a fraction. "Mark the bubbies on that one with the ginger hair! Have you ever seen the like, my lord?"

Roxby had, many, many times, and a great deal better ones, too, but he was far too well-mannered to say so to his guest. Besides, he thought pleasurably, what common rope dancer could ever hope to compete with the extravagant beauty of his own Diana? But then men like Admiral Birtles would never have a chance to see a lady like Diana, and to him a sullen-faced little tart like the one posturing above them was a veritable Aphrodite.

"If the girl pleases you, Admiral," he said delicately, "then an introduction could be arranged."

The girl kicked high, and the admiral gulped. "Aye, my lord, perhaps for you."

"And perhaps for you as well, if you wish it." Idly Roxby rubbed a smudge from the face of the ruby on his finger, giving the admiral time to consider the full possibilities he was offering.

It did not take long. "The devil you say!"

"Not the devil, Admiral," said Roxby, smiling, "only me. The *signora* is an old friend of mine and she is most fond of obliging friends."

"As it should be, my lord, as it should be," agreed the admiral impatiently, craning his neck to watch the dancers as they moved to the other end of the rope.

"Ah, then we are agreed," murmured Roxby. "You see, I have a . . . *concern* that I feel needs addressing, and you, Admiral, may be the one to assist me."

"Oh, aye, my lord, whatever you please," he answered, not really listening. "Though I can't in blazes see what I could do for your lordship."

Roxby shrugged, demurring. Nearly a week spent here in London, and nearly all of it would come down to these next few minutes. "A small affair, nothing more. You have heard I am to be wed soon, yes? My bride was born in the New England colonies, and although I cannot wait for the day when she becomes my wife, I am less than pleased with the activities of several of her family."

The admiral frowned, at last turning toward Roxby. "What kind of activities, my lord?"

"Smuggling," said Roxby blandly. "Thievery. Making general fools of the king's ships in that part of the world. I cannot hold their actions against my innocent bride, of course, but I would not wish such a stain against my lady wife's name."

"What port, my lord?" demanded the admiral sharply. "There's nothing I hate more than a damned thieving smuggler, robbing from his majesty's own pocket! Give me their names, my lord, and I'll see that the scoundrels are brought to justice, strung from my own yardarm if necessary."

"Appledore, near Boston," said Roxby. "The family name is Fairbourne. And I would appreciate your reticence in this matter as well, Admiral, for reasons that are most obvious."

"My word of honor, my lord, my word." The admiral smiled knowingly, and tapped his finger to the side of his bulbous nose. "Hah, haven't I fallen into that hellhole with my own wife! Better to begin on the proper foot with your lady, eh?"

"Exactly so." Roxby smiled, marveling that such an ass could control so large a portion of the country's welfare. But no matter. He'd do whatever Roxby wanted, that was clear enough.

Without that annoying, disreputable nest of Fairbournes to cling to, Diana's loyalty to him would be unquestioning, unswerving, and so would her dependence upon him as well. She'd never guess his part in the ruin of her family, either. He could even play the understanding and supportive spouse if he wished and bind her to him further. His lovely, trusting, innocent Diana—how wonderfully well she'd suit him!

He smiled again, beckoning to Signora Benaccetto so he could arrange the admiral's reward and thinking how much he'd accomplished for the price of one sullen-faced rope dancer.

"I wish you much joy of your evening, Admiral," he said as the ginger-haired girl winked at them over her fan. "You will not, I believe, be disappointed in your decision."

And neither, thought Roxby with considerable satisfaction, would he.

"I do not believe, Diana, that there is one single true gentleman among those despicable admirals, not one!" Harriet Marchmont hurled a crumpled letter to the floor and kicked her slippered foot at it for an additional measure of scorn. "I sent the sweetest of letters, such as a lady might pen to a gentleman, to every last one of them, begging the honor of an audience to discuss the *Amazon*'s future, and not one—not *one!*—of those dirty rascals has had the decency to arrange a meeting."

"Not a single one?" asked Diana, slipping off her cloak and retrieving the balled-up letter at her feet.

Slowly she sat in a chair beside the tea table, smoothing the crumpled paper with her fingers as best she could to read the neat clerk's handwriting. "What excuse did they give?"

Lady Marchmont sniffed and twitched the wide skirts of her dressing gown against her legs for disdainful emphasis. "The usual blather, of course. To a man, they discovered other engagements demanding of their time, and the pressing needs of the country must take precedence over the pleasurable honor of a lady's wishes, your most obedient servant, sirrah, sirrah. It's enough to make me wish to go directly to their offices, baiting them like bears in their dens, the way I did at Whitehall in London."

"You *did*?" Warehouses and counting houses and navy offices: Diana knew from experience that these were all places where a woman's sudden appearance could outrage men instantly, as if they'd somehow been caught standing about with their breeches down in a brothel. "And they received you?"

"Of course not," said Lady Marchmont, setting Chou-Chou over her shoulder and patting his back as if to burp him. "They barred their doors and cowered behind their desks, the filthy cowards, and sent their little clerks out to bow and scrape and make their apologies. I vow, Diana, you look quite dreadful. Are you ill? Shall I send for a pot of tea, or perhaps a cordial?"

Diana shook her head, wishing what ailed her could be so easily remedied. "I was out walking, to see the *Amazon* more closely," she said with vague truth. "I am a bit tired, that is all."

"Then you do need tea." Briskly Lady Marchmont

clapped her hands for her maidservant and sent her down to the kitchen. "But while I do appreciate your fervor, you truly shouldn't have gone down to the *Amazon* unattended. There are *so* many low people here in Portsmouth! If you'd come to any harm, I cannot guess what I'd say to Roxby."

"I wasn't alone," said Diana defensively. She didn't know what to say to Roxby, either, and not just about walking in Portsmouth. "I took one of your footmen with me."

Lady Marchmont rolled her gaze toward the ceiling. "I suppose they're better than nothing, the great foolish brutes. I don't keep them for their, um, cunning, you know. He acquitted himself as you wished?"

"Oh, yes," murmured Diana, wondering guiltily how much the man would volunteer to his mistress. The last thing she wished was Lady Marchmont's interpretation, or misinterpretation, of what had happened between her and James there beside the *Amazon,* especially when she wasn't exactly sure herself.

James. Oh, Gemini, when had she started thinking of him by his given name like that, instead of Captain Dunham? She was going to marry Roxby, and she still didn't speak to him with such familiarity. Granted, Roxby was the one who didn't wish her to, claiming that no wives of titled gentlemen used anything but their titles, but that wasn't the point. Somehow she and James Dunham had begun calling each other James and Diana, just as they'd begun worrying over each other, and falling into walking at the same pace side by side, and oh, worst of all, kissing each other whenever they were alone.

No, she must be honest. The kissing wasn't the worst, not by half.

The worst was how much she *enjoyed* kissing James.

Whenever Roxby kissed her, she always had the uncomfortable feeling that he was holding back a part of himself. She'd told herself that he'd merely been being a true gentleman, deferring to the innocence that he seemed to hold so dear, and in the beginning she'd found that excitingly flattering. But since they'd become betrothed, she'd often secretly found herself longing for more from him—more impulsiveness, more passion, more ungentlemanly desire for her as a woman and less respect for her as his lady bride. Yet the one time he'd done that, she'd struck him for his efforts. And worse, she'd felt absolutely nothing in response.

No wonder she'd never dare confess such shameful longings to anyone else. How could she? For to do so would be to admit how unsuited she was to be Roxby's wife and marchioness, how unworthy she was of his love.

But with James Dunham, she'd never had to hide much of anything, and from that first morning by the millpond she'd never worried about being unworthy or unsuitable or unlike a marchioness. It simply hadn't mattered.

And when they had finally kissed, tumbling headlong into each other's arms, there'd been a wild, untidy quality to it that had made her heart race in a way Roxby's kisses never had done. James had been no more in control of his passion—and yes, there had been passion, however misguided, an excess of passion—than she'd been herself, and that had only served to excite and bewilder her more. Yet how could she feel this way about a crippled navy captain on half pay?

At least it wasn't love. She knew that much. Love was what Roxby was offering her with marriage, fine and elegant, as precious and pure as gold, and the prize that she'd come clear across the ocean to find.

But then what exactly was it that she felt for James Dunham?

And why, God help her, couldn't she *stop*?

"What's that rubbish you're holding?" asked Lady Marchmont curiously. "Some horrid example of our landlady's taste in ornament?"

Diana looked down at the stoneware cat still clutched tightly in her hand, the little head poking out from beside her thumb. She hadn't realized she'd kept it, and she worried what would happen to James without it to guard him.

"I, ah, I found it in a shop," she said, holding the figure up for the other woman to see. "I thought it looked rather like Captain Dunham's cat."

"Humph," said Lady Marchmont, unimpressed. "The same wretched animal that torments poor Chou-Chou so. I wouldn't go wasting my money buying trinkets for that Captain Dunham, either. I've never met such an *unrewarding* man."

She sniffed, tipping the newly brewed tea from her cup to the saucer. "But what concerns me now is trapping these cowardly admirals. Fah, the way they're maneuvering, you'd think they could win any war they pleased!"

"If they're like other men," said Diana, relieved to turn her thoughts away from James, "then they must eat. And if they eat, then they likely dine together in a pack, at the same tavern or ordinary every day."

"They do?" Lady Marchmont cocked her head, considering. "How do you know this?"

"It's the manner of all men, isn't it," said Diana with a shrug, "or at least sailing men. Perhaps it comes from taking mess together on ships."

" 'Taking mess,' " said Lady Marchmont, wrinkling her nose. "How *vulgar* sailors are!"

Diana sighed, knowing better than to take offense. "All I can say is that my father will dine with the same friends at the same time and place and eat exactly the same food, as regular as the sun. If we can learn the tavern that's favored by the higher officers—I'm sure it's well-known—then we shall find our admirals, and without any clerks to keep us away, either."

"My dear Diana, you are brilliant!" cried Lady Marchmont, so loudly that Chou-Chou howled in agreement. "To catch them at their meal, to make them listen to us as they dine and drink their ale or sea water or whatever sailors drink, why, that shall be perfect!"

"They will be much more agreeable when their bellies are full," said Diana eagerly, beginning to share once again in the other lady's excitement. Now that she'd seen the *Amazon* for herself, she understood how important it was that such a frigate be accepted into the king's service, how wasteful it would be otherwise, and she'd say or do whatever she could do to persuade those over-righteous admirals. This was a way she could make Roxby proud of her, too, and redeem herself a bit in her own eyes.

"To tomorrow, then," declared Lady Marchmont, holding up her dish of tea as a makeshift toast. "Tomorrow, and the triumph of the Ladies' Ship!"

"To the Ladies' Ship!" echoed Diana warmly, raising

her own tea. She'd happily drink to tomorrow and the *Amazon* and their success, and to a new chance to put Roxby first and forget James Dunham.

And to love. She'd drink to that as well, and with a wistful smile, she silently lifted her tea toward the little stoneware cat with the raised paw and the white star upon his forehead.

To the triumph of love, and the future.

"You were the *Castor*'s captain, sir, weren't you?" asked the ruddy-faced older man, squinting over his dinner as he appraised James. "The one that kept that brig full of Englishwomen from the French? Fenner's favorite?"

"Aye, aye, sir," said James with the slight formal bow, hat tucked beneath his arm, that admirals required with responses, even in taverns at dinner. Rear Admiral Buttonwood of the Blue, that was what Richard had whispered to him before they'd passed this table. James couldn't recall anything else about the man, but then all he was expected to do was to reply to questions, not initiate them. "I had that honor, sir."

"Hah, more likely they were the honored ones, Dunham," said the admiral with a grunt, "and damned relieved, too, to see you keep them from the hands of those bloody French bastards. But I recall they clipped your wing, didn't they?"

"Aye, aye, sir," said James, painfully aware of how closely Buttonwood was studying his right arm, as if he stared hard enough he could see through the blue wool sleeve to measure the damage and scars beneath. "A starboard gun exploded, sir, and a splinter caught me. But it's much recovered now, sir."

"And a good thing, too. A splinter as long as a lance, I've heard," said the admiral with another appreciative grunt that could have been as much in response to the roasted beef and onions on his plate as anything that James himself had said or done. "I also heard, sir, that you'd taken over the sighting of that gun with half its crew gone, all the time still coolly commanding the rest of your people. Handsomely done, sir, handsomely done."

"Thank you, sir. Good day, sir," said James as he bowed lower and backed away, partly to hide the flush of pleasure he could feel warm his cheeks. Blushing like some giggling girl, now *that* would inspire any admiral's confidence in his abilities.

But he couldn't deny that he was pleased, ecstatic, really. During his long convalescence, he'd had plenty of time alone to go over and over every second of the *Castor's* last hours, agonizing over each decision he'd made or hadn't made and wondering if his fate, and that of his ship and crew, couldn't possibly have been changed for the better. He didn't doubt that the Admiralty Board that had reviewed his report would see all the same wrong choices and bungled chances. He'd never dreamed they'd find any good in a lost ship.

Perhaps he'd have a future and another ship after all. Perhaps his luck really was beginning to change, the way Diana Fairbourne had predicted, and perhaps that little gray cat really had something to do with the change after all.

"There now, didn't I tell you to listen to old Lanker, eh?" whispered his friend as they made their way through the crowded room to find two seats together, back among the other frigate captains and commanders. The Gold Dolphin catered to navy officers, and kept sea hours for dinner, serving the midday meal unfashionably early. "Didn't I tell you to come here with me, to show yourself fit and willing for service?"

"Did you see how Buttonwood stared at my arm?" said James as he swung his leg over the chair. "I half thought he'd ask me to pull up my sleeve, so he could inspect the damage for himself."

"Nay, you had him the minute he spoke of the splinter as being 'long as a lance,' " said Richard with relish as he beckoned to the keep to serve them. "The gore always makes 'em drool. Ah, looks like we're to have the roast beef as well, even at this lowly end of the table."

James grinned at the unlikely connection between battle gore and roast beef, but then right now he'd likely grin at anything. He wouldn't be self-conscious dining among the good-natured din of so many fellow officers. Here, any awkwardness with a knife or fork would be overlooked or even admired, an infirmity earned with honor, and besides, even in the grandest cabins of the ships of the line, the manners at table weren't always the most refined.

"I tell you, Jamie, they'll find you a ship before— ahoy now, who the devil is *that?*"

James didn't have to ask where, because Richard's head and the head of every other man in the room had turned toward the door. All conversation stopped as if by an order, for there couldn't possibly be anything else more exciting than what was happening in the front of the room.

"Dear no, we don't need chairs," the lady was saying

as she fluttered her fan before her face like a nervous butterfly, sweeping into the room after the Gold Dolphin's host. Her voice was sweet, coaxing, but also accustomed to being heard and obeyed. "I should not presume even to ask. Unless, that is, one of these gentlemen is so kind as to offer his."

Immediately thirty-one chairs scraped across the bare floor as their occupants rose in unison. Thirty-one men squared their shoulders and shot their cuffs, then leaned to one side or the other to catch a glimpse of the sweet-voiced lady in need of a chair.

Though James rose with the others, he didn't rush to crane his neck. He was, of course, tall enough to be able to see easily over the heads of the others, but more importantly, he'd already recognized the lady from that sweet, wheedling voice alone. He wanted no part of whatever had brought her here, and he heartily wished her clear to the most remote corner of China.

"Cast your eye on *that* now, Jamie," said Richard with a muted whistle of approval. "What a lovely little creature, eh? I wonder what she's called?"

"That's Lady Harriet Marchmont," said James, keeping his voice low, "and if you're wise, you'll get no closer to her than this."

Stunned, Richard stared at him. "Your dear lady with the randy toes from the carriage?"

"The same," said James. "Though I'd be more likely to call her a meddling little weasel, no matter how she's rigged out."

And Lady Marchmont *was* rigged out, and doubly impossible to ignore. She was dressed in a brilliant crimson silk gown over full hoops, with a short matching jacket that framed her breasts and only a swath of black lace tucked in the front as covering. Her hair was lightly powdered and her lips and cheeks painted the same vivid red as her gown, and to give extra emphasis to her mouth she'd placed several tiny black patches strategically at the corner.

In silk and scarlet goes many a harlot. That was what his sister Celia would say if she were here, and viscountess or not, Celia'd be right.

"I cannot believe you wouldn't oblige her," marveled Richard. "You're a damned saint, you are, else you've been lying and it wasn't your arm that was wounded. Look at her, man! Black hair and blue eyes, breasts made to fill a man's hands, and long legs to wrap around his waist!"

"Black hair?" James frowned and followed Richard's rapt gaze, letting his own mouth fall open with disbelief. "Oh, *hell.*"

While he'd been gaping at Lady Marchmont's crimson petticoat, Diana had come to join her, and if Lady Marchmont had known exactly what to say to steal the attention of a room full of men, then Diana Fairbourne understood how to hold that same attention without speaking a single word.

She stood framed by the doorway, her head tipped to one side and a bemused half smile on her lips that was guaranteed to make every man in the room smile back like a herd of fools. In return James doubted she'd noticed him, lost in the sea of dark blue wool and brass buttons.

But there'd be no losing her anywhere. While Lady Marchmont depended on bright colors and artifice, Diana had the taste and the beauty to choose simplicity instead. Somehow she'd managed to look every bit as fresh as when he'd first seen her on the bank of the millpond, and he felt a sentimental pang for that first morning alone with her when things had seemed so much less complicated.

Her black hair was loosely drawn back from her forehead, her face devoid of paint or powder—Celia would most certainly approve—and her gown was pale blue silk, unadorned except for a single ruffle of white lace at her cuffs and around her low square neckline.

Unadorned, that is, except for the pearls around her throat and hanging from her ears, doubtless gifts from Roxby. Who else could afford to give her pearls, thought James with more cynicism than was good for him, and what better way to mark Diana as well beyond the reach of any other man in this room?

But why in blazes was she here at the Gold Dolphin in the first place?

"She's a bloody goddess, Jamie, no mistake," said Richard, jostling him a bit to get a better view. "How you could ever—"

"She's going to marry the Marquess of Roxby within the month."

"The devil she is!" Richard looked at him curiously. "Not the same bastard who—"

"Aye." The word stood between them as solid and unyielding as a wall of brick, and though Richard's face was full of questions, to James' relief he didn't ask them.

But from Lady Marchmont, the questions had only begun.

"I had been told that I would find certain admirals

dining here," she was saying as she smiled winningly toward the room of adoring faces. "But with so many *handsome* gentlemen in uniforms, how, pray, am I to sort them out?"

"The ones with the most gold lace, my lady," said the host, waving his hand vaguely to the table where a handful of admirals—including the one who'd praised James—were standing as goggle-eyed as their inferiors.

"But that is far too easy, sir!" said Diana, as she stepped to Lady Marchmont's side. "I think rather we should be able to identify them for their wisdom and experience. Surely, surely I can see such merits on the faces of these gentlemen here!"

The four admirals preened and harrumphed at her attention, and James couldn't help but smile. Though he'd never heard such blatant humbug and flattery, he doubted the admirals would see the pit being dug for them before they'd stumbled headlong into it. For that matter, if Diana continued smiling at them with her head tipped to one side like that, they wouldn't care. God knows she'd worked that same magic on him often enough.

"We would be honored to have you join us, my lady," said the youngest of the admirals with a bow. "Most honored."

"Oh, lah, we thank you, we do," chirped Lady Marchmont, "but we never meant to *impose* ourselves upon your company."

"A few words only, dear sirs, and then we shall leave you to dine in peace," continued Diana, holding her hands outstretched with a charming nonchalance. "Only a few words to you wise, kind, clever gentlemen! Now please, sit, please, all of you, and no more ceremony."

Like schoolboys on their best behavior, the roomful of officers who usually barked the orders now sat obediently as told, albeit on the edges of their chairs and benches with anticipation.

And why not, thought James wryly. Everyone in the room knew the *Amazon*'s plight. Every captain wished she was his next command, while every admiral wished she'd never been built. This was better than any play, and free, too.

Until, that is, Lady Marchmont broke the spell.

"You *are* gentlemen," she said, her voice turning unfortunately shrill, "so I am most shocked that no one has told you how vastly *rude* it is to refuse a gift."

The murmur at the admirals' table turned to a low rumble of rebellion, but heedlessly Lady Marchmont plunged ahead.

"A group of ladies wishes to help you fight the French," she said, her eyes round with resentful excitement, "and is offering you a most magnanimous gift, which your *pride* refuses to let you accept. Does the safety of our country mean less to you than that? Must your stubbornness outweigh our patriotism?"

The discontented rumble grew louder, more ominous. No admiral liked being called stubborn, or worse, having his loyalty questioned. Lady Marchmont might not have recognized the danger, but Diana did, and as the first admiral began to rise again from his chair, Diana rushed to speak first.

"You all know the *Amazon*'s history," she said quickly, "most likely far better than I. But I was born in a harbor town, into a family of seafarers back to the fishes themselves, and when I saw this frigate for the first time this afternoon, I knew in my heart, just as you all do, too, that she is . . . *special.*"

She'd lowered her voice to make them listen more closely, and when she came to that last, reverential word, the room had grown so still James wondered if they'd all forgotten to breathe. But it wasn't just an actress' trick that held them spellbound. Her emotions showed bright in her blue eyes and rang true in every word and sweeping gesture.

"You know that a ship has a soul," she continued, her voice rising once again as she let her gaze sweep across the faces before her. "From her very keel, the *Amazon* was built for running fast before the wind, for carrying brave men into battles against the French! But instead of her glorious destiny, she sits idle and useless at her wharf while her soul weeps and her heart aches for all she's missing. As does mine, gentlemen. As does *mine.*"

And at that exact moment she found James, and across the sea of heads her gaze locked with his and did not look away. Her cheeks flushed and a quick little smile meant only for him flickered across her lips, another secret, another connection they now shared.

In return he nodded, offering acknowledgment and encouragement and something he'd a harder time putting a name to. Clearly she remembered what he'd said to her beside the *Amazon,* for she'd come close to repeating the same words now. But was she ready to heed their meaning as well? Did she feel the coming loss of her own freedom as keenly as she did the *Amazon*'s?

And why the hell hadn't fate put her in his path before she'd met Roxby? A half-crippled captain on half pay,

*without a command or a home or a future, instead of a
peer of the realm with a fortune to match? Oh, aye, what a
fate that would have been for her!*

"How wise is Miss Fairbourne!" cried Lady Marchmont shrilly, her voice clearly jolting Diana back to their
cause. "And how vastly *right* she is, too, gentlemen! Is the
fate she describes the one you wish for the *Amazon?*"

"And more, Lady Marchmont," answered Diana
proudly, as she tossed her head back and looked straight
at the table of admirals. "Is this the fate, gentlemen, that
you'd wish for your country against the king of France,
and for yourselves?"

"Three cheers for the *Amazon!*" shouted a man to the
front, whipping his napkin exuberantly over his head.

"Three cheers for the ladies!" roared another, while
other officers stamped their feet and cheered and
clapped and huzzahed their approval.

"Three cheers for Miss Fairbourne!" bellowed
Richard, adding an earsplitting whistle to the din. "I tell
you, Jamie, she's a goddess, a right royal goddess!"

But James barely smiled at all. She was a goddess, all
right, but mostly she was a woman, a woman that he'd
come to care for a great deal more than he should.

And a woman that, God help them both, would never
be his.

10

$"I$ do so enjoy reading letters with my tea," said Harriet Marchmont happily as she made a neat, square pile of the letters that the maid had handed to her on the breakfast tray. "To have the freshest news from one's acquaintances writ in their own hand is quite the best way to begin the day."

To Diana on the other side of the table, Lady Marchmont's acquaintances seemed both prolific and attentive. There were perhaps a dozen letters stacked before her, an astounding number considering that they'd been in Portsmouth for only three days.

But even more surprising were the two letters beside her own plate. Unlike Lady Marchmont, she was an indifferent correspondent at best. She'd written no letters since they'd come to Portsmouth, and she'd expected none in return, either. Not even Roxby himself knew she was here, so she uneasily touched the two letters before her now. The last unexpected letter she'd received had been the hateful one with the lies about Roxby and a mistress.

Still, she'd hate to be thought cowardly over something like a letter, and with a final gulp of tea, she reached for the larger, thicker one. The blob of wax with the Waldegrave crest pressed into it made her groan aloud, and with considerable reluctance she cracked the seal with her thumb.

Guilt, in the form of Lady Waldegrave's precise handwriting, had found her at last.

"Lady Waldegrave wishes me to return to Ashburnham directly," she said with a sigh as she swiftly scanned the letter's three, closely-written pages. "She says Roxby is expected any day, and that it would be unwise for him not to find me there."

"Oh, piffle," scoffed Lady Marchmont, reaching for another spoonful of strawberry jam for her toast. "You know his feelings regarding the *Amazon*. He'll be most pleased to learn what we have done here on her behalf, most pleased indeed."

"I suppose so, yes," conceded Diana. Though she'd enjoyed addressing all the officers in the Gold Dolphin's front room yesterday and the attention that had come with it, she was eager—no, desperate—to see Roxby again. She wanted to prove to him and herself that she still loved him, and to have him put aside all her troubling uncertainties regarding James Dunham. "But I would like to be able to tell it to Roxby myself."

"Ah, spoken like a woman in love!" Lady Marchmont rested one hand over her heart and sighed prodigiously. "And I'll vow that Roxby must be like all besotted men, vexed if his beloved isn't pining by the hearth for him. I suppose there's no help for it, is there? Tomorrow morning, then, if that is soon enough for Cupid, and back to Ashburnham we shall go."

Relieved, Diana nodded her thanks, and reached for

the second letter. This one was slight in comparison to Lady Waldegrave's, a single sheet, and she frowned as she glanced at her name on the front. The handwriting wobbled, as untutored and laborious as a young child's, and only an unadorned wafer held the folded page closed.

The handful of words written inside were no more steady, but even without a signature below, their meaning to Diana was as clear as the morning sky.

YOU WERE MAGNIFICENT, LASS.

Only one man dared call her lass, just as only one man's simple compliment could make her blush like this over breakfast. The shaky penmanship had come not from inexperience, but from a left hand unaccustomed to such work, laboring in the place of the injured, uncooperative right.

And if she'd any doubt left at all that the note had come from James Dunham, he'd added something else that only she'd understand: a small, shaky caricature of a grinning kitten.

She laughed, imagining how he must have smiled as he'd drawn it, then gulped that laugh back before Lady Marchmont could notice. The best way in the world for her to prove her new resolutions about Roxby would be to show James' note to Lady Marchmont, to explain how he'd been among the other officers at the Gold Dolphin, to share the praise he'd sent and to diffuse any special feelings that such a note might raise in her peculiarly misguided emotions.

Yet Diana did none of these things. Instead she tucked the note into her pocket to reread later, and told herself that the words were harmless, the intimacy their playfulness implied only that of a friend.

Liar.

What she was doing was wrong and faithless and wicked. How could she claim to love Roxby, yet keep another man's words in her pocket, riding there warm against her hip? How could she keep the stoneware kitten there, too, wrapped in a handkerchief, a bulky, constant reminder of how they'd kissed?

Before they left Portsmouth, she would send them both, the letter and the kitten, back to him by messenger to his lodgings. She *would*. She'd enclose only the briefest note in return to him, with a marchioness' composed distance, wishing him luck and saying farewell without anything as contrived as a little cat face.

As contrived, and as endearing, and as—oh, dear God help her, all of this was wrong, *wrong,* and as she bowed her head over her tea, her conscience churned and roiled within her.

"Ah, Diana, such luck!" crowed Lady Marchmont, thumping the table with such enthusiasm that the tea tray rattled and the cups jumped. "We have succeeded, my dear! Here, here is an invitation, in quite the nicest phrasing, for us to come call upon Admiral McGillis this morning!"

"About the *Amazon?*" asked Diana, slow to turn from her own worries. She assumed he must have been one of the men from the Dolphin yesterday, but they'd all blurred together so that she couldn't guess which admiral he'd been.

"Whatever else for?" Gleefully Lady Marchmont kissed the invitation and held it over her head as she danced a small jig of triumph before the time on the clock stopped her cold. "But fah . . . fah! How did it come to be eleven, when we are expected to see him at half past the same hour? Oh, we must dress *now*, Diana! This man does not know ladies, of course, else he would never have invited us for such an unseemly hour! Oh, hurry, hurry, *hurry!*"

Hurry they did, and because of their concerted efforts with Lady Marchmont's maid, they managed to arrive at Admiral McGillis' offices only an hour later than his invitation had requested.

As Lady Marchmont vaguely explained to Diana in the coach, this admiral had made certain ill-timed mistakes as a captain, never grave enough to have been court-martialed, but sufficiently bad that the navy had decided to stop his career at sea before he cost them any more men or ships. Because he had high-placed friends, he'd been made an admiral and given a job on land with a grand-sounding title and offices in Portsmouth where, it was hoped, he'd not cause any more damage or trouble—though he could, as Lady Marchmont noted, finally accept the *Amazon* into the fleet.

The offices were close to the wharves and shipyards, in a tall, imposing building of brick and white stone. Every kind of Portsmouth male—officers and shipbuilders and chandlers, clerks and common sailors—seemed to be passing purposefully through the pillared gates.

But what Diana noticed first were the sailors' widows, most with small children clinging to their skirts as they stood toward the far end of the brick wall to beg, some in poignant silence, others offering tearful tales of lost ships and poverty. And these were the proud ones. She knew from her brothers that most of the women who worked in any of the large English harbor's brothels were sailors' widows, too, driven by desperation to selling their bodies. If their husbands had sailed in one of her father's ships, then these women and children would not be suffering now, and it shocked her to think that the families of men who served the king would in turn be served so heartlessly.

"Now that the *Amazon* is finished," ventured Diana as the coach rolled to a halt, "perhaps we could do something else that is useful, such as build a refuge or home for sailors' widows and their children."

"For sailors' widows and orphans?" asked Lady Marchmont uncertainly, wrinkling her nose. "Why, I would suppose there are plenty of other people looking after them already, the churches and almshouses and such."

"If there were," said Diana, "then these poor women wouldn't be here now, nor would we see them begging on the streets, either. Perhaps if the men knew their families would be better looked after, more of them would volunteer, instead of waiting to be pressed into the navy against their wills. Surely that would be better for everyone, wouldn't it?"

"But widows and orphans," protested Lady Marchmont, bending to keep the sweeping plume of her hat clear as she climbed from the coach. "There is nothing grand, nothing glorious, about widows and orphans. I should think we could find a more interesting way to help the gentlemen fighting in the war than that. Now come, come, we must not keep the admiral waiting a minute longer!"

Diana frowned, and considered pointing out that if Lady Marchmont had spent less time before her mirror, they wouldn't have kept the admiral waiting at all. But the viscountess was already sweeping down the path between a row of bowing men, and with a sigh she followed.

"Admiral McGillis has the most lovely hands I have ever seen upon a gentleman," whispered Lady Marchmont as they waited outside the admiral's office while a clerk announced them. "He is not terribly clever, of course, but he is still rather nice."

"You are acquainted, then?" asked Diana with surprise. Sometimes she wondered if there were any gentlemen left in all of England that had not been favored with Lady Marchmont's acquaintance.

"Well, yes, of course," murmured Lady Marchmont with that intentional lack of specificity that always put Diana on her guard. "In regard to the *Amazon* we have met, yes. Ah, my dear Admiral, how vastly *handsome* you are looking this day!"

The admiral bowed elegantly over his leg with a courtier's grace, then took Lady Marchmont's hands in his own and kissed them in turn while Lady Marchmont simpered and cooed. Diana would admit that he did have lovely hands, albeit shamefully white and unscarred for any decent sailor, but the rest of him struck her as unimpressive, a middling man of middling appearance, and obviously, as Lady Marchmont herself had said, not terribly clever.

"Miss, ah, Miss, well, aye, aye, you are here, too?" he stammered as he still clutched Lady Marchmont's hands, his round face full of dismay at Diana's appearance. "Harriet, ah, ah, my lady, I thought only you were coming to ah, ah, speak of the *Amazon?*"

"I came only to offer companionship to Lady Marchmont, sir," answered Diana hastily, realizing now how correct her first speculation had again proved. "She does not need me to describe the *Amazon*'s virtues to you."

Lady Marchmont beamed as she sidled closer to the admiral. "Oh, Diana, you are such an *understanding* friend! Now, Admiral, pray, let us step into your chambers, and I shall explain *everything* to you."

They did not step so much as bolt, leaving Diana to stand in uncomfortable silence before the two clerks at their tall desks, all three of them equally shamefaced at what they'd just witnessed.

"I believe I shall wait for her ladyship outside," announced Diana to no one in particular, and then she fled down the scrubbed white steps and into the courtyard. What kind of world had she climbed to, that high-born women like Lady Marchmont could work for good causes, yet abandon their own families to act like such, well, such *harlots?*

She was almost shaking as she marched through the front gate, her petticoats swinging indignantly as she ignored the waiting coach and footman and went instead to the end of the brick wall where the begging widows were clustered. Only a few now remained, the others chased off as a nuisance by the watch. Wide-eyed, the women shrank back at first, awed as much by Diana's striped silk taffeta day gown, worth more than most of them would see in a lifetime, as by herself.

"Good day," she said, smiling to reassure them. "My name is Diana Fairbourne."

"Miss Fairbourne!" gasped one woman. "You be th' lady what spoke up so proud to th' captains yesterday! Everyone in Portsmouth's speakin' o' you, miss!"

"You be th' one promised to th' Markess o' Roxby!" breathed another, clutching her sleepy-eyed baby tight in her arms.

Diana nodded, pulling her beaded purse from her pocket. "But I'm also a woman from a family of deep-water sailors, and I know how hard it is to wait and wait for a ship to come home."

"My Jemmy's ship went down off Finisterre," said the youngest woman with the baby, her eyes filling with tears. "Only two weeks we had together, my Jemmy an' me, only two weeks as man an' wife afore th' press took 'im."

"I am so sorry," said Diana softly. "To lose him so soon—oh, I am sorry! Nothing I can say or do will bring him back to you, I know, but I hope this shall help, and let you know that I do care for what your Jemmy did for England."

She pressed two gold guineas and several silver coins into the woman's palm, then divided the rest of what she had in her purse among the other women. It was not nearly as much as she wished she'd had to share, and the women's effusive thanks and blessings before they scurried away only made her feel how insignificant such offerings were, and how little effect they'd have on so grave a problem.

"Will you be coming back to the coach, miss, to wait for her ladyship?" asked one of the footmen, as he hovered anxiously at her side. "You will be more comfortable there, miss."

"Perhaps the problem is that I have grown *too* comfortable in that coach," she retorted tartly, "too comfortable by half."

She turned away then, leaving him with his mouth pursed in disapproval. She was far too unsettled to return to the luxury of the coach, especially while Lady Marchmont was doing God knows what with Admiral McGillis. The *Amazon*'s dock was not far from here; she could walk past the frigate one more time before she left Portsmouth. Resolutely she headed toward the waterfront.

"Miss Fairbourne, miss!" called a young woman in a feathery rasp. "Oh, oh, Miss Fairbourne, please!"

Diana stopped, drawn by the edge of fear in the young woman's voice. She was hovering in the shadows of an alley, as skittish as a doe poised on the edge of the forest, and as fragile as one, too. Her once gay clothes hung loose on her small frame and her hollowed cheeks were painted with a false rosiness that warred with the gray rings beneath her eyes. She coughed, holding a grimy, blood-stained knot of a handkerchief up to her mouth, and to her sorrow Diana realized that before next spring the girl would likely be dead. Whether in New England or old, the signs of consumption were the same, and equally fatal.

"You be th' lady that's kind to th' sailors' women, aye?" asked the girl, then bent over, leaning against the wall for support as another cough racked her chest. She shook her head, still gasping for breath, and beckoned for Diana to come closer.

"Please don't try to talk," ordered Diana, hurrying to join the girl in the alley. "If there's anything—*ohh!*"

The man's arm was around Diana's throat before she'd realized the danger, forcing her chin up as it tightened across her windpipe, stealing away her breath and voice as he dragged her backward, deeper into the dank shadows between the two buildings. Another pair of rough male hands was groping at her skirts, pawing and pulling at her rustling taffeta petticoats. Frantically she tried to kick back, trying to do all those things that her brothers had taught her, but the man who held her had learned the tricks as well, and knew how to stand to avoid being struck.

"Quit yer thrashing, woman!" growled the second man. "I though ye said she'd gold on 'er, Annie?"

Diana felt a sharp tug at her throat as the man broke the chain of her necklace, then tore the matching bracelets from her wrists. If she'd been wearing earrings, he would have ripped those from her ears as well.

"Ye said ye wouldn't hurt her, Matt!" cried the young woman, her terrified face rising briefly before Diana. "Ye said—"

"Shut yer trap, Annie, an' shove off for home!" snapped the second man, breathing hard. "Go on, an' leave us to it!"

The girl coughed again, rattling in her chest, then vanished, and as soon as she did, the first man began dragging Diana farther back into the alley. She tried to fight, tried to struggle, but the arm across her throat was making her weak, light-headed, and she felt her knees crumple and her heels skid beneath her.

God help her, she didn't want to die like this, not like this at all. . . .

"Give yer gold to others, did ye," he muttered. "We'll make ye pay on your back then, ye damned fancy bitch, and—"

"*Let her go!*" roared another man, his voice echoing in the narrow alley. "Damnation, let her go *now!*"

The man holding her swore, then shoved her forward and ran, the second man's footsteps following after him. Diana fell against the rough brick wall, catching herself unsteadily with one arm. Gasping for air, at last she felt hot tears of fear and relief spill from her eyes as she pressed her hand over the raw line that her necklace had cut into her throat.

And then somehow James was there, lifting her from the wall, holding her, telling her everything would be fine, that she was well, and brave, and unharmed, and she believed it because she wanted to and because he was the one telling her. For a long time, she stood with her face buried in the front of his jacket, listening to the steady rhythm of his heart and trying not to think of what could have happened to her if he hadn't come. In the shadows, she couldn't make out his face clearly, but even in the darkest night she'd know his touch, his scent, the feel of his body next to hers.

"How did you—why did you come?" she asked finally, her voice still a rough, half-strangled croak. "You couldn't have known."

"I didn't." Gently he smoothed her hair back from her forehead. "I was walking from the wharves, and a beggar girl grabbed my sleeve and said a lady needed help."

"It must have been Annie." Fresh tears welled up in

her eyes. "Oh, James, it was my own fault for being so trusting, for—"

"Hell, Diana, then it's my fault, too," he said bitterly. "Look at me, scuttling along like a three-legged crab instead of chasing after the bastards the way I could have once. The way I *should* have."

"You did all that I needed," she whispered, slipping her fingers into the crook of his arm, needing that contact. "More than enough."

He grumbled wordlessly. "Can you walk now? There's a coffeehouse across the street where we can find you something to drink before we find the constable."

"No constable," she said, shaking her head. "I wouldn't want to make trouble for that poor girl who found you. And no coffeehouse, either. I—I'd rather just walk."

He led her into the sunlight, an afternoon that seemed miraculously to have continued on only a few moments without her, and self-consciously she ducked her chin, again touching her fingers to her throat to hide the mark.

But not before James noticed.

"Jesus, Diana," he growled, his expression black as he gently lifted her fingers away so he could better see the rising bruise. "What in blazes did they do to you?"

"They—they stole my jewelry," she said, shamed by the price of her own carelessness. "Garnets and paste in pinchbeck, nothing of real value except to me. Thank God 'twas nothing that Roxby had given me."

"As if that matters, Diana!"

"It would have to him." She tried to smile, tried to

lighten the mood. "I think they would have left me that if I hadn't given all my money away to the poor women beside the wall."

"The sailors' widows?" He whistled low. "Oh, lass, you're a saint among the officers for what you said about the *Amazon* yesterday. Now you'll be an angel to the seamen, too."

She glanced at him uneasily. To be party to the Ladies' Ship was one thing, but she was unhappily certain that Roxby would not approve of such individual celebrity for his marchioness. "It was only three women, James."

"Three will be enough," he promised, "if anyone else saw. How much did you give them?"

"Only what was in my purse," she hedged. "A guinea or two apiece, plus the silver."

He sighed, and for the first time since he'd found her, he almost smiled. "Then you've earned your halo for certain, and feathered wings to match. Most able seamen earn but nineteen shillings a month from the king."

"Those women needed it more than I."

"I'm not faulting you for being generous, my brave lass," he said, half teasing, half admiring, the dangerously familiar intimacy returning. "It's just not the way of most fine ladies. Myself, I could love you for that alone."

She glanced at him uneasily, wishing he wouldn't even jest about such things, and felt in her pocket. She shouldn't postpone this any longer, and besides, they'd nearly reached Lady Marchmont's coach. It would be much better like this, with people coming and going all around them, instead of their being alone.

Much better, yes, and she sighed forlornly. The thieves had taken her purse, but they'd left the lumpy little bundle that she now held out to James.

"Here," she said, pushing it into his hand. "That's the stoneware Brighty. I cannot accept it, you see, not from you or any other gentleman. I—I *can't*."

His mouth twisted, as if he'd bitten something sour. "Sixteen pounds a month, Diana. That's what a captain earns, and I've only half that until I'm appointed to another ship. Wouldn't pay for even one of your gowns, would it?"

He looked down at the bundle in his palm, poking aside the handkerchief to let the little gray cat's head peep out. "And here I'd thought Brighty had brought us back together again in that alley."

She winced, for she'd thought of that, too. "Lady Marchmont and I are leaving Portsmouth early tomorrow. Most likely I'll not see you again until the wedding."

"The wedding." He squinted a bit as he gazed back at her, from habit or perhaps only the sun, the lines fanning out from the corners of his eyes in a way she'd always liked. "Farewell, then. Best wishes and good luck, and the devil take his due."

"Don't do this, James," she pleaded softly. "Please don't. For me."

"Oh, aye, I've asked the same of you, haven't I?" He looked past her, moody and bitter, and sighed. "But I warrant I'm only entitled to save you once. Not even Brighty could do more, could he?"

She shook her head, and reached out to slip her fingers into his right hand, the one he always tried to hide. He drew in his breath sharply, wary, but he left his damaged hand in hers, a trust she knew must cost him dearly.

"Good-bye, Captain," she whispered, striving to hold back her tears. "Fair winds, and a safe return."

But he wasn't about to let her go that easily.

"Tell me, Diana," he said. "Have you ever thought of what might have happened if you'd met me before Roxby?"

She had, oh, she had, more times that she could count, and each time had been another small sin upon her conscience and a little stab into her faithless heart.

"Yes," she said. "Nothing."

And with that lie to seal her fate, James turned and left her alone in the street.

Awake when he'd rather be sleeping, Roxby sighed restlessly and pushed himself higher against the pillow, his arms folded behind his head. Beside him Justine snored softly, her legs tangled in the sheets and her curling red-gold hair tossed over her bare back, her voluptuously round bottom nestled against Roxby's hip.

She was an uncomplicated little creature, his Justine, exactly his preference in a mistress. Her tendency to fall asleep instantly after sex had, in Roxby's mind, always been one of her most agreeable attributes, for she never began those tedious, weepy, post-coital conversations regarding love, marriage, and babies that too many women in keeping were inclined to start. Most nights—or afternoons or mornings, depending on the timing of Roxby's visit—he fell asleep as well, for Justine was a most enthusiastic lover.

But though she'd served him well tonight, it was his mind that refused to rest, not his body, and finally in frustration he left the bed, taking care not to wake her. He slipped his silk banyan over his shoulders, poured himself another glass of port, and then, because he could not help himself, he once again pulled from his coat pocket the print that Stanver—dear Stanver, the bastard, always eager to be the bearer of unpleasant tidings—had bought for him earlier at Bushell's shop.

Carefully he held the sheet beside the candlestick to study it. As art went, it was crudely drawn and indifferently pulled, the composition crude and the ink smudged. But for Bushell, craft and art mattered considerably less than the haste with which a topical print could be produced and thrust into the market. The event that had inspired this particular print could not have happened more than two days before, yet here it was illustrated already, in his own hands and broadcast all over London.

The centerpiece of the print was an English warship identified as the *Amazon*, the guns delivering a blazing broadside at an already-damaged French ship attempting to retreat in cowardly confusion—a common enough subject these days, though given the ill-fated progress of the war, also a largely fictional one.

But the skirmish was of far less importance than the figurehead of the English ship, a beautiful young woman with flowing dark hair and one well-shaped breast bare in Amazonian splendor as she gazed with fierce delight at the vanquished French. Two sailors on ropes dangled over the prow to kiss the figurehead's wooden cheeks, one exclaiming "Oh, how I do love you, ma'am!" in a balloon over his head. Blazed along the bottom of the print was the title: "The NEW HELEN, or, The Face That

Launched a Single Ship," as sorry and tired a wordplay as Roxby had seen.

Especially when it referred to the woman he was going to marry.

The figurehead's face was undeniably Diana's, her hair and brow and smile, and though Roxby had yet to see her naked breast for himself, he'd guess that that was fairly accurate as well. And in the unlikely case he or anyone else had been too patently stupid to recognize the glorious Miss Fairbourne, the long banner fluttering from the bowsprit proclaimed "The Beauteous New Marchioness of R***y, her Generosity Rewarded."

It was meant to be lighthearted, amusing, patriotic, the kind of print that would find a ready place in rum shops and sailors' boardinghouses.

But the longer Roxby stared grimly at the print, the less amused and patriotic he felt, and his heart was anything but light. The story of Diana and Harriet Marchmont addressing the roomful of officers had fair flown to London from Portsmouth on the delighted wings of gossip, and while his smile had grown less patient by the time the tenth person repeated it to him, he still had been able to find good in Diana's performance. To be identified with the well-bred ladies of the Ladies' Ship, to endorse a project that his majesty himself was known to favor, to let the world see how much he doted upon his bride's whims, to the handsome tune of a thousand pounds—there was nothing ill in any of that.

But to see Diana's face—and her bare breast—made common like this was not to his liking, not at all, and that she'd put herself in such a situation only demonstrated again her sorry lack of judgment. No wife of his should be portrayed as being generous to sailors. He'd trusted her too much. He should have recalled how impulsive she could be, how headstrong, when he'd left her in Harriet's dubious care. Though this trip to London had been a necessary one, he needed to return to Ashburnham at once, before it was too late to check Diana's dangerous independence and she made him a laughingstock among his gloating friends and, worse, his enemies. From the studied expressions on some of their faces today, he might already be too late.

He drank the port, planning. He'd been too understanding. Now he must be firm, the way a good master should. Though their wedding was still a fortnight away, he wasn't going to wait until the bishop married them. That had been Stanver's advice, and for once he was likely right. Roxby would bed Diana as soon as he returned, for the faster he filled her belly with his heir, the more truly she'd belong to him the way his wife and marchioness should.

Fondly he glanced across at the sleeping Justine. He'd have to neglect her for the next few months while he was on his wedding trip with Diana, but he'd compensate her handsomely for her time alone, and besides, when he finally returned their reunion would be all the warmer.

But first there'd be Diana waiting for him at Ashburnham. Gently he swirled the port in the glass and smiled. Diana Fairbourne was the single most beautiful, most desirable woman he'd ever met, and very soon she'd be his forever.

Ah, the next few months were going to be sweet, sweet indeed.

11

"Roxby's home!"

Diana leaned from the side of Lady Waldegrave's open chaise, hoping to catch a glimpse of Roxby himself. He'd not been at Ashburnham long. His traveling coach still stood before the tall steps of the front door, the horses waiting with drooping heads after the journey, while the footmen and grooms together were wrestling the marquess' trunks and boxes from the baggage cart that had followed. Roxby was never a gentleman to travel lightly, but this afternoon it appeared as if he'd had half of London crated and hauled back with him.

"Sit back, child," cautioned Lady Waldegrave irritably, holding her arm across Diana's lap. "His lordship could be watching from a window, and it would not be wise to appear too eager."

"But I *am* eager," protested Diana. She had spent the day dutifully admiring the windows of the cathedral in Winchester, forcing herself to match Lady Waldegrave's stately pace, and after so much well-mannered restraint she was now brimming with energy and impatience. "Why should I pretend otherwise, my lady? Here I am, promised to marry Roxby, and I haven't seen him for a fortnight. The greater problem, I should think, would be if I weren't eager."

The chaise had barely stopped before Diana was clambering down, not waiting for the footman with the step. With her parasol in one hand and her skirts bunched in the other, she rushed up the well-swept steps, her petticoats fanning out around her and her wide-brimmed straw hat falling back from her head to hang over her shoulders by the ribbons.

"Where is his lordship?" she asked the first footman she saw in the hall. "I must see him directly!"

The footman bowed and hesitated, mentally weighing other, earlier orders, then pointed toward the staircase. "He has retired to his chambers, miss. To rest from his journey, miss."

"He can rest later," she said, and ran up the stairs toward Roxby's rooms. Ordinarily she knew better than to go there, not until after they were wed, but considering the circumstances she saw more good to be gained than harm. Her heels clicked on the polished floorboards, through door after open door of the connecting rooms upstairs.

But joyful anticipation wasn't her only feeling. Matching the hasty staccato of her heels was the anxious racing of her heart. She and Roxby had not parted on the best of terms, and he'd stayed away in London longer than she'd wanted. While he'd been gone, her own behavior hadn't been exemplary, either. Now she wanted— no, she *needed*—proof from him that their love really was a love worthy of marriage. She wanted to put her doubts to rest, and she wanted to know that she was making the right decision.

And most difficult of all, she wanted desperately to forget James Dunham.

The last set of doors off the hall were also open, and through them she could hear Roxby's voice, patiently explaining something to his manservant. That patience made her smile and gave her courage, too. Shoving her doubts aside for now, she pulled off her hat and swept into his bedchamber with her arms outstretched and her smile warm.

"Roxby," she called softly. "How glad I am to have you returned!"

He was standing near the tall open window, one hand cocked at his hip. Because the day was warm, he'd already shed his jacket, and his dark red waistcoat was unbuttoned with the throat of his white linen shirt open. For most men this would hardly be noticeable at all—Lord knows that on a summer day, the men working in the dockyards wore little more than their breeches—but for Roxby it was remarkably . . . *undone*, enough so that Diana realized she was blushing.

"Diana." He turned toward her, a single, fluid motion of great elegance, and smiled as he held out his hand to her. "My own bride. So you have missed me, my dear?"

She went to him, though even as he kissed the inside of her wrist the way he always did to tease her, her smile was fading. Why didn't he say *he'd* missed *her*? Why must he ask first if she'd missed him?

And why, why was she noticing such things now?

"Of course I missed you," she said slowly. "How could I not? Ashburnham is a lovely place, but it was so lonely without you."

"I imagine it was," he said lightly, pulling her closer

so she could smell the musky French scent he favored, stronger now because of the heat that rose from his body. "Come, give me a kiss to welcome me home."

Before she could answer, he was kissing her, kissing her so hard that he forced her head and shoulders back over his arm. Surprised, she immediately thought of that awful kiss in the gallery the night of the party, the kiss that had ended only when she'd struck him, and now, once again, she struggled to regain her balance. But clearly he preferred her like this, unsteady and unsure, and with her arched over his arm he pressed his other hand over her breast, pushing aside her lawn kerchief to bare the soft flesh that rose over the top of her stays and bodice.

With a gasp, she pulled her mouth free, twisting away from him. "Roxby, please!"

He frowned, clearly surprised himself. "My little bride is suddenly shy."

Diana tucked her kerchief back in place, her heart pounding. Pointedly she glanced at Roxby's manservant, standing with his expression impassive but his eyes eager. "Before others, yes."

Brusquely Roxby motioned for the man to leave them, making her acutely aware of being alone with him here, in his private chamber with a bed that seemed as wide as a public road.

"I didn't think you, Diana, of all women, would object to performing before an audience," he said testily. "At least not after you entertained the sailors in Portsmouth."

She looked at him sharply, a world of fears racing through her mind, with James Dunham first among them. "I should hardly call what Lady Marchmont and I did 'entertaining the sailors.' "

"What Harriet does is of no concern to me," said Roxby. "She is, thank God, never going to be my wife or my responsibility."

Diana straightened her shoulders defensively. Lady Marchmont might not be Roxby's responsibility, but to his mind she herself most definitely was.

"We went to Portsmouth to see the *Amazon*," she explained, striving to keep her voice even. "Because the officers at the port refused to meet with us, we went to the tavern where they dine and addressed them there. We convinced them, too, for they're finally going to take the *Amazon* into the fleet. Isn't that splendid, Roxby?"

"Oh, vastly splendid," said Roxby dryly. "How busy we both have been, my dear. While you were addressing the fleet in Portsmouth, I was repairing your last little gaffe in London, saying a small word or two here and there on behalf of Captain Dunham."

She nearly gulped, striving to keep her expression unchanged. Was that the only reason he'd done that for James? Or did he wish to see him gone to sea for more selfish reasons, away from her and on a voyage that could last for years?

"You would do that for him?" she asked. "Help him to obtain a new command?"

"It seemed rather the least I could do after your rudeness toward him. Besides, his success then reflects well on Ashburnham and me." He smoothed the lace on his cuff, preening at the thought of what his influence could accomplish.

"That was very kind of you, Roxby," she said wistfully. She could not want a more definite separation be-tween them than having James posted to a new ship, and he would be delighted to be at sea again, fighting the winds and the French. So why, then, did she feel no real pleasure?

"Kindness has nothing to do with it," declared Roxby, wheeling around to face her, "as you, it seems, have learned for yourself, haven't you?"

"I, Roxby?" she asked, abruptly torn back to the pres-ent, and to this dark-haired man who was her betrothed.

Her betrothed. She must remember that, and forget James Dunham.

"Yes, yes, you dearest," he said impatiently. "Who else, pray, is here with us? When I suggested that you join the ladies involved with the warship to help establish your position and station, I'd no notion you'd choose so demonstrative a role for yourself."

"It was all most respectable, Roxby," protested Diana. "You can ask Lady Marchmont if you doubt me."

"Harriet is no longer our guest, Diana," he said, his lids dropping a fraction over his eyes. "She was called away suddenly on, oh, some personal bit of foolishness. She left this morning, while you were driving with Lady Waldegrave."

He turned away to search through a trunk sitting open on the bed.

"But why didn't she stay to say farewell, if . . ." began Diana, then broke off as the truth, or at least a viable suspicion, dawned upon her. "You sent her away, didn't you? You punished her on my account, didn't you?"

" 'Punishment,' my dear, is too strong a word and an entirely arbitrary one as well," he said. "But if it springs so instantly to your thoughts, then I fear I must conclude you have committed some misdeed requiring it."

Diana gasped. "You have no right to be putting words into my mouth!"

"It is not mere words, my dear, that worry me." He turned and handed her a stiff, folded sheet of paper.

Slowly Diana opened it and flushed dark with shame. James had warned her that she'd become the talk of Portsmouth, or at least the naval part, but she'd no idea that the talk had spread clear to London or that the talk now came accompanied with illustrations of her bared breast.

No wonder Roxby was upset. What man wouldn't be? Her father, her brothers—any of them would have sworn to dismantle the shop stick by stick for producing such a print, and the artist with it—but for a gentleman as proud of his family and name as Roxby, the humiliation must go infinitely deeper.

"How did you come by this?" she asked softly. "Do you know how many were printed?"

"Stanver bought it for me at Bushell's himself, malicious little rogue that he is," said Roxby acidly, "and as for how many of them now exist—ah, my dear, even this single one is too many."

She groaned, and pressed her hand to her cheek. "I don't know what to say, Roxby."

" 'I'm sorry' would suffice," he said. "But 'I'll never leave myself open to public caricature again' would also be much appreciated."

"Oh, Roxby, I *am* sorry," she said, reaching out to rest her hand on his sleeve. "I never expected anyone would make such a—a drawing of me."

"They will now, and worse, if you give them reason," he said. "You are not simply pretty Diana Fairbourne. You are—rather, you will be—my wife and my lady, and I will thank you not to forget it again."

He cleared his throat and lay his hand over hers, the stone in his ring catching the sunlight from the open window. "However, there is something to be said for a penitent willing to amend her ways."

Punishment and penitence: hardly words she'd associate with love, but not so, it seemed, for Roxby.

He ran his hand along the inside of her arm, teasing the sharp edge of his thumbnail lightly along her skin up inside the ruffle of her sleeve, and she shivered. There'd been a time, and not long ago, either, when such a touch from him would have made her heart quicken with anticipation. But now every caress and kiss conveyed an unsettling possessiveness that disturbed her far more than it excited her.

Ever since they'd traded the excitement and crowds of London for the comparative solitude of Ashburnham, she'd felt their relationship had altered. She couldn't say exactly what was different, only that it *was*. But was Roxby to blame, or was it she herself who'd changed?

"This is perhaps my fault, too, my darling," he murmured, echoing her own thoughts so closely that she stared at him uneasily. Roxby could play with words more adeptly than any other person she'd met, and she'd learned to listen carefully for what he really might be saying.

"I should not have left you alone so long, Diana," he continued, easing her once again into his arms, her back to his chest. This time she didn't protest. To do so after she'd caused him such grief over the print would have seemed low indeed. "I should keep you with me always instead. But I had certain matters to attend before we could both be free for one other. Together, Diana, as man and wife should be."

"Free?" she repeated, her mouth turning dry, unable to think of anything more as he increased the pressure of his nail moving back and forth along her skin. She was trembling now, enough for him to notice and enough to make him chuckle softly.

"Oh, yes, my shy darling," he said, his words buzzing against the side of her throat. "There were preparations I wished to make for our wedding, certain surprises I have been plotting for you, now that we can—what is this, Diana?"

Self-consciously Diana's fingers flew to her throat. She had tied a length of pink silk ribbon in a bow around her neck to cover the mark left when her necklace had been ripped away. The bruised red line and the swelling had faded, but when Roxby slipped the ribbon aside to kiss the side of her throat, below her ear, he'd noticed it at once.

"When I was walking in Portsmouth, a thief tore the necklace from my throat," she said quickly. "He—he was very bold. But the necklace wasn't of any value, not one of the ones you've given me, of course, but an old garnet one I'd bought myself in Boston and—"

"Were you frightened, Diana?" he interrupted, running his finger almost tenderly along the mark on her throat. "Did it hurt you very much, the chain cutting across your throat like that?"

"Yes, it hurt," she said, trying to tug the ribbon back. "But when it happened, I was more frightened than anything else."

That was all she'd tell him. The part about James rescuing her, and holding her, and calling her his brave lass—all that she'd keep to herself.

But she wasn't sure Roxby was even listening. "Your skin is so delicate," he marveled, his fingers holding the ribbon aside. "It would take next to nothing to bruise you, wouldn't it?"

"I am fair like my mother and her mother before her," said Diana. Skittishly she twisted free, smoothing the ribbon back in place with a small nervous laugh. It seemed odd that he'd concentrate more on the mark than the theft or the fact that she might have been more seriously hurt.

"Faith, Roxby," she said, trying to lighten his mood, "I should think you'd have more interesting things to notice about me by now than how I bruised, as if I were a piece of spoiled fruit."

He smiled then, the same smile she'd first fallen in love with, the smile that now seemed to have lost a measure of its constant charm.

"But I did promise you a surprise when I returned, didn't I?" he said pleasantly, as if nothing else had happened since she'd entered the room.

He went to another traveling chest, unlatched it, and tossing back the lid, lifted out a drifting length of blue gossamer-sheer cloth. It was only when he held it up with both hands that Diana realized the cloth was actually a gown, cut as simply, and as daringly, as a shift without any sleeves and a short jagged hem. Silver spangles covered the skirt and twinkled even without the extra magic of candlelight.

"It's a lovely color," she said, and it was. "But as a gown it's quite impossibly scandalous, Roxby. The way it's cut, I could never wear stays or a shift beneath it, let alone hoops."

"Nor are you intended to," he said, his smile too knowing. "It's fancy dress, my dearest, for a ball that I shall give in your honor for our friends on Thursday. If the world wishes to view you as Helen, then Helen you shall be, and I'll play your Paris."

Anxiously Diana stared at the filmy garment hanging from his outstretched hands. "I cannot wear that, Roxby, not for a ball. I might as well be as naked as Eve instead of Helen of Troy in that."

"Of course you can," he said, that edge back in his voice. "And you will, to please me. It's only among friends, Diana."

"*Your* friends," she said reproachfully, and as soon as she saw how Roxby's face hardened, she wished at once she hadn't spoken, even though she hated what he was asking her to do. Was this to be her penance, then, her punishment, to display herself before men like Lord Stanver? "Please, Roxby. I don't want them ogling me."

"You will do it to oblige me." He tossed the gown at her, forcing her to catch it. "Besides, you'll be wearing a mask as well."

"As if a mask would—"

"My dearest, I find I am most weary from my journey," he said with a monumental yawn as he looked away from her and toward the oversized bed. "Pray excuse me if I do not see you to your own chamber."

She was being dismissed. There was no other way to look at it and no way she would tolerate it, either. Swiftly she bunched the sheer blue gown into a ball and hurled it back at him, and she didn't wait to see where it hit.

She hurried back to her room, hot, unhappy tears of frustration making everything swim and swirl before her. She didn't want to see anyone else, and she certainly didn't want to talk. What had become of the considerate lover she'd known in London, the man she'd agreed to marry? He'd said he was to blame for leaving her alone for so long, but perhaps the blame lay squarely with her, for never being alone with him long enough to truly know him.

Yet when she reached her bedchamber, that door, too, was standing open the way that Roxby's had been, and like Roxby's room, round-top traveling trunks sat open on the floor before the wardrobe. Guilietta was shaking the wrinkles from a green brocaded *robe à la française*, preparing to hang it on the pegs in the wardrobe to join the other gowns and jackets and shoes and hats that were already inside.

"Where are my clothes, Guilietta?" she asked sharply. "What have you done with my belongings?"

The small woman stepped back, curtsyed, then held her hand out to encompass everything in the wardrobe. "Here, *mia signoria*. They are here."

"But these are not my things." Diana thrust her hands into the wardrobe, rapidly shoving through the bright rustling silks—satins and sarcenets, brocailles and brocades—embellished with silver thread and ribbon love knots and drifting cuffs of lace; rich, beautiful mantuas and gowns and petticoats, costly enough, lavish enough, to be the envy of every lady at court.

And not one elegant scrap of it belonged to her.

"You do not like, *mía signoria?*" asked Guilietta, her hands clasped over her apron, her head slightly bowed. "But all is *bellissima, magnìfica, più grande!* From London, this day, *mía signoria,* for you. From *il marchese.*"

Diana took a deep breath, struggling to control both her temper and her fear. "Then what, pray, has Lord Roxby done with my old clothes?"

"*Ma che?*" Guilietta shrugged expressively, eyes raised toward the heavens, making a splendid show of pretending to neither know nor care. "Those things—old. These—new, fit for *la bellissima marchesa.*"

"Oh, yes, very *bellissima.*" Furiously Diana slammed the door to the wardrobe shut. "I'll show the marquess what I think of his precious *bellissima!*"

How could Roxby have dared do such a thing to her? With every step down the long hallway she remembered something else of hers that had been in that wardrobe, something that she'd carefully chosen to bring with her from Appledore.

The satin petticoats that one aunt had quilted for her and the bodice painstakingly embroidered by another, the shawl brought by her brother from Martinique, a handkerchief of her grandmother's that she'd planned to carry at her wedding, the gowns she and her mother had chosen and whose cost her father had grumbled indulgently over—these things were special to her for their associations with people she loved, and who in turn loved her and wished her happiness, people that, in most cases, she'd likely never see again. The clothes had been talismans even more than they'd been garments, reminders of home.

And now all she had in their place was *bellissima*.

"Ah, Diana," said Roxby. Dressed, or rather undressed, in a long flowing banyan, he wasn't resting at all, but reading before the open window, a glass of claret in one hand and his legs crossed before him, the very picture of elegant ease. "Come back to apologize, have you?"

"I have *not*," she said emphatically, coming to stand before him with her hands on her hips. "Where are my clothes, Roxby, my belongings?"

"*I* haven't done anything with them," he said, tipping the open book spine up across his chest. "*I* have only provided you most generously with a queen's ransom of new finery worthy of your new station. Oh, sit, Diana, please, so I don't have to strain my neck at this deuced awkward angle."

"Why should I sit to please you," she demanded, "when you've had all my belongings taken away?"

"Diana." He arched one black brow, linking his fingers into a little tent over the book. "My love. Your temper astounds me."

"Oh, blasted *perdition!*" She reached down and plucked the book from his chest, and flung it across the room onto the bed. "There! Did that astound you as well, Roxby? Did I astound you enough that perhaps you'll begin answering my question?"

Swiftly he rose to his feet, his jaw set against her and his world-weary pose gone in an instant. She could feel his anger coiling tighter between them, but so much a match for her own that she didn't care.

"We have had this discussion before, Diana," he said, each word as cutting as broken glass. "You have accepted me, and now you must accept my wishes as well."

"But my clothes—"

"Are gone," he said, "and by my orders. I am sure you'll find the new ones satisfactory. Now I shall thank you not to mention this to me again."

Gone. She heard the unmistakable finality of that single word. Everything she'd brought from home, everything that had come from her family. He had taken that from her, and as she realized the extent of what she'd lost—of what Roxby had stolen from her—she felt her anger slip away into grief. For a long moment she closed her eyes, shutting him out and struggling not to cry before him.

"My poor little bride," he said at last, so gently now he was almost crooning the words, and tenderly stroked the backs of his fingers over her cheeks. "None of this would matter if we didn't love each other so much."

Confused, she slowly opened her eyes. His handsome face was close to hers, his smile sorrowful, clearly regretting what he'd said and done. She did love him still, didn't she?

Didn't she?

"There's no use in looking back, darling," he was saying. "The past is over, of no account to any of us. Only the future we'll share together is of consequence, Diana. If you can but strive to remember that, then we shall make one another exquisitely happy."

She knew he wanted her to forget her family, her home, everything she'd been before she'd met him, to trade it all for the sake of their love. He'd made that clear enough before. But this time when he'd spoken, his words reminded her of something else.

"Roxby," she said slowly, "when you were in London, did you ask at my father's shipping agent for my letters from home, as you promised?"

Having a father who was a shipowner and brothers who were captains made sending and receiving letters across the ocean as reliable as was possible. Not only would other captains gladly carry letters for her from the Fairbournes, but her mother made sure to send three copies by three different ships of every long, chatty letter she wrote, letters that Diana read and reread, answered, and treasured as her last link with home.

"Roxby," she said again when he didn't answer. "You did go yourself, or send someone to fetch the letters for you?"

He smiled, his eyes half closed. "Of course I did, Diana. But there were, alas, no letters waiting for you."

"None?" she asked wistfully, giving him one last chance. "Not a one?"

"None," he said firmly, his smile not quite reaching his deep-set eyes.

And to her sorrow, she now had her answer.

For what seemed like the thousandth time since he'd left Portsmouth that morning, James shifted on the hard, uncomfortable seat of the stage and tried to inch away from the portly farmer's wife pressed beside him— a nigh impossible feat when there was not a spare inch between them.

Not that James had any more room in the coach for

his legs, either, not with the three freckle-faced sisters and their father, who was eating continuously from the basket in his lap, filling the coach with a peculiar mingled scent of pickled eggs, lavender water, and horse sweat. James had been given this inside seat as a favor by the coachman on account of his uniform, but by now he gladly would have traded places with any of the cheerfully drunk soldiers riding on top, barely managing to keep from tumbling off the side as they passed around a jug of hard cider.

"We're almost t' Ashburnham," said the freckled sister with the window. "I can see th' church tower."

"What I'd give me eyeteeth t' see would be that grand noble wedding they'll be havin' soon at th' Hall," said the middle sister with a sigh of romantic longing. "They say th' bride be th' fairest flower o' th' entire season, an' that th' groom be th' most handsomest, most richest bachelor in all Hampshire."

"*I* heard all England," volunteered the third sister, not to be left out. "Think o' how fine a life she'll have wit' a husband like that!"

They nodded in solemn, appreciative unison, and James barely suppressed his groan. He'd left Portsmouth because he hated the constant associations with Diana that seemed to hover over the entire town. With her gone, he'd felt no desire to stay, either. But returning here to Ashburnham would offer no more solace if the constant talk would be of her coming wedding to Roxby.

To *Roxby*, the devil take him now and be done with it!

There'd been a minute, maybe two, when James had been positive Diana would call off the wedding. He'd seen how she wavered, seen the doubt hovering in her eyes, and he still prayed she'd come to her senses before it was too late to change her mind.

But what if she did, what then? He'd felt the connection to her from that first morning by the millpond, and he knew she had, too. Oh, he still wanted her, wanted her so badly that he woke at night haunted by her body and sweating with his need.

But he also wanted to be with her for the sheer joy of her laugh and her cleverness. When he'd found her in the alley—"rescued," the word she used, was far too grand for what he'd actually done—his first reaction had been blind fear for her, but his second had been unabashed admiration for her courage, and the trust and kindness that had led her to that dangerous spot in the first place. Hell, they'd even fought well together, and he smiled as he remembered her challenging him in the gallery that night at Ashburnham.

All of which had led him to the uncomfortable realization that he was falling in love with Diana Fairbourne. He might already *have* fallen, for what little he knew. Men who spent their lives at sea in the exclusive company of fish and other men didn't acquire much general experience with falling in love, and James had to confess he was no exception.

Not that falling in love, or being in love, or whatever the hell he should call it, was going to bring him anything except more trouble and sorrow. He'd been raised to believe that marriage should follow love, that the first seldom prospered without the second, and that the second didn't last without the first.

But what could he offer a woman like Diana? He'd

been honest with her about how much he earned, but he wasn't entirely sure she'd believed him. How could he expect her to go from the prospect of Roxby's enormous wealth to his modest captain's half pay?

And even if she'd somehow magically agreed to that, he could never expect a woman like Diana to be content with the dull, endless months alone on shore that faced every navy wife, or the constant likelihood that she'd be left a widow. He'd already cheated death once, surviving when he should have been killed. What about the next time, if he wasn't as lucky?

As if he had a ship again, let alone Diana as his wife. He might as well wish for a chest full of Spanish *dólares*, too, while he was dreaming like a moon-calf fool, for that was as likely to fall into his lap as the other two. She'd been perfectly right to send him packing when he'd lapsed into talking nonsense to her in Portsmouth, and he'd be an even greater fool to think or hope otherwise.

Yet still he missed her, and wanted her, and loved her.

God, what an ass.

Finally, in a cloud of billowing dust, the stage lumbered to a halt before the King Henry, the village's only inn. Slowly James pried himself from the other passengers and climbed from the coach, his leg aching and stiff from sitting so long in such uncomfortable quarters. Once he found a boy willing to take his chest to the vicarage, he chose the long way to his sister's house, telling himself he needed to stretch the muscles in his leg, while conveniently postponing Celia's inevitable interrogation just a little longer.

He came by the back lane and through the yard, past

the old weeping beech, and he smiled sadly to himself. He'd never be able to look at that tree again without remembering Diana climbing among the branches like some sort of misplaced wood sprite, ignoring the dirt and damage to her fine clothes as she tried to rescue Brighty from Chou-Chou. No wonder he got along so well with her, with both of them so all-fired determined to save the world whether it wanted saving or not.

Then, of course, he thought cynically, there was Roxby. He didn't want to save the world, just buy it and cart it back home and improve it with a few jewels here and there to make everyone else envy him.

Diana couldn't marry him. Damnation, she *couldn't*.

"James Andrew Dunham, here you are at last!" Celia could have commanded a quarterdeck herself with a bellow like that, and reluctantly James turned from saving the world—or at least the part of the world with Diana Fairbourne in it—to greeting his sister with a dutiful kiss on her cheek.

"I came on the morning stage," he explained. "I'd done all that was reasonable in Portsmouth, and I—"

"Oh, bother with that, Jamie!" she said impatiently. "Besides, I'd an inkling that you were coming back to us today by how that little cat of yours has behaved, yowling and howling fit to burst since daybreak in your chamber. *He* knew you were coming, no mistake."

"He did?" asked James uneasily, and automatically felt in his pocket for the small stoneware kitten. There were a good many things about Brighty that didn't quite make sense, and this sounded like one more of them. "How the devil would a cat know that, anyway?"

"Because he's remarkably clever for a beast, that's

why, and I'm surprised he's not here now to greet you himself," said Celia, looping her arm into his to draw him toward the house. "But hurry, James, there's something come for *you*, not an hour past, something I'm sure you'll want to see!"

Diana, he thought at once, his heart racing with shameless anticipation: *something has come for him from Diana.*

But as he followed his sister into the parlor, and to the sturdy oak table beside the window, his anticipation lurched in another direction. In the middle of the table sat Brighty, his tail curled neatly over his paws and his face composed in a smug feline version of a smile, and beneath him was a large sealed packet, a packet James would recognize anywhere and one he'd feared he'd never see again.

"Shove off, Brighty," he said, sliding the packet from beneath the cat. He opened it awkwardly, the way he did everything now, but this time it was as much from excitement as from any handicap, and when he unfolded the heavy white paper of the new commission, his eyes could barely read the swirling, standardized words that he, like most officers, already knew by heart.

"What is it, James?" demanded Celia, pressing her hands tightly together. "Oh, please, dear Lord, let it be what I believe it is!"

Surprise was far too insubstantial a word for how he felt; *astonishment* was better, but still not strong enough. *Amazement*—aye, he was amazed and stunned and shocked by the blazing bolt of good fortune that had landed for him on his sister's oak dining table.

" 'By virtue of the power and authority to us given,' "

he began reading in an awed voice for Celia's sake, " 'we do hereby constitute and appoint you post captain of his majesty's ship *Amazon*. . . .' "

There was a small note enclosed from Admiral Fenner, too, congratulating him on his accomplishments and good fortune. But it was the first paper that held the magic for James, granting him the ship of his dreams, a ticket to glory and greatness and a fortune in prize money, if he'd but seize it for himself.

And put aside forever all thoughts of Diana Fairbourne.

12

From the open window of her bedchamber, Diana could hear the horses and rumbling wheels of another coach arriving for tonight's ball, the coachman's call followed by the excited chatter and laughter of his passengers being welcomed to Ashburnham.

She should be there at the top of the long stairs beside Roxby, graciously greeting his friends, making sure the footmen took their belongings to the correct rooms, offering the ladies light refreshment after their journey and the men something stronger if they wished it. That was her role, or would be soon, as Roxby's mistress of the house and wife.

Which was why, in a roundabout way, she was hiding in her chamber now, flat on her back in her bed with her arms over her eyes and the curtains drawn tight. She'd asked Guilietta to tell Roxby and the others that she was suffering from the most plaguing headache, and to make her apologies for her.

Roxby had sent his sympathy, and Lady Waldegrave had come herself on tiptoe to peek at Diana through the muffling bedcurtains and whisper possible remedies.

They'd both been kind and solicitous, but there'd also been the unspoken understanding that no headache and no excuses would be accepted for tonight.

Gemini, she was such a coward!

With a groan she rolled over onto her stomach, burying her face in the pillows. It had taken only a moment—a terrible, terrifying moment, true, but a moment nonetheless—to decide that she could not marry Roxby next week. The more time she had spent with him, the more her doubts and misgivings had grown until the only certainty that remained was to put off the wedding.

But that decision, once made, had been the easy part. What happened next would be the real challenge. To break off the match and cancel the wedding so close to the date would be a scandal of the first order. The court and the rest of the fashionable world would be sure to take Roxby's side and close against her, and her brief, exhilarating reign as a great beauty would be over.

She doubted Lady Waldegrave would have anything more to do with her, either. Who would blame her? Diana would have no choice but to return home to Massachusetts in disgrace and face the gossip and raised eyebrows there as well. Most likely she'd never marry now. No decent man would want her. For the rest of her life, wherever she went, there'd always be a taint to her name, whispers about how she'd been too proud and haughty to marry the broken-hearted Marquess of Roxby.

But she wasn't proud and she wasn't haughty. She was scared. Roxby's courtship had been breathtakingly fast, and she'd been so flattered and overwhelmed that she'd accepted just as quickly, without realizing exactly the kind of man her betrothed was. But since she'd come to Ashburnham, she had learned quickly, and although she was certain now that this was not the man she wanted to spend the rest of her life with, she wasn't sure at all that he'd let her go if she finally dared tell him.

And that, really, was what she feared the most. Lady Waldegrave and everyone else had told her that Roxby was the most desirable bachelor in England, and that she'd made a splendid match, far above her station. Roxby *was* handsome, titled, powerful, and rich—everything she'd come to London to find in a husband.

But no one had bothered mentioning that he was also domineering and unyielding, or that he seemed to find pleasure in certain activities that did not seem, well, *right* to her. Diana knew about how men and women loved one another—her mother had explained that—but Roxby had shown her just enough of his inclinations to make her suspect their wedding night would not be the one her mother had described, and that frightened her, too.

She wished her mother were here now. Her mother was a wise, clever woman, no fool when it came to worldly matters. She would have been able to offer Diana exactly the right advice to help her know what to do next.

But her mother was thousands of miles away, and if Roxby had his way, Diana might never hear or read another word from her again. Instead she was more alone than she'd ever been in her life, and, oh, what she'd give to have someone here she could trust and talk to!

Fleetingly she thought of James Dunham, then just as

swiftly pushed the thought away. He was too good a man for her to drag into her private disasters, and she'd no right to let him ruin his own prospects for the sake of her. That was why she'd parted with him in Portsmouth, and why she'd be wickedly selfish now if she tried to turn to him again.

Lost in her own misery, she didn't hear the intruder as much as sense him, the slight, unexpected shifting at the end of the mattress. She lifted her head and twisted around, squinting into the shadows, and as she did she felt his nose butt against her hand, his whiskers tickling her wrist. With a surprised little shriek, she jerked her hand back, but the intruder followed relentlessly, his purring growing more insistent, and more identifiable, too.

"Brighty!" she gasped, reaching out to stroke his ears, exactly the way that he desired. "Brighty, however did you come here?"

She sat up and pulled the little cat into her arms, moving awkwardly on her knees to the edge of the bed to push the curtains aside. There was an ancient holly tree outside her room, one of several around the house, and it was certainly possible for the cat to have climbed up it and into her window. But for him to have come to Ashburnham clear from the vicarage, to have chosen her window among all the others, to have wiggled his way in through her bedcurtains to find her—that seemed outlandish, even for a cat with Brighty's powers.

"This is a vastly long way for a little cat to come, Brighty," she said as she slid from the bed and padded barefoot to the window with the purring cat in her arms. If she leaned to one side, she could just see the drive, and another coach arriving. "You're quite wrong to come calling today, you know, though I cannot imagine how you'll be able to return so far home on those poor paws of yours."

As if in response, he licked a paw and blinked slyly at her with one green eye, enough to make her chuckle. Whether he was magical or not, she did like holding him, as much for the memories of James that he carried with him as for his own warm, furry self.

"Do you miss James, too?" she asked softly, touching the white star on his forehead. "I miss him a great deal more than I should, and I've seen him since you have."

She sighed, sliding the cat up onto her shoulder as she thought of his owner. "I wish I could keep you here, Brighty. We'd be company for each other, wouldn't we? But Roxby would never approve of you as a lowly stray, I fear, and cats make Lady Waldegrave sneeze and weep so abominably that I could never keep you secret."

But she hadn't the heart simply to put him back into the tree and shut her window, and she didn't trust any one of the servants to take him back to the vicarage. For all she knew, it had been one of Roxby's staff who'd tried to drown him in the millpond, only another worthless kitten that no one had wanted. As she hugged Brighty more tightly, she decided what she'd do.

"I'll take you home myself, my little darling, for James' sake while he's away," she murmured into Brighty's fur. "No one expects to see me before this evening, and I can be back long before then. Here, let me set you down while I dress, and then we'll be off together."

Because none of her comfortable old clothes for walking had survived Roxby's purge, she chose the simplest of the new ones she could find, a jacket of Indian painted cotton that fastened in the front with silver gilt buttons—important since she didn't wish to call Guilietta to help her dress, as she'd have to with most of the other new gowns—and a rose-colored silk petticoat bordered with a row of satin-stitched pinks.

A quick glance at her looking glass showed she was more ready for a stroll through the well-tended gardens at Ranleigh or Vauxhall than across the wilder fields surrounding Ashburnham, but she couldn't worry about that now. She scooped Brighty from the bed, drew the curtains closed again so she still seemed to be inside, and slipped out her door into the hall. This wing of the house was one of the oldest, and still kept its own staircase to the back gardens. With her shoes in one hand and Brighty in the other, Diana ran to the outside door, her heart pounding with excitement even as she counted on everyone else in the house to be occupied with the arrival of the guests.

She'd gone walking often enough that she found her way easily, staying to the fields and wooded places and avoiding the open roads where she'd be more likely to be seen. The vicarage was not far from the millpond where she'd first met James, the church having at one time actually stood on Ashburnham land. She spotted the square tower of the church, then the low, yellow-walled vicarage beside it. A vine with red flowers had been trained to grow over the doorway, curling tendrils and trumpet-shaped blossoms filled with fat, lazy bumblebees.

"There now, be a good boy," scolded Diana as Brighty's head popped up at the buzzing and bobbing bees. "I've no intention of being stung simply because you wanted to prove yourself a great hunter."

Though the door was slightly ajar, she knocked, expecting the same slow-witted girl to answer as had before. She waited, and knocked a second time and called, too, but there was no sign of either the girl or James' sister.

"I'll simply have to leave you, Brighty," she said. The cat lay comfortably limp in her arms, batting a languid paw at the nearest silver gilt button on her jacket, and she lifted him up to kiss him on his forehead. "That's for James, for you to give him when he returns. Here now, down you go."

She pushed the door open and bent to set the cat down on the floor. But as she did, Brighty snagged his claw into the thread holding the button, and with a little jerk of his paw the button flew free, bouncing and spinning across the floor. At once he was after it, pouncing on the button just long enough to keep it still before he grabbed it in his teeth and disappeared down the hall.

"Brighty, come back!" shouted Diana. She didn't want to chase after the cat in a house that wasn't hers, but she didn't want to have to explain what had happened to the fancy button, either. Muttering an exasperated oath that she'd learned from her brothers, she gathered her skirts and hurried after the cat, through the parlor and down the hall toward the bedchambers.

"Brighty?" she called again, more tentatively. The house was simply furnished, as was to be expected; there wouldn't be many places for even a small cat to hide. "Brighty, so help me, come here *now!*"

She heard a rustling, followed by a thump, from the last room, and with a smile of triumph she marched toward it.

"Turn over your plunder now," she said as she pushed aside the open door, "you wretched little—*oh!*"

James Dunham was standing beside a low bed, his sun-streaked head barely clearing the sloping ceiling of the added-on room. The bed's coverlet was buried beneath neat piles of folded clothes, with a battered wooden sea chest open and waiting on the floor. Clearly James was preparing for another voyage, for in addition to the clothes, he'd begun gathering other things a captain would take—his long leather-covered spyglass, two pairs of tall sea boots and a pair of dress shoes with cut-steel buttons, a small assortment of books, the triangular box for his uniform hat, and a mahogany case with brass fittings to hold his logs and diaries.

Perhaps because all his shirts were clean and waiting, he wasn't wearing one now, and it seemed to Diana that there was little else in the room beyond that long, lean, broad-shouldered and thoroughly splendid male back. Like so many sailors, he wore his breeches slung low on his hips, hovering right at the twin dimples on either side of his spine, and the small bow that gathered the waistband seemed only to emphasize exactly how closely those breeches fit over his hips and buttocks, ending short of his bare knees and calves.

And, of course, there was Brighty, too, sitting on the windowsill proud as a lord, washing his tail with the purloined button beside him.

But all this Diana noted in an instant, because an instant was all she had before James turned to look over his shoulder at her.

"What—what are you doing here?" she stammered, her face flushing hot.

"I might well ask the same of you, lass," he said sharply, not blushing in the least. "Or is it your usual Yankee custom to wander into houses unannounced in search of plunder?"

"I didn't mean to, James," she said quickly. "The door was unlatched, open, and I was only bringing Brighty back home and he stole my button and ran away with it and I—when I—oh, perdition, I should just leave now, before I make this worse, shouldn't I?"

"Not quite yet," he said, and at last he smiled, an odd, wondering smile that she'd never seen from him before. "Diana, they've given me the *Amazon*."

"They *have?*" she exclaimed, clapping her hands with joy. "Oh, James, that is exactly what you dreamed for, isn't it?"

"It's considerably more than I dreamed, truth to tell," he admitted, so pleased to share this with her that he forgot himself and turned around. "Who would have guessed it when we were all in Portsmouth, eh?"

"Who indeed?" she asked, but her gaze had slid down from his face to his chest. No, not to his chest: he should have known better than that. She was staring at the scars, the livid long zigzags along his arm and side that ran down into the waist of his breeches, scars that the flying wood had carved into him, that the scattered, mottled bits of black powder had burned into his skin, and the lumpy white tucks and pinpricks that remained from the surgeon's labors in the cockpit.

"When do you leave?" she murmured, her eyes still lowered.

"I'll clear Ashburnham at dawn," he said, belatedly reaching for a shirt from his sister's neat piles, any shirt to cover his shameful, scarred nakedness. In Celia's typical efficiency, she'd buttoned the cuffs on the sleeves and at the collar when she'd finished with the ironing, and he fumbled with the tiny thread-work button at the throat now, so desperate to undo it that he tore the loop. "I won't have my sailing orders until I'm back in Portsmouth, but since the *Amazon*'s already fitted out and she already has most of her crew, I expect we'll be off to sea as soon as possible."

"Don't," she implored softly, and not meaning the *Amazon*'s sailing, either. "You don't have to hide yourself from me."

But he did, swearing as he fumbled with the shirt. Once he'd been proud to stand like this before a woman, but not the way he was now. Nor had he missed the other irony, either, that he'd never seen her look more lovely, flushed from her walk and her hair as mussed as if she'd just risen from bed.

"I said you don't have to do that, James," she said, the same soft, wistful voice. "Not today, anyway. Please."

"Diana, you needn't—"

"But I do," she countered. "I do because I care for you, and don't care about—about what happened to you when the *Castor* was lost."

Ah, they were in dangerous waters here, and it had nothing to do with the *Castor*, either. Swiftly he pulled the shirt over his head and over his chest before he turned back toward her.

"I only meant that you were a lady, gently bred," he said gruffly, "and not accustomed to seeing, ah, what can happen in a battle."

"I'm a woman from a family of men who have, it

seems, been fighting the French one way or another my entire life," she said, her blue eyes so troubled that he knew she, too, realized the perils they were skirting. "I don't believe that has anything in the least to do with gentleness or breeding. But then war never does, does it?"

"No," he said. "It doesn't."

He looked down at the waiting sea trunk for want of any place better, thinking of how much destruction and suffering was encompassed in that simple statement. He'd been lucky. He'd lost a great many friends and comrades who hadn't been as fortunate. And he'd seen even more men who'd cried and wept for death as a release from their suffering, their limbs blasted away by cannon fire, or their flesh so burned it slid from their bones as they floated helpless in the icy sea, or their wounds so deep that blood ran like a red river, all from a pistol's ball or a saber's slash.

He knew. He'd been one of them.

It was easy for landsmen, and especially women, to be swept along in the patriotic fever of war, to focus on the red and blue banners and gold-laced uniforms and the glory of a noble death, without comprehending any of the agony that went with it.

But Diana wasn't like the Lady Marchmonts of the country, not about this or anything else. How much easier this all would be for them both if she were!

He felt her hand come to rest on his arm, light as a feather, and by choice on the worst part of the scar. Without looking he knew she'd drawn closer. Her scent was there, and the bell of her skirts brushed against his bare calves.

"If Brighty or fate or whatever it was hadn't brought me here, James, I would not have seen you again to wish you well," she said softly, the sadness palpable in the small room as her fingers curled around his arm. "To see those scars reminds me how fragile life can be, especially for a man like you."

He rested his hand over hers, wanting to say whatever would take that sadness away. "I'm no different from any other man, Diana."

"But you *are*, James, in more ways than I can count," she cried, anguish making her words tumble over one another. "You're good, and kind, and bold, and brave, and because you'll always put others first, you always put yourself at risk. You did so before and barely survived, and now you have been rewarded with another splendid chance to be killed."

"Oh, lass," he said, cradling her face in his hand as he gently turned her toward him. "You make me sound like a saint, when all I've done is what my orders and my honor have asked."

But she shook her head against his hand, unconvinced, her eyes now luminous with unshed tears while she searched his face as if to memorize it for safekeeping.

"Our lives are bound to follow different paths, James," she said, "and oh, we've set different courses for ourselves!"

"True enough," he said, trying not to remember back to the street in Portsmouth where he'd asked something dreadfully close to this. His heart was beating faster with unreasonable hope, and he told himself he'd rather face a Frenchman at twenty paces than have her turn her words, and that same fool's heart of his, inside out again. "But I'd say your future is a sight more glorious than mine, Diana."

She tried to smile. "And only slightly less perilous."

"Damnation, if Roxby's done anything to harm—"

"Oh, hush, James," she scolded gently, reaching up to smooth his hair back from his forehead, her body swaying carelessly against his. "You've dragons enough to slay for the king. But you take care of yourself as well, mind? I could not bear a world that no longer has you in it somewhere."

If James had been the saintly, honorable gentleman she wanted to believe he was, then he would have stopped there. He would have taken her by the arm and steered her from the temptations of his bedchamber to the safety of his brother-in-law's parlor, to compose herself among the books of sermons and cross-stitched scriptures that Celia had lovingly worked and framed.

He would have sent for a hired chaise to take Diana back to Ashburnham, or waited with her until his sister and Oliver returned from their parish calls with the vicar's cart. He would have wished her joy in her marriage; he would have returned to his preparations for his voyage.

Unfortunately, Diana was sadly mistaken about his character, and with her pressing her breasts into his chest, he was neither saintly nor honorable, and certainly not a gentleman. He was only a man, a lonely, uncertain man preparing to return to a war that had already nearly killed him, and he was a man alone with the woman he loved but couldn't have.

Except, perhaps, for now.

And with no other thought than that, James circled Diana's waist with his arm, pulled her close, and kissed her as if nothing else in the world existed or mattered, and for them at that moment, nothing did.

She seemed to melt against him as readily as butter in the sun, her hands sliding around his shoulders and her body shifting closer, meeting his in all sorts of promising little ways. Her lips parted and opened to him, not so much in surrender as in welcome, a welcome made warmer still by the eager touch of her mouth and the throaty little sounds of pleasure she made deep in her throat.

The next step seemed even simpler, guiding her the last half pace before he tipped her backward onto the bed and followed her there, among the piles of new washed shirts still smelling faintly of the grass and sunshine where they'd been hung to dry. Supporting his weight as best he could, he kissed her again and felt her wriggle and shift beneath him, accommodating him, her legs sliding apart, curling around his through the layers of her skirts.

Simpler, and simpler still. A stack of shirts toppled to the floor and he didn't care. The rope springs of the low bed creaked and squeaked in rhythmic protest, and he didn't hear them. When he fumbled with the row of tiny, rounded buttons on Diana's bodice, she helped him, and when he tugged the gathered neckline of her shift down to bare her breasts, licking and teasing her nipples into tight, rosy crests, she gasped with sweet, startled pleasure that betrayed her lack of experience.

She helped with the confusion of her skirts as well, until he was touching the sleek skin above her garters, higher still to the tangle of hair at the top of her thighs and the most sensitive place of all, wet and tight and achingly responsive to his fingers. Lightly he stroked her there, easing her open, and she arched beneath him, panting, and reaching to help him next unfasten the buttons on the fall of his breeches. Even that practical touch of her fingers to his arousal was more than he wanted, and he groaned and pressed against her, instinct and desire driving them both now.

On the faintest corners of his consciousness he remembered her saying how often men wished to kiss her, and though he didn't doubt they wished to do what he was doing as well, he was also certain that, as she'd also claimed, she'd never let them, and as selfish as that certainty was, it pleased him just the same. She could belong to him alone in the most primal male way, and she would, too, as he centered himself between her legs.

"Love me, James," she gasped, trembling beneath him, as ready as he was himself. "Love me now, before you sail!"

A bucket of sea water could not have doused his desire faster, and with a groan he rolled away from her. *Love her before he sailed:* oh, aye, and what a way to show it! What the hell was he *doing,* anyway?

"James?" she asked, more a whimper of longing as she twisted around toward him. "James, please, what—"

"You are still betrothed to Roxby, aren't you?" he asked, his eyes squeezed shut and his breathing harsh as he struggled to control himself.

"Yes," she said in a tiny voice. "But now I—"

"*No.*" He pulled his breeches closed and left the bed, keeping his back toward her so he wouldn't be tempted to return. "You're still his, Diana, as close to being his wife as can be."

"But I swear I—"

"Don't argue with me, Diana," he said, frustration making his voice harsh. "What the hell do you think I am, anyway? Do you think I could take your maidenhead and then leave you to face the consequences when Roxby discovers you're not a virgin on your wedding night? Do you want me to sail away knowing this would be all I'd ever have from you, one afternoon, while Roxby has you the rest of your life?"

She made a sharp, keening cry, as painful as if he'd struck her outright, and against his judgment he looked back.

Her face was pale, her cheeks wet with tears, while her fingers were now the clumsy ones as she tried to rebutton her bodice.

"I wouldn't have done that to you, James," she sobbed. "I swear I wouldn't!"

"Then what would you have done, Diana?" he demanded bitterly. "Come to me again in a hired room when I returned on leave? Or would you have left me to wonder if Roxby's son were really mine, if I'd sired the next marquess myself?"

"I would not do that, James," she said through her tears, "not to you, or me, or any—any child of ours."

She slid unsteadily from the bed, shoving her skirts back down over her legs as she tried to slip past him. He caught her arm, trapping her in the doorway, forcing her to look at him this last time. Her eyes were full of sorrow and shame, her mouth still swollen from his kisses.

"You asked for my love, Diana," he said hoarsely. "But what you had to offer in return wasn't what I call love, not by half."

She dashed away her tears with the heel of her hand,

and lifted her chin, her pride now a match for his own. "You said, Captain Dunham, that you were no different from any other man, no saint. But you *are*. You must be. How else to explain what you've refused this day?"

He didn't, because he couldn't, not without offering his own love for her scorn. Easier to keep his silence, easier still to let her go, and learn to live with the gaping hole in his chest where his heart had once been.

And ignore the reproachful, unblinking eyes of the little gray cat on the windowsill.

"Ah, Diana, here you are at last," said Roxby pleasantly, leaning against one of the oversized marble urns that dotted the formal gardens. "I trust the headache has left you now?"

"Yes," said Diana, praying he wouldn't ask why her eyes were so red rimmed from crying, or her clothes so wrinkled from lying on James' bed. "Yes, I feel much better now."

Over and over she'd been hearing James' words in her head, and over and over she'd tried to find the precise place when she'd erred. But the sorry truth was that he'd been right and she'd been wrong, and now she felt empty and hollow inside, lost and alone with a finality that she'd never dreamed possible. When Brighty had led her to James' room, she'd been giddily willing to believe that, after everything else, fate had smiled and was offering her the real true love of her life.

But it hadn't lasted a lifetime. It hadn't even lasted an hour. How could things between them go so horribly wrong so quickly?

Now all she wanted was to be able to return to her rooms by this back way through the gardens, to nurse her misery in private. She'd never thought Roxby himself would be waiting here for her.

"I am so glad, my dearest." He smiled, studying the roses growing in the urn, critically framing the nearest blossoms one by one against his open hand. "When Guilietta informed me you'd vanished from your bed, I told her not to fear, that you'd most likely gone for a walk through the gardens, as is your custom."

"I am recovered, yes," she answered, not trusting herself to say more. She should have realized that Guilietta would not be fooled by drawn bedcurtains alone, just as she should have known the lady's maid would report directly to Roxby himself. "But I do wish to go now to my bedchamber."

"An excellent idea, my darling. Though in the future, I'd advise you to use the front staircase. This back one strikes me as unsafe, and I have ordered it closed and the door at the end of your hallway locked."

She looked at him sharply. "Are you making me your prisoner now, Roxby?"

"You wrong me, Diana," he said, shaking his head with a sigh. "I only wish to keep the lady I love from harm. The only prisoner is I myself, a prisoner of your love."

Carefully he snapped one of the roses from the bush and handed it to her with a bow. Once she would have been delighted and impressed by his thoughtfulness. Now as she took the rose, she felt more wary than wooed.

"You'll want to give Guilietta time to dress you for the ball tonight," he continued. "I'll be expecting you to look your best. Fair Helen of Troy should be nothing less."

"Less than nothing is what you expect me to wear,"

she said bitterly. She'd been so occupied with what had happened between her and James that she'd forgotten completely about the ball and the scandalous costume Roxby had provided for her. "I've not promised I won't choose a different gown, Roxby."

"Then I shall pray you choose to please me instead," he said, resting his hand over his heart with a courtier's grace while his dark eyes glittered ominously. "Oh, one last bit of news, my darling. Lady Waldegrave regrets that she'll be unable to attend you at the ball tonight. As much as she'd wished to see you in your triumph, she was unexpectedly called back to London."

"Lady Waldegrave has left?" she asked, stunned. "But she would never leave me here alone!"

Roxby shrugged carelessly. "She gave no reason to me, beyond promising that she will return in time for our wedding. She assured me that nothing in heaven or on earth would make her miss that."

"Nothing, that is, except you," said Diana, striving to swallow her rising panic. She and Lady Waldegrave had had their differences, to be sure, but the countess was her mother's oldest friend and her only real ally here at Ashburnham. "You sent her away, didn't you? Just like you did with Lady Marchmont."

But Roxby only smiled and leaned forward to kiss her cheek. "My dear Diana," he said softly. "You worry unnecessarily. All that needs concern you now is that I love you, and you love me. Because beyond that, my dear bride, there *is* nothing."

13

"*Il marchese* is proud of your beauty, *signoria*," said Gulietta to Diana's reflection as they both studied the mirror before them. "You are *bellissima, signoria*, more beautiful than all others. You must be proud, too, and happy your lord loves you."

Critically the lady's maid plucked at one of the sheer sleeves of the gown, making it stand out like a tiny wing behind Diana's shoulder.

"*Bellissima*," she said again nodding, so satisfied that she forgot to be self-conscious about her limited English. "You are ready, *signoria, si?*"

But while Gulietta saw only *bellissima*, Diana stared at herself and felt nothing but shame. It wasn't just the thought of appearing among the other guests wearing so little, but before Roxby himself.

"I cannot go like this, Gulietta," she whispered urgently. "Here, here, help me change into another gown."

"He will only return you here to me, *signoria*," predicted the lady's maid philosophically. "This is what *il marchese* wishes you wear. He will not be content until you obey."

Diana sighed unhappily, knowing the woman was right. Roxby would at once send her back to change if she disobeyed him and wore a different gown. She'd already delayed dressing and joining him as long as she could, longer than was wise. She'd do better for herself not to cross Roxby tonight, or give him any more reasons to suspect her. Without any friends or allies left in the house she needed to be doubly on her guard, and for this last night, she'd oblige Roxby however he wished.

And in an appalling way, the costume he'd chosen for her *was* beautiful. Roxby did have an eye for that, though the only concession to how ancient Helen might have dressed was the gold diadem, bright with diamonds and Roxby's favorite cabochon rubies, pinned into her hair, and the open sandals that laced around her bare legs to her knees.

The gown was sewn with layers of the sheerest fabrics in differing shades of pale blue, arranged one over another so that any motion or change of light made the colors shimmer with the elusive iridescence of a dragonfly's wing. Silver and gold spangles sparkled like scattered stars, and the fabric had been cut so cleverly that it seemed to cling to Diana's body one moment, then drift away the next, a constantly changing, teasing beguilement.

That alone would have been suggestive enough over stays and a shift, but the gown had been shaped to be worn over nothing but Diana herself, leaving her dreadfully aware of how the silk slid and shimmered like a lover's caress over the roundness of her hips and the swaying fullness of her breasts, accentuating them in a way that seemed even more revealing than if she'd walked into the ballroom completely naked.

It was clearly a costume meant for a grand courtesan or royal mistress, or an actress who wished to become one. Only Roxby could conceive of such an ensemble as suitable for his bride, and with an unhappy gulp Diana thought once again of the portrait of his sloe-eyed grandmother in the gallery upstairs.

"Only one night, *signoria*," said Gulietta with unexpected kindness, resting her hand on Diana's shoulder. "These gentlemen like *il marchese*, they like to show to other men what is theirs. But you keep *la fierezza*—your pride, *signoria*. Do not let them see your shame. Your pride, *signoria:* that is what the lady must keep."

She disappeared from the reflection briefly, returning with a white satin half mask and a wide blue shawl that matched the costume.

"*Per cortesia, signoria*," murmured Gulietta sympathetically, tying the mask over Diana's face before she draped the shawl over her shoulders. "These help you, *si?*"

Diana nodded into the mirror, more thankful than the sad-eyed maid could ever know. With the mask to hide her face and the shawl to shield at least the darker crests of her nipples and the shadowy triangle at the top of her thighs, she could perhaps find the courage to stand at Roxby's side tonight. It would be a beginning and an ending that would prepare her for tomorrow, when she meant to be stronger still and tell him the truth.

For tomorrow, by daylight and by whatever means she could, she meant to leave for good.

"*Il marchese* will make a fine master for you," said Gulietta confidently as she tugged the shawl higher over Diana's arms. "*Grandissimo maestro!*"

Diana's shaky smile faded, and so did that elusive pride in herself that she was so struggling to find. It could only be Gulietta's unsteady grasp of English that had made her choose the word "master" to describe Roxby.

Couldn't it?

"Ah, Gulietta, you have performed your attentions most admirably!" exclaimed Roxby from the door, greeting her with languid applause. "*Bene, bene, brava!* You've spent your time admirably. I have never seen Miss Fairbourne garbed to such perfection."

Before Diana could turn to greet him, Gulietta scuttled away, and in her place behind Diana stood Roxby, both of them framed together in the same looking glass. If she was a provocative Covent Garden Helen, then Roxby was Paris dressed as if ancient Sparta were no more than another fashionable new square in west London. True, he wore high boots and three tall white plumes in his hat, sure signs of royalty on the stage or in any masque, but the elaborately curled wig and blue velvet suit, thickly embroidered with silver threads and spangles that matched Diana's costume, were hardly inspired by Homer.

But those were details Diana noticed later. In this first moment, all that registered was the predatory, almost feral, eagerness in Roxby's hooded eyes as his gaze swept over her. She'd often seen men look at her with desire, but never with this level of intensity, and not from the man who was to be the first to lie with her, either. With difficulty she fought the nearly irresistible urge to run and save herself.

"You are perfect, my dear," he said, resting his hands on her shoulders. "Quite, quite perfect."

At his touch she shivered with a mixture of trepidation and revulsion, and immediately she saw the displeasure ripple across his face. Careful, careful, she warned herself, forcing a smile. With Roxby, she couldn't afford to let her feelings show like that again.

"You are most handsome tonight, too, my lord," she murmured, praying he'd hear only conviction in her voice. She knew she could play his game if only she concentrated hard enough. "How could Helen wish for more in her Paris?"

"How, indeed, fair Helen, when I am already your slave?" In the mirror his features relaxed, and with one hand he swept aside her hair and kissed the back of her neck. No, it was more than a kiss, for the first softness of his lips at her nape was sharpened by the edge of his teeth grating over her skin, nipping at her, and with a startled gasp she twisted away, protectively covering the place with her palm.

"Why did you do that?" she demanded sharply. "Faith, Roxby, I am not some cur's bitch to be bitten like that!"

But Roxby merely smiled. "Ah, my pretty innocent," he said, offering her his hand. "We are many things in this life and can be so many more, if we do but dare."

"Daring is one thing, Roxby, but to bite at me—"

"Hush, hush," he said, clucking his tongue with mock disapproval. "Would fair Helen trouble herself with such pitiful scruples? I ask only that you trust me as I do you, and I promise you a night that neither of us shall ever forget."

"I am already rather sure of *that*, Roxby." She was watching him warily, the trust he asked for impossible for her to give. "Everything with you is unforgettable."

He laughed, tipping his head back, the ruby pin at his throat twinkling in the ruffled lace neckcloth beneath his chin. "Well said, my fair Helen, well said. Now come, give me your hand. Our guests are crying out for their first glimpse of you."

The guests. Dear God, she'd nearly forgotten them. Once again she swallowed her fears, spread her shawl to cover more of her body, and slipped her fingers into Roxby's waiting hand.

"Pray, do not be so priggishly shy," he said, frowning disdainfully at the shawl as he pulled her toward the door. "This is hardly the time to play the modest maid, Diana."

"I'm not playacting, Roxby," she said as lightly as she could. "I'm as modest a maid as I can be, even if you have made me dress like a strumpet."

"No, you are not," he said, his fingers tightening around hers as they began down the hall. "You are *mine*, Diana, and I'll ask you not to forget it again."

She wouldn't, not when he was half dragging her toward the sounds of bright music and excited voices and laughter edged with wine. The short petaled edges of her gown fluttered around her knees, goosebumps raising on her bare legs. Her heart was pounding with uncertainty, and she knew there would be no looking to Roxby for any defense from whatever lay ahead. The best she could hope for was that his position, and by extension hers, would protect her from the worst indignities.

The ballroom was in the far corner of the house, rising through two floors. High on one side was a small balcony for the musicians, and opposite it a smaller, curtained second gallery that an earlier dowager marchioness had had installed to spy upon her wayward husband at play. It was here that Roxby brought Diana now, letting them look down on the others without being seen themselves.

"Pity we're so late," drawled Roxby as he glanced carelessly downward. "You would have enjoyed the costumes earlier, I think."

They were nearly level with the coved ceiling, bright with paintings brought from Italy, a different apotheosis over each arched window and a great deal of rosy allegorical flesh—not that it came close to what was being displayed on the polished floor below them, beneath the scores of candles and jingling crystal drops in the chandeliers.

These were not the same guests that had come to Ashburnham to the earlier party in her honor, the local gentry dutifully invited to pay their regards. There was no sight now of the red-faced country squires with their plump wives and simpering daughters, no climbing merchants from Winchester, or elderly rakes banished by debt to the frugal country—people that, on the whole, Diana had liked and had been able to imagine seeing as friends and neighbors.

Tonight's guests were altogether different, London guests, the fast, fashionable crowd that was rumored to revel regularly at Lord Stanver's house. In spite of the black or white half masks that most wore, it was easy to tell that the men were mostly young and mostly rich, and the women unanimously beautiful.

They had, as Roxby noted, all begun the evening in costumes much like the ones Diana and Roxby wore, vaguely Greek in inspiration, but few had seemed able to keep those costumes entirely on their bodies. Most of the women had either lost their bodices entirely, or at least opened them to bare their breasts, while the men were beginning to shed their clothes as well, including a portly young man now garbed only in a wreath of ivy leaves.

That was enough, far more than enough to make Diana blush furiously with horrified embarrassment, for even at the wildest parties and frolics in New England, the guests managed to stay clothed. But what these unclothed bodies were doing with each other—dancing in drunken abandon, kissing and fondling one another in the corners of the windows, even openly coupling on the benches and against the walls, without heed or care of who was watching—was shockingly beyond her experience or comprehension, let alone her acceptance.

She thought of how her mother had described love making, the tenderness and rare joy and passion between two people who cared deeply for one another, and she remembered how closely she'd come to sharing exactly that this afternoon with James.

With James: oh, dear God, if she began thinking of him now, of what she could have had with him and now had lost forever, she'd begin to weep and never stop. . . .

That bliss was what she'd always expected from marriage, and what she'd hoped to find with Roxby, but what she was seeing here was joyless and ugly. No wonder Roxby had only smiled when she'd accused him of behaving like a dog, for here his friends were acting exactly like animals in heat, and with as little decency or respect for one another.

And she wanted absolutely no part of it.

She yanked off her half mask and the bejeweled diadem, tossing them both behind her.

"I'm leaving, Roxby," she said, pulling away from him, so agitated that she felt almost light-headed. "This—these people—you can stay if you wish, for they are your friends, but they aren't mine and never will be."

"Oh, Diana." Amused by her response, he swept his hand through the air, toward the people below. "Does this frighten you, then?"

"It doesn't frighten me, Roxby," she said, hugging her arms and the shawl tightly around her body as she inched back from him toward the door from the little gallery. "It *sickens* me, as it should you, too, if you were a decent gentleman."

"Decency, my dear," he said with a smile, "is for tedious, small souls."

"Then I must be the smallest, most tedious soul alive," she said, her voice quavering as a woman shrieked with noisy delight below them.

"Oh, I would venture you're vastly more innocent than tedious," he suggested. "Untutored, charmingly so. Inexperienced, decidedly. But then, I'd never planned to introduce you as one of our, ah, celebrants tonight."

He reached out and caught the corner of her shawl, twisting the fabric around his finger and pulling her slowly closer.

"You're mine, Diana, my wife and my prize," he said, his dark eyes intent, "and I'm not a man much given to sharing."

"And I'm not your wife, Roxby, not yet," she said, tugging at her end of the shawl, "and I'm not—"

"Ha, ha, you're found out, Roxby!" exclaimed Lord Stanver gleefully as he staggered his way into the curtained gallery. He'd lost his coat, his waistcoat open, and his shirt pulled out from his breeches to billow around his legs, but he'd somehow managed to keep a brass Roman helmet perched at a precarious angle on his wig. "I should have known you'd run with your vixen into this snug little foxhole!"

Roxby sighed, and released his hold on Diana's shawl. Stanver was hardly the champion she would have picked, especially not when he was staring so obviously at her breasts, but perhaps his inebriated presence would be enough of a distraction, and once again she began inching toward the door and the hall.

"You disappoint me, Stanver," said Roxby wearily, having seen this sort of behavior from his friend more times than either of them could remember. "You vowed you'd come tonight in some noble fancy dress, in honor of my bride. Yet all you show her now is a whoreson with a coal scuttle upon his head."

"Damn your impertinence, Roxby, I *am* in fancy dress!" cried Stanver, frowning as he fumbled with the trailing hem of his shirt. "King Mars himself, god o' war, in the very divine flesh!"

From inside his shirt he suddenly pulled out an enormous long-barreled Spanish pistol, covered with gold filigree and studded with gems. Brandishing the gun over his head, he grinned with more of a naughty child's wicked delight than any real bellicosity.

Diana yelped and ducked. Her luck today had

seemed bad enough already without being murdered by a drunken fool with a pistol. Though she hadn't seen whether the gun was primed and cocked, she wasn't going to take more chances.

"You infernal idiot," snapped Roxby, holding his hand out for the gun. "Give that to me now before you blast away your own miserable excuse for brains."

But Stanver snatched the pistol away, tucking it back into the belt beneath his shirt.

" 'Tis mine, Roxby. I won it fairly last night at faro—they say it's worth twenty guineas if it's worth a farthing—and I'll not give it up to you," he said petulantly. "You always claim the best for yourself anyway."

Unsteadily he turned to offer his hand to Diana. "Now who are you, my pretty chick?" he said with a suggestive wink to accompany his smile. "Ah, let me conjure: Venus, sure, queen of beauty and love! Come, give me a kiss to reward my learning."

"You forget yourself, Stanver," warned Roxby, coming to stand behind Diana and slipping his arm possessively around her waist. "Are you so far in your cups that you've forgotten Diana is my bride?"

Stanver's pudgy face furrowed sullenly. "Yours, Roxby?" he muttered. "Why, you wretched bastard."

"Mine," said Roxby firmly, and before Diana realized what he was doing, he'd jerked the shawl away from her body and reached up to cup her breasts, his fingers spreading to lift and fondle their fullness. She gasped and tried to break away, but he held her tightly, his thumbs pinching her nipples to make them jut through the sheer fabric. "You see how fond she is of me, Stanver."

"Not like this, I am not!" cried Diana furiously, spitting each word as she finally twisted free of him, covering her breasts with her arms. "I will not have you use me like this, for your—your *entertainment!*"

"The wench doesn't act like she's yours, Roxby," observed Stanver. "Not exactly."

"No, she doesn't," agreed Roxby sadly. "But then my little bride's tastes are not quite as, ah, *extravagant* as are our own, not yet."

"Nor will they ever be," said Diana fiercely, "not if by 'extravagance' you mean the sort of wickedness I've seen here tonight! You can go to the devil for all I care, Roxby, but you won't take me with you. Now step aside and let me go."

Roxby's expression didn't change, keeping that odd, imperious sadness, but he didn't move from her path, either. Until he did Diana was trapped, and she was quite sure he knew it as well as she did.

"Now, Roxby," she said, striving to equal his *hauteur*. "Or would you have it said that the Marquess of Roxby was less than a gentleman?"

Stanver guffawed, broadly enough that Diana's fear notched higher. "Gad, Roxby. You'll have to oblige her now, won't you? You being such a gentleman and all."

But Roxby only smiled, tossing aside his plumed hat as if to show he'd cast off the ruse of the fancy ball. "I shall always oblige my fair Helen," he said, gallantly holding his hand out to her. "Being a gentleman and all, as you say. I am your servant, Diana. Pray, let me take you from this place, to one more, ah, seemly and decent."

The way he'd used the same words she had rung as

another warning, but before she could decide why, Roxby had taken her arm firmly in his grasp and was pulling her through the door and down the hall, away from the noisy scene in the ballroom below. Without the shawl or mask, she now felt more vulnerable than ever, and overly conscious of how wantonly her body moved without the security of her stays to contain it.

"You're returning me to my rooms, yes?" she asked, daring to hope.

"No," said Roxby, his pace quickening. "I should rather believe mine shall suit us better."

"Yours!" she repeated with horror. "No, Roxby, I cannot, not alone, not dressed like this, and at this hour!"

"Oh, surely you can, lovey," said Stanver, grasping her other arm. "He's going to be your husband, and you must trust and honor your husband, there's a good girl. Or is it honor and obey?"

"But he's not my husband now!" she protested, struggling as the two men pulled her into Roxby's bedchamber. "I owe him nothing, nor will I ever, for I've no intention of ever, ever marrying him after this! Free me, Roxby! Free me *now!*"

"After such venomous, cruel words from you, my dear?" said Roxby, shoving the heavy door shut after them. Swiftly he turned the key in the lock with a decisive click, and set it up high on the molding over the door, well beyond Diana's reach. "When you accepted my offer of marriage, you lost your freedom to refuse me again, for I will not be scorned. Not by you, not by any mere woman."

"*No!*" she cried, kicking and plunging as the two men dragged her toward that enormous bed, the heavy curtains swept aside like those flanking a playhouse stage, the carved, gilded coronet centering the canopy rail an unnecessary reminder of Roxby's station and power. "I am *not* your wife!"

"In the blind eyes of the church, perhaps not," said Roxby, his face flushed as he and Stanver wrestled her flat onto the bed. "But possession counts for far more, my dear, and once you take my body and my seed into yours to bear my son, then you *are* mine. Hold her, Stanver, and mind she doesn't bite."

"You're mad, Roxby!" she cried, somehow terrified and furious at the same time. "How could I ever have loved you?"

She heard fabric tearing and saw Roxby toss aside the top layer of her gown: what was left must be virtually transparent. Trying to writhe away, she sank deeper into the feather bed as Stanver pressed her shoulders down, his body smelling powerfully of his own unwashed sourness and spilled brandy and the cloying, flowery perfume he used to hide the rest.

She had a quick glimpse of Roxby's face, the slight smile of undeniable satisfaction as he pulled his arms free of his coat and waistcoat, tossing them to the floor in his haste, and began opening the buttons on the fall of his breeches.

"It doesn't matter if you love me or not, my dear," he said, breathing hard, lowering himself over her. "All you need know is that I have won, and you are my prize."

"You *bastard!*" she hissed, twisting her face away from his.

"That's it, sweetheart, look to my buttons for divine guidance," said Stanver, almost giggling as he pushed one of the oversized buttons on his waistcoat into

Diana's face. The button was exquisitely painted, a representation in miniature of a tiny Leda being ravished by the amorous swan. "Between us old Lord Roxby and I can show you every cunning position out of Aretino, and a few of our own invention, too."

Even without looking, she felt Roxby freeze.

"You misspeak, Stanver," he said, his voice taut with warning. "Diana will be my marchioness, my *wife*, and mine alone."

"The hell she will," scoffed Stanver scornfully. "Since when haven't we shared wenches, wed or not, even the high-bred ones?"

"Since now," said Roxby sharply. "I'll raise no cuckoos in my nest, Stanver, especially not yours. I want to know my son's mine."

She sensed the change in focus, how they were now more intent on quarreling between themselves than over her, with Roxby easing back from her to concentrate on Stanver.

She swallowed, marshaling both her strength and her courage. She'd only have this one chance, and she'd have to make it count or blame herself the rest of her life.

Once James had called her his own brave lass. For the sake of that memory, she could be brave again, couldn't she?

"Fine words to come from *you*, Roxby," Stanver was saying, not bothering to hide his contempt, "considering how damned muddled your own family is."

Now, she told herself, *now!*

As fast as she could she curled her legs up together and kicked them hard into Roxby's unbuttoned flesh. The heels of her sandals caught him low and off balance, making him grunt with pain. For an instant his face still hovered over hers, his expression of surprised agony most un-Roxby-like, and then he toppled backward, groaning and clutching at himself instead of her.

"What in blazes—" began Stanver, relaxing his grip on Diana's arms as he gawked at Roxby, and as he did she made her hand into a fist and struck him under the jaw and into his windpipe, the way her brothers had taught her. He gurgled and flailed, clutching at his throat, his one thought being to find his next breath.

And Diana didn't wait. As quickly as she could she rolled from the bed and began running as soon as her sandaled feet hit the polished floor. The door to the hallway was still locked, but another door led to Roxby's dressing room, and through it she rushed, heedless of how her tattered clothes were slipping from her body. Maybe her luck was finally changing, for not only was there no sign of Roxby's manservant, but the key to that door was resting in the lock as well. With both hands she slammed the heavy door shut and turned the key, locking them in on the other side, then hurried into the adjoining chamber that served Roxby as a sort of private sitting room and office. But she wouldn't be safe here for long. She could hear the two men recovering enough to begin swearing at each other, and at her.

Her heart racing, she had only a few seconds to decide where to head next. She could, of course, go back to her rooms, where they'd be sure to look first, or return to the ballroom to ask for help from the others—a dubious choice at best, considering those others were Roxby's friends and likely to condone, not condemn, what he and Stanver had been doing to her.

Her gaze swept around the room, settling on the tall

casement windows. Just outside them she could make out the shadowy outline of another century-old holly tree similar to the one near her own window. They'd never expect her to escape that way—what lady would climb down a tree, twenty feet from the ground? As swiftly as she could, she swung her legs through the window onto the broad stone sill and reached back to shut the window after her. She didn't know if Helen of Troy had had to do any tree climbing during her various adventures, but as immodest as the short-skirted gown now was, it made Diana's escape far easier than if she'd been hampered by full petticoats and hoops. Balancing briefly on the sill, she leaned forward to grab the nearest branch and pulled herself past the prickly leaves and into the middle of the tree.

And relished her first, giddy, precarious taste of freedom.

"Where do you think she is, Brighty?" asked James softly, reaching up to stroke the little cat riding on his shoulder. "Take your bearings, my lad, and mark her window for me if you can."

Yet even as James stared up at the sprawling expanse of Ashburnham Hall before him, he was also adding *jackass* to all the other names he'd already been calling himself since he'd let Diana go earlier that day. To have come here at this hour, nearly midnight, to stand here in the dark on the ludicrous hope that a kitten could somehow guide him to Diana so he could apologize to her before he left for Portsmouth—high holy hell, was there anything that better defined blind jackass faith than that?

As if registering his own opinion, Brighty mewed, and pushed his muzzle against James' ear, tickling James' neck with his whiskers.

"Oh, aye, so you're no hunting dog," he said with a sigh, "and there's no saying she'd wish to see my face again if I found her. Looks like they've some grand frolic tonight, doesn't it? Likely that suits her better, too."

The long, low silhouette of the house was punctuated with candlelight glowing through its windows, with the brightest flare reserved for the tall windows in the far corner, where James knew lay the ballroom. The evening was warm, and the windows had been opened, and James could just make out the shapes of guests moving back and forth between the party and the gardens and back again. The sounds of violins drifted erratically on the breeze, though not nearly as strong as the raucous laughter of women and men who'd had too much drink.

"Roxby does know how to amuse himself," said James, trying not to imagine Diana in the middle of all that riotous amusement, and, of course, absolutely failing.

She'd be wearing one of those fine-lady gowns of smuggled French silk, and she'd be laced so tight at the waist that her breasts would seem to spill out from the top, and she'd be glittering with jewels, Roxby's jewels, and when she'd laugh and smile she'd make the candlelight seem dull by comparison. She'd make a man babble all manner of nonsense, just to keep her attention, and he hated thinking of all the men in there now doing exactly that, crowding around her, begging her to dance and smile and laugh at them.

Especially Roxby. What was it, next week, that they

were to wed? Hell, James didn't want to think of that, not tonight, not ever.

But she could have been his. This afternoon, on the same bed where he'd suffered and fought so hard to come back from death to where he now was, she'd made the final, greatest offering of life and love, and he'd turned it down.

She could have been his.

If he hadn't been so damned full of pride—what was it Richard Lanker called it, his overnice church-yard scruples?—he would have accepted the love she'd offered, and if he hadn't been so damned frightened of himself, he would have offered his own love to her in return. Simple, neat, shipshape, and handsomely done.

But he hadn't, and now he'd go to sea and to war, maybe even to his death, never knowing what could have happened, what *should* have happened, while she'd marry Roxby.

"Come along, Brighty," he said sadly, softly. "Let's shove off."

But instead of settling on James' shoulder once again, Brighty yowled in protest, and before James could stop him, the little cat had flown from his shoulder and was racing across the grass, a pale gray streak threatening to vanish into the darkness.

The last time Brighty had bolted like this, Chou-Chou had been in hot pursuit and Diana had been quick to become his champion. But now, although Chou-Chou wasn't chasing him, Diana wasn't here for the res-cue either, and with a disgusted oath, James began following the cat across the lawn at a lopsided lope, already dreading how his leg would feel during the long ride to Portsmouth in the morning.

"Come back here, you infernal beast," he called as loudly as he dared, ducking beneath the prickly branches of a gnarled old holly tree. He could just make out the kitten, standing beside the trunk and peering up into the branches, his tail lashing with excitement. Likely the wicked creature had found some damned squirrel to chase, thought James, and reached to gather the kitten back into his arms.

But as he did, a rattling shower of dried holly leaves rained down on his shoulders. Muttering more oaths upon the squirrel, he straightened, just in time to scowl at Diana as she dropped to the ground at his feet.

"Oh, my, James, it *is* you!" she exclaimed breathlessly. "Oh, Gemini, my luck *must* be changing!"

He gulped, not sure what to say about luck or anything else, and put Brighty back onto his shoulder. It wasn't only that she'd appeared seemingly from the heavens. What stunned him most was that, except for a few filmy scraps of spangled nothingness, she appeared to have done so absolutely naked, a fact that became astoundingly obvious when she threw her arms around him in the fondest embrace.

"Diana," he said, clearing his throat as he touched his hand upon her back in the lightest, most respectful way possible. "Diana, you, ah, surprise me."

"And you even brought Brighty for good luck." She pushed back to look up at him and tried to smile, and only then did he realize she was crying, wet trails of tears glistening on her cheeks. She raised her hands to take the cat from his shoulder, and he used the chance to pull off his coat and wrap it around her, sturdy dark wool over that tattered sheer silk, and not a moment too soon, either.

"You are the perfect hero, James, my hero, coming to me like this, and after this afternoon, too," she said fiercely, clutching the edges of his coat with one hand and Brighty with the other. "How you knew—faith, how you *knew!*"

"Diana, tell me what in blazes—"

"Not now," she said, looking fearfully around as she began edging away from him, toward the open lawn. "We must run now, before they come after me. Hurry, *hurry!*"

"Who's seeking you?" he demanded, following her as she scurried from beneath the holly tree and across the grass. "What have they done to you, Diana?"

"Roxby, of course, and Lord Stanver, too," she said, the tears in her voice as well as her eyes as she seized his hand to urge him to hurry, "and oh, we haven't *time*, James!"

But they were already too late.

The man's untucked shirt billowed around him as he unsteadily stepped into their path, the long barrel and jewel-studded butt of the pistol in his hand catching what light there was.

"Why, you ungrateful little bitch," said Lord Stanver, using both hands to aim the oversized gun at Diana. "How dare you leave poor Roxby like that?"

14

Swiftly James moved between Stanver and Diana, shielding her as best he could. The man was clearly drunk, but what was less obvious was whether the pistol in his hand was even loaded. From the way he was waving it about, James suspected the damned fool wouldn't know the difference when he was sober, either. But he couldn't risk depending on that, not at this close range, and especially not with Diana as his target. And where the hell was Roxby hiding himself in all this?

Jesus, what *had* been happening in the house before she'd fled?

"Take yourself off, my lord," he ordered, using his sternest captain's voice. "Miss Fairbourne's not going anywhere with you."

Stanver snorted disdainfully and waved the gun with an ostentatious flourish. "The devil you say, and to pay, too. I'm the one with the pistol, aren't I?"

"You mean you're the one Roxby's sent to do his toady work," jeered Diana, leaning around James. She didn't try to keep the scorn and bitterness from her voice, and once again James wondered what had happened earlier between them. "Where is Roxby, anyway?"

"He went off to the other side of the garden, while I came here," said Stanver, his scowl blacker than the night around them. "And I am not doing Roxby's toady work. I'm looking for you. Gad, but you're a faithless little piece, that's what you are, and I don't know why he's so damned hot and determined to wed you."

"You don't talk like that to her," said James sharply, his gaze following the oversized pistol. If only Diana distracted him enough—and she was doing a most admirable job of it—then perhaps he could knock the gun from the man's hands. But they couldn't afford to wait too long, not with Roxby prowling about as well. Stanver was unpredictable enough alone, but combined with Roxby he'd be infinitely more dangerous. "You address Miss Fairbourne like the lady she is, mind?"

"And besides," said Diana vehemently, her hand resting lightly on the back of James' waist, "I am not going to marry Roxby, Stanver, and I never will, so I don't give a tinker's damn what you think of me."

"Ehh?" asked Stanver, clearly stunned by such a pronouncement. "You don't want to be Marchioness of Roxby? Every woman in England wants to marry Roxby. Why the devil should you be any different?"

And as much as James loathed having anything in common with Stanver, he had to admit that he was just as stunned, and just as eager to hear Diana's reply.

"Because I'm not like every other wretched woman in England," she declared, and despite the precariousness of their situation, James fair warmed with pride for her independence. That was *his* Diana talking, his lass.

"And," she continued, her voice rising, "because I've found another man I love truly, who'll love me for who I am, not what he can make of me, the way Roxby wants. Can you fathom that, Stanver? I don't love Roxby, not as I should, and now I'm not sure I ever did."

James fought the impossible urge to turn around and pull her into his arms and kiss her. *She loved him!* She loved *him,* and not Roxby, and he wanted to laugh aloud with the joy of it.

But to his even greater surprise, James saw he wasn't the only one experiencing these same feelings, and it wasn't just Diana, either.

"You don't love Roxby?" asked Stanver, his face glowing with bewilderment at what he believed was his incredible good fortune. "You don't love Roxby. Gad."

He took one step toward them, his gaze intent on Diana, then another step. "You love some other, ah, other gentleman instead, a poor fellow who'd love you with all his humble heart if you'd accept him, and not Roxby. True love, oh yes, the truest for you, my dear! And *not* Roxby, hah, hah!"

The pistol began to droop in his hands, forgotten now, and James tensed, ready to lunge, trying not to think of the horrible, twisted mockery of love he'd just heard Stanver describe.

Steady, he told himself, steady, steady . . .

"My turn," muttered Stanver. "True love!"

But with that last "love," Brighty suddenly screamed with a banshee cat's fury and hurled himself from Diana's arms to Stanver's chest, raking the man with his outstretched claws. Stanver howled with pain and surprise and staggered backward, freeing one hand from the pistol to flail at the cat.

At once James lunged at Stanver, reaching for the gun as Brighty jumped clear. James had the advantage in size and sobriety, and as his body struck the other man the two of them fell hard to the ground, grunting and kicking and swinging wildly as they rolled over and over across the dew-wet grass. He was only vaguely aware of Diana's terrified face, glimpsed as she hovered beside them, too afraid of the gun to interfere.

But even as James fought for the pistol in Stanver's hand, relying on desperation and experience, some distant part of his brain made a horrifying realization: Stanver held the pistol tight in his left hand, not his right, his pudgy finger wedged in beside the trigger.

Meaning now that James must use his own right hand to claim the gun, his weak, useless hand, the one with the fingers that couldn't grasp that gun even if Stanver purposely placed it in James' palm.

With a groan of weariness and frustration, James tried to twist around to bring his left hand up, and as he did he shifted his weight just enough for Stanver to lower the gun and aim it point-blank at James' chest. He heard Diana scream, a faraway echo in his head, and to answer he made one last, desperate swing at the pistol, knocking the barrel back toward Stanver.

And as he did, the flintlock clicked, the gunpowder flashed in a puff of acrid smoke, and the lead ball exploded from the barrel. At such close range, the force of it slammed the gun back against James' chest, so hard he was sure he'd been shot himself, and automatically he cursed his misfortune, to have come so close to having Diana and to lose her—to fail her—like this.

But the inevitable, searing pain of a pistol's ball never came. Instead he heard Stanver gasp, then moan, then go slack against him, sliding free. Wet, sticky warmth—Stanver's blood—seeped against James' arm, and as quickly as he could he pushed himself clear of the wounded man.

"*James!*" cried Diana, hugging him close as she sobbed with relief. "You're alive! Oh, thank God, thank God, you're alive!"

"Aye," he said heavily, exhausted, unwilling to look back at the too-still man with the spreading dark stain on his white shirt, lying on the ground behind him. "Aye, this time, I am."

It shouldn't have ended like that. If he'd only been quicker, if he hadn't had to compensate for his useless hand, the gun never would have been fired. As it was, if Stanver wasn't yet dead, he would be soon. No man could long survive a wound like that one.

James rested his arms around Diana's shoulders, too spent now for anything else, even to acknowledge Brighty rubbing against his leg. He'd known he'd be heading back to war in the morning, but he'd never dreamed the killing would start again before he'd left.

"Here," said James softly as he lit the candle beside the bed, the same bed where they'd tussled earlier that day. Brighty had already taken his spot on the windowsill, blinking sleepily with his tail neatly curled around him. "You rest here while I go see if I can arrange for the hired cart to come now instead of waiting for dawn."

"No, James, please don't leave me," whispered Diana forlornly, her hands in tight fists as she stood on the far side of the bed. As long as they'd been moving, hurrying with a purpose across the dark fields back to the vicarage, she'd been fine, but now the cold shock of Stanver's shooting was settling around her. He could see it in her eyes and the way she held her shoulders, lifted and tense, and he could hear it in the quaver to her voice that betrayed how she was trembling.

He could scarcely fault her, either. He'd seen more men die than he could count, yet the horror and the suddenness of violent death always surprised him anew. And he was a man, an officer, trained for such things. What could it be like for a young woman like her?

"Please, James," she said again, more plaintively. "I— I know you've things to arrange for us, but I'd rather not be left alone just yet."

"You'll be safe enough here," he said as he pulled the blood-stained shirt over his head, one more reminder that she didn't need. Once Stanver's body was discovered, and Diana's disappearance linked to his death, there'd be no safe place for them in all of England. His commission, their future together, perhaps even their lives, would all hinge on fate and fortune and how vengeful Roxby would feel after his friend's death and his betrothed's rejection. "Roxby couldn't conceive of you coming here with the lowly likes of me."

"He cannot conceive of me with any man other than himself," she said bitterly. She sank down onto the edge of the bed, her shoulders huddled beneath the bulk of his coat, her unpinned hair hanging tangled around her face as she bowed her head. "But I did not think it would end like that. No, no, not like that."

He sighed wearily, and ran his left hand back through his hair. "I am sorry about Lord Stanver, Diana. I'd never wish for that to happen, especially before you."

"Do you truly believe I'd mourn for Stanver?" she whispered incredulously. "A vile worm of a man like that?"

"I didn't know, Diana, considering that—"

She took a deep breath, more of a gulp, her hands drumming with agitation on her knees.

"James, he helped drag me to Roxby's bedchamber against my will," she said in a frantic rush, "and then he held me down while Roxby tried to—tried to rape me. There, I've said it. He tried to rape me, James, with Stanver expecting his turn after. But I fought them. I did. I wouldn't let them do that to me."

"Jesus," said James, horrified. How could any man, even Roxby, do this to a woman he claimed to love, a woman he'd promised to *marry?* Yet as appalled and as furious as he was at Roxby, he'd have to take some of the blame himself, for he was the one who'd let her go this afternoon, back to Ashburnham and those two bastards and their private little hell.

"First they dressed me like a whore," she was saying, still drumming on her knees, "and then they tried to make me act as one. Oh, James, I'd wanted so much to be a grand, fine lady, but if that is what I must do to be one. . . ."

She let the words trail off, a lifetime of casual sin suggested in the silence, and a life that now she'd be mercifully spared.

"If I'd known," he said, outrage thick in his voice as

he struck his fist against the wall, "I would have killed Stanver outright myself, and Roxby, too."

"Oh, yes, and what good would that do?" she asked with another gulp, her tears leaving two streaky trails down her cheeks. "So that they'd hang you for murder?"

"Then marry me."

She looked up at him sharply, not trusting what she'd heard.

"Marry me, Diana," he said again, coming to sit beside her on the bed. "Honor me, and be my wife."

"Your wife." She stared at him incredulously, the wonder that filled her eyes spilling out in fresh tears. He hoped there was a bit of joy there, too, though by the candlelight, and after all she'd suffered this night, he wasn't sure. "Yours, Captain Dunham?"

"Aye, mine," he said firmly. He'd never given serious thought to asking a woman to marry him, let alone imagined the specifics of the event the way women seemed to, but he was certain it wouldn't have been like this, sitting on the low bed in his sister's back bedchamber, him splattered with a dead man's dried blood and the lady bruised and scratched from climbing down a holly tree, wearing little enough to make a fairy blush. But it was *right*, because Diana was right, the one woman in the world he loved and wanted to keep with him for the rest of his life.

"God knows I'm no prize, Diana," he said, taking her hand as carefully as if it had been spun from glass, uncurling the fingers that were still knotted into anxious fists. "But I love you, Diana, and I swear I've never said that to another woman. I love you, and if you meant what you told Stanver about—"

"About you?" she finished breathlessly. "It was you that I meant, you know. And I meant every last word, James. I love you, and I think I've always loved you, from the first, when you dared me to row you across the pond."

"I'm daring you again, lass, daring you to risk your life alongside mine," he said, his smile crooked with the hope she'd give him the answer he sought. "I'm damaged goods by anyone's standards, scarred and crooked as a jury-rigged ship. I've no title or great fortune to share—I haven't even a house of my own yet for you to mistress—and every time I put to sea there's a better than even chance I won't return. Hell, I cannot even say for certain what's to become of us twelve hours from now."

"You're a good, honorable man, James Dunham, and I won't listen to you say otherwise," she answered fiercely in the way he'd always loved so dearly about her. "You're worth a hundred Roxbys—no, a thousand!"

"But am I worth enough for you to wed?" he asked, his smile fading as he searched her face. "Worth enough to be your husband?"

Her smile wobbled, and she curled her arms around his neck to draw him close.

"Yes, you great foolish man," Diana whispered, her lips brushing against his cheek. "Yes, yes, *yes*."

She curled around to kiss him, daring him as he'd dared her. How could he have ever doubted that she'd accept? Her head had been foolish, true, but her heart— her heart had known from the beginning that he was the one, in a way she couldn't really explain.

But she could show him.

She knew how uncertain their future was, just as she knew the risks that he'd taken to bring her here. She, perhaps more than anyone, understood how dangerous and devious a man Roxby could be. In a twisted way, he'd cared for Stanver as a brother, and he'd wanted her as a wife. Now she and James had robbed him of both, and there was no way under heaven that he'd let them go unpunished.

These few minutes alone here, before they began to flee in earnest, could be the only ones they'd have to share. With Roxby after them, there'd be no guarantee that they'd ever actually have the chance to marry, or have children, or grow old in each other's company— but no, she wouldn't think of that now. If this was all they'd have together, then she was determined to make the very best of it.

She kissed him lightly, teasing his lips to part for her with a featherweight touch. She liked the differences she found, the roughness of his beard so late in the day contrasting to the softness that their lips now shared, and she slid her hands down his back, letting his coat begin to slip from her bare shoulders.

"There now, lass," he said, breaking the kiss and resolutely shifting away from her—away, but not so far that he showed any real inclination to stay apart. "We haven't time to begin this, not the way you deserve."

"Oh, yes, we do," she whispered, trying to be brave and convincing and confident, even though her palms were moist and her heart was beating far too fast. "I know we must be on our way, but I—oh, James, please don't let me have what Roxby tried to do as my only memory."

There, she hadn't meant to let her unhappiness show, any more than she'd intended to weep again. But to her surprise, it was that fat, hot tear of misery spilling from the corner of her eye that finally convinced him.

"Not Roxby," he growled, slipping his hands into his coat to bring her closer. "Us. Damnation, Diana, I want you to remember *us*."

He pushed the coat away and onto the floor and eased her across his lap. Dressed, or undressed, as she was, it was easy for her to slide her leg over his, and sit astride his lap with only his breeches between them and the ragged silk fluttering over her hips in a thoroughly unladylike fashion.

But thankfully she'd abandoned being a lady, and all that mattered now was being herself with James. Even through the cloth, she could feel the heat expanding between them, and the hardness of his erection pressing against her most sensitive places. She remembered how he'd touched her there this afternoon, and how wonderfully fascinating that touch had been. Partly from instinct, partly from experimentation, she moved herself against him, rocking gently, bracing herself with her hands on his bare chest.

He groaned and swore, dark, incoherent oaths of passion and longing that she found wildly exciting, and as she leaned forward to kiss him, she moved over him again.

"Nay, not so fast," he said hoarsely, slipping his left hand beneath the hem of her short gown to find the full curve of her hip. "I know we've not much time, but I won't let you run me aground."

His fingers spread, pressing into her flesh to hold her

there. Without thinking he tried to use his other hand as well, and swore again, this time with frustration, when instead he bumped it clumsily against her hip.

"Here," she whispered, guiding his arm around her waist. "Like that, yes?"

"Like this, aye," he said, and kissed her hungrily, deeply, as his fingers caressed her in impatient circles over her hips and bottom. She could feel the same hot, heavy tension building in her lower body, the overwhelming need to join with him, and when he eased her spread thighs farther apart to touch her, she gasped and clung to him, his shoulders sheened with sweat. He moved his fingers between her thighs now, touching her there, teasing that small, most tender place with the pad of his thumb until she felt swollen and wet and aching for the rest of him.

Yet still he refused to let her break their kiss, taking her startled little moans of pleasure into his mouth as his tongue echoed and reinforced the rhythm of his fingers. Though she felt like she was drowning in sensation, in pleasure, it still wasn't enough, and blindly she reached between them to unbutton the fall on his breeches. He helped her, freeing himself, then raised her until she felt the blunt end of his erection nudging against her.

She held herself there, poised, her breath coming in rapid little pants as he pushed into her. She gasped, trying not to remember Roxby's assault. James seemed a great deal larger this way, and a great deal more forcefully male, and she whimpered with anxiety, her hands clutching at his shoulders. But this *was* James, she told herself, and this *was* what she wanted, and yet things seemed to be happening a great deal faster than she'd thought they would.

"James," she whispered urgently, fighting her panic as he pressed farther into her. "James, I do not believe you shall—*ah!*"

With a single push, he was deep inside her, so deep their bodies now touched with her legs spread wide.

"There you are, my brave lass," he said hoarsely, running his palm along her spine to comfort her. "The worst is over, I promise."

But it didn't feel that way to Diana, not at all. Instead she felt stretched and filled and sore, without any of the joy and blinding pleasure that her mother had promised came with love.

"James," she said again, her voice quavering. "I am not sure I'm doing this properly."

"Oh, aye, you are, you are," he said with a groan. Gently he lifted her leg, shifting her position slightly to ease some of the pressure. He stroked the soft skin along the inside of her thigh, kissing her again as he gentled the tension from her muscles. "Now move again the way you did before, back and forth, as if you're riding the waves."

Privately she thought there was nothing wavelike about this, but for his sake she'd try to do what he'd suggested. She rose up on her knees tentatively, then sank down, and did it another time, then another, the motion growing easier and to her great surprise, more enjoyable.

Much more enjoyable.

He'd slipped the narrow strap of her gown from her shoulder, pulling the silk down to free her breast and taking her nipple into his mouth, licking and tugging at it with his tongue and the edge of his teeth. Sudden pleasure streaked through her, sharp and bright as lightning from her breast to the place where they were joined, and miraculously he no longer seemed too large, but exactly, precisely right for her.

She was gasping for air now, riding him harder, relishing the way he'd sink deep into her each time she lowered herself, slick and yielding, and how as she rose, her body seemed to cling to him greedily, unwilling to give up any part of him.

"This is love, Diana," he said, his voice so raw beside her ear that she could barely make out the words. "*Our* love."

"Oh, James!" she cried out, for he was moving, too, thrusting to meet her. "Oh, James, James, *James!*"

All thoughts fled except for this, and for him, riding the incredible waves of pleasure that kept coming like breakers in a storm, rushing forward each time to carry her higher, and higher still, and when she called out his name for the last time the wave broke, crashing and sweeping everything before it with a blinding rush of purest joy and release.

And love. Oh, yes, *this* was the man she loved the best, and always would.

"I do love you, Captain Dunham," she whispered as they lay together afterward, arms and legs tangled wantonly, her head upon his chest where she could listen to the rhythm of his heart. She felt more at peace here with him, on a low bed with a linsey-woolsey coverlet, beneath this rough sloping ceiling, than she ever had in all the solemn, gilded glory of Ashburnham.

"And I love you, too, Mrs. Captain," he said, chuckling as he gave her ear a small nibble. "Or at least the soon-to-be Mrs. Captain, and a fine thing, too, considering how much we please each other."

"Oh, vastly fine," she whispered happily, "and vastly pleasing, too."

"Aye." He sighed and sat upright, running his hand fondly over her hip. "But as pleasing and fine and everything else as this has been, we'd do well to clear off now."

"I know. We've no choice, not really." Diana sighed, too, as Brighty jumped down beside her on the bed, settling into the warm place left by James. Absently she stroked the kitten's back while she pillowed her head on her arm to watch James as he rose from the bed and began to wash in the basin in the corner. He was a handsome man, her future husband, well-made and well-favored. She was pleased to see how much less guarded he'd become about letting her see his scars, how he trusted her. Strange how comfortable she felt with him, as if they already were an old wedded couple, and her heart lurched when she thought of how soon he'd sail.

"All my things are packed, of course," he was saying, "but as for you, I don't——"

"Take me with you, James," she said softly. "Not just to Portsmouth, but to sea. Take me with you on the *Amazon*."

"To sea?" He turned, frowning. "Diana, I do not believe a ship of war is a decent place for a lady."

"But I'm not a lady!" she cried, rolling over onto her stomach with a pillow bunched in her arms. "That is, I'm not a lady who needs pampering and hot tea in the afternoon like clockwork. You forget my sailor family, James. Why, I've likely put in enough time at sea to stand for a lieutenant's exam! I don't mind storms or rough seas, and I could be useful, too, keeping your log or mending your shirts or——"

"Diana, no," he said gently. "It's not that I wouldn't wish to have you there—God knows how I'm going to leave you behind as it is—but I can't put you at that risk. The first time we engage a French ship, the first broadside we—"

"Then I shall go below into the hold," she answered promptly, "or to the cockpit to help with the surgeon and his mate. You're a captain, and I know that captains are entitled to take their wives with them. I tell you, James, I could be most useful, or leastways I can obey orders to keep clear. I do know how to do that."

He smiled, skeptical of the order-taking, but she knew, she *knew* his resolve was wavering. "What would happen to you if we were captured?"

"What would happen if I stayed here, meek and mild as you wished, and Roxby found me?" she fired back. "I have no family, no friends of my own in Portsmouth, nor in all England, truth to tell. Oh, please, please, my dearest, dearest love, don't leave me behind!"

"Jamie?" The three quick knocks on the door were perfunctory, the knocker knowing her welcome was assured. Without further warning Celia opened the door, an apparition of righteous surprise in a full white night rail and outsized ruffled cap, her hair in twin braids hanging over her breasts and a thoroughly astonished look on her face. "My word, Jamie! I'd no notion you had a, ah, *visitor*."

"This is Miss Fairbourne, Celia," said James quickly, grabbing a clean shirt from a peg on the back of the door. "Miss Diana Fairbourne, of Appledore, in the New England colonies. Diana, may I present my sister Celia, that is, Mrs. Oliver Chase?"

"I am honored to make your acquaintance, Mistress Chase," said Diana, scrambling miserably to wrap herself in the coverlet from the bed. "Vastly honored."

But Celia wasn't in the mood for pleasantries. "Miss Fairbourne," she said with grim disapproval, folding her arms over her chest. "You're the one who's to marry Lord Roxby, aren't you? Then why, pray, are you here *dawdling* with Jamie in his bed?"

Swiftly Diana slid from the guilty bed, no real improvement, for in the process the coverlet failed to cover the tattered remains of her short, spangled Helen costume or the sandals that laced over her bare shins to her knees. To her horror she also realized how much the small, close room smelled of her and James, the unmistakable musky scents of intimacy.

"I was to marry Lord Roxby, yes ma'am," she explained hurriedly, dipping a hasty curtsy, as if that could possibly help. "I was, but I'm not now. No. Now I am going to marry James instead."

"All true, Celia," said James, coming to stand behind Diana, his hands on her shoulders to reassure her. "Miss Fairbourne has done me the honor of accepting my offer of marriage."

Pointedly Celia sniffed, her gaze once again considering the rumpled bedclothes as well as their own disheveled appearances. "I should say, Jamie, that you have had your wedding night well before your wedding. Well, no matter, and nothing that, in this house, cannot be put to rights at once, though it won't be quite proper without the banns and all. I'll go wake Oliver."

"No, Celia, don't," said James quickly. "I don't want

him mired in any of this. He depends too much on Roxby's favor to ask him to risk so much for me."

Celia frowned, the lowered arch of her brows reminding Diana very much of James. "So his lordship does not yet know your glad tidings, or his own loss?"

"I told him, ma'am," said Diana quickly. "But I cannot say that he was pleased."

"I daresay not. Miss Fairbourne, we must find you something more seemly to wear."

Diana flushed, gathering Brighty into her arms to give them something to do. "This was fancy dress, not what I ordinarily wear, of course," she said, chattering from nervousness, "and it was seemly enough for Roxby's ball. I was Helen, you see, and his lordship was Paris."

"Indeed," said Celia dryly, unconvinced. "Better he should have been gotten up as Menalaus. He was the abandoned husband, you recall, the wounded party, whilst my brother, as the merry seducer in this affair, would make the more proper Paris, come to carry off Helen."

"Damnation, Celia," said James, the warning in his voice clear. "That's enough."

"I could say the same to you, brother," answered Celia sharply. "And I will, if—merciful heavens, what happened to that shirt? Oh, Jamie, if that is blood—"

"Burn it," he said curtly. "As soon as you can. All I will tell you, Celia, is that aye, a man did die, but by his own hand, not mine."

"Oh, brother, brother," said Celia unhappily, holding her hands to her cheeks with dismay. "You have ruined yourself over this, haven't you? All you've suffered during your recovery, all you've achieved, your splendid record with the navy, all of it gone, and for what? For what?"

"I love Diana, Celia," he said, curling his arm protectively around Diana's waist. "I would not have asked her to be my wife otherwise."

"And I love him in return," said Diana quickly. "I've given up much for your brother, mistress, yet I do not regret any of it, because I love him, and him alone."

Celia's lips pressed tightly together, more sad than angry now. "Then I pray you'll always be able to say that and believe it with every bit of your heart. Because when this is done, Miss Fairbourne, love could be all that you and Jamie have left to your names, and may God have mercy on your miserable souls if it's not enough."

The surgeon called from Winchester was small and elderly, and so nervous to be entrusted with the care of a nobleman that his wig kept slipping upon the stream of sweat from his forehead.

"Lord Stanver's wound is most grave, my lord," he was saying with another one of his infernal, bobbing bows. "It will certainly prove mortal, my lord. With great sadness I fear I can predict his untimely demise before noon."

What a pompous little idiot, thought Roxby impatiently, looking over his head to where Stanver lay on what would, it seemed, become his deathbed. His face was already as pale as the linen pillow-bier, gray green, really, and the familiar fleshy red cheeks were somehow already diminished and sunken. Each breath was labored and agonizing, another small cheat against death, though he'd never regained consciousness and now likely never would. Beneath the coverlet, the surgeon had contrived a bulky patch of a bandage to absorb the blood that was relentlessly pumping from him, but Roxby had already seen how much had stained the ground where Stanver had fallen——he himself had been the one to find Stanver with the dawn this morning, the one who'd pried the pistol from his friend's chilly fingers——and how much more blood had been swabbed away to make him presentable enough to be put to bed.

It was a miracle the poor bastard hadn't been completely drained dry by now, lustily emptied like the last bumper of the night. If it had been any other man lying there, Stanver would have been the first to make a wager of it, laying odds to the exact hour when he'd leave this life for the next, and precisely how much blood there'd be left in the corpse when it happened.

Not that he'd find any takers from the somber, silent group gathered around his bed——Pember, Barleigh, Walters, even Allington with ivy leaves still over one ear, blubbering worse than the harlots with the lace handkerchiefs——not a one of them with any right to be there, as if Stanver needed mourning before he was even dead.

He'd been so damned proud of that blasted Spanish pistol, waving it about like Dick Turpin himself, and soon he'd be just as dead, the fat, bumbling ass. For that matter, Stanver had been a fat, bumbling ass as long as Roxby had known him. It was one of his especial charms. No, *had* been: Roxby knew he must grow accustomed to the proper tense, just as, somehow, he'd have to grow accustomed to life without Stanver following along in his shadow.

And somehow it was all Diana's fault, might the cunning bitch burn in the deepest, blackest, matrimonial hell that he could contrive for her. For each wracking breath that Stanver now drew, he'd make sure she'd pay double, and the moment he found her and had his fingers around that lovely white throat of hers, he'd—

"*Por favore, mi signori,*" said the small woman with the sad, shadowed eyes, dipping her curtsy so low that her black skirts fanned around her on the floor. "You had asked me to be aware, *mi signori,* to search."

She handed him a crumpled paper, the single sheet still carrying the folds of a letter. Only four words were written inside—YOU WERE MAGNIFICENT, LASS—the handwriting coarse, clumsy, common, most definitely not a gentleman's hand.

God, had she taken one of the footmen for her lover, or worse, a groom from the stable? Had she run off to London with one of them? Ah, he'd believed her to be so pure, such an innocent, when she'd been spreading her legs for any base-born rascal who wanted her.

"Beneath her pillow, *mi signori,*" the maid was saying. "After Portsmouth, with Lady Marchmont."

Portsmouth and Harriet Marchmont, the Ladies' Ship and a town filled with sailors. . . .

Including one sailor with a crippled hand, a great strapping captain who'd write like a child but still could give her enough of what she wanted to be "magnificent," a black-hearted, traitorous rascal who'd tried to give him a cuckold's horns even as he'd curried his favor.

Carefully Roxby folded the letter and tucked it into his pocket, glancing one last time at Stanver, as much farewell as he'd deign to show before the others. Stanver could live for another hour or two, another hour or two that Roxby didn't want to waste.

"Guilietta," he said as he turned away. "Ask one of the men to call for my coach as soon as it can be brought. For Portsmouth, Guilietta. You may tell them that. For Portsmouth."

And for Diana Fairbourne, and for James Dunham.

And most of all, for Stanver.

"Where is Roxby?" demanded Allington as the surgeon closed the dead man's eyes. "He must answer to this. If what Stanver just told us is true—"

"Of course it's true," snapped Barleigh. "Dying men don't waste their breath making up tales. And mind you, Roxby was the one who found poor Stanver in the garden. Even had the audacity to carry that foolish Spanish pistol back into the house himself, bold as you please."

Allington nodded, turning his back as the surgeon pulled away the covers to begin preparing the body. Keeping company with a friend while he passed from one life to the next was a good Christian's duty, but he'd draw the line at attending a corpse, especially one as mangled as Stanver's. "I saw him with Roxby and the girl earlier, in that little gallery in the ballroom. God only knows what games the three of them were about, but even Roxby must answer to this."

The other two men nodded solemnly as the maidservant returned, curtsying before Allington.

"*Mi signori* has gone," she said. "Urgent business in Portsmouth."

"Urgent, ha. He's run," declared Allington. "The action of a guilty man, I'll vow. Barleigh, your horses are the fastest. Send one of your men to follow Roxby's coach to Portsmouth. I'll go to my father directly, at Barchester House."

"You would involve his grace?" asked Walters, more than a little in awe of Allington's father, the Duke of Barchester. "I say, Roxby's always been a friend."

"So was Stanver," said Allington grimly. "My father's the only man of rank higher than Roxby in the county. He must be involved, else Roxby will sail away clean as a whistle. And after what we have heard this night—no, we must act. Upon our honor, we must act now."

15

"*W*e did not expect t' see you back among us so soon, Cap'n Dunham," said the cheerful porter at the door of the Blue Anchor. "Might I take that basket for you, Cap'n?"

The covered wicker basket hissed, swinging from James' hand with sufficient menace that the porter thought better of his offer and backed away instead.

"Will you be bidin' long wit' us, cap'n," he said from a more respectful distance, "or only a night or two?"

"Not even one this time, Abraham," said James, patting Diana's hand where she'd looped it through his crooked arm. "I'm reporting to my new commission today, and I've already shipped my dunnage along. You'll know the vessel, I'm sure. The *Amazon*."

"The devil it is, Captain!" cried Abraham with delighted amazement, quickly muzzled for Diana's sake. "That is, beg pardon, mistress, for speaking so afore you."

Diana grinned back at him, even though beneath the heavy black mourning veil she doubted the man could make out the shape of her face, let alone her smile. She could scarcely see out herself, and without James to guide her she was certain she'd have toppled headfirst from the step of the hired cart into the street.

The black mourning gown and the small brimmed hat with the veil had been Celia's idea of a disguise, and grudgingly Diana had to admit it was a good one. Not only did it hide every inch of her person, but widows in general were nearly invisible in society, sad little harbingers of death that most people seemed to choose not to see at all.

"I'm here for Captain Lanker, Abraham," said James. "This lady and I have business with him. Do you know if he's about?"

"Cap'n Lanker?" Abraham nodded vigorously. "Oh, aye, aye, he be here at table, seein' as it's nearly mess time."

"Tell Captain Lanker I should like to see him," said James. "And privately, in one of the little parlors, too. This poor lady has suffered enough without being paraded before the rest of those rascals at their trough."

Abraham tugged on the front of his knitted cap and ushered them to a small receiving room before he disappeared in search of Captain Lanker. Carefully Diana felt for a chair before she sat, unwilling to trust only to the murky shadows she saw through the veil and fearing to end up sitting on the floor instead.

"Perdition, James," she grumbled crossly as she tried to rearrange the veiling. "It's hot as blazes in here, nor can I see my own nose before me. I do wish you and your sister would have let me dress as your cabin boy, the way *I* wanted. I would have been much happier in breeches and a homespun shirt, I can assure you."

James chuckled, opening the basket to lift Brighty

onto his shoulder. "You would have made the prettiest cabin boy in Portsmouth, and the least likely one, too. There are some women who can pass for men and no one spares them a single glance, but not you, lass."

"But I do not see—"

"Nor would you," he said, running his hand down Brighty's back and scattering gray fur over his dark blue coat. "Your, ah, bottom is not a boy's bottom, and your bosom is not a boy's scrawny chicken-chest, especially not in breeches and a shirt. I'd have to flog the men away from you, rigged out like that. The mourning is much the wiser course."

"Especially since you're not the one dragging all this hideous heavy stuff about with you," she said and sighed wistfully. He was dressed as befitted a successful captain, ready to take command of his new ship, from the crown of his laced black hat to the tip of his presentation sword, to the polished buckles on his shoes, all enough to make her sigh again.

"It's not just the inconvenience of it, James," she said. "I don't like beckoning fate like this, pretending to be a widow when I'm not even a wife."

"But you will be soon enough, love," he said fondly. "My wife, that is. I plan to keep you safe from widow-hood for, oh, at least a good hundred years or so."

"James, you rogue!" boomed Captain Lanker even before he'd entered the parlor, his hand outstretched to clasp James' hand. "Captain of the *Amazon!* How many ladies did you have to please for that, eh? How many—"

"Hold your blasted tongue, Richard," ordered James, and from the belated throat clearing and coughing that Diana heard, she guessed the two men were gesturing and mouthing silent warnings back and forth around her. "I've told this lady you were a gentleman and a friend, and I'll thank you not to make a liar of me in less than a minute."

"My, ah, apologies, ma'am," said Captain Lanker contritely, making some sort of good-natured bow before her. "And my, ah, shared sorrow on your grief. Was your husband another brother officer, ma'am?"

James groaned, while Brighty purred. "I'm not sure this is an improvement, Richard. A mannerly Lanker—next the moon will drop from the sky and pigs shall sprout wings and fly to France!"

"And you, *Captain* Dunham, can kiss my—ah, er, nether parts."

Diana laughed, unable to help herself, and with both hands swept the veil back from her face.

"Good day, Captain Lanker," she said, "and how glad I am to meet you at last!"

But Richard only stared, his mouth gaping open with a kind of worshipful disbelief. He was an enormous bear of a man, with huge hands and feet and a nose to match, and worshipful disbelief did not sit comfortably upon his massive features.

"You, ma'am," he said slowly. "You are—"

"Miss Diana Fairbourne," said James firmly. "Once betrothed to the Marquess of Roxby and now to me. We want you to marry us, Richard. We *need* you to marry us today, as soon you can manage it."

"Me?" If possible, Richard's oversized jaw dropped another fraction lower. "Now?"

"Now," answered James. "Before Roxby realizes he's lost her to the better man."

"But me to do the marrying." Anxiously Richard shook his head. "Why, I've never done such a thing before, James, not for anyone."

"It's simple enough," said James. "The way I've understood it, any captain or admiral on board can do it, and there's no bothering with bishops or banns or such. You've read the service for the dead scores of times, haven't you? It's much the same, perhaps even shorter."

Richard glanced uneasily at Diana. "You said that, James, not I. Mark that well, Miss Fairbourne. *I* never likened marriage to heaving a corpse over the side."

But though Diana told herself he was only jesting, the mention of the corpse immediately reminded her of how terribly fragile life was, of Stanver and the gun and Roxby too, of all she wanted to escape—and almost had. She looked at James standing beside her with his matchmaking cat asleep on his shoulder, his own impossibly dear face so serious that she knew he was thinking the same things. Her fingers crept up to take his, seeking the comfort only he could offer, and she fought the tears that were once again threatening to spill over.

Oh, how quickly life could slide from laughter to tears, from joy to grieving!

"Please, Captain Lanker," she said softly. "I know it is a tremendous favor to ask, but I love James—Captain Dunham—so much, and if I do not marry him now, I am afraid that Roxby will try to stop us, and then it shall never happen."

Richard's face softened, so much that Diana almost wondered if he would shed a tear himself on her behalf.

"Oh, aye, it will," he declared, striking one fist against the open palm of the other. "It will, missy, because I'm the one who'll do it. Hell, we'll do it now, if you wish. I've had my dinner, and I can challenge the entire world once I've a full belly."

"Now?" she asked, her smile wobbling. "Here?"

Gallantly he held his arm out to her, while James offered his on the other side, and with a tremulous grin Diana stood between the two men, glancing shyly from one to the other. Once again she thought of Roxby and Stanver, men graced with every blessing the world could offer. Yet these two common-bred captains were so far their superiors in all the ways that mattered that she could not ask for better, more honorable champions, an unimaginable luxury after having to depend so much on herself. Her future wasn't secure yet, but for the first time she let herself dare to imagine it could be possible, and she squeezed James' arm a little more tightly just to reassure herself.

But they'd barely begun walking down High Street toward the harbor, Brighty once again unhappily confined to his traveling basket, when a dark green coach came to a rumbling stop on the cobblestones ahead of them.

"Captain Dunham, oh, Captain Dunham!" called Harriet Marchmont, and Diana didn't have to see her to know she must be leaning from the coach's window, waving a handkerchief, with Chou-Chou barking furiously on the seat behind her. "Here, here, Captain Dunham, come, so I might congratulate you on your new commission!"

"Ah, I know I've seen this lovely creature before," asked Richard in a loud, appreciative whisper as they walked toward the coach. "Quick, James, remind me of her name, before I make an ass of myself."

"She's the lady with the accomplished toes," said James cryptically. "Good day, Lady Marchmont! Thank you for your good wishes, my lady, and for any efforts you might have put forth on my behalf."

"Oh, yes, yes, you are most welcome," answered Lady Marchmont hurriedly. "But who, pray, is this other splendid, handsome hero? How vastly *epic* you are, sir! An introduction, Captain, I beg of you!"

But Diana was equally impatient, lifting her veil with both hands as she stood on her tiptoes beside the carriage.

"Harriet!" she cried excitedly. "Oh, Harriet, you are exactly in time! Captain Dunham and I are going to be married, this very moment, and Captain Lanker here is going to marry us on board his ship!"

"He *is*?" exclaimed Lady Marchmont, glancing coyly at Richard from beneath the sweeping brim of a low-crowned lace hat. "How wondrously romantic of you, Captain Lanker, for——*whom* did you say you're marrying, Diana? Wherever is Roxby? And why are you dressed in those hideous, hideous weeds?"

"Roxby is at Ashburnham," said Diana, "or at least he was when I——we——left him there last night. Oh, Harriet, so many things have happened since I saw you last!"

Lady Marchmont narrowed her eyes reproachfully. "More properly since Roxby sent *me* away, Diana, packing me off as if I were some squalid parlor maid who'd filched the best spoons! But here, hop in beside me, and tell me all."

"That is kind of you, Harriet," said Diana, hanging **back beside James,** "but since James and Captain Lanker and I are all going to——"

"Oh, piffle, I meant *all* of you!" She unlatched the door, not waiting for the footman who now hurried to unfold the carriage step. "There is quite enough room inside, and I shall take you wherever you need go, as long as I might be one of your witnesses. Yes, I will, do not deny me! Here, Captain Lanker, beside me, we shall be cozy together. Oh, my, Captain, you are *such* a large and well-made sort of gentleman."

But Lady Marchmont's ebullience faded when Diana told her of Lord Stanver's death. While James sat grim faced beside her, Diana also haltingly described her last night at Ashburnham, omitting the most shameful details on account of Richard Lanker's presence. Even then, it wasn't a pretty tale, and the wedding party's mood as they reached the wharf was somber at best.

"I'm sorry you had to hear about Roxby again, James," said Diana softly as they sat side by side on the bench of the cutter that would carry them out to where Richard's sloop *Dragon* was moored. Though she took his hand, lacing her fingers into his, to her sorrow she still could feel the tension in him. "But I thought as our friends, they should know why there is such—such haste to our marriage."

"I do not fault you for telling them, lass," he said, the tension in his voice as well, as he stared past her and over the water. "It's only that hearing again what Roxby and Stanver did to you—I would have killed them if I'd been there, Diana. I would have killed them outright."

"Oh, James, please don't say such things," she pleaded urgently, glancing at the others sitting in the sternsheets with them as well as the men before them at the oars. "If the wrong person heard you—"

"I don't care who hears it, Diana," he said with a tight-lipped smile, "because it's true. Which is why it's probably best if I don't cross paths with that bastard Roxby again in this life. I'd hardly be the husband you deserve if I end up dancing from a yardarm for murdering a peer."

"If I can put behind me everything Roxby did, then I pray you can as well," she said unhappily, wishing he'd stop this black talk on the way to their wedding. "Cannot you think instead of us and our future together as lovers, as husband and wife?"

Still gazing out over the water, he made one of those low, grumbly noises that meant he'd prefer not to answer. Didn't he have enough of death and dying with the war, without looking for more in the guise of avenging her? She slipped her fingers free of his, curling her hands around Brighty's basket in her lap and blinked to keep back the tears.

Lord, Lord, all she seemed to be doing these last days was crying, or trying not to. What was it about love that magnified every one of her emotions, making the joy so perfect but the pain so keen?

Even the weather seemed to have grown more ominous, the clouds gray and threatening, the sea dark and choppy with whitecaps, and the mists on the horizon making the low profile of the Isle of Wight fade in and out of sight. In the open boat, Diana had given up fighting the mourning veil and had pulled it off. Now the wind-blown spray stung at her face and tugged at her hair as the cutter fought its way up and down through the waves.

Sitting on the bench behind them with Richard, Lady

Marchmont was unusually quiet, doubtless struggling to keep from parting with her dinner, but for Diana the endless motion of the little boat was oddly comforting, reminding her of so much that was dear to her. She glanced back at James, at his handsome, stern profile, and with frustration wondered what sort of murderous thoughts he was now considering. Surely no sharp at the gaming table could more ably mask and control his true feelings than a captain in the king's service.

"Would you like to be rowing, lass?" he asked softly, startling her. "Would you like to steal the oar from one of these brawny fellows of Richard's and take his place, eh?"

She looked at him sharply, and saw the bright, teasing gleam in his green eyes.

"I'm sure Richard would permit it," he continued, "as a special favor to my bride on our wedding day. What a bridal gift—a place in the crew of the *Dragon's* boat."

"But I can think of one better," she answered quickly, with a sly, curving smile. "I could be the coxswain for the *Amazon's* boat. What better place for me than guiding the tiller of the Ladies' Ship, with my own captain and commander in the sternsheets?"

He chuckled warmly and took her hand back and lifted it, his lips warm on her chilly skin. "You know that is why I'm marrying you, don't you? To always have a smart, first-rate coxswain that will expect no wages from me?"

"But I'll make other demands, you know," she said, sliding closer so he'd feel the swell of her hip and thigh against his. "I have my rights, sir, and I'll expect certain private compensations."

His chuckle grew into an out-and-out laugh, deep

and warm enough to sweep away her doubts. "No wonder I loved you from that first morning, Diana. A woman who can make me laugh as well as handle an oar—"

"And other things," she added archly. "Mind you remember that."

"And other things," he dutifully amended, but she couldn't miss the love that lay so close to the surface of that teasing. "Ah, lass, what more would I possibly want in a wife?"

"Then you'll have no doubts, Jamie," said Richard, leaning between them, "when you stand before *me*. And mind you, you'll keep any vows you make or answer to me. Ahoy, there, *Dragon!* Rig the bo'sun's chair to bring aboard the ladies!"

Diana and Lady Marchmont were duly swung aboard by way of the bo'sun's chair, a trapeze-like contraption guaranteed to spare ladies the unseemly and risky spectacle of climbing up the boarding ladder in petticoats. Of course Lady Marchmont squealed and shrieked as she was hoisted high over the water and into the air to the deck, while Diana was simply resigned, choosing for once not to prove that she could clamber up the side of a ship faster than most men, petticoats or no petticoats.

Of far greater concern for her was James. Petticoats notwithstanding, climbing up the slippery, curving wall of a ship rocking up and down in choppy water was a challenge for the strongest sailor, with only carved slots in the side for footholds and two dangling ropes for hand guides—a challenge she wasn't sure James, with only one strong hand and a game leg, could meet. As soon as she'd been deposited on the deck herself, she hurried back to the rail, praying he wouldn't let his pride lead him to plunge into the deadly water between the boat and the ship.

"Take care, James!" she called anxiously, watching him poised to make the shift to the ladder. "Oh, please, be careful!"

But all he did was grin up at her and blindly reach for the ladder with the same ease that most people would navigate their bedchamber in the dark. He looped his weak hand around the rope, hooking it within the crook of his elbow, and used the other, stronger hand to pull himself up. It wasn't the most graceful ascent, but it wasn't a disaster either, and though he was winded by the time he met her at the gangway, he was also still grinning with the same wicked grin he'd used to taunt and dare her not so long ago at the millpond.

"You didn't think I could do that, did you?" he asked as she hugged him fiercely. "You dear silly goose, fussing over me like that. You thought I'd tumble into the water like old Humpty-Dumpty."

"I didn't want to lose you before we were wed," she scolded tenderly as she pushed herself back away from him, straightening the lapels on his coat with almost-a-wifely concern. "But *you* let me worry because *you* didn't tell me that you had obviously practiced doing that with one hand, just like I saw you practicing with the sword and the scarecrow."

"Aye, I did," he said, holding her comfortably around the waist as if they were standing before the fire in their own drawing room instead of on the windy, damp quarterdeck of a sloop of war, with the standing rigging singing overhead and the timbers groaning underfoot and a score of sailors pretending very hard not to gawk at them. "Just the way you could row that boat clear back to Massachusetts if you'd a mind to, couldn't you?"

"It's rowing back across the harbor that concerns me," interrupted Richard with a zealously stern *harrumph*, his well-worn Book of Common Prayer in his hand. "There's a good blow coming from the west, and if we don't do this soon, Jamie, you and your bride be spending your wedding night cozy and snug with me here on the *Dragon*."

They made their way down the narrow companionway, crowding into Richard's tiny cabin, where his servant had already arranged a hasty celebration of Madeira and sweet biscuits on a well-polished salver, placed in the middle of Richard's desk-*cum*-dining table. In addition to Richard and Lady Marchmont, the *Dragon*'s first lieutenant and two midshipmen had also been drafted to serve as witnesses, making for close quarters indeed.

"Here now, Diana, let me do what pitiful bit I can for you," said Lady Marchmont, frowning as she turned Diana away from the men. "Something—some *things*—borrowed for good luck and all."

She slipped off her own pearl earrings and hung them from Diana's ears, replaced Diana's plain linen kerchief with her own sheer one trimmed with Valenciennes lace, twisting it artfully around her shoulders and beneath her breasts, and smoothed and patted Diana's hair, pulling a few curls free to twist beguilingly at her temples and over her shoulders. Finally she tore a cluster of decorative silk flowers from the waist of her petticoats and put them into Diana's hand.

"It's a sorry excuse for a bouquet, dear," she said as she kissed Diana on each cheek, "but among all these wicked men, 'tis the best I can do. Be happy, Diana. This may not be the chapel at Ashburnham, but I do believe you have chosen the better gentleman."

"All hands to quarters, ladies," called Richard. "Handsomely, now, handsomely!"

But as Diana took James' hand, a low yowl of indignant complaint rose from Brighty's basket on the deck behind them.

"Gemini, we can't forget Brighty!" exclaimed Diana, freeing him as he chirruped his thanks. Swiftly she tied the silk flowers around his neck and returned to James with him in her arms.

"Brighty's our matchmaker," she explained to a mystified Richard, "the one who kept us on this course. He *has* to be here now."

And Brighty knew it too, settling proudly in the crook of her arm while James held Diana's hand. Nervously Richard cleared his throat once, then began reading the solemn words of the ceremony, words that Diana scarcely heard.

How different this wedding was from the grand event Roxby had planned for them! Here in the *Dragon's* cabin, there were no banks of fragrant flowers to fill the gilded family chapel at Ashburnham, no cream-colored silk gown or diamonds around her throat or in her hair, no bishop to preside or legions of titled guests to help celebrate, no music, no pomp, no splendor, no ceremony to rival a royal wedding.

But there was more love in this little cabin than there could ever be in all of Ashburnham, and as Diana promised herself to James forever, she knew with every part of her being that this was the one man put on earth for her.

"Oh, hell, there's no ring," muttered Richard, scowling down at the open book in his hands. "What in blazes are we supposed to do for a ring?"

"Here," said Lady Marchmont quickly as she stripped off one of hers, a gold band crowned with a flower of pearls centered by a sapphire. "Accept it as my gift, or simply make do with it until you've found something to please yourselves better."

Carefully James took the ring, the little gold circle dwarfed by his hand, and slipped it onto Diana's finger. She stared at it there, realizing how much such a symbol represented no matter where it had come from, and how she'd never wish to part with it because James had put it there.

And, oh, yes, she was crying again, but this time from purest joy, and when at last James bent to kiss her, nothing had ever felt so inexpressibly *right* as becoming his wife. She'd come clear to England to find a title, and she had found the finest in the whole kingdom: Mrs. James Dunham.

16

"*I* love you, lass," whispered James as he held her tightly, or at least as tightly as he could with Brighty squashed between them. "I always have, and I always will."

"All's well, all's well," declared Richard, beaming at what he'd done. "The only fee I'll claim now is a kiss from the bride."

"Gladly given, too," said Diana shyly, disentangling herself from James long enough to reach up and kiss the other captain. "I—*we*—will never be able to thank you enough for this, Richard."

"If I've helped you outfox that bastard Roxby, well then, that's thanks enough," he answered gruffly. "You're rightly wed now, beyond being put asunder and all the rest of it. Leastways you will be once James, ah, does his husbandly duty toward you."

It took Diana only a moment to realize what he meant, and when she did she blushed crimson, and so to her amazement did James. Perdition, they both might as well have *confessed* outright!

But Richard only leered. "So much for the virtuous vicar's son, eh?" he said, chuckling with delight. "I'd say this girl's already made improvements in you, Jamie, and first-rate ones at that."

"Which is exactly why we're clearing off for home now," said James, grinning with more devious anticipation than any vicar's son likely should. "To continue making improvements."

Diana blushed again, but her grin matched his in eagerness. They were indisputably husband and wife and entitled to do whatever pleased them the most. "To the inn, you mean. To our bedchamber there."

"No, to our home," said James. "At least it's our home for now, sweet. The *Amazon*'s cabin. High time we took possession, I'd say."

"Then you're not leaving me behind?" she asked in a breathless whisper, almost afraid to hope she'd heard him right. "You're taking me with you?"

"Aye, I am, my pretty wife," he said, pulling her close again, "for we've both worked too hard at finding one another to willingly stay apart."

"Then you'd best clear off now, before you've no choice," said Richard, glancing past them out the stern window. "That wind's freshening something fierce."

"If you please, Captain Lanker," cooed Lady Marchmont as she let her fingers flutter over his arm. "Such weather frightens me *dreadfully*, and I'd much rather throw myself upon your hospitality. That is, dear Captain, if you have space for a poor lady in distress?"

Of course Richard did, and the last glimpse that Diana and James had of their two friends was them standing in the wind at the rail, waving and thoroughly cheerful to be in one another's company.

"I am not certain we should have left her there,

James," said Diana with concern as they shifted closer together on the bench, sharing a single borrowed boat cloak against the spray. "Lady Marchmont is generosity herself, but she is not exactly trustworthy with gentlemen, and poor, sweet Richard—"

"Richard is a grown man of much experience," said James with amusement, "and while you are the kindest little creature to fuss over him, I do believe he'll survive Lady Marchmont's attentions."

Diana sighed fretfully and wriggled closer, sheltering poor Brighty in his basket beneath her petticoat. "It's just that I am so very happy, James, that I wish all the rest of the world could be as well."

"All I can answer for is you, lass," said James, tenderly turning her face toward his under the tent of the spread cloak. "And that, you know, is more than enough for me."

He could swear to that confidently now, knowing they were wed before God and witnesses. Until then he'd been worried that Roxby would somehow appear to claim Diana, but even a peer could not overturn a lawfully done marriage. Not that their challenges were exactly over. He'd still a new ship and crew to master and fit out for a cruise, orders to follow, Frenchmen to fight in a seemingly unending war. But together he and Diana would make sense of it all. Together, with love on their side, they'd find a way to resolve everything else.

But as they walked down the empty wharf to where the *Amazon* was waiting in the fog-shrouded dusk, his heart was pounding and his mouth dry with excitement as he patted his pocket one last time to make sure his commission was still tucked safely inside. Because he'd sent his belongings ahead earlier in the day, the crew would be expecting him now, on their best behavior and every bit as nervous as he was himself.

"If you wish, Diana, I can find you lodgings ashore for tonight," he said, squeezing her chilly hand. "I can't vouch for what's waiting for us, or even if they'll be able to muster a hot dish of tea for you."

"I'll have you to warm me, James," she said cheerfully, already a sailor's wife through and through. "Unless you wish me to stay ashore and keep out of your way until you've had yourself read in."

"What, and have you miss the pipes and all the thump and crash of the marines?" he said, trying to lighten the moment. "They'll have to concoct a special salute for you, considering—"

"Captain Dunham, sir," said the one voice he'd hoped never to hear again. "I believe you have something that rightly belongs to me."

An unwelcome voice, followed by the scrape of a sword being pulled from its scabbard, and then there among the shifting shreds of fog stood Roxby, dressed entirely in black save for the stark white of his shirt at the collar and cuffs.

"My lord," answered James sharply, shifting his body to shield Diana. He could feel her trembling, hear the rapid panting that her breathing had become. "I believe you are mistaken."

Roxby smiled, flicking the sword lightly before him as he took two steps closer. "And I believe I am not. If you were the gentleman officer that you pretend to be, then I might send my friends to arrange a more honorable meeting between us. But since you have not behaved honorably toward me, Captain Dunham, I see no reason to behave honorably toward you. Unless, that is, you will agree to return Miss Fairbourne to me at once."

"I'm not yours, Roxby!" cried Diana, her voice shaking. "I never was, not the way you think! And now—now I am married to James, and you—you should just go away and leave us!"

Roxby went very still, his smile frozen. "That, my dear, is hardly possible."

"Not an hour past," said James, and held the pause a fraction longer than he should have. "My lord."

"Only an hour?" asked Roxby, his eyes narrowing. "Then you've not had time to—"

"Last night," said Diana quickly, her hands clutching in the back of James' coat. "I went to him willingly, Roxby, gladly, and we made love. *Love,* Roxby. He didn't have to force me."

"Oh, yes, Diana, love was always a great attraction for you, wasn't it?" Roxby sighed wearily and beckoned for her to join him. "But you and your insipid *love* are making it damnably hard to forgive you. Now come with me, you deceitful bitch, where you belong, and I'll let this low-bred bastard *lover* of yours sail away unharmed."

Instantly James drew his own sword, holding it with both hands, strong over weak, on the hilt the way he'd practiced. He hadn't wanted it to come to this. Roxby was known as an accomplished, elegant swordsman, and James was neither, nor had he been before the explosion that had wounded him. This wasn't even the sturdy, familiar hanger James had practiced with, but the presentation sword he used for dress, bright with gold wire and odd little animals. Nothing was as he'd choose it. But on his side was his size and his longer reach and the extra intangible of desperation. Aye, he'd plenty of that.

And he had Diana. Jesus, even the thought of her once again in Roxby's hands was enough to steady James' hands and focus his fury.

"Diana is my wife, Roxby," he said as he tested the sword in his hands, "and I'll thank you not to speak of her with any less respect than she deserves."

"Your *wife*," said Roxby contemptuously. "More like your whore, after I was finished with her."

"Oh, please don't do this, James," begged Diana frantically, trying to tug him away. "Not for my sake, love! Let us return to the street, or summon the watch, or call the men on the *Amazon* for help, or—or—oh, James, he'll kill you!"

"Only if I let him," said James, not letting his gaze shift for an instant away from Roxby. "Which I've no intention of doing."

"But James, please—"

"Now stand clear, love," he said, "so no harm comes to you."

She gave one last strangled sob of sorrow and fear before she finally slipped away from him. He knew how she must hate this, but Roxby had left him no real choice, and they both knew it.

Tentatively the two men circled around the narrow dock, watching, weighing, considering, testing. In the distance, the curious were gathering to watch, standing on barrels for a better view. A pair of gentlemen fighting with swords, one a captain, one a peer, must seem capital sport. That it was also illegal would only add to the interest, and on some idle level of his consciousness

James hoped the wagers the spectators were inevitably making were for him.

"Is that how they teach you sailors to hold a sword, Dunham?" sneered Roxby. "Two hands, like a farmer with a cudgel? No wonder His Majesty is faring so badly against the French."

James' sword sliced through the air, the arc ending with a jarring clash as Roxby parried with his own blade, forcing James to jerk to one side to save himself. He swung again, and again the blades scraped against each other. It was hard work, this kind of fighting, hard, numbing, exhausting work, and despite the cold dampness of the evening, James felt the sweat prickle on his neck and back, his heart racing with excitement and exertion.

"Did she scream for you, Dunham?" demanded Roxby, though his breath was coming faster now too, white puffs before his face in the chill air. "She did for me, and for Stanver, too."

"You lie," spat James, and angrily lunged forward. A mistake. With a dancer's agility, Roxby stepped around him, his sword singing through the air as he caught James in the upper arm, the blade nicking through the sleeve of his best bespoke uniform coat to draw blood, and a keen bolt of pain with it.

Concentrate, damn you, James ordered himself. *If you begin listening to his lies, then you will die.*

He twisted, just in time to avoid Roxby. Again and again he backed away, so far he nearly toppled off the edge of the dock. The wound wasn't deep, but his sleeve was soaking fast with blood, clear to the gold lace on the cuff, and each time he lifted the sword now the pain shot down his arm.

"No one—no one screams for Stanver now," he said, breathing hard. "Rotting in hell, that's where your friend Stanver is, and where you'll go next."

"Stanver was a—was a gentleman," said Roxby furiously, "and worth a hundred of you and your—your whore."

Impulsively he lunged toward James, the first real mistake Roxby had made, and James seized it, his blade cutting deep into the other man's shoulder, enough that James felt the instant he hit the bone, enough that Roxby cried out with pain and clutched blindly at the wound as he staggered backward.

"Swear you'll never—never come near my wife again," demanded James harshly. "Swear her name will never cross your—your foul lips again."

But Roxby wasn't listening. "Stanver tried to stop you, didn't he?" he said, swaying unsteadily on his feet. "Stanver knew what—what a gentleman must do for his friend's honor."

An unearthly yowl, almost a scream, suddenly echoed across the dock and over the water, a banshee's wail rising high and fit to raise the dead. A banshee named Brighty, thought James, all too familiar with his various protests. Doubtless he was fighting Diana even now to escape his basket.

But Roxby didn't recognize the sound as a cat's yowling, and his eyes grew wild with terror as his gaze swept over the dock, searching for a different explanation.

"What—the devil was that?" he demanded hoarsely, his dark hair disheveled, his fingers now red with his own blood as he sank to his knees. "By God, Stanver, if you've come back to haunt me here . . ."

Yet it wasn't Stanver's ghost that bolted across the dock between them, but Brighty, and worse, Diana racing after him, determined to save him and heedless of herself. She reached for the little cat just as Roxby reached for her from his knees, and before James could stop him he'd grabbed her skirts and jerked her off her feet, dragging her back against his chest. For an instant she fought, her arms thrashing wildly to free herself, until she felt the blade of the sword pressing flat across her chest, the edge directly below her throat. Silently she beseeched James, her eyes bright with tears, Roxby's blood already marking the white skin of her throat.

And James had never felt more hideously helpless in his entire life.

"Let Diana go, Roxby!" he ordered urgently. "Let her go *now!*"

"Stanver—Stanver wouldn't want that," said Roxby, his face twisted in a grimace of pain. "He—he warned me she'd bring me to sorrow."

"Free the woman," thundered another voice behind him, echoing James, a voice weighty with authority. "At once, Roxby. Do not make this worse for yourself than you already have."

The horror on Roxby's face now shaded with awe and fear.

"Your Grace," he said with hollow formality. "I am honored."

James turned and marveled at all he hadn't heard. Behind him on the dock had gathered an entire crowd of men, some with lanterns, but the one man in front carried his own glow of righteousness. The Duke of Barchester was an imposing older nobleman in a wig that flowed luxuriously over his brocaded shoulders, his bearing as ramrod straight as his beliefs and politics—and the one man in Hampshire whose title ranked him higher than Roxby.

At his side stood the Earl of Allington, his son and heir, pink cheeked and plump as a girl, and two other younger gentlemen that James couldn't identify. Behind them were a half dozen red-coated marines with their sergeant from the Portsmouth garrison, the bayonets on their upright muskets gleaming in the lanterns' light.

"You say you are honored, Roxby," said the duke, biting off every word. "I say you are most grievously wrong, sir, for you have this day blackened both your honor and your family's name beyond redemption. You've led us a merry enough chase to find you here, Roxby, and now it is time for you to explain yourself."

Roxby tried to smile with his usual charm, the result more a ghastly grimace, his face sheened with sweat as he pressed the blade of the sword more tightly against Diana's skin. "Because I was betrayed by the woman, this woman, that I'd honored as my bride? For that I am dishonored?"

"No, Roxby," said the duke with no attempt to hide his disgust. "For the murder of Lord Stanver."

"No!" cried Roxby with real anguish. "How could I have killed Stanver? He was my oldest friend, more than a brother!"

"But Stanver told us himself," insisted Lord Allington, his round cheeks flushed red as he motioned to include the other two gentlemen. "You'd left, Roxby, but we stayed with Stanver, and just before he died he told us how he'd tried to defend Miss Fairbourne here against you and how you damned him for his trouble, then shot him. We heard him confess and swear to it, Roxby. We all did."

Roxby shook his head in disbelief. "That's a lie, Your Grace!"

"No man dies with a lie in his mouth, Roxby," said the duke sternly. "Not when he knows he'll soon face his Maker. Do you deny that you quarreled with Lord Stanver over Miss Fairbourne, or that later you alone appeared to summon help, or that when you did, you were still carrying the gun in your hand? Can you deny that you fled here to Portsmouth, seeking a ship to the Continent to escape your crime?"

"None of that means anything, Your Grace!" cried Roxby, desperation making his voice ragged. "You cannot believe—"

"Lord Roxby," interrupted the duke imperiously, the marines coming to flank him. "I charge you in the name of His Majesty King George with disturbing the peace and good order of this kingdom in the murder of Lord Stanver. Because you are a peer of the realm, you are spared the common gaol, but you will remain in my custody until you can be tried by your fellow lords. Now release Miss Fairbourne at once, Roxby. *At once.*"

Roxby bowed his head over Diana, his hand trembling as he still held the sword to her throat, whispering something that made her close her eyes, her mouth twisting with sorrow and regret.

Watching, waiting, James fought the almost irresistible urge to rush forward and pull her free, away from Roxby's grasp forever. Roxby's own life was in shambles, ruined by the final betrayal of the one man

who'd shared all his sin and shame. James had been startled by Stanver's deathbed accusation, though not surprised, not after remembering how spitefully Stanver
had coveted Diana for himself.

And yet as much as James might wish to see Roxby
ruined, no matter how much he hated the marquess, his
conscience refused to agree. What was happening here
wasn't justice, but a dead man's revenge, and while irony
played well on the stage, James' own sense of honor and
truth would not let him remain silent.

"Roxby!" called the duke again, the warning clear in
his voice. "Free Miss Fairbourne, or prepare yourself for
the consequences of your refusal."

One of the marines stepped forward, his musket
ready. Yet Roxby did not move, his head still bowed over
Diana, his sword, though unsteady, not moving to let
her go. He was like a fox at the end of the hunt with the
dogs baying for his destruction, and as unwilling to let
the dogs see his fear. He had nothing else left to give,
nothing else to take except, if he chose, Diana's life, and
to James' horror, he saw Roxby's shaking fingers flexing
one last time around the grip of the sword.

His Diana, his wife, his one love. . . .

"Lord Roxby didn't kill Lord Stanver, Your Grace,"
James announced, his voice loud and steady as he seized
and offered the truth, the murmur of amazement rip-
pling through the crowd immediately. "Lord Stanver had
been drinking, so far in his cups that he killed himself by
accident with an unfamiliar gun. My wife and I were with
him, and I will swear that in any court in this land."

"You lie, Dunham!" shouted Roxby furiously, outraged. "Why the devil should I believe any of what you

say, when you have stolen my bride! Why would you come here now to slander Stanver, a man who cannot defend himself? *For God's sake, not Stanver!*"

His face was filled with hatred, blind and impassioned and directed solely at James, hatred so strong that it lifted him, challenging, onto his unsteady feet again to charge forward, his sword aimed straight at James' chest. Forgotten, Diana slipped unharmed—*safe, safe at last!*—from his grasp to the dock, and the shot from the marine with the musket was easy and straight.

One shot, echoing over the water, the acrid scent of gunpowder mingling with the salt of the sea.

One shot, and Roxby cried out as a gruesome blossom of crimson exploded from his chest and his head snapped backward. The force of the ball threw him backward like a broken puppet, tossing him off his feet and to the dock hard, leaving him sprawled and still, dead in an instant.

One shot, and once again Roxby was joined with Stanver, this time for all eternity.

And Diana, in James' arms at last, safe and unharmed, was finally his for all time as well.

Epiloque

One Week Later

"*E*nter, Captain Dunham," said the clerk, glancing up at him expectantly over the tops of his spectacles. "They're all within, sir, and waiting."

James nodded curtly and squared his shoulders. This wasn't exactly a court-martial waiting for him on the other side of that heavy paneled door, but it was the next closest ordeal. A group of admirals and senior captains were gathered to decide how best to resolve his complicated fate. They had let him keep his sword, and for the moment they'd let him retain his commission as captain of the *Amazon*. What happened beyond that was anyone's guess.

Though no other officers were waiting in this particular antechamber, James had seen enough of his peers in the Blue Anchor and around the harbor to realize that although their sympathy might lie with him now, they were also mentally framing their condolences for his career. His Majesty's navy did not approve of scandal, and because in a mere seven days his scandal had mushroomed to a stupendous size and fame, he was already being treated as a doomed man, his commission in peril and his future in ruins. No wonder he paused before knocking on that heavy door to beg admittance, tapping his fingers on the pommel of his sword for luck.

"You have nothing whatsoever to fear, James," whispered Diana, and he permitted himself one last, fond glance over his shoulder, infinitely more reassuring than any mere sword pommel. She was dressed in pink, as bright as a May primrose against the dark, spindle-back bench, with Brighty in her lap. And when she winked and blew him a kiss from beneath the curving brim of her straw hat, he could almost—almost—believe that he truly did have nothing to fear.

Until, that is, he stepped through the door and heard it close behind him with all the finality of a tomb. The room was narrow and plain, the floors and windows bare, and the walls decorated only with charts and maps. Sunlight streamed through the tall windows, and gulls danced on the breeze beyond the panes, but inside sat five grim faced senior officers in tall-backed chairs, their hands clasped on the table before them.

James' hopes plummeted even lower at the sight of those cheerless, unencouraging faces, and might have dropped clear through the floorboards if the sixth ruddy face hadn't been all smiles beneath bristling white brows, beaming with unabashed pleasure to find him, even in these circumstances. Because Admiral Fenner had been at sea on blockade duty, James had not seen him since the blackest days of his convalescence, and to have him here now, a friend and an ally when he needed one most, was nearly as reassuring as having Diana sitting outside.

"Sit, Captain Dunham, if you please," said the nearest

grim-faced officer—Admiral Carter, it was, his sallow skin never having recovered its former color after he'd had yellow fever in the Indies—with a weary wave of his hand. "We have a great many things to discuss with you, sir, and in light of your recent wounds, it would be impolite of us to require you to stand."

"Thank you, sir," said James as he dutifully sat in the proffered chair. Carefully he arranged his sword to one side and his hat in his lap, and braced himself for the worst.

"You are at present the captain of the frigate *Amazon*?" continued Carter, referring to the thick sheaf of papers before him. "You received your commission for this vessel only recently, sir? A week ago, by my reckoning?"

"Aye, aye, sir." James had to be careful to answer only what was asked and volunteer no more. Yes or no: that was all that was expected here.

"The same day as that damned brawl on the north wharf," noted another grim face, this one with a band tied over one blind eye and the other as sharp as an eagle's. "Whatever devil possessed you, Dunham, to pick a fight with the damned Marquess of Roxby—"

"Which is not what we are here to discuss, Captain Hervey," interrupted Admiral Fenner smoothly. "It's the question of these orders that we must address."

"Aye, the orders," said Carter, tossing a single sheet across the table to James. "These were to have been your orders for the *Amazon*, Captain Dunham, until it was recognized there might be certain, ah, irregularities about them."

"Irregularities, hell," sputtered Hervey. "They're deuced queer, no question about it."

James had wondered why there'd been no orders forthcoming when he'd taken over the *Amazon*, and he read them carefully now, making sure he understood each word of the Admiralty clerk's flawless penmanship, and with each word his anger rose.

The *Amazon* was not bound for the Mediterranean to prowl the rich shipping lanes, or to patrol the coast of France, or even to carry dispatches to the various kingdoms in Italy. No, according to these orders, he was to have sailed across the Atlantic to New England, to play rat-catcher for half-penny smugglers and tariff dodgers. With unusual precision, he was ordered to end the trading of a certain family, to imprison them if necessary or destroy their homes and warehouses as he pleased: the Fairbournes of Appledore.

Diana's parents, brothers, uncles. His own newly minted father-in-law, the grandparents and the cousins of the children he hoped to have with her.

"Queer as they come, I say," repeated Hervey furiously. "And completely that rascal Lord Roxby's doing, of course."

"Oh, of course," agreed Fenner expansively. "Rumor is that he bribed old Birtles with a dancing girl—a *dancing* girl, for all love! One would have thought Birtles would have sold his soul for a higher price. Still, I suppose Roxby thought this was one way to deal with a difficult mother-in-law."

The older men laughed together, but James did not join them. Roxby's actions had nothing to do with his future wife's family. Rather, it had been one more way he'd tried to control Diana, and it sickened James to realize how close he'd come to succeeding. If these orders had come to any captain other than himself, he doubted they would have been questioned until it was too late, if even then.

"No, no, indeed," continued Fenner, taking the paper back from James. "In light of Lord Roxby's death and your marriage, we have decided to amend these orders. We can hardly send you out to annihilate your bride's family, can we, eh?"

"No, sir," said James, the sick feeling remaining behind his impassive face. "Not at all, sir."

"No one outside this room need ever know these orders existed," said Fenner, tapping his forefinger on the table for emphasis, "and if that doesn't keep the peace with your bonnie little wife, then I do not know what will."

"No, sir," said James again. He had promised Diana he'd hold no secrets from her, but this one—this one he'd never be so cruel as to share, and for her sake he'd take it with him to his grave. "That is, aye, aye, sir."

"But then what in blazes are we to make of you, Captain Dunham?" demanded Carter. "We can hardly reward an officer who goes about skewering marquesses over ladies, no matter how many times the Duke of Barchester swears it was justified."

"Barchester," grumbled Hervey. "How I do hate it when the titled bastards meddle in our affairs!"

Carter shook his head. "But we can't send a vessel that's become as notorious as the *Amazon* into the heat of war, either. How could we pretend she's only one more anonymous ship in the line of battle, a vessel that's called after *ladies?* It couldn't happen, Captain Dunham, and it wouldn't do."

"No, sir," said James, certain now that they meant to take the *Amazon* from him. How could they not, really? He'd told himself to expect it, to accept it when it happened. But then he thought of how Diana already regarded the frigate's cabin as their first home as newlyweds, of the little improvements she'd lavished on the cabin to make it their own, even how she'd placed the stoneware figure of Brighty on a special shelf over their bunk. It would break her heart to be ordered from the *Amazon,* nearly as much as it was going to break his. "No, sir, no."

"It's for the good of the service, James," explained Fenner kindly. "Especially now, with the French at our throats, we cannot afford to make individual allowances. You understand, I'm sure."

Oh, aye, James would understand, his expression studiously blank. What he understood was that, in this, Roxby had won after all, and he had lost.

Fenner rang the small brass bell to summon the clerk.

"Please ask Mrs. Dunham to join us," he said, and as the man bowed and left, Fenner smiled at James. "If you do not object, that is. But I felt that since our decision will have such an impact on your dear lady, she has every right to hear it explained."

Oh, aye, thought James miserably, better to tell her to her face that her husband has no future and her home's to be taken back.

"Good day, gentlemen," said Diana, smiling brilliantly as she swept into the room, her pink silk skirts rustling and Brighty tucked neatly beneath her arm. The six senior officers rose in unison, and in unison they were ready instantly to lay down their hearts and lives for whatever cause she wished. She had that power, his wife, and any other time James would have smiled to watch her. She would have made a splendid marchioness, but her talents would not be wasted among the admirals, either.

"How very kind of you to include me here, sirs," she said, tipping her head beguilingly as she smiled and settled Brighty in her lap. "I did not expect such a favor."

Yet as James gave her his chair, moving to stand behind her with his hands on her shoulders, he saw the quick, anxious glance meant for him alone. For all her smiles, she understood what was as stake here. How much he hated her having to hear what would inevitably come next!

"We are the ones who are honored, Mrs. Dunham," said Fenner, adding a small, stiff bow. "Given the, ah, interest surrounding you and your husband during this last week, we have decided it best that he be removed from the public sight for a time, perhaps a year. For the good of the service, ma'am."

"A *year!*" cried Diana, shocked. "How can you toss James out on his ear like that after all he has done for you?"

"Oh, we're hardly tossing him out, my dear," said Carter with a sly glance. "He's far too valuable for that. No, we are merely sending him on, ah, special orders."

"To give the gossips and the scandal sheets time to forget." Fenner passed the new orders to James. "I trust, Captain Dunham, that these will be more to your liking."

Quickly James scanned the page and smiled, relief washing over him in waves. He was not ruined. He was not dishonored. He was still the *Amazon*'s captain, still worthy of Diana's love.

"What is it, James?" demanded Diana. "Gemini, don't keep it a secret!"

"We are bound for New England and Halifax, sweet," he said, handing her the orders to read for herself. "To disrupt the French in those waters, to intercept their shipping—that means prizes, love—and to serve Admiral Person in Boston however he sees fit. I suppose now I shall have to meet your family as well."

"Oh, James," she gasped. "You are taking me home— *home!*"

"Only for a visit, Mrs. Dunham," said Fenner, smiling broadly as he rose to signal the end of the meeting. "We'll be wanting him back in these waters next year. And when you return, James, I expect to stand as godfather to your first son."

"I *told* you there was nothing to fear," said Diana as soon as they were alone in the hall, and as soon as he'd kissed her, too. "I told you they'd make it all right!"

"You might have told me, but you didn't believe it," he teased. "You were every bit as worried as I."

"Not by half, Captain." Impishly she grinned up at him, running her hand across his chest. "I cannot begin to guess what my family will say when they see me sail into Appledore in the *Amazon*! And, oh, what they shall say when they meet you, for you are not at all what they expected."

"What they should do is compliment you on your good sense and judgment." He could smile now that everything was settled; he could even tease her. "And they should be grateful for how you have improved the family in general by introducing a king's officer into their rascally midst."

"Braggart," she said, and swatted his chest. "What worries me most is how you've promised a godchild to Admiral Fenner by the time we return when you've already sworn the same to Richard."

"Twins," said James blandly, fighting with little success not to laugh outright. "It's the only answer I can see. Fortunately, a crossing to New England at this time of year could take weeks."

"Months," said Diana cheerfully. "A good thing, too, if we are expected to produce twins. We shall have to make the most assiduous use of every moment we are alone together."

James nodded gravely, then spoiled the effect by slipping his arm around her waist and kissing her until she giggled. "Fortunately, as you might recall, the woman I have married is no ordinary chit."

"Fortunately, too, my husband is no ordinary rogue, either." She smiled, her happiness radiating from her entire being. "Which is precisely why I love him so very much."

"And why I love you, too, lass," he said softly, and when he kissed her again, he knew he'd found the brightest star in the entire sky.

And there was nothing ordinary about it at all.

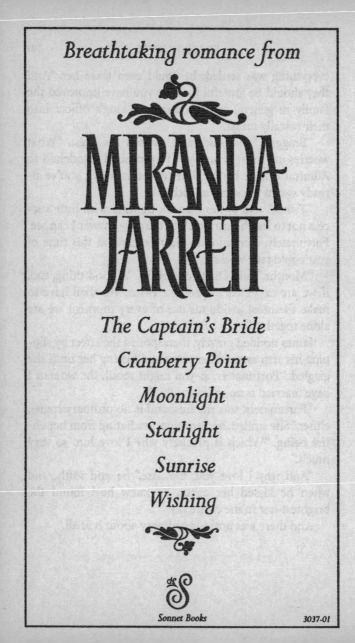

Breathtaking romance from

MIRANDA JARRETT

SONNET BOOKS
PROUDLY PRESENTS

SPARKLE

Miranda Jarrett

**Coming Soon in Paperback from
Sonnet Books
Published by Pocket Books**

Turn the page for a preview of
Sparkle. . . .

Naples
The Kingdom of Two Sicilies
November, 1798

*H*eedless of the lurching progress of the hired cart, Captain Lord William Ramsden absently traced the gold lacing on the sleeve of his dress-uniform coat and thought of all he'd survived in these last eight weeks. For that he could thank fate, and damn her, too. Even here in Naples, he felt the chilly memory deep in his bones, where not even the bright afternoon sun could warm it away. He'd seen too much blood spilled, heard the screams of too many dying men, for it to be otherwise. His body might have escaped unwounded, but his soul was exhausted.

He frowned, once again struggling to put the memories behind him, his fingers still tracing the intricate gold braid. He'd already seen to the repairs the *Centaur* had needed after the battle, completed his reports, and visited the wounded among his crew in the hospital on shore, called upon the ambassador and his wife, composed letters by the score to be sent back to London. He'd always been thorough that way, taking care of the things he could control in a life so full of uncertainty and risk.

But it still wasn't such a bad showing, even for a fourth son, and gradually William's frown relaxed. He was a captain and commander in His Majesty's Navy; he'd just helped win one of the greatest victories of this war against the French; he was, God forgive him for being honest, even a hero. Perhaps he *was* entitled to a small respite, even a bit of out-and-out idle amusement. Not even Admiral Lord Nelson was devoting every waking hour to thinking of ways to confound the French.

All of which was why William sat riding in this shabby hired carriage behind a pair of white Neapolitan mules, listening to his old friend Captain Henry Pye babble on about their plans for the rest of the day.

"You can go wherever you please in Naples, Will," Henry was intoning with a ponderous, wine-induced solemnity. Their midday meal at a waterfront taverna had been lengthy, the local marsala splashing freely and often into their glasses. "If your heart's set on gawking at one more broken-down pagan temple, then go. I'll not stop you. I'll damn you as a buggerly don and a low-bred prig, but I won't stop you. Myself, I'm bound for Signora Francesca's most illustrious *studio d'artista*, and if you've half a drop of red blood left in you, you'll come with me."

"Shall I now," said William mildly. He'd known Henry since they'd both been midshipmen, far too long to take his slander seriously, and besides, the tavern's rich, plummy wine had worked its magic on him as well. "So is that what they call a whorehouse in this benighted city? A *studio d'artista*? I should watch my purse if I were you, Henry. Artistry like that sounds costly."

"*Bordellos*," said Henry with excruciating patience.

"That's what the brothels are called. *Bordellos.* I've only told you that at least a thousand times, Will. Not that you care. No whore's fine enough for your tastes, anyway."

"None that I've met, no," agreed William. He'd always preferred females who could hold his interest in conversation as well as in bed, a discernment that marked him as a curiosity among his friends. He'd no patience with the tawdry, mercenary women that preyed upon sailors in every port—the common ones here in Naples had shown their gratitude to the English by giving at least a third of his crew the pox while stealing the purses of the rest—nor had he any interest himself in privately entertaining the more expensive doxies, the greedy local actresses and opera singers, in his cabin, the way other captains did. "Consider it a favor that I've left all the more harlots for you."

"But I say, William, Signora Francesca's not some common harlot," insisted Henry. "She's a whole other breed of wickedness."

"There are degrees in Naples?"

"Hell, yes," said Henry righteously. "Signora Francesca's establishment is a family concern, you know, inherited from her late, lamented father. I wonder that your brothers never told you of it."

William's smile grew guarded, the way it always did when his brothers were mentioned. Younger sons, even the younger sons of dukes, were generally regarded as a burden to their families and a trial to genteel society. As the fourth son of the Duke of Harbrough, William had understood this truth from the distant time he'd been a tiny boy, barely breeched, when his oldest brother had made it forcefully clear one afternoon behind the stables. There would always be three others—three tall, terrifying, older others—between William and the end-less bounty and good fortune of being a peer of the realm in the greatest country in Christendom, that most obviously being England in the reign of His Majesty King George III.

It wasn't fair, of course. William knew that. Little in life was, especially for fourth sons. As befitted their sta-tion, his oldest brother Gervase, the heir, and St. John, the second son, had both been sent across Europe to complete their education and wallow in all the usual temptations that catered to young English gentlemen. His third brother, Markham, had been bought a com-mission in a fashionable regiment.

But their father had watched his farthings and pence with exceptionally unducal precision, and he'd deemed it an unnecessary expense to squander such costly blan-dishments upon his extraneous fourth son. Instead of a grand tour with a tutor and servants, William had been sent alone to sea on his tenth birthday, a newly minted, brokenhearted midshipman in His Majesty's Navy. He'd never seen his father again, and he'd never returned home to Harbrough House, either. There'd been no rea-son to, especially not after his father died and Gervase inherited the title, nor did William see a reason for ex-plaining any of this to Henry now.

"My brothers and I have never had the pleasure of discussing Naples," he said instead, "let alone something as sordid as this particular young woman."

"But that's the best of it, Will, leastways for someone as particular as you!" exclaimed Henry, his round, ruddy face glowing with excitement. "The signora's not sordid at all. She's a great beauty, *and* she's half En-glish."

"One glass of wine, Henry, and they're all beauties to

you," said William, relieved to be able to shift the conversation away from his family. "Half a bottle, and this woman would be Venus herself."

"I am quite in earnest, Will, even if you choose to mock me," said Henry, scowling. "The girl *is* beautiful, in a Latin sort of way. Even you must remark it. But that's not the reason for calling on her. One goes to Signora Francesca's to view the paintings."

William raised his brows with amusement. "Since when did you become such a connoisseur, eh? Must we search your cabin for plundered Titians or Guidos before we sail again?"

"Not paintings like *that*," said Henry, leaning forward and lowering his voice in eager confidence. "You wouldn't want these paintings hanging in the parlor at home. Not at all! Signora Francesca's paintings are more what you'd have about for, ah, entertainment. For gentlemen. You know, for amusement."

"Henry, I don't see—"

"Will, they're lewd," said Henry bluntly. "The paintings, I mean. Like *Fanny Hill* and Aretino, only in the antique style."

"The signora traffics in wicked pictures?" asked William incredulously. "Your fair young goddess?"

"There you go again, Will, twisting my words about to make me sound like a damned fool," said Henry with a wounded sniff. "The lewd ones aren't the only ones she has. They say she has more polite ones, too, along with heaps of other old rubbish for sale, for the Neapolitan ladies who visit her studio. And Lady Hamilton, of course. They say the signora's a special favorite of her ladyship."

William made no comment beyond a discouraging shake of his head. Lady Hamilton was an uneasy subject for English officers in Naples, what with their very married admiral so openly enamoured with the equally married wife of the English consul.

But what could this young signora with the peculiar mixture of goods in her studio have to attract a worldly woman like Lady Hamilton? Was the girl herself that clever, that witty, or simply so beautiful that her company would be irresistible to women as well as men? If that were so, how could such a winsome creature maintain a business on her own? William frowned again, thinking. He liked reason and logical explanations, and he'd always been fascinated by the puzzles people made of their lives, trying to decipher why and how they chose the paths they did. From Henry's telling alone, this beautiful half-English signora with the lewd pictures was offering more questions than answers, and that was enough to intrigue William mightily.

Or at least mightily enough for an afternoon's diversion. What more, really, could he want?

The cart lurched to a halt, the driver grinning and sweeping his whip to the right to indicate they'd reached their destination in this crowded, close-packed street. The house was typically Neapolitan, narrow and three stories high, the stucco painted a pale candy-pink with carved, curling flourishes over the door and square windows like swirls of white icing.

In the slanting sunlight, striped curtains fluttered at the open sashes, and even though it was November, lush red flowers still spilled cheerfully from the window boxes. The homely smell of frying onions and fish mingled with the salty, damp air from the sea, and the street echoed with sounds of stray dogs barking and vendors shouting and children shrieking and women gossiping in the accelerated southern Italian that William couldn't begin to understand. It was all unabashedly domestic, and not at all the place one would expect to visit to view lewd pictures.

That is, *one* might not expect it, but Henry certainly did. In a single enthusiastic leap, he'd hurled himself from the cart to the street with the same eagerness that he'd use for boarding an enemy ship, and with another two strides he was up the steps and pounding on the door's heavy iron knocker.

"Subtlety, Henry, subtlety," cautioned William as he paid the driver and followed his friend up the steps. "We're here to view the signora's wares, not make a prize of her house."

But the maidservant who opened the door to them more than matched Henry's cheerful enthusiasm, her grin wide to make up for her haphazard English as she took their names, then showed them up the staircase to a large parlor that ran the width of the back of the house.

"D'you think this is the signora's studio, eh?" asked Henry hopefully as soon as the maidservant left them alone.

"It's not exactly her kitchen, is it?" With unabashed curiosity, William gazed around the cluttered, high-ceilinged room, so different from the cramped but tidy spaces between decks where he lived himself.

The yellow walls were covered with paintings of every sort—martyred saints, landscapes and sunsets, still lifes of decaying fruit, maudlin little girls clutching kittens—except, of course, the subjects that Henry was so eager to see. Pale marble statues in familiar classical poses were arranged around the room like unwelcome guests, staring bleakly through blind white eyes at the additional disembodied fragments—an orator's hand, a goddess's sandaled foot, a headless satyr propped in one corner. Black and red painted antique vases were displayed on a green-draped table along with small mosaic medallions and twisted chunks of volcanic rock from nearby Vesuvius. In a tall cage, two crested, white parrots preened and screeched, and the fragrance of the red flowers at the open windows hung heavily in the warm, sun-filled room.

Cautiously Henry leaned over one of the black-figured vases, keeping his hands clasped tightly behind him as if he were a small boy warned not to touch.

"I say, these aren't exactly wicked," he said, clearly disappointed. "How's a fellow to be interested in a jumble of old pots like this?"

"Perhaps the signora keeps the wicked ones for private viewing," suggested William dryly. Although he couldn't claim a true collector's eye, most of the signora's paintings struck him as second-rate or out-and-out reproductions. Privately he was beginning to doubt that her more lurid wares even existed; it wouldn't be the first time that English gentlemen had exaggerated what they'd seen or done abroad. "For only her most especial customers."

"By Jove, then I hope she approves of us," said Henry, anxiously smoothing the front of his dark blue uniform coat. "There, William, can you see the spot from the sauce last night?"

"For God's sake, Henry, you look more than well enough. The woman's a wretched shopkeeper, not the queen." William sighed and shook his head over his friend's uncertainty, as if this woman's opinion actually *mattered*. Not that he'd never worried like this himself; when he'd been younger, much younger, on leave in London, he'd spent any number of hours in any number of elegant parlors, waiting for some young lady or another to deign to show herself. Strange how they'd all blurred together in his memory, those blue-blooded Georgianas and Charlottes with golden hair and angelic smiles. They'd been so endlessly desirable to him then in his lovesick youth, and yet so perpetually unattainable, too, more prizes reserved for his more fortunate brothers. For no matter how many Frenchmen he'd managed to dispatch, even the greatest heroics had always paled before the prospect of a dukedom.

"Ah, good day, good day, my most gallant and deserving of gentlemen heroes!" exclaimed a woman's voice behind him, followed by some garbled, gulping reply from Henry.

Roused from his memories of the young ladies in London, William smiled wryly, thinking of how not one of them would dare greet strange gentlemen with such scandalously warm enthusiasm. He was smiling still as he turned toward the woman, yet as soon as he did, the image of those sweet-faced young ladies in white muslin was instantly banished by the sight of the signora before him.

She was younger than William had expected, taller, her figure more rounded and lush, and if the quality of her paintings had been exaggerated, then the promises of her beauty most certainly had not. Her skin was golden, burnished with rich rose, her eyes as dark and fathomless as midnight. Her hair was black as well, glossy and gleaming and parted in the center, exactly like the woman who'd posed for a Raphael his uncle owned. They could have been sisters, this young woman and that long-ago Renaissance model, with the same warm, glowing beauty, the same exotic, sensual promise.

And her dress—Jesus, he'd never seen a woman

dressed in such a fashion, a mixture of Turkish fantasy and fancy-dress costume that somehow managed to be both alluring and enchanting, and completely her own. Her gown was peacock-blue satin looped over a yellow-striped petticoat, the sleeves trimmed with brown fur cuffs and the bodice cut low over a sheer, linen shift embroidered with scarlet silk. She'd wrapped another length of striped silk into a turban and pinned it into place on the back of her head, with a black plume and a garnet brooch, and from her ears swung large gold hoops strung with single pearls.

Everything—the silk and the gold and the fur and the pearls—seemed to shimmer and glow as she walked, emphasizing the rich curves of her body and the warmth of her smile, and it took every bit of William's well-practiced reserve not to gawk outright. It didn't matter that the paintings and sculpture in her studio were trumped-up trash; she was the one true work of art, and a most rare one at that.

"Captain Pye, is it not?" she was saying breathlessly as she curtseyed before poor dithering Henry, granting him a stupefying view of her bosom in the process. "How honored—most genuinely honored!—I am to have you grace my little studio! For what your brave navy has done to save this kingdom, to fight back those evil French and their hideous republic—why, whatever you wish, dear Captain Pye, whatever you crave, is yours—yours!"

It was humbug and nonsense, every last pretty word of it; William could see that at once. She didn't have the slightest intention of giving away one broken-down saint, and she wouldn't have to, either, because Henry was already reaching for his purse, so starry-eyed and besotted that he'd gladly give her double whatever she tried to refuse. The more she fluttered and blushed and praised his gallantry, the more Henry would be willing to pay, and it wouldn't be until later, when he'd found himself in the street with some bastardized portrait of Aphrodite and an empty pocket to show for it, that he might—*might*—begin to realize what had happened to him.

Not, of course, that William had any intention of letting that happen. This woman might be the most enchanting female ever put on this earth to bedevil honest men, but he'd extricated Henry from worse disasters in the name of friendship.

"Good day, signora," he began, purposefully keeping his voice stern and his bow as perfunctory as possible. "I am Captain Lord William Ramsden. Your servant, ma'am."

"Oh, my lord captain, I am the one who must serve you!" She smiled brilliantly and tipped her head to one side as she spread her satin skirts and dropped him a curtsey. But she couldn't quite keep the wariness from her dark eyes when her gaze met William's, or the brittleness from her voice as she tried to flatter him with the same charm that had worked so well with Henry. "An English lord in my humble little home! How my dear, late papa would have loved to live for such a great day!"

"Indeed," answered William with another cursory bow. "And how proud, too, he would have been to see his daughter in so thriving an enterprise."

She flushed, his meaning all too plain, and William almost regretted his words. But still she held her ground.

"Indeed he would," she answered, her ear-bobs swinging against her cheeks. "Though he passed most of his life here in Naples, he never forgot his English home, or put aside his loyalty to his English sovereign."

With a graceful sweep of her hand she gestured toward an engraving of King George on the crowded wall. Cynically William wondered how long it had actually hung there—since Lady Hamilton's first visit, perhaps, or only since the English fleet had sailed into Naples to refit earlier this autumn?

"If dear Papa could but see me here now," she continued, somehow managing to bring the brightness of tears to her eyes, "in conversation with a gentleman who is next to royalty himself, the son of an English duke!"

"Only a fourth son, ma'am," said William curtly, wondering if she kept a copy of the peerage in another chamber for assessing her customers. "A powerfully long step from royalty, ma'am. Far better you should honor how I serve His Majesty as a captain in his navy."

She nodded in silent agreement, her only answer. But there was a new interest in her eyes as she appraised him again, an expression that, in an odd way, put William more on his guard than before. Why would he wish the regard of a female rascal like this one?

"Here now, signora," said Henry importantly, clutching a small stone cupid in his arms. "I'd wager my sister in Brighton would fancy such a gewgaw in her garden, there among the hollyhocks. What's he cost, eh?"

"This little fellow?" she asked, fondly running her fingertip along the statue's nose, and not quite accidentally brushing her plump, bare forearm over Henry's hand. "He's very old, you know, very ancient, at least from the time of Hadrian. But would your sister welcome the mischief such a statue would bring with him? Cupid is Venus's son, you know, and given to making us mortals fall into love most inconveniently."

She smiled coyly, and Henry grinned back, as ripe and simple a mooncalf as William had ever seen.

"Give me that infernal thing, Henry," he ordered, wresting the cupid from his friend's arms. "Before you hand over your gold, use your eyes instead of your— well, use your eyes, damn it. This is no more from ancient Rome than you are yourself. Mark how these stains in the marble look like someone's spilled tea on it, trying to make it seem old. And here, see how clean these chisel nicks are in the stone. Wouldn't you think they'd have worn down a bit in, oh, the last thousand years or so?"

Henry scowled down at the fat-cheeked cupid, then up at William. "What are you truly saying, William?" he demanded petulantly. "That I'm a right royal jackass? That the signora here is lying?"

William sighed with exasperation, and awkwardly shifted the offending cupid to his other arm, where its stone wing wouldn't poke him. "What I'm saying is that perhaps you're, ah, confused. Aye, confused. And so's the signora."

The signora smiled with surpassing sweetness, turning her face upward to William, as if fair begging to be kissed in the most innocently cunning way imaginable.

"An English ship captain who is also a connoisseur, a scholar," she purred. "Oh, lah, how I do marvel now at your great gifts, my lord!"

"I make no such claims, ma'am," he said as brusquely as he could, concentrating on the nodding plume of her turban instead of the myriad of temptations offered below. "But I do know I saw this exact statue in the garden of the British ambassador's villa last week. What are the odds of there being two such here in Naples, eh?"

"Oh, my lord!" she gasped, her hand arching over her breasts with surprise and a certain undeniable emphasis. "To think that a great scholar such as the ambassador has been taken in by a counterfeit!"

"Damnation, that's not what I'm saying at all!" exclaimed William. "What I'm saying, ma'am, what I'm *trying* to say, is that—"

"Is that this Cupid and the one in the ambassador's garden are both the work of the same master carver." She laughed merrily, and William had the uncomfortable feeling for the first time since she'd entered the room that her smile was genuine, a gift intended for him, a gift he most certainly didn't want. What had happened to his logic, his reasonable explanation?

"Signora," he said as sternly as he could. "You misconstrue my words, ma'am."

"Oh, I rather think not." Gently she took the statue from him, cradling it in her arms as if it were a real baby, the stone eyes turned adoringly up at her. "I beg you to remember that you are in Naples, my lord, and that here anything—anything!—is possible."

Look for
SPARKLE
Wherever Paperback Books Are Sold
Coming Soon
From Sonnet Books
Published by Pocket Books